Wolves at Our Door

Wolves at Our Door

A Novel

B. J. Carr

iUniverse, Inc.
New York Lincoln Shanghai

Wolves at Our Door

iUniverse books may be ordered through booksellers or by contacting:

iUniverse
2021 Pine Lake Road, Suite 100
Lincoln, NE 68512
www.iuniverse.com
1-800-Authors (1-800-288-4677)

ISBN: 978-0-595-43456-5 (pbk)
ISBN: 978-0-595-87783-6 (ebk)

Printed in the United States of America

1

Zane watched as the big bull Elk emerged from the chaparral brush. His breath caught at the beauty and majesty of the animal.

At that instant a rifle shot range out and the big bulls front legs buckled and he went down on his side and his legs twitched as he drew his last breaths.

"Congratulations!" Zane said to the man who had just snuffed out the life of the bull.

"Thank you!" Grinned the man. Zane had guided the Texas hunter into the basin where the bull was killed.

"Now the work begins." Zane said as he and Dan Scott made their way the two hundred yards down the ridge to where the bull lay dead. Zane put his back-pack down and began to take out knives and hatchets. He had guided the man to the bull now it was his job to dress it out.

"Looks like a nice five points! Did you bring the camera?" Dan asked as he lifted the bulls' head to examine his trophy.

"Yeah." Zane said, removing the digital camera out of his pack. The man from Texas posed several shots with his Bull and rifle. Once Zane finished the pictures to the hunters satisfaction Zane began the task of dressing the Bull. Although he had done it hundreds of times, he felt a tug of sadness at the majestic bulls death. Zane always felt better when he had reduced the bull to quarters and the majestic animal became another carcass. Then Zane faced the task of getting the carcass out of the basin he had guided the Texas hunter into where the bull was killed.

Dan sat and ate a snack as Zane dressed and quartered the bull.

"How are we going to get him out of here?" Dan asked?

"I'm going to have to back pack him out." Zane told him. "It's too rough down in here to get a pack horse to the carcass. Zane took his two-way radio out of his pack and got Jack Cutler on the radio. Jack Cutler was the man that owned the Guide service Zane guided the hunter.

"What have you got? I heard a shot out of the hole below road 13." Jack asked on the radio.

"Five points, it's going to be a back pack. Bring the four wheelers to that main ridge off road 13." Zane told Jack as Dan Scott, the successful hunter listened in.

"I'll come right away!" Acknowledged Jack.

Zane wrestled a front quarter onto his shoulder and back and told Dan. "Let's get out of here."

The Texas hunter started back out of the basin up the ridge they had come down. Dan Scott was a man in his forties. Zane Adams was a bigger younger man in his late twenty's.

After about a hundred yards the man from Texas stopped to rest. Zane waited patiently with his hundred-twenty-five-pound, pack, on his shoulder and back. Zane watched Dan Scott, Texas hunter, carefully. One never knew about the physical condition of those Dudes as Zane referred to them. Coming to Idaho for an Elk hunt from all over the United States, it was the guide's job to watch the hunters and be prepared to pamper them or in an emergency to administer life saving CPR.

Dan Scott appeared to be in fairly good condition for a Dude. After a brief rest they climbed another hundred yards. It took nearly an hour and a half to top out on road 13 where Jack Cutler waited on the four wheelers. Zane threw the front quarter of the Bull on the front rack of the machine.

"Made it huh?" Jack grunted when Zane and Dan topped into the old roadway.

"Yeah!" Zane said. Relieved to be rid of his heavy pack. He also knew there was to be four more trips back to the carcass before he was done.

"I'll take Dan and this quarter to the lodge and be back by the time you make the next trip." Jack said as he allowed Dan Scott to climb, on the back of the machine.

"Okay, see you next trip." Zane said with a grin and he headed back down the ridge toward the basin to get another quarter. He thought with dismay that he had to resort to entering the damnable hole Dan had shot the elk in. A few years ago the Elk were more plentiful and more accessible. That was before some idiots decided to introduce Wolves back into Idaho. The worst part of the plan was that there were already wolves in Idaho. There had been wolves all along. Not many and those, that were here, had migrated from Canada or Montana and Yellowstone.

The Wolves that were brought in under the reintroduction program from Canada had proliferated and nearly all of the local sportsman and even the Idaho fish and Game realized the Elk herds were being decimated by the Wolf packs. The wolves were also responsible for the Elk being driven into brushy inaccessible basins and holes where they could better protect themselves.

Such a place Zane Adams spent the rest of the afternoon back packing Dan Scott's Bull out from.

It was nearly dark by the time Zane got the carcass out. He rode behind Jack Cutler the last trip on the four wheelers to the lodge. Zane was tired. Jack sent him to the kitchen for a hot meal while he and another hand skinned and finished taking care of the Elk that Dan Scott had tagged.

Jack Cutler came into the kitchen just as Zane finished eating. He handed Zane five hundred Dollars. "You're, bonuses from Dan Scott. He said to thank you! He has already left, we are to send the processed carcass and horns to him."

Zane put the money in his wallet. He had worked hard that day and was tired. "What's up for in the morning?" He asked Jack.

Jack got himself a cup of tea and sat down at the table with Zane. "We have a guy and his daughter coming tomorrow from Michigan. Jody is in Spike camp with the fellow from Arkansas. I have two guys set up on the main ridge in the morning. Might be a good time for you to take a day off if you want to?"

"Yeah, I think I will. I'll run in and give Mom this bonus money and be back out tomorrow evening. Will that work for you?"

"Yeah that will be about right. You can take over the Michigan hunter the next day. You did a good job today Zane and I appreciate it. You deserve the bonus Dan Scott left. Take a breather and I'll see you, tomorrow evening." Jack sipped his tea as Zane got up and went to his room to shower and change his clothes. It was after eight by the time Zane got in his truck and headed for town.

On the edge of town Zane decided to stop at Pete's Bar and have himself a beer before going on out to the ranch where he lived with his mother. Zane's Dad had died in a truck crash a few years before and Zane stayed on the Ranch and ran cattle with his mother.

His job with Cutlers guide and outfitter worked into his helping his mother on the ranch. The slow times coincided with the winter hours when he needed to feed the livestock. The slow summer months with no packing and guiding gave Zane time to get the hay in for the cattle in winter. With what the livestock provided for income and his job with Cutler Outfitter, it worked out.

There were not many vehicles in the parking lot as Zane went into Pete's Bar. A couple guys sat at the bar and a woman and man sat at one of the tables. Pete was behind the Bar and spoke to Zane as he came in.

"How is it going for the big white hunter, Zane?" Pete laughed. Fetching Zane, a Coors light as Zane slid up to the bar.

"So, So! Would be better if not for the damned, Wolves"

"Yeah," Pete said. "All the hunters are griping. Looks to me like you have had a rough day?

You look tired. Oh God, here comes the Bombshell! Pete swore.

Zane looked around and seen Gina Daniels coming through the door. Zane knew Gina. She was a good-looking gal married to Punk Daniels. Punk had a reputation for being a sore head scrapper but everyone knew it was mostly because Gina, his wife was always on the make and causing trouble. It was easy for her to do so because she was very good looking and according to those who seemed to know very hot and easy. This led to many a brawl with Punk her husband involved. Punk worked in the woods and often was out in camp somewhere staying in his camp trailer.

Gina made straight for Zane Adams when she saw him at the bar. Pete looked at Zane, shook his head and smiled.

"Well hello, Adams," Gina said climbing up on a stool beside him.

"Hello Gina, how about something to drink?" Zane asked and motioned Pete over to get her something. Zane had never had anything to do with Gina but Zane also appreciated the fact she was a very good-looking woman. She had dark hair and eyes and pretty features. She had a heck of a good body on her. Gina had no trouble getting men's attention, a fact that caused Punk to be constantly scrapping over her. Gina seemed to enjoy having Punk fighting over her because she often instigated it. On this particular evening, Zane noted she appeared to be alone and no sign of Punk.

Pete brought her a beer and Zane paid for it. "What is the mountain man doing down from the Lodge?" Gina asked Zane.

"A rare respite, just heading for home, and what are you up to Gina?" Zane smiled with amusement.

"What makes you think I'm up to something?" She said tossing, her head. "You want to play some pool?" She asked.

"No thanks." Zane said.

Gina jumped off her stool and rubbed her pubic bone against the side of Zane's leg. "Oh come on Adams. One game?" She begged.

Pete smiled and Zane found he was reacting to Gina's provocative rubbing against him. It had been some time since Zane had been with a woman and Gina with her good looks was affecting him. Reluctantly Zane agreed to game of pool if for no other reason than to avoid Gina rubbing on him. He ordered another beer for himself and Gina.

During the pool game Gina made sure Zane got his eye full looking down her blouse, at her full breast, as she leaned over the pool table. Zane was aware she was seducing him but it had been a long time since he had been with a woman and Punk was nowhere in sight!

Zane stayed longer at Pete's than he intended. He also drank more than he intended. He also found himself going out the door with Gina. When they got in Zane's truck, Gina was all over him. The rumors about Gina Daniels weren't exaggerated. She was hot all right!

Hey, we aren't running a race here! What's your hurry?" Zane laughed as he started his truck.

To say Gina had Zane flustered was putting it mildly but Zane had no intentions of laying her in the street in his truck. Zane drove to his house. The house was dark.

"We have to be quiet. My Mother is asleep." Zane said, trying to ignore Gina's hands roaming and groping at him.

"Your Mother!" Gina giggled.

"Yeah, my mother." Zane got the steaming hot Gina out of the truck and quietly with him holding her hand they stole through the house and up the stairs to Zane's room. Rachel Adams room was downstairs on the other end of the ranch house.

Once inside his room Gina began to tear at his clothes. "Slow up here, we have time, there isn't any rush I know of." Now that Zane had the hot and attractive Gina in his bed he intended to make a night of it. "Where's your husband?"

"At camp. He won't be home until the end of the week." Gina panted. Gina began to strip her clothes off. Zane turned on a night light in the dark room. He didn't like groping around in the dark.

Gina now naked stood by impatiently as Zane began to undress. She watched him with excitement. Zane was tall and long bodied. Although strong he was not the biceps bulging, muscle bound, type of man but was long armed and legs with a broad back and chest. He wore his hair quite long. It was blond and curled. He had a ruddy Scandinavian complexion and good features with a square jaw.

Zane was not necessarily worried about a future confrontation with Punk Daniels as he could very well handle himself.

Zane pulled the bed covers back and Gina jumped in. She was still in a hurry to get at him. She knew Zane Adams but had not ever had anything to do with him. Now that she had her hands on him she was in a hurry.

"Now what are you doing?" She complained.

"Putting on a condom."

"Oh God, that's like taking a bath with your clothes on." She bitched.

"Sorry but there is no way I'm having sex with you without it." Zane told her grimly. Finished he climbed in bed with Gina and took her in his arms. She was frantically all over him. Zane was trying to get her slowed down. He kissed her slowly and passionately and Gina was trying to squirm under him and capture his manhood between her legs. She was wet and hot.

"Come on Gina, let's enjoy this! What's your hurry to get it over with?" Zane nuzzled her breast and she arched her back toward him. She wanted it and she wanted it now!

Impatient Gina crammed him inside her with her hand. Zane took a deep breath and held himself in check. He intended to make it last. He was moving slowly and Gina was squirming against him frantically. He felt her orgasm shortly after they began. Zane clinched his jaw and kept his release in check. He felt her swell with the orgasm and he slowed to allow her to relax once she was done. Slowly he began to move again as she began to relax. "Come on Baby, stay with me!" He whispered and Zane felt her respond. This time Zane took control. She began to moisten as her heat, begin to rise again and Zane continued to keep a tight rein on his own release. Soon Gina was again aroused and panting with desire.

"Hang on, hold it long as you can" Zane coaxed her. He knew the longer they could delay gratification the more powerful the release would be when it came. Zane felt Gina again getting close to orgasm and he knew he couldn't hold her off so he let go of his control and went with her. Zane was right, when they released it shook both of them and Gina gasped with the force of her climax.

Zane wasn't the kind of lover that was done when he finished. He kept caressing and kissing Gina and made her feel she was still important to him.

"My God Adam's, you are something else!" She murmured so contented she was about to purr.

"So are you!" Zane rolled off her and gathered her into his arms and held her tenderly. Gina snuggled in against Zane. Zane was weary beyond belief. The whole day packing the Elk out of a damnable hole and the alcohol and his tryst with the hot Gina, Zane could barely keep his eyes open. He fought sleep until he knew Gina slumbered peacefully in his arms.

"What the God Damn Hell, do you think you are doing!" Zane struggled out of deep sleep to find his mother standing over his bed.

"Jesus Christ Mom, get out of here, can't you see I need some privacy? Zane grumbled.

Gina had sat bolt, up right in the bed when Rachel Adam's began to curse. The fact she was buck-naked didn't dawn on her and her breast, were exposed above the covers. Gina was so startled she didn't attempt to cover up.

"Zane, what the hell you doing with Punk Daniel's wife in your bed?" Rachel demanded of him!

Zane rolled over and dragged Gina back down beside him and tucked the covers around her naked breast.

"You get out of here and we'll be down in a moment." Zane told his mother calmly. "You make any coffee?"

Rachel, "harrumph" with disgust and turned on her heels and left the room slamming the door behind her.

Gina looked at Zane wide eyed.

"We better get dressed." Zane said calmly swing out of bed and putting his own clothing on.

"Is it going to be safe to go down there?" Gina asked still wide-eyed.

"Yeah, Mom's bark is worse than her bite." Zane grinned.

"If you say so Adams!" Gina said struggling into her wrinkled cloths she had thrown around the room the night before.

Zane with Gina trailing behind him came down the stairs and into the cheerful kitchen. Seeing them, Rachel Adam's got up and poured two cups of coffee. Zane indicated Gina to sit at the table with him and Rachel plopped the cups of coffee in front of them. Her lips were compressed in a thin line of disapproval

"Good morning, to you mother, apparently you know Gina Daniels?" Zane said. He had amusement in his blue eyes at his mother's obvious disapproval.

"Hi." Gina said nervously concentrating on sipping her coffee, thereby avoiding Rachel Adam's withering look of disapproval.

"What you doing with her?" Rachel asked Zane.

"Nothing at the moment." Zane said. "I plan on taking her into town when we finish our coffee." He grinned slightly.

"I'll take her in when she finishes her coffee." Rachel said with finality. It was not up to any other discussion as far as she was concerned. She had visions of Punk Daniels chasing her son down the street with a shotgun!

"What do you think?" Zane asked Gina. "I can run you in if you don't want to ride with my mother?"

"I'll go with her." Gina agreed. She had every reason to believe Punk, was on his job but just in case she decided it best to accompany Zane's disapproving mother.

"I'll change and then we'll go!" Rachel left the room.

"Will I see you again?" Gina asked Zane eagerly. They're lovemaking fresh in her mind.

"I have a couple more months in camp. I don't think it would be a good idea unless you are trying to get me killed?" Zane grinned.

"Punk doesn't need to know." Gina sighed with regret. She wanted to be with Zane Adam's again some time. She would make sure Punk didn't find out or it would ruin her chance of getting her hands on the sexy Adam's again!

Rachel returned and herded the reluctant Gina out to her car. Zane sighed with relief. He had not been looking forward to hauling Gina back into town in broad daylight. She was a hot lay but Zane had no intentions of pushing his luck and fooling around with Punk Daniel's wife again. He would try to stay out of Gina's sight until she cooled off from their night together.

Zane went out to the barn and checked to see if the horses had water. The water trough was full. Apparently Rachel had already been out doing chores. With Zane's truck in the yard she had no way of knowing he wasn't alone and she had no doubt done chores realizing he needed rest before she came in to awaken him only to find Gina in his bed.

Zane laughed, to himself when he thought about his mothers, indignation, upon discovering Gina Daniels in his bed. Zane didn't make a practice of bringing women into his bedroom but at the age of twenty-eight he thought himself too old to need his mother's permission.

Zane had been the breadwinner and man of the house since his father's death ten years before.

He had not had to stay, he could have done as his older brother Matt and continued on to have a life of his own. Zane had wanted to stay and he and his mother were very close but he was not going to tolerate her dictating his personal life. He knew he should not have been messing around with Punk Daniel's wife. He wasn't making any excuses for himself. His physical, needs and lust had clouded his judgment and he would try to avoid it happening again. But the fact was he was paying the bills in the household and his mother was not going to decide who was or not going to be in his bed. If he had felt, otherwise he would have not brought Gina Daniels home with him.

Zane messed around doing a few odd chores until his mother returned. He saw her drive in and go into the house. He went inside also expecting her to have something else to say.

Rachel had put her purse and Jacket away and was in the kitchen when Zane came in.

"Did you have, any trouble, getting Gina home?" Zane asked?

"No. But what were you doing with her?" Rachel asked her lips still thin with disapproval.

"I don't have to explain the facts of life to you, do I? Zane grinned with amusement.

"I can't believe you would be foolish enough to screw around with Punk Daniel's wife!"

"Not much choice around this small town." Zane grinned. "You have an alternative solution?"

"Well why can't you find a nice girl?" Rachel wanted to know.

"How do you know Gina isn't a nice girl?" Zane rolled the girl part sarcastically.

"Well for one thing she has a husband, and a very ill tempered one from what I hear."

"Forget it! It was a lapse of judgment on my part. I'll try to control myself from now on. But I don't expect you to be making my decisions about it." Zane took the five hundred dollar bills from his wallet and laid them on the table. As far as Zane was concerned he was done, discussing it with his mother.

Rachel still had a look of disgust in her eyes but she knew Zane had come to the end of discussing any more about Gina Daniels. Rachel just hoped he would not end up in an altercation with Punk. "When are you going back up to the lodge?"

"This evening. I have a new guy coming in from Michigan. I told Jack I would be back this evening so I can take his hunter early the next morning. Anything you need me to do before I go?"

"You can go up and clean up your love nest, as I am not going to do it!"

"Yes Mother dear!" Zane grinned and went up to straighten his room. He would have without her saying anything. After all he had some condom wrappers and things to dispose of. When he entered the room, it smelled like sex. He thought it was probably worse earlier when his mother found him and Gina in the bed. Zane stripped his bed of sheets and went down and crammed them in the washer. He rummaged around in the linen closet and found laundered sheets and went up and made his bed. When he was finished, he went out to the garage and found some tools. He needed to clean the battery terminals on his pickup before he got stuck along the road back in the mountains.

Rachel came out of the house while he was working on the battery terminals and asked, "What he wanted her to do with the money?"

"Put in the savings until we need it." Zane said.

"If you have time, there is a hole in the back of the hay field fence, maybe you could mend it. It isn't time yet to let the cows start coming in."

"I'll do that soon as I finish here."

"Thank you. Will you be here for dinner?"

"No I'll have some lunch before I leave but I want to get back to the lodge before dark."

After finishing the battery cables Zane got the four wheelers and took some fencing tools. He went around the back of the hay field fence and found the place and repaired it.

Zane went in when he returned and his mother and he had some lunch. There was not much they needed to talk about so lunch was pretty well silent. After lunch Zane packed some clean clothes and made ready to go back to the lodge.

About three in the afternoon Zane decided he would go. He went in and kissed his mother on the cheek.

"When will you be back?" She asked.

"When you see me! You know how it is this time of year."

When Zane drove back through town he went by Pete's Bar but thinking better of it decided he wouldn't stop. He headed out to the mountains toward the Lodge.

Zane pulled into the Lodge about dark. He saw Jody Miller out by the meat house and figured one of Jody's hunters had luck. Jody Miller was the other guide that worked for Jack and Annie Cutler. Jody was part Nezperce Indian. Jody was a very good hunting guide and he and Zane got along very well. Jody had been up at Spike Camp when Zane left the day before. Jody had taken a hunter from Arkansas.

Zane parked and walked over to the meat house. Jack and Jody were skinning the quarters of an elk. The head lay there and Zane could see it was a four by five. Not a big rack but he imagined the Arkansas hunter was pleased.

"Did you have any trouble getting, the carcass out?" Zane asked Jody.

"Nope, got the pack horse right to it." Jody grinned. "I hear you had to pack one on your back for the Texan?"

"Yeah, I took him down in that basin below road 13. I knew damned well when I went down in there it would be a backpack. I don't know what else we are to do if we want any hunters to come back another year."

"Yeah." Jody agreed. "But if things continue there might not be much to hunt if they do return next year. This situation is getting grim. If not for the good season we had on the bow hunter's Jack might have to think about closing the doors. The rifle hunters have been at a definite disadvantage. We can't call those bulls up out of those brushy holes after they are done, rutting."

"Maybe we should start after the season hunting those damned wolves and pack a shovel to bury them. I'm afraid we are in danger of losing our Elk hunting in Idaho." Zane said.

"Yeah," Jack Cutler chimed in, "The Idaho Fish and Games hands are tied with Federal protection on those wolves.

"I guess with no hunters they also will be out of a job." Jody said. "I can't believe my people were one of the main driving force behind this wolf introduction. How dumb is that? You would think us Indians would have better sense than anybody of the consequences"

"Well I hope this has shut up, the ones also wanting to bring the grizzlies in here." Zane said.

"I wouldn't count on it." Jack said. "Some son of a Bitch in Washington, D.C. doesn't care what the consequences are, to the inhabitants of Idaho. Just the idea of bringing back grizzlies seems romantic to some environmentalist sitting in an office in Washington."

"The idea my mother might be out trying to take baby calves away from a pack of wolves doesn't set too well with me." Zane said with disgust.

"Yeah, wonder what the proponents of the wolf recovery, are thinking these wolves are to eat when the game is gone?" Jody wondered.

"Livestock and peoples pet. Maybe even peoples kid." Jack said.

"Did my hunter come in from Michigan?" Zane asked.

"Yeah he is in the lodge. If Jody can finish up here, I'll take you in to meet him and you can put together plans for in the morning."

"Go ahead, I got it." Jody said. Jack and Zane headed for the lodge.

There was a big fire roaring in the fireplace of the great room in the lodge. Jack introduced Zane to George Belmont, from Michigan.

George Belmont was an attractive man Zane guessed to be in his middle forties. His daughter a attractive blonde girl looked to be in her middle twenties. Zane thought George must have been quite young when his daughter whose name was Bethany was born. Either that or Bethany looked to be much older than she actually was.

Zane found out George was the only one that was going to hunt. Bethany was along just for the trip into the Idaho wilderness. Zane visited with George trying to get an idea of what the man's expectations were. That was important to a guide to find out if the patron was looking for a trophy animal or just wanted to shoot an Idaho Bull elk. George Belmont was just looking to bag a bull. He was not looking for a trophy but made it clear he would not pass one up if the opportunity arose.

The daughter Bethany was quiet and did not have much to say. She was checking out Zane and he could feel her interest in him. That was another rule there was to be no interaction of a personal nature with the patrons or members of their family.

This was sometimes a problem as some hunters brought their wives and some of the wives acted as if they were very interested in the Guides. Zane thought wryly they were fascinated by the impression they were some kind of sexy savage

George and Zane made plans to leave before daylight. Zane had plans to take him into some big fern glades. Perhaps he could get George his elk without having to drop down into one of the basins like the one he packed the Texans Bull out of on his back.

With plans made Zane retired. Jody had just finished eating after tending to his hunters elk and both guides headed for their rooms where they bunked together.

"You went into town, anything interesting going on in civilization?" Jody asked as he crawled in his bunk

"Nope, same old things, "Zane said. Zane was thinking about Gina Daniels. She would be a damned good lay if she would slow down a bit. Zane hoped Punk wouldn't get word of him screwing around with his wife. Zane didn't like to brawl but he could if he had to. Zane heard Jody snoring in his bunk so Zane turned over and went to sleep. It would be an early rise.

2

Rachel Adam's watched Zane drive down the driveway. She had a frown on her forehead as she thought about finding him with Gina Daniels upstairs that morning. Rachel hoped Zane had the good sense to protect himself from disease. Hard to tell what that promiscuous woman was packing around. She also hoped Punk Daniels would not find out. She was sure Zane could handle himself but the idea he would have to brawl with Punk over Gina would be known all over the small town.

Rachel realized it was hard for Zane to meet eligible young women his age. He was too old for the high school girls and most girls were married or went off to college and didn't return because there was little work in the area.

Logging and the local businesses, was all there was. The logging was getting scarce as protesting environmentalist was blocking the federal timber. There were a few remaining sawmills, one of which Rachel's other son Matt worked.

Rachel had seen many new people moving into the area there were many retirees coming into the area because of low property values. It seemed every time California had a quake, there were more Californians in the area. The Californians were aggravated at the poor condition of the local roads but without the taxpayers to provide the funds the solution was simply more people for more taxes. Then the Californians would find the reason they moved out of California, Too many people!

A few stump ranchers like Rachel's property were producing a few heads of cows but they could not survive without Zane's earnings with his job for the Cutler Guide business.

Rachel herself worked in the local grocery store for a few days a week. Her old friend Chuck Danner and his wife Mabel ran it. Rachel had known Chuck all of her life. They had gone to grade school together. Chuck had married Mabel when he left for the service during the Vietnam years and brought her home when he was discharged. Mabel's health was declining. There were days she could not get to the store and it was those days Chuck called on Rachel to come to the store and help.

Rachel had married Walter Adam's right out of high school. His family had the ranch where Rachel and Zane now lived. Walter and Rachel had two sons,

Matthew, Matt as he was nicknamed, now thirty-five and Zane twenty-eight. Zane was Rachel's, baby, the last-born and her favorite all though she would deny it.

Walter had worked in the woods as well as run cattle on the Ranch. Walter had also loved his liquor.

More than his wife and children because it finally killed him as he drove off the grade one night intoxicated.

Matt had married right out of high school and went to work in the sawmill. Zane had just graduated High School at the time of Walters' death. Zane had always been interested in the outdoors. He worked briefly for a logger but when he was given the chance to work for Cutler Guiding and Outfitting he took it.

Chuck Danner had called the Adam's resident for Rachel to come in.

Rachel was still a very attractive, woman. She had worked hard on the Ranch and was slender and had a good shape. Her blonde hair had a few streaks of gray but she still had the fine features she had as a young, woman. She had a nice smile and her eyes were blue and bright, she was a long way from old age and Chuck wondered why no man had become interested in her.

Actually it was Rachel's own doing. There had been plenty of men, some very much younger interested. She had not been receptive. After Walt's death Rachel had to deal with many years of a bad marriage so she concentrated on running the ranch and had her son Zane with her to do so. Since she didn't feel the need to have financial support she chose to ignore her physical loneliness and was content the way things were.

Rachel hurried into the store to help Chuck. He was waiting on a customer at the check stand when she came in. She went to the back room where the office was and hung up her jacket and stored her purse. There were a desk and a safe for the store money in the back room. There were also a couple extra chairs for sitting.

Rachel put on her store apron and went up front to help Chuck. The customer was just going out the door. "Mabel sick again today?" Rachel asked?

"Yeah, seems she is getting worse. Those new pain pills she's on for her pain knocked her on her back."

"That's too bad, I don't suppose she can do without them?" Rachel said with genuine concern. She liked Mabel and Chuck both.

"I don't know." Chuck said tiredly. Actually Chuck didn't think Mabel needed to take that much narcotics for her pain but he didn't say anything disparaging about her to Rachel.

"Didn't I see your car in town this morning? Chuck asked.

"Yes. Seems my son had a woman of disreputable character in his bed when I went up, to awaken him this morning."

Chuck laughed. "I'm sure that made your day! You know Zane can take care of himself if anybody can. You can't keep him, your little innocent boy forever!"

"I know, but I wish he would be a bit more selective."

"How in the name of God is he going to do that in a town this size. I won't ask who it was but I wouldn't be too surprised to hear about it. Nothing much goes on around here without it being known. The guy has to do something, you don't expect him to be celibate if he has a chance at something?" Chuck grinned and shook his head.

"I know, and as Zane pointed out it isn't my business whom he has in his bed, but a mother can still worry can't she?"

"Sure but it won't do you any good." About that time a customer came in and Rachel took over the check stand. Chuck walked off to help the customer.

Danner's store stocked groceries, clothing, hardware and hunting supplies. Being the only store in town, they tried to stock enough to keep the small town population from having to drive fifty miles to a larger one. Rachel smiled at Chuck's reaction to Zane's disreputable bed partner. It was typical for a man. It seems that men had a different outlook on obtaining sex than women. Rachel hoped Chuck would not hear who was in Zane's bed. If he were to, Punk Daniels would also and then Zane would be in a fight.

Rachel got the duster and thought she would dust before the next customer came in. Chuck was still helping someone back at the meat counter. She dusted the canned goods and shelves and she heard Chuck check the customer out. Rachel went in back and got the stepladder and proceeded to dust the fluorescent light fixtures. She didn't hear Chuck until he was under the ladder. She was thinking about Gina and Zane. When Chuck went to say some thing, she was startled and fell off the ladder and Chucks caught her in his arms.

"Well for Gods sakes, how clumsy of me!" Rachel laughed grateful Chuck had saved her from a nasty fall.

"Yeah", Chuck said reluctant to let Rachel out of his arms. She was light as a feather and smelled so good. Reluctantly he put her down. "You need to be more careful, it would be a good idea not to get on the ladder if you're here by your self." He grinned. He thought if he had to catch his hefty wife she would have knocked him flat. Chuck was of the opinion most of Mabel's problems were her weight. Because of his feelings for Rachel Adams Chuck allowed Mabel to stay at home whenever she whined she didn't feel well.

Chuck liked working alone with Rachel. He knew he would never do anything about his feelings but daydreams but he did plenty of that. He had no idea what he would do if Rachel ever became interested in somebody else!

Rachel noticed something in Chuck's eyes when he caught her and it seemed he delayed in letting go of her. No! It must be her imagination. She and Chuck had been friends too long for what she imagined she saw in his eyes.

Rachel thought Chuck was still an attractive man. He had a full thick head of graying hair and had begun to thicken somewhat around his waist but he still moved like a man with energy and his eyes were bright and hazel colored. They went perfectly with his thick head of salt and pepper once dark hair. Chuck still had a square jaw line and was not yet beginning to show the sagging jowls some men his age did. Rachel had been fond of Chuck since they were children and she also was fond of Mabel, Chuck's wife.

Mabel Danner had a heart of gold. She was generous to a fault. Rachel Adams was a close friend; Mabel had no idea that her husband had feelings for Rachel. Mabel trusted Chuck completely, they had been married for thirty-five years and it had been a very good marriage. They had not had children but they had a wonderful life together and she never once suspected Chuck of having feelings for her good friend Rachel.

Maybe Mabel had let herself go in the last ten years and there were times she stuffed herself with food to make up for the loss of children and the possibility of grandchildren but she knew her husband to be of faithful and loving disposition. In her wildest dreams she would have never suspected him of harboring feeling for Rachel.

Mabel and Chuck had often discussed Rachel's unhappy marriage and life to the drunken Walt Adam's but both agreed she was lucky to have her son's. That Rachel loved her sons were obvious, nearly every thing she did was for or with her sons. Rachel was even blessed with a couple of grandchildren from Matt and his wife Susie.

Matt and Susie lived in another small town about twenty minutes away from Adam's farm. With Zane still at the Ranch with her and her and Zane working the cows, Mabel didn't feel Rachel's life was as empty as hers even though she had her husband Chuck, or at least she believed so.

Little did she know she had him in body and not in his mind? Actually Mabel had little of Chuck in body either. It had been several years since there had been any intimacy in their marriage. Mabel was too sick or too tired and just not interested. Small wonder Chuck was left to day dreams about Rachel Adams.

Rachel was not the kind of woman that would ever betray a friend and she was disturbed with what she saw momentarily in Chuck's eyes when he had his arms around her. Rachel put it out of her mind, it must be her imagination but she still felt Chuck's arms around her. It had been a very long time since she had a man's arms around her and she craved to be loved but not by betraying her good friend and employer.

Zane got up well before daylight and him and Jody had breakfast in the kitchen of the lodge while Annie served the hunters in the dining room. Jack sat at the table with the guides.

Jack wasn't eating but drinking coffee. Annie had complained to him about it but he was noticing extra weight around his middle and was trying to cut down. The fact Annie was an excellent cook didn't make it easier.

"What have you got in mind for the Michigan hunter? Jack asked Zane.

"Going to take him over below the high Ridge into the big fern glades. I hope I can find him something this time we can get a pack horse to."

Jack laughed. "Yeah, we hate to have you waste your time being a pack horse or should I say Jack ass!" Jack laughed.

Jody laughed also. Zane grinned. "Well you got to go, where the Elk are and I hope I don't have to go into some hole with this George guy from Michigan. But I will if I have to." He added.

"What's your plan?" Jack asked Jody. Jody was usually very quiet. He didn't spend a lot of time talking and Zane wondered idly how he got along with the hunter he had taken to Spike Camp. When Jody was in Spike camp Jody had to do the cooking and guiding. On his last trip there with the Arkansas hunter he had been successful in getting the hunters Elk but Zane bet their conversation was limited. Maybe Jody wore the hunter out and he was ready for sleep after they ate.

"I'm taking one of those guys you had over on the main ridge the day before into Breakfast Creek. He acted like he was discouraged after sitting a stand off the main ridge."

"Good idea." Jack agreed. "Break those two I had over there on the ridge up. I'll take the older guy with me on the four wheelers down into the meadows. See if we can find him some shooting."

"Good luck!" Zane said pushing from the Breakfast table and going out to the supply shed to get his pack. The guides were not allowed to carry rifles but Zane always carried three fifty-seven-magnum pistols, as a side arm. He picked it up and grabbed his pack. As he came out of the supply shed, the man from Michigan had come out the front door of the lodge and was waiting for Zane. Zane surmised Annie must have told he, they were getting ready to go.

"Good morning George!" Zane greeted the man from Michigan.

"Good Morning." The man said curtly. No smile on his face and Zane surmised this guy was all business.

Zane opened the door of one of the Suburban with the Cutler Guide and Outfitters' insignia on the door and started the engine to let it warm up.

"We are driving?" George Belmont asked.

"Yeah, just over on the upper road where we can go down through those big fern glades, I told you about last night."

George Belmont looked the tall rangy blonde guide over and decided he looked like a man that could handle himself. Actually with his hair-curled down on his collar and side burns, he looked like what George Belmont from Michigan would expect, an Idaho Mountain guide to look like. George handed his rifle to the guide and climbed into the Suburban that was beginning to warm up. It was still dark out but the sky was beginning to show signs of light in the east. It appeared to be partly cloudy and the temperature was a few degrees above freezing.

Zane put Georges Rifle, in the gun holder in the suburban and got behind the wheel and backed out. They drove up the gravel road from the lodge a short distance and turned uphill on a dirt road.

The road appeared to be well packed and not muddy. The fall rains had not been plentiful and mud was not yet a problem. The lack of rain had made it difficult for the hunters to move in the woods because the rains had not softened the grass and brush and moving was very noisy. Especially for two men, which was always the case for a guide service.

The fact that the majority of game was taken during the season by a lone hunter was well known by Zane but as a guide he needed to be near or with his hunter at all times. Sometimes guides could leave hunters on stands but they never let them move through the woods alone.

It was just breaking day as Zane pulled over in a wide spot on the high road. He and George would be dropping off and hunting down the hill through a series of fern glades and patches of timber and of coarse the usual patches of brush. The elk were beginning to feed on the edge of the glades to garner the last remnants of edible grass. They were also feeding on a brush that still had leaves and buds attached.

By the time it was light enough that one could discern if an Elk had horns or not Zane and George broke off the road and started down into the canyon below.

George Belmont had loaded his gun upon leaving the rig and Zane paid particular attention to make sure if the safety was on. Zane didn't like the Dudes, following him with a loaded gun if the safety wasn't on. They could easily fall and cause the weapon to discharge.

As they made their way down Zane was aggravated with the noisy conditions. Before breaking out into a large glade Zane stuck his reed from his pocket in his mouth and blew a couple of cow Elk calls. He listened carefully to see if he got an answer.

"What is that?" George Belmont asked.

"Cow Call. If there is anything in the glade below some times they will assume we are other elk coming in. If a Bull it will sometimes stop them from slipping away if they believe, we are just another elk." Zane, whispered so his voice wouldn't carry down into the glade below.

Not hearing anything Zane motioned George to follow and they broke out into an open glade about ten acres covered with bracken ferns. The bracken ferns were about six feet tall. Zane left the reed in his mouth. Often, times, he could stop a bolting elk with a call from the reed in his mouth.

Zane and George Belmont made their way through the big fern glade. It was riddled with Elk trails and elk droppings. Zane detected the smell of Elk hanging in the glade and he knew they were not far behind them.

The hunter and guide made their way through a patch of trees and Zane suddenly heard a stick crack in the stillness of the morning air. He stopped dead in his tracks. Carefully he stepped forward and called a short call with the reed in his mouth. A cow below answered.

Zane motioned his hunter to go ahead of him. Cautiously they sneaked through the remaining trees until they could see into the next glade below. Zane's practiced eye picked up the tawny body at the edge of the clearing below. There were also several cow and calf elk out in the clearing. It was the lighter color of the larger animal below next to the timber drew Zane' s attention. He tugged on Georges Jacket and the hunter from Michigan followed the direction of Zane's gaze. There stood a rag horn Bull. He was about two hundred yards below and standing broadside.

George took the safety off and pulled down on the Bull. Zane watched with concern as the rifle roared and the Bull disappeared like a shadow into the trees. Zane knew George had not taken the time to make sure of his aim. The shot was too hasty and Zane knew it.

"Did I miss?" George asked as the cows and calves also disappeared out of the glade into the trees.

"I'm afraid you did. But we need to go see." Zane said calmly. He knew it was a clean miss but Zane also knew from long experience to check every shot out. He and George crossed the glade where the bull had been standing. The Bulls hooves had dug in as he bolted and Zane followed his trail for about a hundred yards and there was no sign the Elk was impeded or was there any sign of blood.

"Clean miss." Zane told the Michigan hunter. "You'll get him next time." Zane could see George was disappointed.

"Will there be a next time?"

"Let's hope so, I'll do my best." Zane grinned.

"Well you did your job this time, I guess I'm the one that messed up." George said gloomily.

Thinking it might be the time to mention it, Zane said. "It happens all the time. The next time you get one in your sight's take a second to make the first shot count. That extra second can make all the difference."

"Thanks! I'll remember that. Thanks for the chance."

"We'll find something, you have a week. Actually you were lucky to even get a shot your first day out. Let's go on down through here as I planned and Jack will come, and pick us up in the bottom."

Zane was again in the lead as they went through trees and stopped at the next glade. Zane whistled the cow call and there was no answer. They continued on down the ridge. Into the next group of trees two cow Elk and a calf come running horizontally around the hill but there was no Bull with them. They went on down into the next glade and finally came out on an old road down below.

"Are you hungry?" Zane asked digging in his pack for the sandwiches that Annie had sent.

"Thanks." George said, and accepted a sandwich.

Zane got the radio out and called for Jack to pick them up. Zane got a sandwich out and sat down on the old road bank to joined George Belmont.

"How long does it take to learn to use those Elk calls?" George asked Zane.

"A long time, according to my mother." Zane laughed. "I've been doing that since I was a little kid. She bitched about me making noise with those things all the time. She particularly hated the Bull bugle. She used to hide them from me so she could get some peace and quiet!"

"Sure did sound exactly like that cow that answered you before we saw the Bull." George had finished his Sandwich. "When do you use the Bull bugle?"

"Usually only when the Elk are rutting. They won't pay any attention any other time. There are some bottles of water or soda in my pack." Zane told him.

"Water will be fine, thank you."

"You're paying for it." Zane grinned. About that time Zane heard the whine of the mule, a vehicle that could haul four persons on a back trail. Jack came around the corner in it and Zane began to gather up his pack.

"Any luck?" Jack asked.

Zane looked at George and grinned "Not yet"

"That's not true," Gorge Belmont, confessed, "I had a shot at a Bull and missed."

"Happens all the time." Jack said, taking Georges Rifle, and checking it to be sure there was no shell in the barrel before he put in on the machine in a scabbard.

When they got back to lodge Zane told George, he would talk to him about planning something for in the morning later in the evening in the great room. Zane went on in the kitchen. Annie was busy at the stove working on the evening meal.

"Some fresh rolls, and coffee, Zane?" She asked.

"Thanks Annie." Zane said helping himself to the rolls and coffee. "Jody came back in yet?"

"No he is still out. Jack was out with the older fellow but he was back in time to go get you and the Michigan man. Any luck? She asked.

"George missed a four-point, shot too quick." Zane said.

"Oh that's too bad, sorry Zane."

"Just have to figure where to take him for another chance. I'm not wanting to head into one of those backpack holes. What do you do to keep Georges, daughter, entertained? Zane asked.

"Nothing, I haven't seen her out of her room since breakfast. I went up and told her when lunch was ready but she didn't open the door, just told me she wasn't hungry. I hear the Television on but I haven't seen her."

"Didn't it seem to you she is a little old to be Georges, daughter? Also George is dark complexion and dark hair and she is as blonde as they come." Zane mused.

Annie looked at Zane intently. "Now that you mentioned it, but that isn't any of our business." She rolled her eyes and smiled.

"Yes, I know that. Just interesting though!" Zane grinned. "Wonder why they bother, if she's his mistress or secretary, why bother lying about it? Is Bethany registered as Belmont?"

"I believe so. Maybe he is just older than he looks or maybe she is younger than she looks. As for the blonde that can be out of a bottle?"

"I guess it doesn't matter as long as I can find him another elk. We don't want any more hunters leaving empty handed." Zane was finished speculating about George and Bethany, whoever she was!

Jody came through the kitchen door about then and Zane could tell by the frown on his face he had not had any luck, with his hunter either.

"See anything at all" Zane asked as Jody got coffee and a roll and sat down to the table with Zane.

"Nothing up on the mountain, but Wolf tracks. We went into Breakfast Creek and there have been a few elk in there but also the Wolves."

"Yeah they have the elk down in those brushy holes where the wolves are unable to do anything with them. The Big Creek guide told me they found a wolf in a brush patch that had been trampled to death." Zane said.

"Somebody is going to have to do something or we are going to find ourselves out of a job." Jody said. His black eyes were gloomy at the prospect.

"Mom seen three in the hay field behind our house just out of town." Zane said. The idea they would have to begin to guard the cattle and ranch dogs from marauding wolf packs did not make Zane one bit happy. The mountains, were full of wolves were bad enough but just out of town!

"What you figuring to do with your Michigan fellow tomorrow?" Jody asked Zane.

"I hope to improve his patience and marksmanship." Zane scowled

"He got a shot?"

"Yeah, a good one too, about two hundred yards broadside, he just was in too big a hurry."

"Jesus, that's too bad Zane, I suppose you could have got a horse there also?"

"Yeah, right to it. I just hope I don't have to go back into one of those holes. I think I'll take him over on Isabelle and off that high ridge. There are glades much the same as we were in today but it is too far for Jack to bring the mule. Could I get you and Jack to get a rig down in there on that lower road so we don't have to climb back out?"

"Sure, I'll talk to Jack about it. I'll try to figure someplace along in there to take my guy so we can get a chance for both of them and I'll still be able to pick you up."

"Sounds like a plan. I'll run it by Jack before I talk with George Belmont."

"You need me to do anything Annie?" Zane asked.

"No," Annie said busy at the stove. "Jody, did you do the horses? I'm not sure Jack got to them?" Jody Miller took care of the packhorse string. Jody was good with horses and mules and enjoyed working with them.

"I'll go now." Jody said finishing his roll and getting up from the table and going out the back door. Zane followed him to see if he could help. Zane spotted Jack out by the meat house and went over to fill him in on Jody and his plans for the morning hunt. The Cutler Guide outfit did not take hunters out for an evening hunt. Jack had bitched he had spent too many hours in the dark looking for a wounded animal.

Often they would take them in the afternoon but not out just before dark when the game liked to move. That time of evening was a favorite for the local hunters but Jack wouldn't usually allow the Dudes to go.

Zane filled Jack in on him and Jody's plans. "Whatever you think." Jack knew his guide was a better hunter than Jack was himself. Jack also knew he wanted to groom Zane to take over his guide business when he retired. He and Annie had discussed it on several occasions.

That evening after the Lodge had their evening meal, Zane went to the Great room to talk with George Belmont. He found him sitting by the fireplace with his blonde daughter. George had a glass in his hand. An alcoholic drink, which Zane surmised was whiskey by the smell. Bethany Belmont sat in a chair by the fire also but she didn't seem to be drinking anything. She looked up, when Zane came. When he took a chair to talk with George, she looked away.

Zane noted she was a very pretty young woman. He still doubted she was Georges Daughter but like Annie had pointed out it was none of their business. Zane filled George in on his plan and he noticed Bethany kept her eyes downcast and didn't look at Zane or George either one.

The next morning in the early morning while still dark, Zane, Jody, George and an older hunter named Sherman left in the Suburban. It was further over on the high road above Isabelle than they went the morning before. Jody was driving and Zane sat in back with George.

Zane and George got out on top. They had to wait about ten minutes for it to get light enough to start down off the high ridge. They were in glades, much the same as they had been the day before. They spooked out a couple of mule deer but there were no elk and there was no fresh sign like Zane had found the day before. Jody picked them up in the bottom.

Jody called Zane aside and said Jack had called and George Belmont's wife was at the lodge. She had appeared unexpectedly and his daughter was holed up in her room.

Apparently Annie had not mentioned Georges Daughter, but she had spoken to Bethany about Marion Belmont's appearance and Bethany told Annie not to mention she was there. Seemed Zane observations were correct. Bethany was not George Belmont's daughter!

Zane grinned and shook his head. "Just as I figured. I'll have a talk with George and see what he wants to do."

"George, can I speak with you before we load up here?" Zane asked Belmont. Zane took George aside so Sherman wouldn't hear and give him the bad news.

George Belmont's face turned white when Zane told him his wife was at the lodge and Bethany was holed up in her room.

"What do you want us to do?" Zane asked.

"Marion doesn't know Bethany is at the Lodge?" George asked.

"No, Annie told Bethany and she is holed up in her room."

"Well that's a relief. We may have a murder about to happen if Marion finds Bethany. Have you got some place we can hide Beth?" George asked. His color had turned from white to red.

He was obviously embarrassed and caught in a trap of his own making.

"We will have to get her out of the Lodge. There is no place for her around there. There are no accommodations, in town, as it is too small. I can take her to my mothers and see if she can accommodate her until you figure out what to do? She lives alone and has room."

"Shit, guess I have my self in a pickle here. I appreciate it if you can hide Beth. This situation could cost me a large fortune as well as a divorce, very easily." George Belmont found himself between a rock and a hard place.

Zane went back and got his radio out and got Annie on. He told her to keep Bethany hid until they got back. Zane told her to Put Mrs. Belmont up in George's room.

"We will try to keep things under wraps until Mr. Belmont gets back." Zane could hear Annie suppressing a giggle.

The hunters loaded up and headed back to the lodge. When they returned, Belmont went to his room to see his wife.

Zane found Bethany whatever her name stored away in him and Jody's room.

"George asked me to run you into town. We have a place you can stay." Zane told her. Her eyes were large and her face was pale. Obviously she also realized George Belmont was in a hell of a messy situation with the potential for big trouble.

"I can't get out of here without Marion recognizing me. You have a hat or something to cover my hair?"

"I'll check with Annie. We will get your luggage for you later. Right now it is important for me to get you out of the Lodge." Zane went to talk with Annie about some clothing and a hat.

Annie came up with some Camouflage clothes and a large hat.

Zane took the disguised Bethany out the kitchen door and drove off with her in his truck. Once out of sight of the lodge she removed the hat and let her Blonde hair loose.

"Sorry about this. You must think quite badly off me." She said obviously embarrassed

"I don't get paid to think! I'm a hunting guide!" Zane said. He kept his eyes on the road, as he didn't want Bethany, whatever her name to see the amusement in his eyes.

"I do need to know your name though because I'm taking you to my mother's and I need to introduce you to her."

"It's Bethany Robins."

Bethany Robin's was quiet the rest of the way into town. Zane noticed his mothers' car at the store so he pulled in. "I'll be right back, anything you need? Something to drink?"

"A soda if you don't mind. Citrus kind." She added.

Zane went in the store. Rachel was at the check counter. "Hi Mom, I hope you don't mind but I've brought you a guest for a couple days."

"A friend of yours? Why isn't he staying at the lodge?" Rachel was glad to see Zane.

"It's a girl and she isn't a friend of mine but a friend of a friend. Is that all right?"

"Sure. I'm rattling around alone. Are you bringing her in here or taking her out to the house?"

"I'll run her to the house. Her name is Bethany Robin's and I need to get back to the lodge. We forgot her luggage and I'll get it in this evening." Zane pecked Rachel on the check and started back out the door when he remembered the soda. He went back to the cooler, got the soda and dug in his pocket for change. He handed his mother a handful of change. "See you this evening."

Zane went out and handed the soda to Bethany. He started the truck and headed for the Ranch.

"You will be here by yourself until my mother comes from the store. Her name is Rachel. Make yourself at home."

"What did you tell her?" Bethany asked.

"That you are a friend of a friend and you need place to stay. I'll be back this evening with your things. Annie will have them boxed by then. I'll talk with George and see what he wants to do."

"Don't bother with George. I'll decide from here what I am to do. Have George call me and I'll deal with him."

"You're choice." Zane drove up to the Ranch house and helped Bethany Robin's get out of the truck. He took her in the house.

"I hate to leave you here alone but I have to get back. It should not be more than a couple hours until mom comes. See you later."

"Thank you Zane. I will be fine. I appreciate you getting George out of trouble."

"You aren't in trouble?" Zane asked. Surprised she referred to George as the only one with a problem.

"No, I'm not the one with a wife or husband. I'm only in trouble for being foolish." Bethany smiled and Zane noticed she looked more at ease than she had since she first came to the Lodge with George Belmont.

"See you later." Zane left Bethany Robins standing in the middle of the Ranch house. He knew when his mother came she would be in good hands. He chuckled to himself on the way back to the Lodge. These Dudes. He wondered how much George Belmont stood to lose if Marion Belmont had found Bethany at the lodge. By Georges reaction he bet it is a lot!

3

Zane returned to the lodge. As he went into the kitchen, he saw a couple, large boxes stacked on the floor. He surmised it was Bethany's luggage.

"Well is it quiet on the western front." He asked as Annie turned from the stove with a mischievous grin on her face.

"First of all, I owe you an apology about telling you it wasn't any of our business about George's daughter! It seems it quickly became our business when Mrs. Belmont showed up.

Boy, is she a piece of work. I can't blame George for sneaking around with that sweet girl after getting a load of his Mrs."

Zane grinned widely. "I figured she wasn't his daughter. She is kind of a quiet shy girl and not at all the kind you would expect some rich guy from Michigan to be tangled up with. Do you know what he does for a living?"

"No but from the rags that wife is wearing I'll bet he has some big bucks. By the way those boxes go to your mother's house, Bethany's suitcases are inside and speaking of big bucks there is a thousand dollars in that envelope on top."

"Is that for Bethany's lodging?" Zane asked.

"No, Belmont said he would take care of that separately. That is your money for getting her out of here and saving him a big scene."

"I'll share it with you. You did as much as anybody to save his sorry ass." Zane laughed.

"No need. I have my own thousand thanks to Mr. Belmont. Also Jack said for you to gas your truck out of the fuel tank as this running back and forth is Lodge expense." Annie turned back to her cooking. She was just taking up the evening meal.

"You better eat before you take those boxes in."

Zane sat down to eat and Jody came in with a grin on his face. "You get your freight delivered?" He asked sliding into the table for his dinner.

"Not all of it." Zane grinned, indicating the boxes stacked by the door.

"You going to have time to get a hunt put together for the Michigan guy or is he tied up with his wife here?" Jody asked as he shoveled in his dinner.

"I have to run in town and won't have time to confer with him. Can you do that and ask him if he wants to go? I can take him back into the glades where he got the shot. That should be calmed down by now and there are elk hanging around in there."

"Yeah, I'll go talk with him. You'll be back tonight or in the morning?"

"Probably tonight. I hate making the drive early before a hunt, but I will be here." Zane promised. "Thanks Annie." Zane got up and grabbed the boxes and headed out the back door and put them in the truck. He pulled over to the gas barrel and fueled up his truck. He noticed George Belmont had come out of the lodge and seeing Zane he headed for him.

"Is everything all right George?" Zane asked trying to keep the amusement out of his voice.

"Thanks to you." George said with relief visible on his face. He took a check out of his pocket and told Zane, "Give this to Bethany."

Zane noticed the check was made out for $5000 dollars. "Bethany asked that you call her." Zane gave him the number. "Jody will talk with you about tomorrow if you still want to hunt?"

"That's what I came here for." Belmont said.

"See you in the morning." Zane wondered if that's what he came for why had he brought a liaison along with him. Belmont headed back into the lodge and Zane got in his truck and headed for the second time for home.

"It was well after dark when he pulled into the Ranch. He packed the boxes in and heard women laughing from the kitchen. Zane stepped into the kitchen and found his mother and Bethany Robins apparently enjoying each other visiting over some tea.

"Back with your luggage." Zane said and kissed his mother on the cheek.

"Beth and I have been having a very nice visit. "Rachel told Zane. Zane could see his mother liked Beth as she called her, very much. "You have time for a cup of tea?"

"Sure Mom." Rachel got up to get the tea and Zane took the check Belmont had given him for Bethany out of his shirt pocket and slipped it to her.

She stared at the check without expression and tore it in half and stuffed it in her pocket. Her expression didn't change.

Rachel returned with Zane's tea. "Thanks" Zane said not taking his eyes off the face of Bethany or Beth as his mother had referred to her. Apparently she had told Rachel to call her Beth. The phone rang about then and Rachel answered it.

"For you Beth" Rachel handed the phone to Bethany. Beth looked around the kitchen and put her hand over the receiver. "Do you have another extension?" She asked.

Zane jumped to his feet and herded his mother out of the kitchen. "We'll give you some privacy." He said realizing it was no doubt Belmont on the phone.

In the living room Zane took the thousand dollars out of his billfold and gave it to his mother. "Some of that you can use for Beth's board and room." He said. He realized Beth was not going to use any of the check Belmont had sent with him.

"That isn't necessary Zane. Beth has already given me $500.00 dollars. She is a very nice young lady and the way she talked she doesn't have any money problems. She indicated to me she would like to stay a while if I would have her and I told her it would be fine. She will be nice company for me here all by myself. You know we have plenty of room."

Zane didn't know what to make of the situation. Apparently Bethany Robin's was not dependant on George Belmont for money but there was little doubt her presence at the Lodge was a threat to Belmont's financial security when his wife showed up.

"I guess that is up to you, Mom. But I have to tell you I don't know this young lady very well.

She needed a place to stay temporarily and there are no accommodations around so I offered. I 'm sure you already know more about her than I do."

"Yes I do. And I'm positive she is a really nice young woman, so don't you worry. I and Beth Robin's will get along just fine."

Zane trusted his mother's opinion of people. She had good instincts and Zane was a bit confused about the entire situation but he needed to get back to the Lodge. "All right mom, just so you know, I don't know much about her."

"We will do just fine. I'll tell Beth you said goodbye, unless you want to your self?"

"That won't be necessary. You tell her. "Zane kissed his mother and left Beth Robin's in her capable hands, he headed back to the Lodge and his early morning hunt with George Belmont.

When Zane got back to the Lodge it was late and he went straight to bed to get a few hours of sleep before his hunt with Belmont.

The next morning at Breakfast Zane was tired. He had not slept well. Used to physical exercise he found his involvement in George Belmont's personal affairs and his two trips to town to be tiring.

George however was alert and looked as if he had slept well and he was anxious to get back into the area he missed the Bull.

As he and Zane drove up to the upper road. George asked Zane if he had given the check to Bethany. Zane told George, "She tore it up and put it in her pocket."

"That doesn't surprise me. Bethany isn't my daughter but she isn't what you guys' think either."

"I don't think much, I'm a hunting guide." Zane grinned.

"Bethany Robins is the daughter of my dead business partner. I'm her Godfather and Bethany has no family. I've tried to take care of her since Doug died, as she hasn't any other family.

However my wife has never believed the closeness between me and Bethany was innocent and if she found out Bethany had come on this trip my marriage would be over. I doubt, if her divorce attorney would believe our relationship innocent either. However it has only been a few months since Doug died and I thought this trip would help Bethany deal with her fathers loss."

"Why did she tear up the check you sent her?" Zane asked.

"Bethany's father left her a great deal of money. I guess she didn't want me to help because the way it may look. It didn't look good, did it?"

Zane grinned and shrugged. "None of my business. My business is to find you an Elk."

"I just wished Marion would realize that Bethany is like a daughter to me. I've never had children and Bethany is as close as I am going to ever have a child. Marion and I have only been married for five years and she is insanely jealous of that girl. It would not have been pretty if she found her at the lodge. Thanks for getting me out of that pickle. Who knew Marion would follow me to a hunting lodge. Maybe she knew Bethany was also out of town and surmised I had taken her with me."

"Well Beth is safe at my mother's and your wife is snuggled in at the lodge. Now let's see if we can find you an Elk!" Zane grinned as he parked on the high road and him and George Belmont made ready to go back down through the fern glades.

"She must have told you she prefers to be called Beth." George said as he got his rifle out.

"No, she told my mother. Actually she has not said much of anything to me. She was very quiet when I took her into town yesterday."

"She is a bit shy and doesn't talk much. She has finished college though and is twenty-two years old. She just never has much to say. I don't know of another living soul she is close to but me. I have never met any of her friends. What's more I don't know if she has any. She was devoted to Doug since her mother died. I'm afraid she is a very lonely young woman and with Marion's attitude I'm not sure there is much I can do to help. I don't want to lose my wife over trying to look after Bethany. Besides Bethany is old enough to start finding her own way.

Enough of that! Let's find me another Elk and see if I can screw that up also."

Zane grinned and shook his head. He was beginning to feel sorry for George Belmont wealthy Michigan Hunter that had so many problems. One of which was in his own house with his mother.

George and Zane dropped of the high road and once again started down in the fern Glades. In the distance Zane heard a wolf howl and others join him. By the sound they were hot on some prey in the far distance. George looked at Zane with a question in his eyes.

"Wolves", Zane said and proceeded down the game trail. George followed behind. Soon the wolves were quiet. Either they gave up or made their kill. There was fresh, elk sign. Zane was right! The Elk were still in the glades. The single shot George had fire that day had not caused them to move out of the area.

The further down the glades they moved the more signs the Elk had recently been there. Zane heard a faint sound below. George did not hear it but when Zane held his hand out to stop his movement George stopped. Zane blew the cow call with the reed in his mouth. There was immediately an answer below. George and Zane both got up on a downed log and were peering over into the fern glade below. Zane's practiced eye found the lighter tawny body of a bull. He motioned toward it. George this time took his time and when he fired Zane seen the Elks legs' buckle. Zane jumped off the log and at that instant Zane heard another rifle crack. He watched in horror as he saw George Belmont, throw his rifle in the air as he was blown backward off the log they had both been standing on. Zane had no idea where the second shot had come from but he knew immediately that George had been hit.

Not sure if more shots were to come, Zane crawled over to George Belmont and could see from the hole in George's side that there was little he could do for him. George Belmont was dead. Zane didn't know how or where the shot had come from but he struggled his pack from his back and got the radio out.

"Jack, I got big trouble. George Belmont has been shot!"

"What!" Jack came on the radio. He thought he was hearing things.

"George Belmont has been shot and killed. I don't know where the bullet came from but he's dead. You better get the sheriff up here!"

"Holy shit! Are you all right?" Jack asked?

"Yeah, I'm still down below this log but I'm all right. George just shot an Elk and we were both up on a log. The shot came from my side, if I hadn't stepped off it would have hit me instead."

"I'll get the Sheriff and Coroner up there, right away." Jack said.

Zane knew there was nothing that could be done for George Belmont. He scanned the direction the shot had come in from. Zane could see nobody. He got on his feet and crossed the glade with his pack and began to dress out the elk George had shot. He was not about to let the animal go to waste no matter what the circumstances. While Zane dressed out the elk he wondered if it had been a stray bullet that had accidentally struck George Belmont. He knew if he had not at the exact right time stepped off the log it would have hit him instead of George. It was the first time Zane had been around a hunting fatality.

By the time Zane had dressed out the elk and propped the brisket open he heard the helicopter. Zane moved out into the fern glade and began to wave the orange vest he had taken from his backpack. It would be difficult for the chopper to spot a hunter in camouflage clothing such as Zane wore. The chopper set down in the big fern glade.

Zane recognized Sheriff Anderson as he exited the chopper. He also recognized Alan Sharp the Physician, Coroner.

The helicopter pilot cut the engine to the chopper.

"Hello Zane. I hear you have a fatality here? "Sheriff Anderson had known Zane and his family all of Zane's life.

"Yeah, my hunter from Michigan took a bullet. His name is George Belmont and he is laying over here behind a log."

The pudgy Sheriff huffed as Zane took him up the glade and showed him where George had fallen. Zane had not moved him, as he had known at first glance George was dead. George's rifle also was lying where George had thrown it when he got hit.

Alan Sharp the coroner got out his death papers and started filling them out. He also knew there was no doubt George was dead.

Sheriff Anderson began to take pictures and drew a diagram with Zane's help where they had both been when the bullet came in that hit George.

Zane and Sheriff Anderson both looked over toward the area from where they figured the bullet had come from. "We'll ask around and try to figure out what other hunters were in this area." The Sheriff said. "Also we might get lucky and find out what caliber of a rifle the fatal bullet came from. What do you know about this hunter?"

"Just that he is from Michigan. I think he was pretty well off. He checked in with his partner's daughter but she left yesterday. His wife showed up yesterday and she is still at the lodge as far as I know." Zane said.

"Does she look, like someone that would shoot a man?" Sheriff Anderson grinned.

"I don't know. I haven't seen her yet." Zane said. "Belmont had just shot an Elk a split second before he took the bullet. I dressed it out. I guess we need to find out what his Mrs. might, want done with that?"

"Always the hunter. Aren't you Zane? Most guys under these circumstances wouldn't think to take care for a carcass."

"It kept me occupied, so I didn't have to sit here waiting and looking at my dead hunter."

"Well tell Jack I'll be at the lodge soon as I take the Body out. The Coroner could go with the chopper but I'm too fat to walk out of here with you. Guess I'll drive up after we get back to talk with Jack and the dead guys' wife.

"You need help getting Georges body on the chopper?" Zane asked.

The overweight sheriff agreed and the helicopter pilot and Zane put the Body of George Belmont on the basket under the chopper and they lifted out leaving Zane with Georges Elk and rifle.

Zane got on the radio and asked Jack to send Jody with a couple packhorses.

"Yeah, he just got back. I'll send him. What you need the pack horses for?"

"There is a Bull elk laying here George just shot before he got hit. I guess you can inform Mrs. Belmont. The Sheriff will need to speak to her."

"What about the girl?"

"I'll take care of that once I get out of here." Zane said. If what George said was true, Bethany Robins would be dealing with yet another loss.

It was after noon by the time Jody came riding into the glade on one horse and leading two more with packsaddles.

"Hear you have been having a very unusual morning." Jody grinned.

"Boy, you can say that again!" Zane said. "We have an Elk to pack and my dead hunter is already in the morgue. What about Jack and Annie, they having a hard time with Mrs. Belmont?"

"Yeah, they had to get a doctor up there to sedate her. She wanted to hell out of there to go to the morgue but she wasn't in any condition to do that. It's a hell of a mess. This the first time you see someone get killed?"

"Yeah! I knew he was dead as soon as he hit the ground. Must have been a fast big gun because it literally blew him off the log he was standing on."

"Where were you?" Jody asked.

"Standing beside him, as the bull went down, I jumped off the log and Belmont took it in his left side. A few seconds before it would have been me."

"Your lucky day, I guess." Jody began to load the elk Zane had quartered on the packhorses.

Zane walked up by the log and picked up Belmont's rifle. He brought it down and tied it on top one of the meat packs.

With a half Elk on each horse Jody offered to let Zane ride out behind him on the third horse.

"I believe I will. This has been one bitch of a day." Zane got on behind Jody and the two guides rode out with Belmont's Elk behind them on the other two horses. When they topped out with the pack horses they unloaded the meat into the Suburban, Zane and George had left. Jody took the truck, trailer and horses back to the lodge.

When Zane and Jody got to the lodge, Zane went to the kitchen. He needed a hot cup of coffee. When he came in Annie come and put her arms around him and gave him a hug.

"Been a bad day for you, I'm so sorry Zane."

"Thanks Annie, Can't be too easy for you and Jack either."

"We've lost a couple hunters through the years but this is the first one that has been shot. That must have been hair-raising, ordeal for you?"

"It would have been me, if I had not just jumped off the log. How is Mrs. Belmont taking it?"

"Not good but she is very glad she came out here as she got to spend one last night with her husband. She is very much a woman, grief stricken. We had to get Doc Barns out to sedate her.

Sheriff Anderson wants to speak to her soon as he can. I think they are going to rule it an accident. Apparently they need to have a Coroners' inquest to determine the cause of death."

"I'll help Jody get the meat hung and then I better go talk with Bethany Robins. She is apparently Belmont's late partners daughter. He had recently died and Mrs. Belmont is jealous of Bethany. Belmont swore his interest in her is paternal as she is his God daughter."

"It will also be difficult for her. I see no reason we need to tell Mrs. Belmont she is here. Do you?" Annie wondered.

"That information can only hurt Belmont's wife! I agree there is no reason to tell her. It isn't as if she had anything to do with his death." Zane agreed.

Zane went back out and started hanging the Elk quarters in the meat house. He had started skinning when Jody showed up to help after taking care of the pack animals.

"Can you finish up here Jody?" Zane asked. "I have to go in and let the girl know about Belmont's death."

"Sure, you got it hung it won't take me long to get the hide off. What are we to do about a tag on this animal? In case the game warden comes around checking."

"The Sheriff knew Belmont shot it and I had dressed it by the time they took his body, I would imagine that Mrs. Belmont will have to decide what we are to do with it." Zane grinned and shook his head. It was new to him he had never had a situation like this day, in his life. It was even worse than the day before which in itself was no ordinary day. Zane hoped he never again have a day as this one had been and it was not yet over. He still had to deliver the bad news to the girl in his mother's house.

Zane went in and showered before he headed for town. It was after eight that evening when he got home.

As he entered the back porch he could see his mother and Beth sitting at the kitchen table. When he came in the back door, Rachel jumped up. Glad to see him, she went to give him a hug but she knew by the set of his jaw, something was amiss.

"What's going on Zane?" She asked. Concern on her face.

"I'm afraid I have bad news for Bethany."

Bethany Robins looked at him expectantly. Her mind ran wild. Was he going to ask her to leave his mothers house or what could he know that could affect her or be bad news?

"I'm sorry to have to tell you George Belmont was killed this morning."

Bethany stared at Zane Adam's. He could tell it wasn't registering. Slowly realization dawned on her. Tears welled in her eyes and her lips trembled. "How?" She said in a trembling voice.

"He was shot by a stray bullet." Zane looked away as he saw the grief in her eyes.

Her hands fluttered aimlessly. The tears began to roll down her face. "He was like a father to me." Bethany got up and ran blindly out of the room. Zane looked at his mother helplessly.

Rachel stood not quite understanding the scene she had witnessed." Is that her father's partner?" She asked Zane?

"Yeah, I didn't know their connection until George told me this morning before we went hunting. Apparently George's wife hates Beth and she showed up yesterday. George had brought Beth with him on this trip to get her out of Detroit after losing her father recently. Because of the jealousy between them, I brought Bethany here to keep Mrs. Belmont from finding she had come with George. We all thought something underhanded was going on but I believed George when he told me this morning what the deal was."

"Poor girl, no wonder she is devastated. I'll go see if I can help." Rachel went to find Beth.

Zane got a beer out of the refrigerator and sat down to the kitchen table. "One hell of a day" he muttered. After Zane finished his beer, he called the Lodge. Annie answered.

"Hi, Annie, this is Zane. I don't believe I will be up until morning."

"That's fine, we weren't expecting you to return tonight and take your time coming in the morning. Jack still hasn't scheduled anything for you. Sheriff Anderson was here and spoke to Belmont's wife. I believe she is leaving in the morning for Michigan, Get some rest Zane!"

Zane hung up and went upstairs and crawled in his bed. It had been a day he hoped to never have again. Although exhausted Zane could not sleep. In his mind he still saw George Belmont as he threw his rifle in the air when he was blown off the log. Zane thought he would return at first chance and try to figure out where that fatal shot had come from. It was obvious that Sheriff Anderson was not going to inspect the area the shot could possibly come in from. There had to be something where the shot was fired. Boot tracks, rifle casing or something. When Zane returned, he wanted to investigate and try to figure out what happened.

The hunters within that area had been scarce this year because of the abundance of wolves and the shortage of game. Also the high gas prices had cut down on the amount of hunter's that far out. It is not often that a stray bullet accidentally hits a hunter. It happens but the odds of a single shot finding a human on a missed animal are astronomical.

There had been very few hunting fatalities in Idaho by hunters mistaken for game since the days they quit hunting any Elk and now hunted only Bulls. That restriction caused most Elk hunters to be positive of their target.

Zane was uncomfortable that George Belmont could have been a deliberate target. If that were the case, the bullet would not have likely hit Zane if he had not moved in those last seconds.

If Belmont was the target there had been other chances that he had been open for a shot and away from Zane. Zane could think of no reason anyone would want to shoot at himself. It must be the fluke of a missed shot but Zane would return to see what he could find.

He thought about Beth Robin's and wondered if she was going to return to Michigan to attend Belmont's funeral. He thought about what George had said about her having nobody. He wondered what kind of business George and Robin's were in and if that meant Bethany and Marion Belmont was now partner's in that business.

Zane found himself getting a headache thinking of all of the things or ramifications of George's death. He got up and took a couple aspirins. He finally drifted into uneasy sleep. He dreamed of George Belmont's death and awoke bathed in sweat. He was unable to return to sleep and finally as morning broke he heard his mother downstairs moving around in the kitchen.

Zane got up and dressed and went down to see if Rachel had coffee.

"Good morning Zane, you look as if you didn't get much rest." Rachel put a fresh cup of coffee in front of Zane as he sat down at the table.

"I didn't." Zane said gloomily. "I kept seeing George as he took that bullet. How is your Beth girl taking it?"

"Not good, apparently this George was very important to her."

"Yeah, according to what George said, she is the closest thing he had to a child of his own."

"I think she felt the same about him." Rachel said. "I don't think she got much rest either."

Somehow Zane felt a sense of responsibility to George Belmont where the girl Bethany was concerned. Zane didn't know what he was to do about her loss but he was willing to help her any way he could. He was glad that his mother seemed to have a rapport with the girl.

"I wonder if she will return to Michigan for the funeral?" Zane asked Rachel.

"I'm sure she will by the way she talked last night. She offered to give me more money for the use of the phone but I told, her that wasn't necessary. To use the phone as she needed."

"This is going to impact Jack and Annie at the lodge. Maybe it won't this year but certainly next year. That is if the wolves haven't put them out of business by then."

"Always something to cause a person worry." Rachel said. Zane looked at her sharply. He well knew his mother had more than her share. He hoped his bringing Bethany Robin's into their home was not going to cause her more!

"Good morning Beth, I hope you got a little rest, you, poor dear." Rachel said as Beth came into the kitchen. "Would you like coffee? Or I can fix you tea?"

Beth Robin's took a chair at the table with Zane. She was looking right at Zane. "Coffee will be fine, thank you Rachel. Her voice was soft but steady. Without taking her eyes from Zane she asked? "Where you with George when he died?"

"Yes, it was just George and I. He had just shot an elk when he got hit." Zane saw her flinch when he said he got hit.

"Did he suffer?" She asked? Her voice was still steady and calm.

"No, I don't think he even knew what hit him. He died instantly. He had talked about you before we started hunting and told me he felt you were the closest he would ever have for a daughter. I know he was sincere. George Belmont didn't act like a man who didn't mean what he said." Zane didn't know what else to say to her.

Her gaze remained steady. "He was important to me and my father both." She said softly. She looked down as Rachel put the coffee in front of her.

"I appreciate your mother and your kindness," She said again looking at Zane.

"I wish we could do more. Do you plan to return to Michigan for Georges funeral?" Zane asked.

"I'm not sure. I will need to make some calls. I'm sure Marion will hate it if I am there, but she will need to deal with me on some level, it seems we will now be partners in business."

"What business were George and your Father in?" Zane asked sipping his coffee.

"Manufacturing. There is a factory in Detroit that we handle military contracts and manufacture supplies."

"Will you be expected to handle that?" Zane asked. He hoped he was not being too nosey but the young woman sitting at his table with visible signs of grief did not look as if she was up to handling the running of a factory.

"No, of coarse not. There is a CEO and a board of Directors, Neither Marion nor I will be required to do anything but listen to the accounting reports and attend the board meeting of the Director. We are the major shareholders."

"That might prove to be awkward if you and Mrs. Belmont don't get along?" Zane wondered.

"She will not have to put up with me. I might stay out west here. This is the first place I have felt welcome since my father died. That is if Rachel would be kind enough to tolerate me until I find a place."

"It will be no problem at all! Beth, please stay as long as you want. You have been welcome company to me." Rachel smiled at Beth Robin's warmly.

Zane was flabbergasted at his mother's apparent fondness for the girl she had just met. All though Zane felt a certain responsibility for Beth Robin's he had no idea why his mother was so taken with her.

"Thank you. I will need to go today some how and take care of a few things. Is there a car rental around?"

Zane chuckled. "You stand a better chance renting a jackass to ride around here than you do renting a car. I don't know where the nearest rental agency is, Maybe Lewiston?" He looked at Rachel.

"Well is there a dealer? I could buy a car? Also, I need a cell phone and a laptop." Beth looked worried as she realized she was as far into the wilderness as she could get within the continental United States.

"I'll take you into Lewiston and we will see what can be done." Rachel said.

"Are you going back to the Lodge this morning?" Rachel asked Zane.

"They aren't expecting me. Annie talked last night like things were at a stand still until the Coroner rules on Georges death." Zane looked at Beth. "Sorry about having to keep bringing it up."

"I must learn to deal with it." She said sadly.

"I'm going to call Chuck and see if he can get by without me today? Mabel has been down for several days." She explained to Zane. Rachel went to the phone to call Chuck.

Zane studied the pretty blonde girl that obviously had to deal with complicated situations that Zane, as a country boy had no idea what it might entail. One thing Zane was certain, was that the young woman appeared to be composed and knew what she needed to do.

Rachel got off the phone and told Beth she would be able to take her into Lewiston to take care of her business. Confident Beth Robins was in good hands with his mother Zane planned to go back to the Lodge. He was anxious to get into, the area the shot that killed George came from.

Zane felt in his gut there were many questions to be answered if one was to track down where that fatal bullet originated?

4

After Beth and Rachel left for Lewiston, Zane did the farm chores. His mother had not had time. When he was finished taking care of the animal's Zane, got in his truck and headed out. Going through town and seeing only one rig at Pete's Bar Zane decided to stop and find out what Pete had heard.

As he came in Pete was alone behind the bar. He had been watching as Zane got out of his truck." Well there's the mountain man! Heard you lost a hunter yesterday?"

"Yeah, but until they are done there isn't anything I can talk about." Zane sat on a stool and Pete set him up a beer. Zane nearly refused but decided one wouldn't hurt anything.

"What have you heard?" He asked Pete.

"Not much except your hunter took a stray bullet. Is that all there is?"

"Pretty much the story for right now, they are to have a Coroners inquest and I can't talk about it until after that." Zane grinned. He could see Pete was about to burst wanting to know more.

"What the hell did you do to Gina, the bombshell?" Pete wanted to know quickly changing the subject. Zane wondered if that was the reason why Pete looked about to burst.

Startled by the question, Zane said. "Nothing! Why?"

Since nobody was in the place, Pete told Zane what had been going on. "Usually anybody screws with that Gina, she runs home and tells Punk so she can turn them into Punks punching bag! I haven't heard a damn thing about you and her from anybody but Gina herself. She has sneaked in here a couple times to ask me if I had seen you? Gina is being damned awful quiet about her leaving the other evening with you. What did you do to her? Pretty hard to keep that one quiet, she thrives on causing trouble."

"I don't know." Zane grinned. "What makes you think I did anything to her?"

"Aw come on Zane, she had you so hot you were about to have a melt down when you two left this place! You can't shit an old shitter like me. I know something happened between you and Gina but I don't know why she is keeping it quiet?"

"Maybe you don't know as much as you think you do!" Zane grinned. Finishing his beer, he got off the stool and paid for his beer and proceeded out the door leaving Pete alone behind the bar.

"What do you want me to tell her?" Pete hollered after Zane.

"Tell her, you seen me, or whatever you like!" Zane grinning went out and got in his truck and headed to the lodge.

On the way to the lodge Zane began to think about Gina Daniels. So, she had not run and told Punk. Maybe he wouldn't have to battle Punk over that hot piece after all. But if Gina was being quiet he knew it was because she was hoping to get her hands on him again sometime. Zane had no plans for that to happen. As he told Rachel, it was a lapse of judgment on his part. But he smiled remembering being with Gina. She was a very satisfying lay! He would sorely be tempted not to refuse if she caught him in need or the right frame of mind!

Zane got back to the Lodge just after lunch. He went into the kitchen to find Annie at the table having Coffee.

"Where is everybody?" Zane asked sitting down at the table with Annie Cutler.

"Jack took Mrs. Belmont to Spokane to catch a flight to Michigan. She is going to make arrangements for her husband's body to be sent back. Jody took Sherman down on the creek. This is his last day. Jody is hoping to get him a shot at least. The only other Hunter is the Guy from Pennsylvania that just came in. He is resting in his room. Somebody will need to take him in the morning?

Did you get rid of your house guest, the blonde girl that came from Michigan with Belmont?"

"No, I don't know what is going on there. It appears my mother is about to adopt her. For some reason Mom has taken to her like I've never seen her take to someone." Zane grinned and shook his head. It was beyond him.

"What about you Zane? She is a very pretty girl!" Annie smiled.

"I guess I hadn't noticed that. I sort of feel responsible for her after what George told me, but I guess with so much happening I had not paid much mind to what she looks like. I think she is tougher than she looks. Mom took her to Lewiston to get her a car, cell phone and laptop. Seems her and Mrs. Belmont jointly owns a factory in Michigan."

"That should be interesting if Mrs. Belmont hates her?" Annie smiled.

"Maybe with George dead her reason for hating Beth is also gone. Beth made the remark Marion Belmont would have to learn to deal with her as they are now partners in this factory."

"When does the girl plan to return to Michigan?"

"I don't know. She is forming an attachment to my mother and my mother to her. Beats the hell out of me?" Zane said. "I'm going over into the glades where George got shot. I'll take my radio. Give me a holler if you need me." Zane got up and went in and got his backpack and his side arm pistol. He took his truck and drove up on the high road and parked where he and George parked that fateful morning.

Zane made his way down through the glades where he and George had went the day before. When he got down to where George was killed the Raven's flew up off the gut pile where Zane had dressed our George's Bull.

Zane took the bright orange vest he had signaled the chopper with and laid it on the log where he and George had been standing when the bullet struck!

Zane took his pack and headed East toward the area the bullet came from. He crossed down into a chaparral draw and climbed up on the next ridge. It was about two hundred yards back and Zane could clearly see the vest on the log where he had left it, from that vantage point Zane was certain he would have noticed another hunter if one had been on that ridge. There was not much that escaped Zane's attention despite the fact the Elk were in the glade at the time.

The shot would have had to come in from this ridge or the next. Zane was almost certain the shell had not traveled over four or five hundred yards. Not with it blowing the left side of George Belmont's body out. Zane was sure even a magnum would have not had that much power if it had traveled more than five hundred yards and do the damage it did!

Zane had dropped low enough on the ridge that as he made his way up he could detect any sign on top of the ridge consistence with the route of the bullet, which would be on target toward the orange vest.

Zane had tracked animals for many years and he paid no attention to the animal tracks. He made his way up the ridge until he was above where the bullet path could have been. He had not found any sign of any foot tracks on that ridge whatsoever.

Zane dropped down into the next brushy draw and climbed the next ridge. When he topped the next ridge, he worked his way up until he could see the orange vest on the log in the distance. He carefully scoured the ground as he worked his way up. Suddenly he saw a track in the moss that was not made by an animal. Zane cursed the dry conditions that made reading tracks so difficult. He spent some time trying to determine which direction the single track had come in from?

Zane looked over in the distance at the orange vest. He took out his range finder and figured the range to the vest was 430 yards. If the shot that killed

George was deliberate, it was an easy shot for someone very good with a rifle. If it were by accident, the hunter would have been further to the east shooting uphill for the trajectory of the bullet to come into the area of the orange vest.

Zane concentrated on the foot track he had found. He tracked several feet in a widening circle and found a couple more tracks. It did not appear whoever, had made the tracks had not been hunting but had walked around aimlessly.

Zane finally happened onto an area that was trampled down in a circle as if someone had waited and trampled the grass and weeds and paced in a circle for some time as if they waited in that spot. The tracks appeared to be just over twenty-four hours that would mean it could very well be the tracks of whoever fired the fatal shot.

Zane frowned as he wondered who would be laying in wait?. And who was the target? Certainly George Belmont had taken the bullet but a few seconds before it would have been Zane. Zane could think of no reason why anyone would be laying in wait, to kill him?

Zane looked to see how the person could have gotten to that vantage point. Who would even know that he and George were going in those glades? It would have to be someone with knowledge such as someone from the Lodge. The whole idea was ludicrous.

Someone could have come from the road down below that came out on Stoney Creek. It would be only about a quarter of a mile onto the ridge overlooking the glade. The problem was that nobody had a reason to want Zane dead and if someone wanted George Belmont dead they would not have had access to the knowledge to get it done from where Zane found there had been a person. Such a person would have to have known that Zane and George would be in that area?

Zane looked around for any tangible thing. A shell casing, a candy wrapper, a cigarette butts. There was nothing but the trampled grass to indicate there had been someone on the ridge that could have fired the fatal shot. The only clue was in one place Zane could make out the round knobs from hiking boot tracks. This tread was widely used by makers of all kinds of boots. That did not give Zane much to go on.

Zane was certain there had been someone there but unable to figure out why he or she were there and discounting that anyone had reason to want him dead, Zane decided to pull out of the area and keep what he discovered to himself. None of it made any sense.

Zane crossed back down across the two draws and returned to the fern glade where the shooting took place. He picked the orange vest off the log and put it in his pack

He climbed back up to the high road where he had left his pickup and returned to the Lodge. His trip into the glades had caused more questions than answers. He wondered if anyone would ever know the reason George Belmont was shot?

When Zane returned to the Lodge Jody had come back with the older hunter Sherman. Sherman had bagged a nice buck. No elk but he was happy with the Buck and Jody was busy skinning it out at the meat house.

"Where did Sherman get the Buck?" Zane asked.

"Down on the creek. I saw your truck over on the high road. What were you doing? Did you forget something down in there, yesterday?" Jody asked.

"No just looking around. Still trying to figure out what happened. Did you see where a rig had been parked over on the Stoney Creek side of those Glades?" Zane asked.

"No, but then I didn't pay much attention, you think that is where the other hunter came in from?" Jody asked.

"I don't know. I reckon we are never going to know. Bugging the hell out of me though. I hate it because I lost the hunter while he was in my charge."

"I can about imagine. It would bother me also. I hope it never happens to me."

"I hope so also. It doesn't feel good. You need some help?" Zane asked. The two guides always worked together to get things done.

"Thanks! I got it now. You going to take the new guy from Pennsylvania in the morning?"

"You want to take him?" Zane asked.

"Yeah I can, that way if there is anything left to be done on the Belmont death you will be available." Jody smiled. He hoped he was being helpful. He could well imagine what Zane was feeling losing a hunter.

"The blonde girl, take off for Michigan or is she still at your mothers?"

"Still with my mother. I think my Mother is planning on keeping the girl and adopting her. Seems Mom is quite taken with that Beth."

"What about you, She's a looker! You probably aren't too unhappy with her around!" Jody teased his dark eyes sparkling with amusement.

"I haven't seen much of her and I well imagine she will be heading for Michigan and Belmont's funeral. If you are taking over tomorrow I might go back home and see if I can help get her ready to leave. I might have to take her into Spokane if she flies. Especially if Mom has to work at the store."

"Go do what you have to. Don't worry, with one hunter we can manage without you."

"Thanks Jody, you're a good friend and partner."

Zane went in the kitchen to discuss his plans with Annie. He told her Jody was taking over for him and he was going home to help his mother with Beth Robins. "If anything comes up and you need me, back here just call." Zane said. He wanted to know if Jack had returned?

"No but he is back in town. He got Belmont's wife out on an afternoon flight. They are going to let her have Belmont's body before the inquest and Jack figures they are going to list it as a hunting accident fatality. The inquest will only be a formality where you tell what happened to get it on the record."

"This could hurt the Lodge in another year if the Wolves don't put us out of business first." Zane told Annie regretfully.

"It won't make much impact. We may not have many Michigan hunters sign up from Detroit but they come from all over the country. Word doesn't spread in the outside world like it does in our little corner of the world." Annie said.

"Our little corner of the world is thousands of acres of beautiful country, with probably more Wolves than people out here."

"Yeah but wolves don't carry tales." Annie laughed. "I'll call you if we need you, don't be so hard on yourself Zane, Jack and I value you and love you like the son we never had. Don't worry things will get back to normal soon." Annie hugged Zane as he left. She knew the young man was upset over losing the hunter. It didn't change her and Jack's opinion of Zane Adam's one bit. He did not yet know it but he would someday be the future of Cutler guide and Outfitters.

Zane drove back into town. When he returned to the ranch Rachel and Bethany had not yet returned. Zane did the evening ranch chores and rummaged in the refrigerator for an evening snack. He went in the living room and turned on the Television. He laid his long rangy frame on the sofa and because he slept very little the night before he fell asleep on the Sofa.

Rachel and Beth returned about eight o clocks and awakened him. They were laughing when they came in the door.

"Well it seems you two are having a good time." Zane yawned without getting off the couch.

"Beth bought the town of Lewiston." Rachel laughed. "Suppose you can lend us a hand getting those packages in?"

"Sure", Zane went out and found not one car full of packages but Beth had also bought a brand new Toyota Camry and both cars were full of packages.

"I did not bring much with me when I came with George." She explained as she looked guilty as Zane packed packages crammed nearly everywhere in both cars.

"I guess a woman, need more stuff than men." Zane thought there must have been a small fortune spent on the stuff in both cars. Beth also had her cell phone and her laptop. "I won't be running your mother's phone bill up since I have my own phone." She explained.

After the house was strewn with Beth's packages Zane told her Marion Belmont had flown out of Spokane for Michigan and he asked if she had found out when the funeral was to be.

"It will be Monday next week. I plan to drive to Spokane and leave my car at the airport until I return." She told him. From all appearances Bethany Robins had every intention of staying an undetermined time with Rachel Adams.

Zane could see Rachel was very happy and excited about the girl staying with her. Zane didn't understand it but he supposed it was all right as long as it was making his mother happy. He still had no clue why Rachel had taken Bethany Robins under her wing.

It didn't bother Zane as he was often gone and he knew it would be nice to have Beth with his mother. She spent way too much time alone. Zane didn't know how he felt about the young woman being in the house but he supposed it would be no bother for him also. He did wonder what Beth Robins was going to find to occupy her in such a small town.

He would think someone from Detroit would probably be bored in a short time if she could find nothing to do. He wondered if she planned on flying in and out of the wildernesses in Idaho to handle the details she would need to handle in her corporate world. Zane knew nothing about what that entailed. He was merely a mountain man and Elk guide and a part time small rancher.

It would not be long once the Lodge finished the season Zane would be on the Ranch full time taking care of the small herd of cattle.

He wondered how Beth Robins Corporation Owner, would adapt to a very different world than where she had come from.

Once the packages were in the house, Zane excused himself and went upstairs and went to bed. This time he slept soundly.

The next morning Zane came down the stairs to find the shopping clutter was gone and things were again orderly. Rachel had coffee but he didn't see his mother anywhere so he helped himself to a cup. He saw the new white car was still in the drive with his mothers.

Rachel came in the back door from the porch. She had a basket of eggs. She had apparently been in the hen house.

"Where's your girl?" Zane asked. "Still sleeping after all that shopping?"

"No, she's out on the porch with Thumper." Rachel smiled as she set the eggs down.

Zane looked out on the front porch and the blonde girl was sitting with the big tabby cat in her lap. She was sitting on the steps leading onto the porch and petting Thumper, her long blonde hair cascaded down her back. She was smiling and seemed to be loving playing with the cat. Thumper, looked also if he also was enjoying the attention he was receiving.

About that time Maggie the Ranch Border collie came up to see if she too could solicit some attention. Beth Robin's petted Maggie also but Thumper decided he was not willing to share the attention and he reached out and slapped Maggie on the nose with his paw, claws, extended. Maggie jumped back and curled her lips and showed her teeth at the cat.

Seeing they were about to fight over the attention Beth laughed and put Thumper down and got up and came in the house. Zane had been watching the city girl with the animals; when she came toward the house, he turned away.

"Those animals act like they are jealous." Beth said as she came in the door.

"They are, they don't want to share your attention." Rachel smiled.

"We never had animals in the city. We always lived in a high-rise apartment. Sometimes I would see animals being walked in the park but we never had any." Beth's face was flushed from the cool air. She looked very pretty. Zane had thought she always looked to pale but with the flush in her cheeks he had to admit she was a very pretty girl.

Beth Robin's was also a tall girl. She did not have to look up at the tall lanky Zane but was able to look at him near eye level. Zane figured she must be about five ten at least. She was slim hipped like a boy but she filled out her blouse and was not exactly flat chest, like most tall slim hipped girls. Zane remembered George telling him her age and that she had finished college.

"You want some coffee?" Rachel asked.

"Thank you I can get it my self." She went over and helped herself to the cups and filled her coffee from the carafe. Beth had become familiar with Rachel putting the coffee in the carafe.

Zane had sat down at the table with his coffee after watching the girl play with the farm pets.

"I had never been in a chicken house until I went with your mother this morning." She told Zane her eyes sparkling with adventure.

Zane smiled with amusement. He had never thought about a trip to the chicken house could be exciting for anyone." What did you take in College?" He asked.

Beth looked at him surprised. "I majored in History and English literature. I also, took business administration. George must have told you I went to college?" Beth wondered just how much George had told the hunting guide about her? "That leaves me with enough degrees to teach school." She added.

"Did you plan to teach?" Zane asked.

"I had not yet planned to do anything. Daddy expected me to go to college. He never had, and neither had George. An education was important to both of them." Beth began to look, sad, thinking, about her father, and George both now gone. The color was beginning to fade from her face and Zane wished he had not reminded her.

Rachel had been fixing breakfast as Beth and Zane sat at the table. Sensing the girl was sinking into sadness Rachel asked her to set the table?

Beth got up and began to get plates from the cupboard. She seemed to already be familiar with where Rachel kept things.

By the time the three sat down to a breakfast of bacon, eggs and toast Beth had some color back in her face. It seemed Rachel knew what to do to preoccupy her mind.

"These don't taste like any eggs I have eaten before." Beth told Rachel as they ate breakfast.

"You probably have never had a fresh egg." Rachel smiled. "Now that you know the difference, it will ruin you for anything but a fresh egg." She added.

"What is your plan for today?" Rachel asked Zane.

"We only have one hunter and Jody is taking him. I told Annie to call if she needed me. Other than that do you have something you need me to do?"

"I have to go in and help Chuck. Maybe you can keep Beth Company?" Rachel suggested to Zane.

"I don't need anybody to watch over me." Beth protested.

"I didn't mean that you do," Rachel said. "I just thought it isn't good for you to sit around and dwell on your loss. You need to stay busy." Rachel was certain she knew what was best for the young women.

Zane wondered how his mother expected he was to keep Beth entertained.

"I can do some house work if you tell me what needs to be done and later I could drive in and help you at the store?" Beth was not sure she wanted to spend the day with the hunting guide.

Being shy and the circumstances she had met Zane under, she was not quite comfortable in his presence. Although Beth found Zane to be attractive, he had a way of looking directly at her as if he could see through her and even see what was in her mind. Zane Adam's blue eyes were very observant and penetrating. He didn't seem to miss much. Beth was completely comfortable with Rachel Adams but Zane was another matter. He had been kind and considerate but she found him not to be the open caring person his mother was. She sensed he was guarded when around her.

Zane was guarded around Beth Robins. He didn't understand his mother's sudden attachment to the girl. He knew Rachel perceived she was a girl pretty much an orphan. But she was twenty-two years old and from an entirely different world. He wondered if it had something to do with Rachel never having a daughter. Zane was aware the two women had formed an attachment that he couldn't understand. He wondered why he should even be concerned about it. He tried to weigh what ramifications could develop, from their growing attachment. The worst that could happen would be that Rachel would have a new friend. Even if Beth went back to Detroit it would only mean there was someone was in Detroit his mother liked and cared for.

Zane decided he would quit worrying over it, his mother and Beth Robins were both adults and he could think of no harm from their growing fondness for each other.

"What are you frowning about?" Rachel's question jarred Zane out of what he was thinking.

"Nothing," He said looking around and finding both Beth and his mother looking at him questions in their eyes. "Sorry, just thinking of something else."

"Well I have to get ready for work." Rachel said getting up from the breakfast table.

"I'll clean up breakfast." Zane said getting up and taking his plate to the sink.

"I'll clean up breakfast." Beth said starting to stack the dishes on the table.

Zane looked at her with amusement. He decided he would stay and help her. He could do the barn chores but he would do that after the dishes were done.

Beth and Zane cleaned the breakfast dishes without conversation. They were just finished when Rachel came out of the bath ready for work. They were standing in front of the sink along sides each other as Rachel came and pecked Zane and Beth both on the cheek.

"Now, you kids remember no fighting." She laughed as she went out of the door.

Zane grinned at Beth with amusement. She smiled back at him. "I'm going to the barn and take care of the horses." Zane got his jacket and asked Beth, "You coming?"

"Yes." She smiled and hurried to get her coat. Beth and Zane walked out to the barn. Zane noticed Beth was wearing white sneakers and he thought wryly she could well get some horse manure on them. He didn't say anything. The cool night had put a skim of ice on the horse trough. Zane broke it with his hand, as it was thin. He picked the pieces of ice out of the trough and discarded them. Beth watched.

Zane went into the horse barn and opened the top of a metal barrel that held grain for the horses. He filled the pan in the grain barrel and put it in the wooden grain boxes for the horses. Beth followed him and watched.

Upon hearing the grain barrel lid two big Bay horses came tromping up the ramp from the pen behind the barn. Beth scrambled to get out of the way as the horses crowded into their stalls to get their morning grain. Zane smiled with amusement when he saw her blue eyes wide with fright once the big horses crowded into the barn.

"They won't hurt you," He chuckled as he put the grain bucket back in the barrel and fastened the hasp on the top so the horses could not get in it. Horses would founder if they got into all the grain they wanted and it was important the barrel top be securely fastened.

Beth had backed over to the door her and Zane had come through. Her eyes were large in the dim light of the barn. Zane could tell she was unsure about the presence of the big horses.

Beth stayed by the door as Zane climbed a wooden ladder up into the top of the barn. The hay was stacked to the rafters; He threw a bale of hay down into each manger by the Bays where they were eating the grain in their boxes. Horses seemed to know which manger was theirs. Zane climbed down from the hayloft and took his pocketknife out of his Levi's and cut the strings on the hay bales. He put the strings with others hanging between the stalls and knotted them together.

Beth still stood uncertainly by the door. "That's it here." Zane smiled with amusement. Beth had not moved from in front of the door. Zane walked up to her and still she stood looking with eyes wide. Zane reached over her shoulder and pushed the door open. She seemed to be glued to the spot but once he opened the door she turned and went out first.

Zane wondered what she was thinking. Hard to know what a city girl was thinking of. It was a routine Zane had known since before he could remember. Beth had appeared to be frightened by the big horses.

"You ever have been around a horse?" He asked as they walked back to the house.

"Never," She said.

"I guess we will have to see about getting you on one someday!" Zane grinned.

Beth looked at Zane and wondered if he was being facetious? It was hard to tell looking at him what he was thinking. "I'm looking forward to it." She said smoothly. She hoped he had not noticed how frightened she had been when the horses come tromping into the barn.

Zane had noticed her fright but he grudgingly conceded she had covered it up well. The girl from Detroit was out of her element but she was trying. Zane still wondered why she didn't just fly back to Detroit and leave this bit of wilderness she seemed to know nothing about.

Once back in the house Beth disappeared down the hall to the room she had been using across from his mothers room. Zane went upstairs and gathered clean clothes and he went in the upstairs bath and took a shower. He straightened up his room and made his bed. He heard the phone ringing downstairs and hoped Beth would answer it. It quit ringing and he supposed she did.

Suddenly Beth appeared in the door to Zane's room. Zane had not yet put on his shirt from his shower. He grabbed his shirt and hastened to put it on when he saw her. He blushed at being caught without his shirt.

"Someone is on the phone for you named Gina." Beth said noticing Zane's color at being caught without his shirt.

"Tell her I'm not available to come to the phone." Zane said his color deepening. He wondered how Gina knew he was home.

"As you wish." She said and went back down the stairs.

Goddamn it, Zane had not thought about Gina calling the house. He knew if she did when Rachel was home Rachel would tell her off in no uncertain terms. He was sure Rachel had ragged on Gina the morning she gave her a ride into town. Zane went down stairs.

"Your friend Gina did not like me telling her you weren't available to come to the phone."

"Why what did, she say?" Zane tried not to show Beth he was aggravated.

"She demanded to know whom she was speaking to?"

"What did you say?" Zane fastened his eyes on Beth's face and waited expectantly.

"Nothing, I said Goodbye and hung up." Beth had an amused expression in her eyes as she studied Zane.

"Thanks." Zane said. "Tell her the same if she ever calls again." He added. He glanced at Beth sharply when he heard her giggle.

Beth could tell by his actions Zane was aggravated by the call. She looked away but couldn't help but let the giggle escape when she realized Gina must be someone very interested in speaking to Zane and Zane was very much not interested in speaking with her. It did not take much for Beth to realize what was going on.

Zane Adam's was obviously, embarrassed and Beth intended to let him out of the situation. She had her coat on and her purse in hand when he had come down the stairs. With his hair still damp and beginning to curl around the bottom of his neck the confident, hunting guide, she was used to looking at, looked very much like a little boy doing something he didn't want anyone to know about. Beth suppressed another giggle.

"I'm going to the store to visit with your mother and see if she needs help." She told Zane.

"Okay." He said. Relief was apparent in his blue eyes.

"Beth went out and started the Toyota she had bought the day before. It smelled like a new car. She wrinkled her nose at the smell and reminded herself to get an air freshener at the store. She found it hard to believe people actually bought the new car smell in an air freshener. When she backed out, she noticed Zane watching out the window.

Beth parked at the store and went inside. Rachel had just finished checking a customer and smiled when she saw the girl.

"How was your morning with my handsome son? Did you help him take care of the horses?"

"Yes, they frightened me when they came in the barn."

Rachel laughed. "Yes it doesn't take long for them to hear the lid on the grain barrel. That grain is their daily treat. We try not to give them too much because if they aren't being used much they get frisky on it. And Zane, what is he doing?" Rachel asked her eyes twinkling. She had felt Beth and Zane were uncomfortable with each other. She hoped leaving the two together would begin to make them more at ease.

Beth didn't know if she should mention Zane's phone call but she found she was curious so she told Rachel, "I hope you don't mind but I answered the phone while Zane was upstairs."

"Of coarse not dear, make yourself right at home. Someone call, for me?"

"No, a woman named Gina, for Zane."

Rachel's eyes snapped as she looked at Beth and her lips flattened out in a disapproving line.

"Did he speak to her." Rachel asked?

"No, he said to tell her he wasn't available."

"He's not to her, the woman has a husband. And a mean one at that! I'm glad Zane didn't speak to her." Rachel didn't offer any more information but Beth had a good idea why Zane had not taken her call. "Is there something I can help with?" Beth asked.

"If you wouldn't mind. We could stock some shelves until Chuck gets back from lunch."

"Be glad to." Rachel and Beth worked companionably until Chuck came back into the store from his lunch break. He was pleased at the amount of stock Rachel and Beth had put away while he was gone. Chuck had met Rachel's houseguest the first day she came. He made the remark if she was to keep helping he would have to put her on the payroll.

Rachel laughed thinking of Beth Robin's factory owner and wealthy young woman on the Danner's store payroll.

"I wonder if I applied at the School when I return from George's funeral if I could get on as a substitute teacher?" Beth said when Chuck mentioned giving her a job.

"That might be a very good idea Beth. The school district has a hard time getting teachers, I'm sure they would be glad to have access to someone qualified for a substitute."

Chuck watched Rachel and her young houseguest. He had met Beth the day she came to Rachel's. He wondered how Rachel knew her? He wondered if she was a girl friend of Zane's?

Chuck told Rachel she could take off the rest of the afternoon. When both of the women drove toward the Adams ranch Rachel noticed Zane's truck at Pete's bar. She hoped he wasn't going to be messing with Gina Daniels or worse, Punk Daniels!

5

Zane had a beer at Pete's and decided he would head back to the lodge. Pete was still trying to figure out what Zane had done to keep Gina Daniels from spreading around town about her leaving with Zane one night.

The big tall rangy Adam's was not giving an inch as Pete tried to pump him for information. Pete finally had to give up and decided if he was ever to know what shut Gina's mouth he may have to resort to asking Gina herself.

Zane had one beer and then walked over to the store to tell his mother he was going back to the Lodge. She was not at the store. Chuck Danner said she and Zane's girlfriend had left for the ranch.

"Not my girlfriend!" Zane said to Chuck with an amused grin. "Where did you get that idea?"

"I just thought it. Nobody, give me that idea." Chuck said. He was embarrassed that he had reached the wrong conclusion about Rachel's young visitor.

"Can I use your phone?" Zane asked.

"Sure, sorry about the mistake about the girl Zane. Don't tell your mother on me."

Zane grinned; he called the ranch and his mother answered. "Hi Mom, I'm heading to the Lodge, anything you need me to do? I seemed to have missed you some how?"

"I saw your truck at Pete's when I came home. No, there isn't anything but I'll call the lodge if anything comes up."

"Okay, I'll see you in a couple days." Zane hung up and thanked Chuck and left.

Chuck watched him pull out. He shook his head and grinned. Boy, was he way off base where Rachel had gotten the girl.

If the young woman was not a friend of Zane's where did she come from? Rachel had introduced her to Chuck as her friend. She was not a relative or Rachel would have said as much. Chuck had also noticed on this day, the girl was driving what looked to be a new car. She had not had that, the day she came with Rachel. Wherever the girl named Beth, had come from it was obvious to Chuck, Rachel was very fond of the girl.

Zane drove to the lodge. He found Jody and the Pennsylvania hunter at the meat house. Zane parked his truck and walked over to see what they had.

"Had some luck this morning, huh?" Zane said. There was the head of a four-point laying in the back of the suburban and Jody had the four quarters of meat already hung in the meat house and was skinning on them. A man in his fifties stood by with a grin on his face.

"Yeah he was standing in the middle of a skid trail over on Stony Creek when we went this morning. Luck is what you call that." Jody introduced Zane to Pennsylvania, happy successful hunter. His name was John Bell.

"Are you done or you going to stick around for a deer?" Zane asked Bell.

"I don't know about a deer, but I'm going to spend the week I have reserved. Beautiful Country around here, I may as well enjoy it." John Bell said. "If nothing else I will get some rest and take some pictures."

"You need some help with that hide?" Zane asked

"Sure," Jody said. Zane took a skinning knife of the rack on the wall and proceeded to help Jody skin the remaining three quarters of elk.

John Bell watched for a few minutes and started for the Lodge. Zane saw that Bell's game tag was already securely attached. Once skinned the meat rolled on a track into the cooler part of the meat house. Then the hides were bagged and sent to a leather processor if the patron didn't want them.

"Should be getting some White tail hunters pouring in here over these next two weeks?" Zane said to Jody.

"Yeah, we are about to wrap this Elk Hunting season up! A good thing, we had a good Bow season or we wouldn't have filled many Elk hunters. Jody said as he finished up the last quarter.

"Yeah let's hope the buck hunter's do better against the wolves." Zane said.

"They should. The bucks don't travel as far as the Elk to get down in those big holes. I was sure glad my hunter got this one. I don't think I could pack an elk out of a hole like you did for the Texas hunter." Jody grinned. Jody knew he didn't have the strength for back packing that his rangy partner did.

"Yeah, I hope we don't have any more of that. But at least the Texan got out of here with a nice rack. He hopefully will bring us some Texas hunters next year."

"Yeah, that will be nice as long as we don't have to take them into those brushy holes. You get rid of that Michigan woman yet. She probably left for Michigan by now hasn't she?" Jody asked changing the subject.

"She hadn't gone yet this morning but I imagine she will have to go soon if she plans on attending the funeral. Although I believe, she plans to return after the funeral.

Jody's eyes widened. "What for? She doesn't know anyone here does she?"

"No, just my mother. She went to Lewiston with mom the other day and came back with a new car and a whole load of stuff."

"She is staying here on your account?" Jody teased Zane.

"Nope, she doesn't have much to say when I'm around. She is rather quiet. She just seems to really like my mom. Beats the hell out of me. George did say that last morning she didn't have any family and she was close to George and didn't have anybody else."

"Yeah, wonder how close to him she really was?" Jody laughed suggestively.

"George said it wasn't like that and I kind of believed him. He told me she was as close to his own child as he would ever have. Turned out he was correct about that." Zane said gloomily thinking about George Belmont's last few hours on earth.

"Well if she is getting close to your mother at the very least you will be able to look at her. She is damned good to look at." Jody grinned.

"Yeah, she's easy on the eyes all right. Quiet too. Don't have to listen to her yakking while I'm looking at her." Zane grinned and took the knives to the sink and began to clean them putting them back in the rack. Jody crowded in beside him and began to wash his hand. Jody smelled of Elk. Some times the guides used Elk scent when in the woods but in this case Jody smelled like Elk because he had been handling one.

Once finished the two guides headed for the kitchen door to the Lodge. Annie Cutler was putting their evening meal on the table as they came in. Another day was about finished in the Bitterroot Mountain range

While eating Jack came in and sat down with Zane and Jody. Annie got him a plate of food.

"I just brought three more guys in. We have a few days left of the Elk season and two of them are after Elk, the other one is a Buck hunter. He is from Connecticut and wants a big rack white tail. He was telling me they have deer back there but no trophy racks and he wanted to take a week of vacation and hunt for a big rack Buck. Since you are the Buck caller, I'll turn him over to you Zane."

"What about the Elk hunters'?" Jody asked. "You want me to try and handle both of them?"

"No, I'll take the older fellow and give you the younger one. You lucked out and filled the guy from Pennsylvania, good job Jody. Hope you can find something for this last guy." Jack finished his dinner. The plan was in place and now he was hoping they could send another happy Elk hunter out for their business advertising for next year.

Jody got up from the table and went to his room. Jody never had much to say in the way of conversation. He talked more with Zane than he did anybody else at the lodge. Jody had worked for the Cutler and Guide business a couple years longer than Zane.

Jack Cutler appreciated the fact that Jody Miller was a capable and loyal employee. Jody was not good with the clients though. He was often sullen and quiet. He didn't develop a rapport with the hunters as Zane Adam's did. Zane was the perfect person for the Guide business. He had skilled hunting ability's and got along easily with the clients. Zane was also intelligent and a fast learner. Jack was confident he would one day be able to turn his business over to the capable hands of Zane Adams. If Jack had a son, he would have wanted him to be a man just like Zane Adams.

After Jody left and went to his room Zane and Jack sat and visited about an hour. They ran over plans and generally laughed and enjoyed each other's company. Jack also asked Zane about the blonde girl. Zane told him the same as Jody. He had no idea why Beth was growing close to his mother. Zane mentioned that he thought Rachel had always wished she had a daughter. Rachel had not developed a close relationship with Matt's wife Susie. They got along but they weren't close. They were much to different sorts of people. Susie was also resentful of the close relationship Rachel had with her Matt, but Rachel was close to both of her sons.

Zane mentioned to Jack that he would not be surprised if Beth Robin's didn't return to the Ranch after Belmont's funeral.

"What does this Beth, do for a living and where's her family?" Jack asked.

"George told me that last morning she didn't have anybody but him. I don't know as if she has to do anything for a living. George said her father left her wealthy and she now owns half of a factory in Detroit with Marion Belmont."

Jack laughed. That should be interesting if this Marion dislikes the blonde"

"None of that is any of my business, "Zane mused. "But when she returns and moves into the house with my mother and me, I might have to try to find out more about her? I can't imagine what a young woman from Detroit would be interested in hanging out on a stump Ranch in Idaho? Why would she want to hang around here?"

"Maybe she is interested in you." Jack grinned.

Zane's face reddened when Jack mentioned that but he shook his head. "She seems to want to avoid me and is really quiet when around me. She is most animated when she and mother are together."

"Maybe she is becoming attached to Rachel as a mother figure? Especially if what Belmont said is true about her having no family." Jack mentioned, noticing Zane seemed a bit concerned.

"Maybe she won't return when she goes to Michigan." Zane got up from the table.

He was finished talking about Bethany Robins.

"See you in the morning. Goodnight." Zane headed back to his quarters.

Jack looked at Annie and smiled and shook his head. He neither had any idea why the girl would want to stay in Idaho.

The next morning the guides and clients headed out. Zane took the hunter from Connecticut. The Hunter was a man in his forties. Zane noticed he was quite a bit over weight and Zane started thinking of the places he could take him, which would be easy access.

The hefty pudgy hunter worried him. Zane sure as hell didn't need a heart attack fatality on top of the shooting fatality. Zane took him to a place where he knew there was a nice Buck hanging around a meadow. Where it was easy access. Because of the weight of the hunter Zane give up the idea of putting him in a tree stand.

Zane had begun to see the paw marks the Buck's left under trees when they were about to begin the rut. The rut was not in full, force yet and Zane was not certain he could get a buck to pay attention to rattling horns or Buck grunts. The rut had to be going strong before those methods worked well in luring Bucks.

Zane decided to put his fat hunter on a stand and see if he could circle around and run something to him.

The Connecticut Hunter was happy to get set down and seemed to be some what relieved that he was not going to have to try and keep up with the rangy hunting guide.

Leaving his hunter on the stand, Zane checked the wind and headed out so the wind would be coming from Zane and away from the hunter in the stand so the game might pick up Zane's scent and move toward the hunter on the stand. Zane walked about an hour circling around. He heard a couple deer burst out of the brush in the direction he had left his hunter but he didn't hear any shots.

Deciding he had pretty well routed the area, Zane returned to Charles, the Connecticut hunter and found him still sitting where he left him.

"See anything?" Zane asked Charles when he got back to him.

"Yeah, I saw a doe and fawn and a small buck about a four point, go through here but nothing I wanted to shoot." Charles said.

"Well I have run this area so I think we should go to another. I know there is a pretty nice buck hanging in here but don't know where he is at the moment.

"Sounds good." Charles said, struggling his portly body on his feet. They walked back to the Suburban and Zane took him to a couple other places and routed them also without success.

They drove back to the Lodge and Zane told Charles he would take him over to watch the edge of a clear cut that evening. He also told him they would try the Buck grunt and rattling in the morning. Charlie had told Zane the small buck, that he had seen run out had a swollen neck. With that information, Zane hoped they were getting into the rut, enough to respond to the grunt tube.

Jody and Jack both returned from their morning Elk hunts without success. Jack, Zane and Jody gathered in the kitchen to plan something for the evening. Zane told them he planed on taking the portly Charles over to watch the timber edge of a big clear cut.

Jack and Jody both decided to take their hunters over on the opposite side of the same of mountain, to watch another clear-cut for perhaps an Elk to sneak out about dark. Jack hated the evening Elk hunts but it was getting near the end of the season and it was the only coarse of action that made sense. They didn't want the clients very far off the road for fear they could underestimate getting out before darkness fell. Looking for Dudes in the darkness is a guide's worst nightmare.

Over the next two days Jack managed to get his older hunter a Bull. It wasn't a big rack but the client was happy with it. The guy from Pennsylvania finished his week up and left with lots of scenery pictures. He also went with Jody one night in the darkness and recorded the Wolves howling. The Wolves, howling was music to the Dudes ears and a source of aggravation to the guides who knew the object of their livelihoods was falling prey to the howling wolves.

One frosty cold morning Zane was able to grunt a nice five point Buck into a meadow for his portly hunter from Connecticut. Charlie was glad to have a rack to take back with him. He gave Zane a $200.00 dollar bonus.

The elk season in the area came to a close. Only deer hunters remained. The Lodge had several deer hunters but most of them were interested in laying around the Lodge and over indulging in whiskey and chowing down on Annie Cutlers good cooking. It was this type of hunter that came for the luxury of the accommodations and took the opportunity for a vacation under the guise of a hunting trip.

Zane had one serous Buck hunter. A young rich man from Alabama and he seemed to know by looking at a Bucks horns the points of rating the rack would get. He was not interested in just shooting a buck but was looking for a trophy kind of animal. Zane grunted and rattled in a lot of Bucks for the young man but he took none because he didn't find what he was looking for. He also left giving Zane a bonus not because he found success but he was an experienced hunter who appreciated the effort Zane put in him in trying to get him what he wanted.

It had been over a week when Zane again headed into town to check with his mother and give her, his bonuses, to put in the bank. It was after the first of November and he also had his monthly check from the Lodge.

Zane didn't stop at Pete's bar when he went through town. He would have liked to have a beer but didn't want to find his mother already in bed so instead he went straight out to the ranch.

It was dark when he arrived home. The white Toyota Beth had bought was parked at the house. Zane went in the front door and found Beth and Rachel in the living room. The Television was on. He went to his mother and gave her a peck on the cheek.

"Hello, stranger," she smiled. "I thought you got lost out in the woods."

They both laughed. Zane had not been lost in his life. His mother was being facetious and Beth looked on with amusement.

"You change your mind about going to Detroit?" Zane asked.

"No," She smiled. "I've been there and back."

"How did that go?" Zane asked sitting down in a chair.

"As I expected. But I'm glad I went. I left things in the hands of my attorney. My father's estate is finished and probated. My attorney can deal with Marion. I actually felt sorry for her, I think she loved George and I know he loved her." Beth said wistfully.

"No confrontation with Georges Wife?" Zane felt he was prying by asking but he had not forgotten George's reaction when Marion showed up with Bethany at the Lodge.

"Of coarse not. I didn't sit with George's family. I also didn't speak with Marion. I stayed out of her way and just attended the funeral. I can't believe he is gone." Bethany Robin's was sad about George's death and Zane and Rachel could plainly see she was affected.

"Beth has applied for a position as substitute teacher." Rachel said, changing the subject.

"That could be something to occupy your time." Zane said. "There isn't much to do in this area."

"Seems nice to have a slower pace of life. Your mother, certainly stay busy." Beth pointed out.

"My mother has always stayed much too busy. Don't let her fool you, she is a work addict. I have never known her to take time for herself ever." Zane grinned. Maybe Beth Robins could get Rachel to slow down and enjoy herself once in a while. She seemed to be relaxed and happy when the girl from Detroit was around her.

Zane took his check and bonuses out of his pocket and laid them on the desk in the living room. "You can take that to the Bank?" He asked Rachel.

"I'll do it tomorrow. Rachel said.

"Put my check in checking but the other in savings," Zane told her. Zane went into the kitchen to see if he could find a beer. He asked the two women in the living room if they wanted anything?

Rachel said no, but Beth Robin's indicated she would join Zane in a beer. Zane returned with two beers and a glass.

"I didn't know if you wanted a glass." He said, handing her the beer and glass.

"Thank you." Beth said. Zane sprawled his big frame on the Sofa and drank his beer. Zane thought the three of them sitting in the living room watching Television kind of strange but Beth downed her can of beer as if she enjoyed it. Zane idly thought he would not have figured her for a beer drinker.

Rachel finally got up and said good night to Zane and Beth and went to her room. Beth and Zane looked at each other waiting for the other to say something.

"Another beer?" Zane asked getting up and heading for the kitchen,

"Yes, Thank you." Beth got up and followed Zane into the kitchen. While he got the Beer from the Refrigerator Beth sat down at the kitchen table.

"I'm glad I have this chance to speak with you," She said.

Zane handed her the beer and sat down across from her at the table. He looked at her with his steady gaze waiting for what she wanted to talk with him about.

"I hope you don't mind if I am staying here at your home with your mother." Beth said looking at him directly. There was no expression in her eyes that gave Zane any clue what she was thinking or feeling.

"Why are you here?" He asked.

"I have grown quite fond of your mother and I enjoy spending time with her, I don't have any family left and I was not anxious to return to Detroit. I hope I'm not imposing on your home. I have the financial independence to go any place I wish to go but your mother has made me feel very much at home here, and I would like to stay a while but not if you feel I'm imposing." Beth's gaze was straightforward and Zane felt she was being sincere in asking his opinion and permission to stay in his home.

"I guess it is up to my mother. I can't see how you being here, has any ill effect as far as my mother is concerned but I am not understanding why you would want to stay, As you said you can go where you want. Why here?" Zane looked at the pretty blonde girl waiting for an answer to what he had been thinking?

Beth looked down and when she looked up Zane could see tears sparkled in her eyes beneath the surface, She struggled to hold them back.

"I lost my mother a long time ago and Rachel reminds me very much of her. I promise I won't be any trouble for her and I think your mother is also very lonely. We get along great and I would love to stay…." She trailed off and looked down at the beer Zane had given her. "I know this might seem strange for you but you have probably had a family and don't know what it is to not have one." Beth looked back to Zane and Zane realized she was begging him to understand.

"Well I don't really have an opinion one way or the other. As you have seen, I am often gone and yes I know my mom is lonely at times. But soon I will also be here through the winter so it won't just be my mother but you will also have to put up with my presence. Did mom mention that to you?"

"Yes, she did. But she told me I could stay as long as I wish. I can pay for my keep and I won't be a burden. If you don't want me here when you come for the winter, I will leave. Just please be honest with me about that."

"Sounds fair enough. You aren't going to be always drinking all my beer?" He asked

"I'll buy some tomorrow." Beth said anxiously.

Zane laughed. "I'm kidding! If you are going to be around, I guess you better get used to that!"

Beth smiled tentative, realizing Zane was indeed teasing her.

"Stay as long as you and Mom decide. Goodnight Beth." Zane got up from the table and went upstairs. Zane got in bed and laid thinking for some time before he finally fell asleep.

It was about five in the morning when Zane got up and went down the stairs. The house was quiet. Zane tried to be quiet as he fixed a couple pieces of toast and fried a couple eggs. He ate his breakfast and put the dishes in the sink. He wiped the oilcloth kitchen table off and was about to go out the door when Beth appeared in the doorway to the dining room wearing a robe and pajamas. Her hair was tousled; she had just crawled out of bed.

"Sorry I woke you. I was just leaving. Tell mom I said goodbye."

"Okay, you didn't wake me." She said softly. She looked very young and still sleepy.

Zane squeezed by her and went out the front door into the still darkness of the cool morning. He started his truck to let it warm up. He wondered if snow was in the forecast, it felt this morning to him like snow. Zane backed out and went to the Lodge. He arrived just after daylight.

Jody had already left with a hunter. Jack was fueling up one of the Suburban. Zane walked over and asked Jack what he wanted, him to do?

"Take this guy I was going with. He's a buck hunter. They are rutting to beat hell, you shouldn't have too much trouble getting him one, and as good as you are with that grunt tube."

"Okay," Zane said. About that time another heavyset guy came out of the Lodge with his rifle. Zane looked at Jack and grinned. Another fat guy! No wonder Jack wanted Zane and his grunt tube.

The next week Zane grunted in Buck's for three different hunters. Jack and Annie made ready to close the Lodge for the winter. They planned to be out by November 20th when the deer season closed. Zane had to go to the county seat one day and testified before the coroner's inquest into George Belmont's death. As expected it was ruled accidental hunting fatality. On his trip into the inquest Zane swung by the Ranch and found Rachel and Beth both gone. Zane called Danner's store and spoke to Rachel. She said Beth was at the school. The school board had been happy to have a substitute on call and because of the approaching Thanksgiving holiday and they had indicated they would need her often.

Zane saw the cows had come in off the open range behind the house and were in the hay field. He also noticed Rachel had begun to put out hay. "Do you need me to leave the truck and take your car?" Zane asked.

"No, she said, I have the wagon on behind the tractor, and I'm not feeding much yet. It will be all right until you come home. I have Beth to help."

Zane grinned, thinking about Bethany Robin's factory owner helping his mother load hay bales onto the tractor wagon.

"I'll be done and out in about three days." He told Rachel. "Annie and Jack are already closing things down. We have about a foot of snow at the Lodge. It will be here soon. Do you and Beth have your snow tires on?

"Yes, Beth took her car to Lewiston one day and got studs. She took my car another day and got them on it also."

Zane hung up and thought maybe Beth would be a real help to Rachel. What remained to be seen was when she had to coexist with Zane in the house for the winter. Zane grinned, thinking about the pretty girl from Detroit being in his house for the winter.

Zane went back to the Lodge and over the next three days finished helping Annie and Jack close up the Lodge for the season. He and Jody bid each other goodbye for the winter and Jody headed for the reservation where he lived with his family.

Jody Miller was the eldest of his siblings. He had several brothers and sisters. Zane had met a brother one time but he had never met any other members of Jody's family.

The muzzleloader season opened as the late deer season closed in Idaho. Jack Cutler didn't solicit hunters for the muzzleloader because the lodge was being snowed in by that late date. Jack and Annie had a winter home in Lewiston. They planned on spending their golden years there. Lewiston was known as the banana belt and rarely did they even have snow.

On November 21 Zane came down from the mountain for the last time for the year. He had all of his stuff in the truck. Zane Adam's hunting guide would now be Zane Adam's cattleman through the winter into the spring. When the spring Bear season opened around the 10th of April Zane would once again be back in the woods for Jack Cutler's guide business. There was also a spring Turkey season but the Cutler's didn't mess with Turkeys. They had to plow snow in April at the lodge to accommodate the Bear hunter's but the hunters were hauled back down into the lower elevations to hunt Bear, as it was still too early at the elevation the lodge was at.

When Zane reached the Ranch both Rachel's and Beth's cars were gone. Zane put his stuff away and went out and checked the barn to see how much hay his mother and Beth had fed. When the cows saw Zane, they crowded along the fence by the Barn lot and bawled at him as if they expected him to feed them. Zane saw they still had hay out in the field from the morning. The cows recognized both Zane and his truck from years past. He grinned that those girls thought they could con some hay out of him when he could plainly see they had some.

The two Bays tromped up into the barn stalls and he also ignored their wide-eyed begging for grain. It was only in the mornings they were grained and he also saw they had hay in the mangers. Zane wondered who climbed the ladder into the loft, his mother or Beth?

Zane went back to the house. It was a quarter to four when he saw Beth come driving in. When she got out of her car, Zane saw that she was wearing a dress.

She was also wearing flat shoes. He thought the tall girl would look really tall to the school children if she wore much in the way of heels.

"Hi," Beth said as she came in the door.

"How is the teaching going?" Zane asked.

"Good, I like kid's very much, excuse me." Beth went down the hall to her room. Zane sat at the kitchen table drinking a beer. He noticed, there were several cans in the refrigerator and he surmised Beth had bought beer.

Beth came back from her room; she had changed into jeans and a sweater. She went to the refrigerator and got herself a can of beer. She sat down at the table with Zane.

"You home for the winter now?"

"Yeah, you and Mom won't have to feed the cows. That will be me from now on. Unless you want to help?" He asked as he noticed she seemed to look disappointed that they would not be feeding.

"I enjoyed helping feed." She said.

"Yeah, you might change your mind about that when it gets twenty below zero and the wind is blowing." Zane grinned.

"It is often very cold in Detroit also." Beth said. "It is a different cold blowing off those lakes. The humidity is high back there and it feels much colder than here. Have you ever been in the east?"

"No, I used to think the edge of the world was across the Clarkston Bridge, until I was about twelve years old." He laughed. "I've been into Spokane a few times to meet clients for Jack at the Lodge but for the most part I've been wandering around in the woods and back country here in Idaho my entire life. I've lived here in this house since I was born. My father lived here before that. We Adam's are known here about as aborigines."

Beth smiled. "So Rachel has told me." She looked at her watch." Rachel should be coming soon. I'll call and ask her what she wants, me to do about dinner?" Beth went to the phone and called the store. She asked about dinner. Zane heard Beth tell Rachel "He is here."

Beth hung up the phone and got some Potatoes to peel. She put them in the sink. Zane got up and took a paring knife out of the knife case and shouldered in beside her and began to help.

"I can get these," She said, having, to look up at him. Although Beth was tall, she had to look up at the six-foot three, Zane when he was standing next to her.

"We will be done twice as fast." He said and continued helping her, peel on the potatoes.

"Can you cook?" She asked.

"Of coarse, Mom has worked at the Danner store since my Dad has been gone. Often I fix supper when mom has to close the store." He smiled at Beth with an amused look.

Beth Robins felt a bit flustered with Zane crowded into the sink next to her. She hoped she would get over that as she became more acquainted with him. She did acknowledge to herself he was very attractive, but she would have to ignore that and develop a friendship with him as if he were a brother. She had never had a brother but she knew being physically attracted to Rachel's good-looking son could be a problem she would need to overcome.

"What about you? Can you cook?" Zane smiled at her amused.

Beth grinned. The question was fair; he did not know her either. "Not much. I've learned most of what I know from Rachel."

"What else did she say she planned for dinner?" Zane asked.

"Some pork chops in the fridge." Beth said.

"We will put some water on these potatoes but won't turn them on until Mom comes home." Zane said. Beth got out of his way. Obviously he knew more about the cooking than she did. Beth gathered the two empty beers' can from the table and put them in the garbage. She wiped the table off. Zane went in the living room and turned on the Television. When Beth came in he had his big frame sprawled on the sofa and was watching the evening news. Beth also took a chair and they watched the television without talking until Beth heard Rachel's car. Beth got up and went to greet her. Zane watched the girl leave the room.

Damn, but she is great to look at!

Zane stayed in the living room as Beth and Rachel finished dinner. The three of them ate. Zane used to helping his mother got up when finished and started helping clear the table. With Beth, Rachel and Zane all trying to do the cleanup Rachel said. "Hold it, there are too many of us in here! We are running into each other, why don't you go sit down, Zane?"

"Why don't you go sit down?" Zane said to Rachel. "You've been on your feet more today more than I have, Beth and I can handle this."

"All right, I'm going to take a hot bath!" Rachel left the kitchen to Beth and Zane.

"You wash or dry?" Beth asked.

"I'll do the washing." Zane said and he went to the sink and began to run dishwater.

"You aren't afraid to get dish pan hands?" She laughed.

Zane smiled and shook his head with amusement. This was going to be an interesting winter to say the least!

Zane and Beth cleaned up the dinner dishes. When finished Zane went back to the Television. He thought about driving down to Pete's Bar but wasn't in the mood for beer after his dinner.

Beth had disappeared in her room. Rachel came in wearing her robe and pajamas after her bath.

What do you hear from Matt?" Zane asked.

"He calls regularly and they were all here with the kids one Sunday. We plan to have Thanksgiving here."

Zane grunted. They always had Thanksgiving at the ranch. That was less than a week away.

"I'm going to bed. Good night Zane."

"Good night Mom." Zane watched the Television and wondered if Beth had also retired for the night. Soon Beth came into the living room and sat down in a chair. She had a cup of tea. She noticed Zane look at it.

"I'm sorry," she said. "Do you want a cup of tea?"

"No thank you." Zane said and went back to watching a documentary on the discovery channel. When his program was finished, Zane got up and handed the remote to Beth, "Good night Beth." He went up the stairs and got in bed.

6

The next morning Zane arose at daybreak and went downstairs. The house was still quiet so he started coffee and put on his boots for the barnyard. He went out and started his truck. While it warmed up he went on out and turned the barn lights on. He grained the bays and they came tromping into the stalls.

Zane went back and got his truck and pulled side ways below the loft door high up on the barn. He climbed the loft ladder and opened the loft door and started throwing bales down into the back of the pickup. When he had twenty bales thrown down, he climbed down and got into the back of the truck and began to stack them.

"Do you need help?"

Zane looked at Beth, she was standing behind the truck toward the house.

"Sure, can you climb the loft and push bales out of the loft door?"

"Yes I can do that." Beth went in the barn with the Bays and climbed the ladder into the loft.

"How many do you want down there?" She asked.

Having finished stacking what he had thrown down, Zane told her about ten more.

Beth pushed ten more down out of the loft. Zane was able to catch and stack them as she pushed them out. "Is that all?" She asked.

"Yeah, latch the door on the loft before you come down." Beth swung the door shut to the loft.

Zane jumped down and went around to get into the truck. He waited to see where Beth was before he started it. Beth opened the passenger's door and got in the truck with him. Zane looked at her and grinned as she looked as if she had just awaken. He started the truck and backed around and pulled up to the gate into the field. The entire herd, of cows was lined up at the gate. Zane whistled for Maggie and she came streaking by and pushed the cattle back from the gate. Maggie held them at bay and looked back to see if Zane was coming in the gate. Maggie understood her job and she knew the truck needed to be through the gate before she allowed the cows down along the fence.

"Can you drive the truck?" Zane asked Beth.

"I think so. It is an automatic?" She looked over at the transmission guide. Zane pushed the four-wheel drive lever forwards and told her to drive it in low range. Zane got out and opened the gate as Maggie held the herd at bay. Beth pulled the truck through the gate and Zane shut the gate so the cattle could not get into the barnyard. Zane walked up and opened the door and Beth went to slide over.

"No," He said. "I want you to drive slowly out the field and make a circle and come back to the gate. She nodded and Zane jumped up on the hay load and began to cut the strings with his pocketknife. By the time Beth drove the truck down the field and back to the gate Zane had cut the strings and fed the bales to the cattle. She stopped before the gate as she could see the hay was gone from the back of the pickup.

Zane jumped down from the back and opened the gate and motioned for her to drive through. She stopped the truck in front of the barn and put the transmission in the park position. Zane opened the door reached across her and turned the ignition off. "Thanks Beth, that helped and made it easier."

"What do you want me to do now?" She asked.

"Nothing, I'll bring the truck out when I am done." Zane grabbed the hay stings from the back of his truck. He put them together and tied them in a knot. He went in the barn and put the stings in a bag that held other strings. He then climbed the loft ladder and put two bales down into the Bay's mangers. When he climbed back down, he cut the strings and tied them to the ones hanging over the stall edges. When he left the barn, he turned out the barn lights. It was now daylight enough to see. He noticed the lights still on the truck and hoped his battery had not been sapped enough to need the charger.

Zane cut the truck lights and waited a moment before he hit the starter. The truck started and he pulled back out of the barnyard and took it out of four-wheel drive. He left the truck running to charge the battery. Zane went to the house to look for the coffee he had started before leaving to feed the stock. He slipped out of his barn boots and carried them in his hand into the house. The house smelled of fresh coffee and bacon frying.

Beth was sitting at the table and Rachel was at the stove. Beth jumped up when she saw Zane come in and got him a cup of coffee.

"Thank you! I guess that's about all I've said to you this morning. Good morning mom. Good morning Beth." Zane smiled at sat down at the table. The kitchen was full of women; Zane thought this might be all right!

"Where is that damned speckled ass cow and her calf?" Zane asked Rachel.

"She has not come in. What do you suppose that means?"

"I don't know but hardly ever is one cow still out all by herself. I might have to saddle a horse and go into the canyon and see if I can find her."

"With all of those cows out there how can you tell if one is gone?" Beth asked.

Rachel smiled at her indulgently and said. "The same way if you came to the breakfast table and one of your children was missing, you get to know them all by sight and their calves. If one is gone, it sticks out like a sore thumb."

"Really," Beth said. "They just look like just a bunch of cows to me."

"They don't when you spend a winter every morning feeding them. There is no calling in sick on this job. Those cows don't care if your dying, they expect to be fed and at about the same time each day. They even know when it's time." Zane laughed." If your fifteen minutes late they begin to bawl for their breakfast! Not only does each of them look different but they also have their own personalities. You would be surprised how one gets to know every one of those cows."

Zane could see Beth had an incredulous look on her face. "It isn't only us, everyone that has cattle will tell you the same thing. A cow, also have very long memories. If a cow gets it in for you, like one year an old red cow lost her calf, it died. Somehow she got it in her head it was my fault she would chase me every time she saw me. Finally we had to sell her."

"I must say, it was nice I didn't have to get dressed this morning and go help." Rachel smiled.

"Thank Beth, she did your job." Zane said. Rachel began to put breakfast on the table. Zane looked at his watch. "No school today?" He asked.

"Today is Saturday." Beth pointed out.

"In guiding and ranching that doesn't mean anything. I never know what day of the week it is."

"Chuck is going to open, but I have to go in this afternoon and close for him." Rachel said. "What are your plans for today?" She didn't indicate she was speaking to Zane or Beth. They looked at each other expectantly.

"Zane?" Rachel said.

"I need to change oil in my truck. If I have time I might go into the canyon and look for that cow. Do you know how old her calf is? Maybe she has calved early and her last calf hung up with her?"

"I'll look the calendar up and see when we have finished breakfast."

After they had eaten Rachel got the calendar from the desk in the living room. "She calved in February. If she bred right back, she could have a new calf. I can't imagine why she is missing. I might think something happened to her but her calf would be here if that was the case. Hardly ever are we missing both the cow and calf."

"Well if I don't go today I will tomorrow. Best find out where she might be." Zane said.

"What do you want me to do today?" Beth asked Rachel.

"You can vacuum the living room and maybe dust it. It hasn't been dusted since spring. With the holidays coming it is about time. You know where the vacuum is don't you Beth?"

"Yes, I do. I used it the other day in my bedroom.

"You might think about doing that someday in your bedroom." Rachel said looking at Zane.

"Yeah, needs done once every ten years whether it needs it or not." Zane grinned.

Once again all three got up to clear the table. This time Rachel run Zane out to the garage to change oil in his truck. Zane saw Beth, come out in a while and go to the hen house. He heard the feed barrel lid rattle as she filled the chicken feeder. He saw her come back to the house with the eggs.

Zane worked on his truck the entire morning. He went in the house for lunch. Rachel had made some potato soup and some scrambled egg sandwiches. While they were eating, she asked Zane if he was going to look for the cow.

"No, I'll go in the morning after breakfast so I have all day. Guess I can clean that room you were bitching about!"

"I wasn't bitching." Rachel said with an amused smile. "Just suggesting."

"Whatever," Zane said. "I'll get it done. I packed a bunch of junk up there, stuff I moved down from the Lodge yesterday. It needs to be put away. You didn't wear the vacuum out in the living room, did you? He asked Beth with an amused grin. Zane knew his mother had little time to vacuum in the living room. It very occasionally got tended to. But also with Zane always gone and Rachel often there by her self it never had anybody in there for days at a time. Nobody even turned on the television much in the summer.

Rachel went in the afternoon to Danner's store. Zane dunged out his bedroom and vacuumed the rug. He then took a shower and changed. He decided to drive into Pete's Bar and have a beer. When he came down stairs, he found Beth was sitting at the kitchen table.

He had not planned to ask her but when he saw that she was sitting there he asked.

"I'm going to Pete's Bar, you want to come with me. Get a look at the local wild life." He grinned.

"Sure," She said much to Zane's surprise. "Do I have time to comb my hair and change?"

"Yeah, but you don't need much fancy, this is the local watering hole." He smiled.

Beth went in and returned shortly wearing jeans and a sweater. She was wearing a denim jacket and Zane noticed she had some makeup on. She was a very pretty girl. Something for the local guys to get a load of Zane thought wryly.

"Take my car?" She asked.

"We can, it's up to you?"

"Okay, I'll drive or do you want to?" She asked. Beth knew some men felt diminished letting a woman drive with them in the vehicle.

"You can drive. It's your car." Zane said and got in the passenger seat. He had to push the seat back to accommodate his long legs.

Beth drove to Pete's and parked the car. She had noticed the Bar when she drove into town. It was the only bar in town. Further down the street there was a café. Other than that there was only Danner's store and it was down and just across the street from the Bar.

There was this time half a dozen vehicles at Pete's Bar. The season was on for the loggers to be out of the woods. They would not return to work in the woods until the ground froze. That was often around the first of the year.

Zane and Beth sat down at a table. When Zane was alone, he usually sat at the bar. Pete came with Zane a can of Coors's light but he didn't recognize the girl so when he sat the Coors in front of Zane he asked the pretty blonde girl what she was having.

"Bring me the same as his" She said. Pete went back to get it and Zane took money out of his wallet. Beth offered Zane a twenty but he shook his head no and gave her a look, he hoped would discourage her from repeating that gesture any time soon.

"You done in the Mountains for this year, Adams?" Pete said as he returned with Beth's beer and a glass.

"Yeah, I'm, done for this year. Now I'm going to feed cows." Zane said. Zane had not offered to introduce Beth.

"I don't believe I know this young lady?" Pete said.

"I'm sorry Pete. This is Beth Robin's." Zane did not say anymore and other than her name, Pete still didn't know anything. Being a nosey old fart he was disappointed he didn't learn more about the pretty blonde. Zane Adams was always that way though. He didn't ever volunteer much information. Information was soul food for nosy old guys like Pete. Although he was, nosy Pete didn't spread information around as gossip. What he learned in the Bar, he kept to himself. He just liked to know every thing about everybody.

Beth smiled at Zane with amusement. She knew he had told Pete very little and she also knew Pete had been fishing for more.

Zane smiled back at her. He also knew Pete would be right on him for more information when he caught Zane without Beth with him. Zane looked around. He knew about everybody sitting in the bar. He also had seen Punk Daniels sitting at the bar. Thank God Gina wasn't with him.

That situation changed a moment later when the dark and sultry Gina came sailing through the door to join Punk. She had noted when she came in that Zane's truck wasn't there and when she spotted him at a table with a pretty blonde she stopped dead in her track! She had been looking for Zane for better than six weeks and there he sat with some pretty blonde. Gina's dark eyes flashed fire!

Pete noticed Gina immediately as well as Beth Robin's. Zane was sitting with his back to the door but when he noticed the look on Beth's face he turned around and seen Gina glaring at him. Zane quickly turned back around and looked at Beth.

Gina made straight for Zane. "Aren't you speaking to me, Adam's?" She said. "Who's your friend?" Her dark eyes flashed, as she demanded to know who the blonde was.

"Gina, this is Beth Robins. Beth, this is Gina Daniel's." Zane said calmly. He gave no outward sign Gina had disturbed him in the least. Beth looked at Zane with admiration. He was apparently good at keeping his cool. She knew from what Rachel said, exactly who Gina was!

"Nice to meet you," Beth said sweetly. "I believe I spoke to you on the phone one day?" Beth looked at Zane for conformation.

Gina whirled in a snit and headed over to the bar toward Punk. Oh God, thought Zane. He knew this day might come the night he left the bar with Gina. He would have to pay a price for messing around with her and Zane had never fooled himself that it would be otherwise!

Of coarse at that time he did not even know Beth Robin's but by Beth's reaction he knew his mother had told Beth who Gina was. Beth must have mentioned to Rachel that Gina called the house that day when Zane refused to speak with her.

Mean while nosy Pete was very much interested in what had happened when Gina came through the door. Pete knew with certainty if trouble started from Gina, Zane Adam's was most likely capable of knocking the hell out of Punk Daniels.

Zane stayed calm. He looked mildly amused at Beth. So, he wondered what Rachel had said about Gina. He doubted if she would tell Beth about her being in Zane's bed but she probably told her Gina had a husband and should not be calling Zane.

Zane had to admit he admired her sweet attitude toward Gina if Rachel had told her that Gina was married. Beth was apparently quick to size up a situation.

Zane motioned for Pete and Pete came with two more drinks for Zane and the pretty blonde woman. Zane picked up the twinkle in Pete's eyes. He knew the old fart was having a good time. After all the pumping he had done, trying to find out from Zane what went on between him and Gina, Pete knew he was close to finding out the whole sordid story.

Somebody put some money in the jukebox and the place began to get noisy as more people came in. Zane saw Gina talking earnestly to Punk. He also saw Punk glancing Zane's way with a scowl on his face.

Punk Daniels was a robust barrel chest stout built man about four years older than Zane. Punk had graduated about the time Zane started high school. Although Zane and Punk knew each other, Zane's brother had been a classmate of Punk Daniels. Punk wasn't his real name but he had been called that so long nobody knew any longer what his real name was.

Punk had a reputation for being tough and he was often scrapping over something Gina started. Nobody knew where Gina Daniels came from. She had appeared in the area when she and Punk married. They had been married about five years, there were no children and both Punk and Gina spent a lot of time hanging out in Pete's Bar.

With trepidation Zane saw Punk headed in his direction. Zane knew full well it was something Gina had said. He knew Gina was mad when she saw him with Beth. Zane also knew trouble when he saw it coming!

Punk Daniels came right up to the table.

"Hello Punk." Zane said calmly even though he knew a scene of some kind was coming.

"What's this about you screwing around with my wife!" Punk said. The bar suddenly became very quiet except for the Jukebox playing.

"Where did you hear that Punk?" Zane asked.

"Are you denying it?" Punk demanded his face flushed with anger.

"I don't think this is the time to discuss this," Zane said. "As you can see, I'm sitting here with somebody."

"Yeah, well if you've had your hands on my wife, maybe I get to dance with your woman."

Punk started to reach for Beth's arm.

"Don't put your hands on her!" Zane didn't raise his voice but the warning cut through the air like a knife.

Punk laughed and reached for Beth Robins.

Zane came up out of his chair and hit Punk Daniels twice in the face with a one, two punch.

Both blows smacked like the shot from a rifle. Stunned and surprised Punk staggered backwards and into and through the huge plate glass window that was the entire front of the bar. The window was safety glass and when it broke it disintegrated into a pile of small pieces. Zane followed Punk through the broken glass where Punk had landed outside in the gravel parking lot.

Gina Daniels screamed and ran out the door where Punk lay in the parking lot unconscious. Zane, bent over and checked Punks pulse, he was satisfied Punk was not seriously injured just knocked unconscious.

"What the hell did you do that for?" Gina screamed at Zane.

Zane satisfied that Punk was all right except he was knocked out, said softly to Gina.

"Well isn't this what you wanted?" Gina was shocked at the cold hard look in Zane Adam's eyes. She knew in that instant any chance she had of being with Zane Adam's again was gone!

Gina began to cry. Several other patrons' had come out to see how badly Punk had been injured. Punk was coming around but he was disoriented. Zane helped him to his feet. He helped him into his vehicle and Gina got behind the wheel and drove off with Punk. Zane sighed with regret. He hoped this was the last of it but he doubted it. Punk Daniel's was too much of a sore head to take being knocked out cold and also out through Pete's window.

Zane went back inside to see what Pete wanted to do about the window. The glass was about six feet square and the cold November air was quickly cooling the Bar off. Beth was still sitting at the table where she and Zane had been. She looked surprisingly calm.

Zane walked over to the Bar where Pete still stood frozen in his tracks. "I guess I owe you for a window?" Zane said. "What have you got to put over it until the glass can be replaced?"

"John, go to the store and get a roll of that clear plastic. Don't worry about it Adam's. I have insurance for that sort of thing. My God, remind me not to get you riled. I never saw anybody get hit that hard in all the years I've been behind the Bar. I've heard of people being knocked into next week but that's the first time I saw it! Is Punk all right?"

"Yeah, he was just knocked out. With his hard head he probably won't even have a headache.

Bring us a couple more beers." Zane went back to the table where Beth still sat. She had not moved and it was hard to tell by her bland expression what she was thinking. Zane sat back down unruffled except for a couple skinned places on his knuckles where he had hit Punk.

"Well, I guess I needn't worry about my safety when I'm with you!" Beth smiled a slight smile.

"You guys have heard we are in the twenty first century. That looked like a scene from the old westerns."

"We are in the west. Do you want to leave?"

"No, not on account of that. Whenever you're ready?" She smiled.

"In that case I ordered us another beer. Sorry your first trip to the watering hole was upsetting." Zane grinned.

"Well, as you mentioned I got a good look at the wild life. I just had no idea the wild life would come through the door with me!" Beth began to laugh.

Zane grinned at her observation and dug money out of his wallet for the drinks.

"Wonder what is taking John so long with that roll of plastic?" Pete said as he delivered the drinks.

Zane's eyed widened as he realized John had went to the store. "Oh shit, Mom is at the store. I suppose John is telling her the whole sordid story."

"I didn't see any sordid story," Beth said. "I just saw you knock a man through the window to keep him from bothering me. I can't believe Rachel will think that is sordid. In fact it is kind of chivalrous." She giggled. "Unless he tells her the part about Gina Daniels being involved, what is the story of you and Gina, if you don't mind me asking?"

Zane's face reddened at her question. "Let's just say it was a lapse in judgment on my part, one time."

"Okay. It really isn't any of my business." Beth smiled.

John returned with the roll of plastic and Zane went to help Pete get the front of the bar sealed off. They stapled the plastic with some stripping over the gaping hole where the window had been. "Might be a good idea to put some inside as well to help from losing all your heat." Zane told Pete.

"Yeah, I'll call and get the glass company here on Monday. Thanksgiving will be Thursday and I hope they can get to it by then." Pete said.

"Sorry," Zane apologized again.

"Well I knew there was bound to be a ruckus, the night you went out the door with Gina. She does it every time. She was quiet for a long time. I guess that blonde you are with is the straw that broke the camels back." Pete grinned.

"Yeah, I also knew there was going to be a confrontation when I left with Gina. I just hope this is the end of it."

"If Punk has any brains left in that thick head of his, he would do well to stay to hell away from you. As I said, I have never seen a man hit so hard! Guess that comes from wrestling those Bulls around up there in the mountains. You are one son of a Bitch I wouldn't want mad at me." Pete grinned.

"Well, let me know, I'll make it right on the window." Zane went back inside. Things had returned to normal except for the view through the plastic was not as good as the glass but the place had once again begun to warmed up.

After finishing their beer Zane and Beth decided to leave. "Guess I've done all the damage I can here." Zane grinned as he helped Beth into her coat.

Pete watched with interest through the plastic as Zane and the blonde girl went out and got into a new Toyota Car, Pete noticed the girl got behind the wheel but when they pulled away the car had local plates on it. Pete had never seen the girl before but he ginned, she was a real looker. Small wonder Gina had a fit!

Zane and Beth did the evening chores when they returned to the ranch. They had just finished when Rachel came in the door. One look and Zane recognized the thin line of her lips. She looked that way when she disapproved of something. She had heard all about Zane knocking Punk Daniels through Pete's window.

"I told you this was going to happen." Rachel reminded Zane.

"Yeah you did." Zane was not going to argue with her nor was he going to explain what happened. As far as Zane was concerned it was also his business. If he had been the cause, he would handle it.

Beth thought with admiration he had handled it very well. She felt Zane Adam's was a man she could feel safe with wherever they went. She didn't know much about bar room brawling but she knew Zane Adams had hit Punk Daniels harder than she could imagine it could be done.

Rachel seemed unaware that Beth had been with Zane at Pete's bar. If she knew about her being with Zane during the incident she did not mention it. They ate dinner and Zane went out and checked the cows. The cows still had feed from the morning.

When he came back in the house Rachel and Zane talked about getting the cows off the field and into the feedlot.

"I can do that tomorrow when I'm on the horse after looking for the spotted ass cow and her calf."

Neither Zane nor Beth mentioned anything further to Rachel of the incident in Pete's Bar.

The next morning Beth showed at the barn before daylight to again help Zane feed the cows. This time Zane only fed half of their hay so he could lure them into the winter feed lot after he returned out of the canyon.

Zane haltered and tied the Bay's in their stall while they ate their grain. After breakfast Zane saddled the Bay gelding called Sonny, he left the other bay a mare whose name Beth found out was Dolly, tied in her stall. Zane told Beth if he didn't tie her she otherwise would tear around the horse pasture and raise hell for not being allowed to follow.

"You ever ride a horse?" Zane asked her as he saddled Sonny.

"No, I haven't been around horses until I came here. Cows either." She added.

"I don't suppose you have never been around a brawl like the one at Pete's yesterday. Folks are probably civilized back east?" He grinned.

"Sure, back east in Detroit we have gangs standing on street corners. They don't fight with their fist but guns, AK47's and knives. You have no idea! Yesterday was like in the movies and the old west!" She laughed.

"Glad you enjoyed it!" Zane grinned, shaking his head in amusement. It was obvious they were from two different worlds. Zane led the Bay out saddled and swung up in the saddle. "Now it's old west time. "He laughed. "See you later and he headed down a dirt road that went around the hay field toward the canyon Maggie the farm dog trotted happily along.

Beth laughed. It indeed was like the old west. She had noticed the firearm strapped on his hip when he mounted the horse. Zane Adams mountain man and guide looked very much like Zane Adam's cowboy. Yesterday he had looked like a prizefighter. Beth found there were many interesting facets to Zane Adam's and she found herself attracted to all of them.

Beth had originally planned to become acquainted, with Zane, as a brother, was not working. There was no way that Beth could look at Zane Adams as a brother. Her attraction to him was growing daily. She did not know what she was going to do about it. With her staying in Rachel Adam's home when she was becoming more attracted to Zane, she felt was somehow dishonest to the relationship she had developed with Rachel. Beth may be forced to discuss, her feelings with Rachel. Sadly she thought she might even have to leave Rachel's house. She had never had a real home and now that she did, she was reluctant to give it up!

Zane rode down the old road. The canyon below him appeared to be huge but Zane had been over nearly every foot of it either horseback or on foot. Adams, cattle had ranged into the canyon since before Zane was born. Zane first learned to hunt game in this canyon. There were abundant white tail deer and a sizable Elk herd. The canyon elk herd often moved up on top into the winter wheat fields. When that happened there were sometimes as many as eighty or ninety heads. Their appearance of coarse did not make the wheat farmers happy.

Zane rode and backtracked the cattle's tracks, from the direction they had come from a couple weeks earlier. He hoped to find signs of the missing cow from wherever the cows had come from. The most likely spot, they usually hung out at that time of year was on the south slope of the other side of the canyon.

It was about seven miles down and across the creek and up the other side. Maggie trotted along happily. This was the highlight of her existence when Zane took the horse and she got to go looking for cows. Maggie knew what Zane was looking for. However she did not necessarily know which critter they were searching for. At least Zane did not believe she did, but he often pondered how much she really knew. Dogs were smart; maybe she did know what cow he searched for. It took Zane a couple hours to ride over on the other side. He went to the salting places. He rode, in on five heads, of Elk on a bench where they salted. There was also a pond in the area. Knowing cattle always need water, he checked the pond for tracks. He did not pick up any fresh cow tracks.

He rode around through an old homestead. There were lots of apple trees planted long ago by the homesteader. The cattle, deer, and Elk also frequented these places to eat the apples that had fallen from the trees; On one occasion he had seen a cow elk on her hind feet picking apples from the trees.

There was no sign of recent fresh cattle's tracks. Zane noticed some Ravens working below him on a bench, beneath the old homestead. He rode down to it. There he found the spotted ass cow or what remained of her. Zane knew at a glance she had been killed by wolves.

Zane knew there were Wolves in the canyon as Rachel had told Zane she saw three Wolves in the field behind the house. The cow had been hamstrung from behind and brought down. She was half eaten. Zane could see where the ground had been torn up as the cow put up a fight. It had been a couple of weeks. Zane figured the wolves bringing down that cow might have been what prompted the other cows to head for home. He took the ear tag out of the cow's carcass and got his camera out of his pack. He took pictures of the kill site. He still did not know what had happened to the calf? As he scoured around he found the calves scull and also took the ear tag from it. The calf could have been the first killed and then the cow, as she tried in vain to protect her calf.

Zane felt anger. It wasn't just the loss of the cow but she was a young cow and it was also the loss of the ten calves she would have over the years. And the loss of their off spring as well. Zane cursed the dumb bastard's that brought the Wolves back.

He was seeing the adverse effect on the Wild life and now he was feeling the loss in his own pocket. What the hell did those idiots' think the wolves were to eat once they depleted the game herds?

Zane knew as well as most folks, by Lewis and Clark's journals there were not many game animals in this area of the mountains. The game had proliferated and adapted to this area as they were driven back off the plains by population expansion. The few wolves the homesteader encountered when they settled this area were quickly eliminated for a very good reason. There was not enough here for man and wolves.

Maggie was also very nervous about being in the area where the Wolves had brought the cow down. She could still pick up the scent of the Wolves even though it had been a couple weeks.

Zane mounted Sonny and headed back across the creek toward the ranch. Maggie began to settle down once they left the scene of carnage. Zane could now quit worrying about the whereabouts, of that cow and her calf.

He knew if he saw a wolf he would not hesitate to pull the 357 from his hip and kill it; Federal offense or not. He would need to be careful if he did such a thing as he could lose his license to Guide. The wolves were an impending threat to both of his livelihood.

It was afternoon before Zane and Maggie returned from the canyon to the ranch. He put Sonny into the stall and started his truck to load hay. He threw ten bales down into the truck.

He drove the truck into the lot where they wintered the cows. The cows had lined up along the fence and were watching. When Zane opened the gate they came eagerly through the barnyard and into the lot with the hay on the truck. Zane shut the gate behind the cows and fed the bales off his truck. He gathered the strings and pulled the truck back into the Barnyard.

Zane went in the barn and unsaddled Sonny and rubbed him down. When finished he let both the Bays loose into the back lot. He shut the gate to the hay field. He would not have to drive back into the field. From now on the cattle would be restricted to the feedlot below the barn until spring when the grass once again began to grow. The feedlot was sloping and was in size about ten acres.

There was a pond for water. When ice began to appear on the pond, Zane would need to chop holes in the ice for the cattle to water.

Zane took his firearm off and put it back in his pack. He took the pack and went to the house. Rachel's Car was gone and also Beth's. Zane went upstairs and put his pack away. He went down and laid the two ear tags he had taken from the wolf-killed animals on the desk.

Zane heard a car drive in and he looked out and saw Beth getting out of her car. Damn she was good looking he thought. He was very much attracted to the young woman but knew he had best keep that to himself.

Beth came through the door. "You find your cow?" She asked.

"Afraid so, the Wolves got her and her calf both."

"I'm so sorry. Why are there, wolves around here?" She asked.

"Because some damned environmentalist thought, we need them!" Zane said. "Is that stupid or what? Is Mom at work?"

"Yes, I just came from there. Got tired sitting here by myself."

Zane went to the Fridge and got a beer. He began to look for something to make a sandwich. It had been since breakfast and he was hungry. Not finding anything he got out some eggs and started fixing some scrambled eggs. He would make a sandwich out of those.

Beth came back in the kitchen from putting her coat away. "You need help with that?" She asked.

Zane smiled with amusement. "No Thanks. You want some, I can cook enough for both of us?"

"No thanks, I had lunch." She said but she got in the refrigerator and also got a beer. "You want another?" She asked. Zane had downed his, as he was thirsty when he got back from his ride.

"Yes, thank you." Zane scooped his scrambled eggs into a bowl and got some bread and mayonnaise out and fixed himself a sandwich. He sat down at the table to eat.

"Sure you don't want something?" He asked.

"I making you nervous watching, you eat?" Beth asked with a grin.

"Yes." He smiled.

Beth got up and made her a half sandwich out of the left over scrambled eggs. Sitting down with it she said, "Feel better now?"

"Yeah," Zane grinned.

They finished eating and both cleaned up the kitchen. Zane headed up the stairs. "Think I'll take a nap."

With her hands on her hips Beth grinned, "I suppose you want me to help you with that also?"

"Yeah, that would be nice!" Zane laughed and went upstairs. As he lay on his bed, he began to think about having Beth to help him with his nap. He grinned and knew he would indeed enjoy having her in his bed. He went to sleep. He slept for a couple hours and when he came downstairs his mother had come home from Danner's store.

Beth had filled her in on Zane finding the carcass of the cow and her calf. "What are you going to do?" Rachel asked Zane.

"I took plenty of pictures and I'm going to call the Federal guys about it. There may be a fund to reimburse for the cow but we are going to be out all of the calves she would have had. These damned wolves are going to be the end of every thing I do for a living. Once they have decimated the wild life, then our livestock will be their food supply. Unbelievable that they have brought those damned things back into Idaho. The Wolves, they have brought in from Canada are a breed that is huge. They aren't small like the wolf that we already had in Idaho.

Why in the hell couldn't they have left things alone? Now we are going to be faced with a problem it will cost the government to remedy, not to speak of the cost of the program to reintroduce them in the first place."

Rachel listened as Zane ranted on. It was no secret he was very unhappy about the wolves. Zane was not alone, all of the locals that knew the problems already beginning were also unhappy.

The fact that the program had been carried out without even consulting with the residents of Idaho was a sore point with nearly all of the residents. There had been a grass root, movement to get an initiative on the fall ballot to remove the wolves but had failed because too many people signed it that was not registered to vote.

After dinner Rachel, Zane and Beth watched a little television. Zane went upstairs early. Shortly after Beth retired also.

Rachel thought about Zane and Beth. She felt both of the young people were attracted to each other. Rachel wasn't unhappy about it. She felt Beth was a wonderful girl and it was way past time for Zane to get involved with a nice girl instead of a wanton sexpot like Gina Daniels. Rachel fervently hoped the fiasco yesterday at Pete's Bar would be the end of Zane's association with the likes of Gina Daniels.

Rachel finished watching her program and she also retired for the night. She reminded herself before falling asleep to take the turkey out of the freezer and put it in the fridge to thaw. She would have her entire family for Thanksgiving dinner and also Beth. Rachel was very fond of Beth and had always wanted a daughter. Aware of the growing attraction between Zane and Beth, Rachel was not going to encourage or discourage a relationship between Beth and Zane. She decided to let nature take its coarse.

7

Thanksgiving day. Zane as usual fixed coffee before he went out load hay to feed. Beth came right after him. Zane grinned when he thought about the city girl up sloughing through the cow manure in the early hours of the morning. He didn't know if she had an alarm or she heard him come down the stairs. She was always there. The school had not called her and Zane imagined if she had to go to the school she would not be out at the barn.

Zane no longer had to tell Beth what to do. She would go in and climb the loft ladder and push the bales out the barn loft door.

Beth no longer drove the truck since the cows were into the lower feedlot. Zane drove while Beth rode in the passenger seat until along they parked along the feeders. Then they both climbed into the back of the truck to fill the feeders. Maggie still kept the cows back from the gate and away from the truck.

Beth now had a pocketknife so she could cut the strings. When Zane got in to pull the truck forward, Beth was not paying attention to him moving the truck and fell out into the mud and cow manure.

Zane, seen her fall and he jumped out to see if she was hurt. The city girl from Detroit was using some unsavory language as Zane went to help her up.

"Are you all right Beth?" Zane figured by her profanity she was not injured. But obviously covered with mud and manure her dignity was ruffled. Zane began to laugh and couldn't stop laughing.

"What the hell you think is so funny, Zane?" Beth sputtered.

"Nothing. As long as you aren't hurt." He chuckled, getting back in the truck and pulling down to the next feeder. Beth walked behind and got up in the truck and helped him fill the next feeder.

"This time, hang on!" Zane said as he got in and pulled the truck up to last feeder. He was still laughing when he got out and climbed up along side the muddy Beth to finish the feeder. "I don't know if I'm going to let you ride in the truck or haul you to the house in the back!" He laughed.

"Fine, I'll ride in the back." She rolled her eyes at him but Zane noticed a sheepish smile. When they finished Zane told her to just take her muddy coat off and get in the truck. He wasn't laughing but worried about her getting cold in the back of the truck. Beth shed her muddy coat and gloves and threw them in the back of the truck. They would need laundered. The front, of her jeans were muddy but because it was very cold and she climbed in the truck with Zane.

"Sure you're all right?" He asked.

"Yes, I'm fine and I will see that does not happen again!"

When Zane and Beth got on the porch, Zane slipped out of his barnyard boots. Beth had retrieved her muddy coat and gloves and stood watching him slip out of his boots.

"What am I supposed to do, undress to get in the house?" She asked?

With a big grin Zane said. "I guess you can if you like or you can run in there and take a chance my Mom doesn't catch you tracking mud."

Beth slipped out of her boots and stuck her nose up and went into the house. Zane followed her laughing. Rachel immediately saw her with mud all over the front of her jeans. She also had mud and manure on her face and in her hair.

"What happened?" She said with concern, giving Zane who was laughing, a warning look. Zane went on to the kitchen to find his fresh coffee.

Rachel came in and Zane supposed Beth had headed for the bathroom. He still had a wide amused gin on his face.

"She could have gotten hurt Zane! It isn't funny, quit your silly laughing." Rachel said but Zane noticed her eyes twinkled and he knew she was also was about to laugh.

"One thing about falling in mud and cow shit, it's soft." He chuckled.

Rachel had just finished putting the turkey for dinner in the oven. She had not yet cleaned up the mess from making the stuffing for the turkey. "You want me to start Breakfast?" He asked.

"No, I'll get to it soon as I clean up this mess. Besides Beth will need time to Bathe. You in a hurry for your breakfast?" Rachel asked.

"Nope, we can wait for the women to get the shit washed off." And he began to chuckle about it again.

Beth finally came from the bathroom. She had on clean clothes and her long blonde hair was freshly washed. Zane tried unsuccessfully to suppress a grin. He did get up and get her a cup of coffee and put it on the table for her. He couldn't contain himself and begin to chuckle again.

"Zane, shut up about it." Rachel complained.

"Sorry mom, but I haven't had this much fun since the hogs ate my kid brother!

"Zane! Don't pay any attention to him, Beth. And no hogs ever ate his kid brother!" Rachel was trying to smooth things over for poor Beth and stop Zane from poking fun at her.

With a sip of coffee and a fresh bath Beth surveyed Zane with benign tolerance. "So glad you have had so much fun this morning. Kids should be allowed to have fun on Thanksgiving." She allowed graciously. Beth and Zane sipped their coffee and eyed each other with merriment.

Rachel started breakfast. "At least I've had my Thanksgiving bath, what about you?" Beth wrinkled her nose at Zane with distaste.

"I'll get around to it before dinner," He grinned. Zane thought to himself not only was Beth good looking but after her spill in the manure and her composure that day in Pete's bar the girl also had a sense of humor. A sense of humor was important in the Adam's family, without one, life could at times be trying.

Matt, Susie and the two Adams grandchildren, Levi and Jason, showed up for dinner about 1p.m. Beth had met them before when Zane was at the Lodge. The house smelled of Turkey. Beth and Rachel had worked on pies the day before.

Zane had taken his shower and was sprawled in front of the Television watching the football games. Matt came in to join him.

"Hey, I haven't seen you all fall." Matt said as he flopped on the sofa with Zane. The two brothers resembled each other but Matt wasn't as tall and rangy as Zane. Matt also wore his hair cut short and he had darker hair and complexion than Zane. The Adams boys had always been close. Matt had moved out of the house before Walt died. He and Susie had married at that time and Matt had worked at the sawmill since he graduated high school.

Matt came to the Ranch in the spring and helped Zane work the cattle when they branded and castrated. He also came if Zane needed help with anything like roofing a barn or shed. Matt spent more time in the fall at the Farm than Zane did, as Matt hunted the canyon that Zane had ridden into the day before.

Matt also gave Zane a hand on weekends when the hay needed to be put in the barn. As they watched the football game that day Zane told Matt about the wolves killing the spotted ass cow and her calf.

Susie joined Beth and Rachel in the kitchen. Rachel had the girls get out the good china and set the dining room table. The dining room table was never used except on holidays.

The boy's Levi and Jason migrated into the living room with Zane and Matt. Beth stepped in and asked Zane "Are the lions winning?" Four pairs of male eyes stared at her.

"You like football?" Zane asked. He found it very unusual that Beth would like football!

"Yeah", She grinned. "I like watching big strong guys shove each other around!"

Matt rolled his eyes and looked at Zane. Zane stared at Beth. Why did he have a feeling she was not just referring to football! "I'm afraid your lions are getting their butts kicked!" Zane said.

Beth looked disappointed and went back to the kitchen.

"What was that about?" Matt said looking at Zane. Zane shrugged but he had a feeling she had subtly referred to the fracas at Pete's Bar. Maybe she was getting even with him for laughing at her over her spill in the mud and manure?

Two p.m. Adam's family and Beth sat down in the dining room to Thanksgiving dinner. Rachel had Matt carve the turkey.

"Why me? You should give the knife to Zane, he is always carving on something." Matt objected.

"Because you are the eldest." Rachel said.

After the delicious dinner the males again sprawled in front of the Television. The women cleaned up after the dinner. Once the kitchen was restored to order the three women invaded, the living room and piled in front of the Television with the men and boys.

About five in the evening Matt and his family left for home. Beth, Zane and Rachel remained in the living room. Rachel excused herself in about an hour and went to her room. Zane looked at Beth. "Is mom feeling all right?" He asked.

"Far as I know." She said.

Zane got up and went and knocked on Rachel's door. "You feeling all right Mom?" He asked.

"I'm fine Zane. I'm reading a book. Goodnight Zane."

Zane went back to the living room and shrugged and told Beth she was reading. Zane sprawled back on the sofa. "Something you want to watch?" He asked Beth.

"What is on?" She asked.

"The schedule is over there, he indicated the stand on the other side of her on the end table. Beth was sitting on the other end of the sofa. Beth picked up the television guide and went to open it.

Zane reached across and picked it out of her hand.

"Hey, give that back to me." Beth tackled Zane and began to try to get the Television guide back from him. Suddenly Zane was looking at Beth and the look in his eyes was not to be mistaken. "Sorry" Zane said backing away.

"Don't, be sorry, please?" Beth said softly. Her voice was as soft as a caress. Beth reached up and pulled Zane's head down and kissed him. Zane pulled her into his arms and kissed her back softly and gently. She folded into his chest and put her arms around him. He drew her closer. There was so much desire in that kiss Zane felt he could hardly get his breath. Zane pulled away.

"Beth, I can't put you on the spot here, you're a guest and I'm not taking advantage of that!"

Zane got up and went upstairs without looking back.

Beth didn't know what to think. She knew what she had felt in his arms but she didn't know why he backed away. What did he mean by taking advantage? Did he think she would feel obligated to receive any advancement he would make? Beth felt like crying. She had known her attraction was growing for Zane but she had no idea she would feel such a overwhelming desire for him. Beth got up and turned off the Television and went to her room. She put on her nightgown and crawled in bed. Her body ached with desire. She had not wanted him to stop and now she felt he had somehow rejected her.

Beth heard Zane come down the stairs and go out the door. She heard his truck start and heard it leave. She wondered where he was going? She got up and put on her robe. She went out and knocked on Rachel's door.

Rachel told her to come in. Rachel was sitting in bed and had been reading a book that now lay on the bed beside her. "Was that Zane I heard leave?" She asked.

"Yes", Beth said. She still felt like crying. "Something happened."

"What do you mean Beth? Something happened? Rachel could see Beth appeared pale and upset.

"Zane and I were kidding around over the television schedule and we kissed." Beth looked at Rachel helplessly.

"What is wrong with a kiss?" Rachel said. She felt like smiling but clearly Beth was upset.

Beth sank down into a chair. "It wasn't just a kiss, I can't explain. I am very much attracted to Zane and he just got upset and left." Beth looked at Rachel helplessly.

"I know Beth that you and Zane are attracted to each other. I've known that for some time. Why was he upset?"

"I don't know!" Beth said weakly. "He just pulled away and said I was a guest and he wasn't going to take advantage of that."

Rachel was thoughtful. "I think perhaps he feels you would feel obligated to return his.… Well whatever went on between you two, it affected Zane deeply or he would have laughed it off. I'm afraid Zane has deep feelings for you Beth, and he does not yet know what to do about it. It must have been some kiss!" Rachel smiled and shook her head.

"It was!" Beth got up and turned to go to her room. "Do you want me to leave?" She asked.

"Of coarse not!" Rachel said. "I would be delighted if you and Zane could have something satisfying between you. I have wanted Zane to settle down for a long time but obviously Zane hasn't come to terms with what he feels for you or he has just realized he has feelings for you. Give him time he will work it out. I don't want you to feel you need to leave. I want you to feel you have a home here as long as you want. What happens between you and Zane has nothing to do with that, please believe me."

"Good night Rachel. Thank you for the lovely dinner." Beth went to her room but she could not sleep. She lay awake. It was after midnight when she heard Zane returns and go up the stairs.

She finally fell asleep once she knew Zane had safely returned.

The next morning Beth heard Zane come down the stairs. She hurriedly dressed and she followed him out shortly after he made the coffee. Zane was still warming up his truck when he saw Beth come out and go to the barn. He saw her turn on the barn lights and he assumed she climbed the ladder to the loft.

Zane had gone the night before to Pete's Bar. Everyone but Zane and Pete was at home full of turkey. Zane seemed to be in a mood of sorts and Pete ended up sitting and pretty much talking to himself. Zane was always quiet but last night he seemed to be brooding. Pete had gotten the window in and Zane got out his checkbook and tried to pay for the window. Pete wouldn't let him. He told Zane, he paid outrageous insurance premiums and it was the first time he got any of it back.

When Zane returned home, he had not been able to sleep. He kept thinking about Beth. He knew he had deep feelings for her but he didn't know what to do about it. He did not want to put her into a position of having to leave. He also didn't want her to feel she needed to be receptive to him to stay. He was in an enigma where Beth was concerned. He guessed he would ignore that the kiss had occurred. He didn't know how he was going to do that but it was the only coarse of action that made sense.

Zane pulled the truck out to the barn and got in the back and started stacking hay as Beth pushed them out. When loaded Beth came down and got in the truck with Zane. Neither one said anything. Beth got out and opened the gate while Maggie held the cows back. Beth and Zane fed the cows without speaking. When finished Zane pulled back to the barn and he went in to grain the Bay's and turn out the lights.

When he finished and was about to turn out the lights, Beth had come into the Barn. They had not spoken. Zane looked at her and reached up to turn out the barn lights. A tear slipped down her cheek. Zane froze for a second and then he went to her and gathered her in his arms. He buried his face in the fragrance of her hair. He felt her shudder against him. There was no way on earth he was going to be able to ignore that kiss between them. He sought her lips and tasted the salt of her tears. He knew as they kissed she was not feeling it out of obligation. After they kissed Zane held her for a second.

"Let's go eat breakfast," He said gently and he reached up and turned out the barn lights. It was all too sudden and Zane needed to slow it down before he dragged her into the haymow.

Neither of them said anything as they went to the house. When they entered the kitchen, Rachel was up and busy in the kitchen. Zane poured coffee for him and Beth both. They sat at the table and drank their coffee while Rachel fixed breakfast. Rachel kept up a stream of chatter but neither Zane nor Beth was listening.

After breakfast Rachel asked Beth. "Are you going to get ready? We are going to be too late for the sales and could get trampled by the crowds?"

"Will just be a jiffy." Beth said, heading back toward her room.

"What's going on?" Zane asked. "You girls going shopping?"

"Yes, Beth and I planned on going into Lewiston. Today is the big day for the Christmas sales. We had planned it for some time. Chuck let me off from the store." Rachel was looking forward to spending the day with Beth and shopping. It was something she rarely did.

"You need some money?" Zane asked.

"No of coarse not. Besides if I did, I know where the Bank is?" Rachel smiled at Zane indulgently. He looked as if he did not sleep well. Rachel said nothing to him about her conversation with Beth. She would not interfere. What was going to develop between Zane and Beth would be their business. Rachel would not interfere!

Beth came out and Rachel and she took off in Beth's car. Zane puttered around the entire day with small jobs in the shop and barn. The women did not return until late. Zane had already fixed himself a bite to eat and cleaned the kitchen and went upstairs to his room. He was still awake when he heard Rachel and Beth downstairs. From the trips they made out to the car and the laughter he wondered if they had bought the entire town. Zane turned over and went to sleep.

The next morning Zane fixed the coffee and headed out to feed. Beth came as usual after he warmed up the truck. She shoved the bales out. As they were filling the feeders, Zane noticed one of the cows had birth membranes hanging from behind. He knew she had a new calf. He wondered if she was early as he had not noticed her springing and making bag as if she was about to have a calf.

"You want to take the truck out Beth?" He asked. "I have to go look for a calf."

"Sure, do you need, me to help?" She asked.

"No just leave the truck in the barn lot and grain the Bay's."

Zane and Maggie headed down the hill to scour the pasture. In the further-most corner near the fence Zane found a small black calf. At first he didn't think it was alive. When he examined it the calf blinked his eyes but didn't move. The calf was lying prone and not curled up as he should be. Zane stuck his finger in the calf's mouth and found the calf's mouth was cold. He knew the calf had not been up and had not had anything to eat. Zane picked the calf up and began the trek up out of the hole to the barn

The calf only weighed about seventy pounds and Zane carried him to the barn easily. He stopped at the feeder and made a bawling sound to see if the mother would respond. She did. Zane put the calf down and she came and smelled of him and licked it. Zane picked up the calf and packed him out of the feedlot to the barn. The cow followed worried about her calf.

Beth had just come out of the Barn when she saw Zane with the calf in his arms and the cow behind.

"Would you shut the gate, to the feed lot?" Zane asked. Beth hurried to shut the gate to the feedlot. She skirted around the mother cow that was following Zane with her calf.

Zane packed the calf into the barn. The mother cow followed Zane and bawled for her calf as Zane entered the barn. Zane grabbed a handful of hay from the Bay's manger and give it to the cow beside the barn. He opened a small pen just inside the door and laid the calf on the hay and shut the gate to the small pen so the Bays could not get in.

Zane headed for the house. Beth came behind him. He went in the back door into the porch behind the kitchen and got a plastic bag container with a plastic tube about two feet long attached. He rummaged around and took out a bag of the colostrums and went into the kitchen.

"You want to heat some quilts, Mom? We got a new one that is a little early and he is cold mouthed." Zane drew some warm water in a pitcher and mixed the powdered colostrums with a whisk. He pored it into the plastic bag with the tube. He rummaged in the refrigerator and put two bottles of vaccine in his pocket. He also took some syringes from a drawer. Beth had followed Zane into the kitchen.

"You want to bring those quilts when Mom gets them warmed? Beth nodded that she would.

Zane headed back to the barn with the bag of colostrums and his vaccines Zane picked the calf's head up and put the tube down the left side of the calf mouth. He was careful not to tip the bag up until he was certain he had the tube down the calf esophagus and not into the trachea to his lungs. The calf tried to protest with a weak bawl and Zane knew, from that he was in the esophagus, He tipped the bag up and began to empty the warm colostrums into the calf's mouth.

Beth came in the barn with the quilts as Zane was emptying the colostrums from the tube feeder.

"Put the warm quilt over him." Zane said. Zane began to plug in a heat light over the calf. Once the heat light was plugged in, he began to fill the syringes he had taken from his pocket.

"What are those for?" Beth asked.

"One is Bose, a selenium vitamin shot for white muscle and the other one is vitamins A and D.

Do you want to go to the house and ask, mom to send the vitamin B and the fifty-milligram needle?"

"Will the calf live?" Beth asked.

"I don't know. Depends on how long he has been laying out there on the cold ground and how soon we can get him warmed up."

As Beth left the barn, the calf's mother had finished the hay. She bawled at Beth and shook her head. Beth hurried toward the house uncertain what the mother cows' intentions were.

She returned with the stuff Rachel had given her. She handed them to Zane. Zane had been rubbing the calf trying to get some circulation going. The calf was responsive when Beth entered the Barn and the calf's eyes followed her but the calf had not tried to get up.

Zane filled the big syringe and put the vitamin B in the calf with the needle. He pulled the loose skin up on the calf neck and injected the fifty milligrams under the skin.

"Well I guess that is all we can do." He said.

"Poor little thing, was that milk you gave him in the bag?" Beth asked." And will that mother cow chase me?"

Zane smiled with amusement. "That milk was a colostrums that is a cow's first milk and it has antibodies that protect the calf from infection and sickness. Sometimes a mother will get riled but this cow is a gentle cow and she knows something is wrong with her calf. She had licked it dry but I don't think she is riled enough to chase anyone as long as Maggie stays away from the barn. Maggie knows and usually stays back from newborns."

"How does she know that?" Beth asked.

Zane shrugged, "I don't know, it is instinct in some Border Collies. She has been here since she was born and probably knows more about cows than I do. Let's go find some coffee, there isn't anything more we can do now, that heat lamp will warm the calf."

Zane and Beth walked to the house. "How is the calf?" Rachel asked as they came in the back door.

"Done what we can do, will have to wait and see?" Zane said. He went to the sink and began to wash the plastic tube feeder. Beth got coffee for her and Zane. Zane took the syringes out of his pocket and laid them on the counter. He took his coat off and hung it on the chair and sat down to drink his coffee. "Well did you girls buy the town of Lewiston yesterday?"

Rachel laughed. "We tried but I'm afraid we nearly got stampeded over by shoppers. I think I bought more than Beth did.

"That's because I don't know what to buy." Beth smiled. "The most fun was having lunch and letting someone else wait on us."

"Yes," Rachel smiled. "The entire day was fun, we'll have to go again, one of these days."

Zane rolled his eyes with amusement. He wondered what it was that women enjoyed about shopping. Zane hated it. He wanted to get what he went to the store for as soon as possible.

Rachel put breakfast on the table and after they ate Zane went back to the barn to check the calf.

When he approached the barn, the cow bawled at him. From within the barn Zane heard the calf answer. He went in the barn and the calf was not up and walking around but it was no longer laying prostrated on its side but was curled up like a calf is supposed to lay. Zane stuck his finger in the calf's mouth and felt his mouth that was now warm. Zane picked up the quilts and felt of the calves body. It also had begun to feel warm.

Beth stepped in the barn. Zane was bent over the calf. He gave her a smile. It was reassurance the calf had improved. "Well, maybe we saved one?" Zane said.

"Now the problem will to be to get him back with his Mama. I, sure as hell can't do as good a job raising him as she can do."

"Can't you just put him back out here with her?" Beth asked.

"Not yet. He has to be on his feet and stronger. We might try by tomorrow if he continues to improve." Zane went over and took more hay out for the cow in the barnyard.

Beth and Zane walked back to the house. "We might try giving him some milk in the bottle after while if he gets on his feet." Zane told her. "Just hope I don't have to put the cow into the squeeze chute and milk her."

"Why would you need to do that?" Beth asked.

"Because if it isn't her milk going through that calf she might get it in her head he isn't hers. In that case I will need to milk the cow to keep her from drying up and feed her milk to her calf. They will sometimes claim their own calf after rejecting it if their milk begins going through the calf. Some times you can get a cow to adopt another calf by feeding the cows milk to it."

"How long does it take to learn all this stuff?" Beth asked.

"Zane smiled and shook his head. "I'm still learning. Every year with cattle it's something else to be learned. Some times, such as me telling you, one can learn things. I'm sure I would have learned more from my Dad if he had lived longer."

"How did your father die?" Beth wanted to know. She had not heard Rachel mention it.

"He was a drunk and killed himself in a truck wreck one night on his way home."

"How old were you when that happened?" Beth asked.

"Eighteen, just out of high school." Beth and Zane by then were going back into the house.

Rachel came from the bedrooms. She had her coat on and her store apron over her arm. "Chuck called and wants me to come in and I imagine it will be all afternoon. You and Zane can pick on the Thanksgiving leftovers if Zane didn't eat it all yesterday." She told Beth as she hurried out the door.

Zane laughed. "I would have had to eat steady all day yesterday to eat all that stuff."

Beth grinned, "In that case we might have something to eat."

Zane went upstairs and decided to shower. He had mud and manure on his clothes from packing the calf. He wondered what he and Beth were to do all afternoon alone in the house. Zane thought he could go into Pete's but he wanted to keep an eye on the new calf. Maybe he would find something to read in his room.

Beth found that Zane was gone for a long time. She wondered if he had lain down for a nap. She hoped he was not hiding out upstairs to avoid her. She went in the living room and turned on the Television. It had been an interesting morning at the ranch. Beth wondered why anyone would wonder what there was to do in the country. Thinking of that she decided to go check the hen house. Since they had been busy with the calf maybe, Rachel had forgotten.

Beth was surprised that Rachel had forgotten to care for the hens. She fed them and packed some water for them and filled the water pan which sat on a heated base this time of year to keep the water from freezing. There was a heavy smell of urine about the house and Beth wondered how often they had to clean out the hen house. She had noticed a pile of manure and litter out behind so she knew they cleaned it, how often she didn't know. When she remembered it to mention she would ask Rachel or Zane.

When she came back inside Zane, had come down the stairs. "I'm going to check the calf." He said putting on his coat.

"I'll go with you"' she said since she already had on her coat. They walked out to the barn. The cow bawled at Zane and Beth. Beth thought it sounded as if she was asking for her calf.

When they entered the barn, the calf was standing up under the heat lamp looking around.

"I wonder if we should try and see what the cow would do with him?" Zane said. He opened the gate and picked the calf up and carried him out and set him down. The cow came right to the calf and began to lick it. Zane went back in the barn and him and Beth watched as the cow licked the calf. She tried to get the calf to go with her and he did but the cow soon found out she could not go far as she was shut in the barnyard. They continued to watch her through a crack in the barn door. The calf got around on the side of the cow and it was obvious she wanted him to nurse but the calf didn't.

Beth looked up at Zane to see what he was going to do.

Zane, wasn't looking at the calf, he was looking at Beth. The look in his eyes was unmistakable. Beth walked into his arms and they kissed. Zane pressed her against him and she felt him shudder. The heat was growing between them and this time it was Beth that pulled away. Their breathing was ragged in the stillness of the barn. "What are we going to do?" Zane voice was thick with desire.

"I don't know." Beth was shaking, she knew they had to break it off and stop before neither one of them could. Beth went out the barn door and headed for the house.

Zane stayed and watched his calf. He began to get his feeling under control. God he wanted her bad, but he still wasn't sure it was something they should do with her as a guest in his house. He wondered what his mother would think if he knew he desired her friend and guest.

Zane caught and carried the calf back into the barn. The calf had still not nursed but the cow knew it was her calf and sooner or later he would nurse. In the meantime Zane decided to try the calf on the bottle. The calf was getting stronger but he needed more nourishment.

Zane went to the house. He heated some milk and put a quart in the nursing bottle. Beth came in to see what he was doing.

"Do you want to feed him?" He asked.

"Yes," She put on her coat and went back to the barn. Zane straddled the calf and wrestled his mouth open and stuck the nipple in. He had to squeeze some milk from the nipple into the calf's mouth but the calf got a taste of it and began to suck the nipple. Zane grinned and Beth laughed. He turned the bottle over to Beth. The calf sucked away at the bottle greedily, Beth laughed with delight. Zane smiled. He was glad the young woman was enjoying feeding the calf.

The calf emptied the bottle in short order. When Beth tried to leave the pen, the calf tried to follow her. Zane shoved him back and shut the pen gate.

"Now he thinks you're his mamas!" Zane laughed. Beth and Zane went back to the house and Zane washed the bottle.

"When will we feed him again?" She asked.

"This evening we will try him on two quarts, but I'll put him out first thing in the morning and see if he won't get after the cow."

Zane went in and sprawled on the Sofa. The television was still on. He grabbed the remote and began to surf, the index for something to watch. He tried to keep his mind from thinking of Beth Robin's and how much he wanted her.

Beth holed up in her room until she heard Zane in the kitchen. She went out and they set out the leftovers and ate in silence. Zane didn't know what to say neither did Beth. Each of them wondered how long they could control the sexual tension between them.

They cleaned up after they ate. Zane went back into the living room. He sat in front of the television but he wasn't aware of what he was watching. As the afternoon wore on he became more relaxed as he knew Rachel could come from the store at any time. Before dark he mixed a bottle for the calf. Beth was holed up in her room. Zane went and knocked. She opened the door

Wondering what Zane wanted from her. Zane was standing there, holding the nursing bottle.

"What did you expect?" He said. He had an amused look on his face as Beth smiled with relief when she realized he wanted her to feed the calf.

Beth began to laugh with relief as she got her coat on. She was almost giggling hysterically when they went to the barn to feed the calf. The calf this time readily took the bottle and with eyes rolled back emptied it. Zane thought he would wait until morning to put him out with the cow. Zane checked the Bays water and hay and climbed the loft and threw a bale of hay out for the cow. They walked back to the house. Zane washed the calf bottle and Rachel comes driving in from the store. Both Zane and Beth were relieved she was back!

8

Rachel fixed herself a snack once she found that Zane and Beth had already eaten. Beth was in the living room. Zane was not in sight and Rachel figured he was in his room.

Rachel and Beth visited and Beth told her about feeding the calf. Clearly Beth had enjoyed her experience with the calf. Rachel wondered how Zane and Beth had handled the aftermath of the kiss that had upset Beth enough for her to talk with Rachel about it.

Rachel did not mention it to Beth, she had decided to stay out of it and let the young people work it out.

It was still early when Rachel begged off and went to her room. The days were quickly getting shorter. It was dark by shortly after five p.m. in the evening. It was about seven when Rachel went to her room. She had not seen anything of Zane. He had stayed in his room and Rachel hoped, Beth and Zane had not had another confrontation trying to deal with their feelings for each other. Rachel knew dealing with sexual frustration was trying. She also had been dealing with it since she had discovered Chuck had such feelings for her the day he caught her when she fell from the ladder.

The major difference was aside from their age was that Chuck had a wife that which Rachel was very fond of, while Beth and Zane were both young adults, with young adults driving needs.

Rachel knew with certainty that Beth and Zane would be unable to resist each other. Rachel knew Beth and Zane had strong feelings for each other and it palpitated between them every time they were together. Rachel had no idea how they were dealing with it during the hours they were alone.

Zane slept fitfully. He didn't know how long he had slept when he heard a light knock on his door. He turned on the lamp expecting his mother was home by now. "Come in" he said. He was shocked to see Beth come in.

"Is something wrong?" He asked. Beth stepped in and shut the door. She was in her nightgown. She came to the side of the bed and stripped her nightgown off over her head.

Standing there nude in her loveliness. Zane was speechless.

"Can I get in with you?" She asked softly.

"Oh God Beth, you know I can't stop this even if I wanted to, and you know I don't want to!"

Beth slid into his bed with him. Zane pulled her beautiful body next to him.

"I don't know if this is right or wrong but God how I want you! Are you sure of this Beth? He asked.

"Yes, I'm sure Zane. We can't fight this and you and I both know it. I know I want to be with you and I hoped you would want me also!"

"Why would you even wonder? You know you've been driving me nuts!" Zane was used to being in control with a woman but with Beth in his bed he was afraid he was on the verge of being beyond control. He tried to calm himself and get control. He knew he wanted to please her as much as himself. It was important that he maintain some control over what was happening but she had caught him totally off guard.

Zane decided he had best engage in some foreplay and try to maintain some control. He tried not to picture her beautiful body as she had taken off the nightgown. He concentrated on caressing and kissing her. He didn't want to pounce on her, he wanted to please her and he wasn't sure how he could control himself if he entered her and started having sex with her.

Zane had learned early on when he became sexually active if he gave more thought to his partner he could better control his own pleasure.

Beth was eager but she let him take the lead. He knew she was heated but he still didn't want to hurry what was happening between them. He had never before been with any other woman that he had so much feeling for as he did this girl from Detroit.

Beth meanwhile was so heated she thought she was going to pass out. Finally Zane tried to enter her but he was feeling resistance even though she was slick and moist with desire.

"Beth, have you ever had sex before?"

"Yes, once." She was nearly panting and Zane had not yet started doing anything.

"Am I hurting you?" Zane was pushing in but she was extremely tight and he was afraid he was hurting her.

"No, you're not hurting me, you feel good." Beth was beginning to fear he would stop but Zane carefully pushed in and stopped to give her a chance to relax and receive him. When he felt, she was relaxing and accepting his intrusion into her body he began to make love to her. He took his time, he wanted to make it pleasurable for her first, He could get his satisfaction from her pleasure if he could get her to feel, what he hoped, she would feel. She was responding. Zane kept a tight hold on his control until he began to feel her tissues began to swell. He could feel she was nearing her orgasm and he was afraid she would scream. When it hit her, he kissed her to keep her from making a noise as she climaxed and she bit down on his lip. It didn't really hurt but it excited him and his orgasm came with hers.

"Oh Beth, he murmured and continued to caress her beautiful body. He made no attempt to pull away from her and she clung to him. He kissed her gently on the lips and her eyes were dilated and she looked at him with wonder.

Bethany Robins had just experienced her first satisfying sexual experience and she was awed by their intimacy. Her body felt as if it had melted and flowed into a heap of contentment.

Beth' made it easy for Zane to not have to pull away from her. She was tall enough that he wasn't smothering her as he had found in the past happened with shorter girls.

He finally rolled up on his side but he held her with him and he still did not pull away from her.

The way Zane felt with Beth in his arms he didn't care if he ever pulled away from her.

He ran his hands gently down her back and over her firm buttocks and down onto her thighs.

She smiled a slow lazy smile of contentment. He kissed her and she began to respond with the sparks of a renewed longing. He could tell the way she pressed into him and arched her back she was becoming aroused again.

He had been drained the first time but he began to feel passion returning as she took the initiative and began to explore his body with her hands. He had not pulled away from her but she got her hands into his groin and began to softly caress him. Her hunger for him was not shy and reserved and he found himself responding to her wandering hands. He began to grow inside of her. Her eyes widened with that and a slow and sexy smile crossed her lips. Zane covered those tantalizing lips with a kiss. He rimmed her teeth with his tongue and she seemed to like it.

Beth liked every thing about this man and she had never felt what she was feeling and she never wanted it to stop. Their second time was every bit as satisfying as the first and she stayed with him until way late in the early hours of the morning. Finally she got up and put her nightgown back over her beautiful body. She leaned over and whispered softly "I'll see you in the morning at the barn."

Zane smiled at her lazily and said, "Don't be late."

Beth slipped back down the stairs and into her now cold bed. The night was short when she heard Zane come down the stairs and make coffee but she had slept very soundly after leaving him and felt surprisingly rested. She arose and dressed to help him at the barn.

Zane was warming the truck. He got out and let the truck run and they both walked to the Barn. The mother cow bawled when she saw them and within the barn the calf answered. Before they went into the barn Zane pulled Beth to him and kissed her. "Good morning Beth."

"Good morning Zane." They went in the barn. The black calf was standing under the heat lamp. When he saw them, come in he bucked a couple jumps and shook his head.

Zane laughed, "It looks like El Toro is hungry. He opened the gate and gathered the calf up and put it out with the cow. She went right to the calf. "I'll get the truck. Zane went back and pulled the truck into the barnyard under the loft door. Beth had climbed the loft ladder and opened the loft door. She began to push the bales out and Zane began to stack the hay. By the time they were loaded and Beth came back in the truck Zane could see the calf was along side the cow.

"We won't have to feed him on this morning." Zane laughed.

"How can you tell, I can't see if he is nursing or not?" Beth asked.

"Look at his tail. See how he is wringing his tail? That means he is sucking."

Zane pulled the truck up to the feedlot gate. Maggie had come, slipping a wide berth away from the mother cow and calf and quickly made the cows get back from the gate.

"Leave it open so the cow will come back in here with her calf." Zane told Beth as she got out to open the gate.

As they filled the feeders, the cow came with her calf and went down the hill out of sight. Beth worried about that and mentioned it to Zane.

"Oh she will hide that calf so I can't take him away from her. It might be several days before she lets him run with her. I'll just have to hunt him up and keep an eye on him. Looked to me like he was pretty frisky."

"He was so cute when he shook his head at us." Beth laughed. They finished feeding and when Zane pulled out Beth shut the gate. Zane went in and took care of the Bays. Beth followed him.

"How do you feel this morning?" Zane asked, his eyes soft and his voice gentle.

"Wonderful!" She said.

Zane put his arms around her and kissed her again. He laughed when he began to get aroused with her long body pressed against him. "We better go find coffee and breakfast."

"What are we going to do about your mother? She is going to know as soon as she sees us?" Beth asked.

"Nothing! We are adults. My mother doesn't control my personal life. She and I have had this conversation before. She won't say anything even if she knows."

Zane and Beth headed for the house. As they slipped out of muddy boots on the porch, Rachel heard the young people laughing. No tension between them on this morning she thought.

Zane and Beth come into the kitchen and from the smiles on their beaming faces

Rachel knew something had happened between them. She suspected since she did not see Zane when she came from work it had been yesterday. She had not noticed anything different about Beth but now the young woman was glowing with happiness.

"How is the calf?" Rachel asked as Zane and Beth got coffee and sat down to the table.

"Back with his mama." Zane said as he sat down with his coffee. Rachel studied Zane and Beth for a moment and then she started making breakfast. Zane and Beth had both blushed as she looked at them and Rachel was now certain some thing had happened between them and what ever it was they were both happy about it.

Over the next couple weeks the Adams house was full of laughter and happiness. Zane and Beth went into the canyon with the truck and came back with a Christmas tree. Beth teased Zane it was a "Charlie Brown!" Christmas' tree but Zane was convinced it was good enough. Beth and Rachel decided once they got it decorated it would be good enough.

One Saturday evening Zane asked Beth if she wanted to go with him to Pete's Bar. He said there was a local band going to be there with live music. "You do dance, don't you?" He asked.

"Of coarse," she laughed. "I had dance lessons, What about you?"

"I just get out there and stagger around. No dance lessons." Zane grinned. He reminded himself the dance lessons, was another sign that he and Beth had come from different worlds.

The evening Zane and Beth went to Pete's; Beth was gorgeous in a black cashmere sweater and black slacks. She wore a pair of Italian leather boots with heels.

Wearing the heels, she looked tall and beautiful. The heels put her height at six feet, only three inches shorter than Zane. Rachel thought Beth looked like one of those models in the fashion, magazines.

They agreed to take Beth's car. Zane's truck was full of hay and cow manure. On the way into town Beth asked Zane, "You are not going to knock anyone through Pete's window this time are you?"

"I will if I have to and the way you look I may have to!" He grinned.

The place had begun to fill up when Zane and Beth came in. Pete noticed them right away. He had not seen Zane for a few days and he recognized the Blonde that Zane had knocked Punk through the window over. As tall as the couple were, they stuck out easily in the crowd. Pete came with the Coors's light and a glass when he seen them come in. They had to hunt to find a place to sit. Zane held Beth by the hand. Pete could see the relationship between Adams and the Blonde woman had changed since the last time he had seen them together. He grinned, he could not blame Zane for that, and the Blonde was a looker. Pete still did not know where she had come from and neither had anyone else. She was seen with Rachel Adam's and it was known that she was living at the Adams Ranch.

Punk and Gina were also in the crowd. Punk deliberately ignored Zane and Gina glared at the couple. She was jealous of the tall Blonde that was obviously with Zane.

During the evening Gina sidled over to Zane and tried to get him to dance with her. Zane was polite but he refused. The Blonde looked down on Gina with a haughty stare. Gina noticed when Zane and the Blonde danced he held her as if she was precious and she also noticed during a slow dance there was no distance between their bodies. Gina knew Zane and the Blonde were intimate and she bet by the looks of it they could even be in love. Gina felt like crying. She would never forget how she felt that night with Zane Adam's.

Beth and Zane had a good time that night and when they got home they went up the stairs to Zane's bedroom. Rachel heard them come in and heard them go up. She decided she would bring up to Zane what his intentions were with Beth. She could tell the two young people were falling in love and Rachel was happy about that. But she also didn't like the idea Zane was just going to carry on an affair. If he were going to be sleeping with Beth, he would have to make a commitment to her.

A week before Christmas Beth asked Rachel what she thought she should get Zane for Christmas. "Well, Beth that is your decision. I have a hard time buying anything for Zane. He never mentions wanting anything. Besides I think he has every thing he wants." Beth was picking up Rachel's insinuation clearly. "Don't you have some thing you would like to get him?" Rachel asked.

"Yes, I would like to buy him a new truck."

Rachel's eyes widened and her mouth dropped open. "Oh Beth, that is way too much! I don't think Zane would allow you to do that. A new truck could be thirty or forty thousand dollars!"

"Yes," Beth said. "But Rachel I have millions and it would not be much money for me!"

"Millions?" Rachel said. She knew Beth's father had left her money but she had no idea it was anything like that.

"Our company is a fortune 500 company and my dividend checks annually are in the millions."

"My goodness, does Zane know this?" Rachel asked.

"Zane and I have never discussed my finances. He knows I, own half the factory with Marion Belmont but I don't think he knows how wealthy the company is?"

"Oh, dear! This could be a real problem between you and Zane. He is not going to be happy knowing how wealthy you are. Zane is very proud. I was going to speak to Zane about his intentions toward you, as I know you have been spending time in Zane's bedroom. But if Zane realizes how wealthy you are it could change his view of his future with you."

Tears had come to Beth's eyes. "I love Zane, and it isn't my fault I am rich. Why should it be something that comes between us?"

"I don't know Beth but I'm afraid it could be a problem for Zane. I think Zane is in love with you and I don't think he has given much thought to you're having money. Besides if I had no idea you are that wealthy, I can't imagine that Zane would realize?."

"Maybe I should not tell him? Maybe I should get rid of the money?" Beth said gloomily.

"He would never allow you to do that. He isn't asking you to do any thing like that but I think you should refrain from buying him anything very expensive. He will then have to face the fact you may have all this money. He would not like people to think he is associated with you because you're wealthy!"

"I wouldn't want them to think that either! I know Zane and I have true feelings for each other and I would get rid of every dime before I lose him!" Beth had never considered the problem her money would cause in their relationship. Beth gave up the idea of buying Zane a truck but she bought him a watch and had it inscribed. Zane would not think about it being an expensive watch. In Beth's world of wealth and privilege it was not an expensive watch.

Zane meanwhile bought Beth a sweater he had Rachel chose for her. He also bought her a bottle of the perfume he, knew she used and he was taken aback at the price of it.

Beth was called several days to the school during the month of December and Zane found he missed her out in the mornings helping him feed. Beth continued to give Rachel $500.00 per month for her board. She tried to get Rachel to accept more. Beth insisted she could not even pay rent for that amount in the city but Rachel would not hear of taking more.

Beth stayed in touch with her advisers and Attorney in Detroit by email and occasionally she received correspondence. Beth spent the money she earned at the school for things she, knew they needed about the household.

Beth and Zane were falling more and more in love. Zane knew he wanted Beth in his life and he began to wonder about if they were to get married. He was still aware she was a factory owner with Marion Belmont but Zane had not comprehended the extent of that. He had no idea that Beth Robins the sweet and wonderful women he craved to be with was among one of the wealthiest young women in the country.

Gina Daniels was the one that discovered who Beth Robin's was. Gina was reading a magazine one-day about wealthy people and there before her eyes, was a college photo of Bethany Robin's the blonde that lived at Zane's house.

Gina busted her ass down to Pete's Bar to tell Pete about the Blonde Zane had at his house.

"You must be kidding." Pete said. "Among one of the wealthiest, people in the United States?

"Yeah!" Gina said. "Among the top 500. We aren't talking millions but nearly a billion according to the article I read, there was even a picture of her. She graduated from some big shot college."

"No shit!" Pete said. "How did she get here on the Adams farm?"

"I haven't a clue," Gina said. Now that she knew who that rich girl was she was certain even though she had observed Zane seemed to be in love with her, The Zane Adam's, Gina knew wouldn't marry some heiress!

Beth and Zane became closer as the winter wore on. Beth was always out in the morning to help Zane with the cattle. She had on several occasions helped him with a cold helpless calf like the black one she had helped with the first time.

One morning she went down in the hole below the feeders with Zane and he put a pair of chains on a pair of calves feet sticking out of the cow that was down on the ground. Zane pulled and the calf finally came out. On that occasion the calf was still alive. Another time when Zane pulled a calf in the same manner the calf was already dead.

It seemed to Beth that they were always busy with something. A farm was a place that people struggled daily to feed and watch after the well being of its inhabitants. Beth mentioned to Zane how often they needed to clean the hen house? Zane indicated it was past due; he planned to get to it! Zane got after it one morning after they were done with the feeding. Beth helped him.

"I don't think you know what you're getting yourself into?" Zane laughed when Beth insisted on helping. Beth soon discovered shoveling out the hen house was a stinky labor-intensive job. But when they were finished and had spread new straw on the floor, Beth felt a sense of accomplishment. She laughed when the hens happily began to scratch around in their new dry litter.

Rachel continued working regularly at the Danner Store. Rachel knew Beth was spending many of her nights in Zane's bed. She did not talk to Zane about it but she could plainly see he was very much in love with Beth. She wondered what he was thinking about him and Beth's future?

One night Zane brought it up to Beth. "Beth, I'm in love with you and want to spend the rest of my life with you. What about you? Is this the kind of life you would be happy with?"

"Oh, Yes Zane, I could be happy with you here the rest of my life."

"What about your interest in Detroit? What do you intend to do about that? Can you sell your part of the business with Marion Belmont and put the money into an account for your own use?"

"I can't do that Zane. The business is tied up in trust and we have stock on the stock exchange. It isn't that simple. Also, there is a great deal of money involved. We have a board of directors and a stockholder meeting. Right now my Attorney has my Proxy but I am going to have to go to Detroit before April for a meeting."

"How big a business is this factory you own with Marion Belmont?" Zane asked. He had not thought about it for a long while.

"Do you know what the Fortune 500 is?"

"Yes, it is a list of the 500 largest Corporations in the country." Zane eyes widened as he looked at Beth. "You and Marion's Factory isn't on that list, is it Beth?"

"Yes it is." Beth said.

Zane reared up in bed. "What the hell are you doing in some poor dirt farmers bed in Idaho?"

"Because I love you Zane Adams and I happen to be right where I want to be!"

"Jesus Christ Beth, it's a wonder we don't have the paparazzi out here in the yard!"

"We would have if they knew where I was." Beth said gloomily. Beth pulled Zane back toward her and wrapped her arms around him. "I love you Zane, none of that out there in the world matters to me. Only you and me and the way we feel about each other." Beth, hung onto Zane and fear rose in her, as she knew Zane was nearly in shock from what she told him.

"Oh God Beth, what are we going to do?" Zane pulled Beth close to him. He felt as if what he now knew about Bethany Robin's world was trying to tear her out of his arms. His mind whirled as the enormity of their situation sank into his consciousness.

The Beth Robins that had fallen out of the back of his truck into the mud and manure was a heiress and worth millions. Zane had planned on asking Beth to marry him but now with this knowledge he didn't know what to do. He knew he loved her. Beyond that he felt as if he were sinking into a quagmire.

"Zane, we could run away, some place and get married and change my name? Maybe nobody will find out who I am?" Beth hung onto Zane, as she was afraid someone would snatch him from her.

Zane pulled away and looked at her. She looked like the woman he loved but he was suddenly seeing her differently. He was looking at her as a very rich woman. He remembered George Belmont telling him Bethany's father had left her a lot of money but this was mind-boggling. He suddenly realized why she had wanted to stay at the Adams farm. Out in her world every thing she did was scrutinized under a magnifying glass. She had sought refuge and anonymity in this farm in Idaho. What if she became tired of the drudgery of their simple life and wanted to return to her world of wealth and privilege? Would she walk away and break his heart? One thing he was sure of was that he would never be able fit into her world.

Suddenly, afraid he was in danger of losing her Zane wanted her, he wanted to make love to her. He wanted her to reach out to him for the pleasure he could give her and the pleasure she could give him. He wanted to put it out of his mind and get lost in the rich essence of her body.

Beth wanted the same thing. There was desperation to their lovemaking but as always they gave each other pleasure.

In the morning as Zane and Beth went down the stairs to feed the cows, they both felt that their small world had changed. And somehow it would never be the same as it had been the day before. Zane put the coffee on and started his truck.

Beth went out and climbed the loft ladder. Zane pulled the truck out under and she put the hay out as she had for the last two months.

After they fed and grained the Bays and before Zane reached for the light to turn them off, Beth put her arms around him and searched his face. A tear slipped down her cheek. Zane remembered that time after their first kiss when those tears on her face had melted his heart. They melted his heart this time also. He pulled her against his hard body and her softness melded into him. He didn't ever want to let her go. Somehow they would have to find a way to hold their two very different worlds together.

"Let's have, our coffee." He said softly and releasing her he turned out the barn lights. Hand in hand they walked into the house.

When they entered the house, Rachel knew immediately something was in the air. Something had entered Beth and Zane's happiness. Rachel was afraid it was most likely that Zane had found out about Beth's fortune. She could think of nothing else that would cause the serious look on the two young peoples faces.

It was a couple days later when the school called Beth, that Rachel was able to ask Zane about it. "You find out about Beth's business in Detroit?" Rachel asked as him as Zane sat at the kitchen table.

"Yeah, seems the woman I love has an interest in a fortune 500 company." Zane said gloomily.

"I'm not sure what that means?" Rachel said, "But I know at Christmas Beth said something to me about her having millions."

"I guess I should have known it by what George Belmont said to me that morning he died. George had given me a check for $5000 to give Beth and she had torn it up when I gave it to her. George mentioned when I told him she tore it up that her father had left her very well off. I guess I had not comprehended what that meant. It doesn't change the way we feel about each other but it could change the way we live if someone finds out who she is?"

"Whatever do you mean by that, Zane?"

"I mean Mom, that the damned paparazzi could be camping in our yard."

"Oh my God Zane, she isn't that rich is she?"

"Yeah, she is that rich! We are talking about assets near a billion dollars!" Zane shook his head at the enormity of it!

"I guess I had not realized. What are you and Beth going to do?"

"Slip off somewhere and get married and change her damn name before someone finds out she is Bethany Robins! We could do that in Nevada, but I can't get away right now. They don't pay that much attention down there and it isn't as if she is a celebrity but is just a very rich girl. That is fodder for the paparazzi when she is involved with a poor dirt farmer from Idaho!

"I am so sorry, Zane. I know how happy you and Beth have been. But I'm glad she told you because sooner or later you would need to deal with it. It isn't something that will just go away."

"Yeah, that's how I found out. I asked Beth to marry me and suggested she could sell her little factory and put the money in an account for her own use. I found out it wasn't that easy when she told me the size of that Corporation. I asked her what she was doing in Idaho with a dirt farmer?"

"What did she say?" Rachel asked.

"That she loves me and she is where she wants to be. I feel the same way but it isn't any longer that easy. You have any ideas?"

"No, it would sound like a dream come true for most people but I know how proud you are and I can kind of feel what you are concerned about. It is what others will think about it, isn't it?" Rachel said.

"I don't give a damn what others will think. I'm worried Beth coming from wealth and privilege will get tired of scraping by like we do. It would break my heart if she wanted to return to that life of wealth and privilege. I would never be able to fit in there. She is the one that is making all the sacrifice."

"Everyone who contemplates marriage has to make sacrifices. You can't second-guess Beth's love for you. It will cause trouble in any relationship even when there is no money involved. Forget about Beth's money. It should be a source of satisfaction and independence, for the two of you. At least that it is one problem you will not have to face. It is hard to build a life when one has to always be worrying about finances. It sounds to me as if you are worrying about your own sense of self worth. If that were any doubt in Beth's mind, she would have not fallen in love with you. Don't look upon that wonderful girls' good fortune as a source of misfortune but thank your lucky stars that she fell in love with you. You are a wonderful loving young man and I well imagine that is what Beth saw in you. She isn't just slumming here, I know she loves being here and I also know she loves you. You can work it out."

Zane smiled. "I do believe that is the longest lecture you have ever delivered, to me."

"Life is short. Make the most, of it. Just make sure you communicate! Now I have to get to work! Think also about that girl with all of those millions down at the schoolhouse-teaching children. She doesn't need to do that! That should tell you what a rare young woman she is!"

Rachel went in and got her store apron and her purse and coat and went to work at Danner's store.

Zane puttered around and waited for Beth to come home. When she finally came Zane met her at the door and kissed her passionately. "Am I going to have time to get my coat off?" She smiled coyly.

"I missed you! I had to feed the cows all by myself." Zane smiled happily. He was so glad she was back.

"Poor, baby, had to load all that hay by your self." Beth teased him.

Zane grabbed her and headed up the stairs with her in his arms. "There is no baby able to pack a long tall blonde like you up the stairs." He laughed as he dumped her onto his bed and piled on top of her. Her response to him was quick, immediate and passionate.

After they made love and lay in each other's arms Beth wanted to know what had put him in such a good mood?

"My Mother. She pointed out to me how lucky I was to have you and love you. More importantly she pointed out how lucky I was that you love me. And as usual she is right!

Also, I can't resist a tall blonde teacher wearing a dress!"

Zane and Beth laughed but hurried to get dressed when they heard Rachel's car drive in.

9

Gina Daniels, was telling everyone that would listen about the rich girl staying at, the Adams farm. Nobody paid much attention to what Gina had to say. Pete at the Bar knew it was most likely true but Pete always kept what he found out to himself. A bartender that carried tales soon had no customers if he spread rumors, so Pete said nothing about the rich woman.

Pete figured out that Zane had most likely met Beth Robins through the hunting lodge. He didn't know how but to Pete, it seemed the most plausible explanation. He was the only one that seemed to give any credibility to Gina's story.

Pete was not seeing much of Zane these days and when he did see him he was with the blonde.

So Pete had not had a chance to tease Zane about it.

The winter dragged on. Beth was still helping Zane feed, every chance she could. Only when she went to the school was she not out with him in the mornings. When the temperature dropped to twenty below Zane tried to get her to stay in the house. Beth would not. If she was physically able to be out with him she was.

Around Valentines day Zane called Matt and had him come over one weekend and do the chores. Beth and Zane went into Lewiston and stayed at a nice motel and dined out. They saw a live celebrity country western singer who was starring at one of the nightclubs on a Saturday evening. They also ate at some of the better restaurants and of coarse stayed in bed late.

In March the weather began to break. Signs of spring began to slowly appear in the Northwest.

An occasional robin could be seen. The ground was no longer frozen but that meant there was mud up to the axils on the truck.

Zane started the old ford tractor and moved the feeders into a little dryer ground so the cows weren't wading in the mud and getting it on their bags. The mud on the cow's bags would cause a calf to have the scours. Their manure would get loose and runny. If left untreated it would also get blood in it and the calf could be very sick and possibly die.

Zane packed a package of probac powder in his pocket. It was a natural bacterial culture containing acidophilus and was most often in the form of a red powder substance. He would catch the calf and put a tablespoon down its mouth. If that did not cure the diarrhea, which it usually did, then he would resort to giving the calf a couple big blue, scours pills he had gotten from the veterinarian.

The Adams farm did not have the facilities to keep the herd Bull separate from the cows; the calves were being born at various times throughout the winter. This had been a very good season. Zane with Beth helping had only lost two calves. The one that Zane pulled that was dead and another cold weak calf they doctored as they had the first one in November. That calf did not get on its feet and died. Beth cried when it happened. But Zane tried to console her with the fact they had done all that they could do. They just had not gotten it soon enough to save it.

Zane and Beth had not discussed Beth's business since Zane had been told Beth's company was a fortune 500 companies. Zane preferred to not think about it. Beth also didn't think much about it.

Beth also knew the time was growing near that she would have to return to Detroit for the Stock holder's spring meeting. Her adviser's and Attorney she should attend had told her. Beth desperately wanted Zane to go with her. She knew Zane would not have to attend any meeting and he would not need to meet any of the advisers but she wanted him to go with her. She also wanted him to meet her Attorney. Beth had decided she wanted Zane to have her assets if something should happen to her. She did not mention it to Zane and she prayed it would not come to pass. The only way he would know is if God forbid, something happened to her.

Zane and Beth still talked of marriage. Rachel wasn't happy they continued to spend their time together in Zane's bedroom without making some commitment but she did not interfere. She knew Zane loved Beth, but she also knew he was holding back because of Beth financial status.

One evening in March Beth asked Zane if he would go with her to Detroit.

"I want to think about that." Zane said. "If, and I'm only saying if I go with you I won't have to do anything as far as this business of yours is concerned will I?" He asked.

"No, all you would have to do is be with me. We could fly into Detroit and go to the penthouse and you would not have to go, to the corporate offices. No boardroom or anything?" She smiled. "I love you Zane Adams and I want you to go with me. I don't want to go alone. I've been alone most of my life. Only since I've been here, have I felt I have a family!" A tear slipped down Beth's face.

Zane groaned. That tear on her face melted Zane heart every time. He loved Beth with all of his being. He decided he would try to get away and go with her. Zane had never been in an airplane in his life. He had barely been out of Idaho. Now he was thinking of getting on a jet with one of the richest woman in the country and flying to Detroit

He reminded himself that woman, was Beth the girl he loved, the girl that fell on her face out of his truck into the mud and manure. The woman that had shared his bed through most of the winter and went with him nearly every morning before daylight to feed the cows, The women that always sat on the porch and loved Thumper the farm tomcat. Yes, the least he could do is go with her if she wanted him.

Beth was ecstatic when he agreed to go. She made the plane reservations for the first week in April. They would be gone five days and Beth made the reservations round trip for their return.

Zane made arrangements for a teenage boy to come and help Rachel two mornings with the cows. Matt would drive over two mornings on the weekend.

"I am not going to have to wear any damned thing like a neck tie, am I?" Zane asked.

"No Zane, you can wear any damned thing you like. The only thing I would object to is if you were to wear nothing at all!" She laughed.

Zane and Beth both were dressed in jeans and regular clothing the morning they drove to Spokane in Beth's car and boarded the plane. They were flying first class but Zane who had never been on an airplane didn't know the difference. He was interested in looking out as they lifted off. They had to change planes in Chicago and Zane thanked God Beth seemed to know what they were doing. He found it all very confusing. The size of the Chicago airport was mind-boggling. From Chicago they landed in Detroit. After claiming their baggage they went out and hailed a cab. Beth gave the cab an address.

They pulled up in front of a large brick building several stories high. It was by then dark and Zane had no idea how tall the building was. There was a man in a uniform that opened the cab door. He recognized Beth.

"Why, Miss Robin's, nice to see you! It has been some time."

"Thank you! Fred, nice to see you." Zane helped the driver get their baggage and Fred looked at Zane strangely as Zane handled the baggage while Beth paid the taxi. Beth smiled sweetly as she realized Fred had expected to handle the luggage. She said nothing and Fred opened the door for them. The lobby was plush and had sofas; it was very luxurious and looked expensive. They went up in the elevator. Zane lost count of the floors they went up but the elevator finally stopped and he packed the luggage as Beth fished a set of keys from her purse and unlocked a door. "How many rooms on this floor?" Zane asked.

"Just this one Apartment." Beth said opening, the door.

They entered a foyer and Zane followed Beth into an expansive living room. Beth began to open the drapes and windows lined the entire side of the room. They were very high up in the building and Zane could see the lights of the city below as far as he could see.

"What is this place?" He asked.

Beth put her arms around Zane's neck and said. "Welcome to Robins Penthouse."

"You mean, there is nobody else on this flour?" He asked.

"Nobody but you and me!" Beth said kissing, him hungrily.

Zane kissed her back, "Where's the damned bedroom?" He asked.

"There are several, which one would you want?" She laughed.

"The one with you in it!" He said.

Beth took him to the master bedroom. They stripped their clothes off and fell into a huge bed with satin sheets. Zane had never seen such opulence in his life but the main thing he was interested in was the woman in his arms. After they had satisfied themselves with each other, they laid in the big bed in each other's arm. "Can we stay here the entire five days?" Zane asked.

"You can if you like. I have a couple of meetings."

"What do you do for food around here?" He asked.

Beth laughed. "When I left last fall there was a staff here but through the winter there has only been the housekeeping since I've been gone. Are you hungry? I can phone some thing to be brought?"

They had eaten on the plane. "No, I'm not hungry. I'm worried what we are going to do for coffee in the morning?" Zane smiled. He was thinking about he was the one that always made coffee. He wondered if there was even a kitchen in this place?

"We will have coffee one way or the other!" Beth assured him.

Beth had made arrangements for the essentials to be available at the pent house when she knew Zane was accompanying her.

The next morning Zane walked out to the living room and stare in awe at the expansive view of Detroit. There was no other building nearby that was the height of the penthouse. "I could have come out here naked without anybody seeing me." He grinned. Zane had on his Levi's but no shirt and no shoes. The rooms were carpeted in thick plush carpeting.

Beth went down the hall naked and came back wearing a silk mauve robe tied loosely. She looked very appealing. Zane resisted the temptation to gather her up and return to the big bed.

He followed her and they went through a door into a kitchen gleaming in stainless steel and granite counter tops." Wow, wouldn't Mom love to have a kitchen like this?" Zane said in admiration.

Beth found the coffee maker and a can of fresh coffee. She fixed the coffee.

"Well it looks like you know your way around here?" Zane observed.

"I used to live here in another life!" Beth said with amusement. "Another unhappy life." She added softly and put her arms around Zane. Zane held her and tried to imagine why Beth was happy on his dirt farm when she had all this opulence in her life.

"Why were you unhappy here?" He asked.

"I was always alone. Alone except for all the people around to wait on me. But I was very lonely after Dad died. I hope I never have to come back here alone. It feels much better with you here. I'm not alone even here, when you are with me."

Zane held her and Beth finally pulled away and said, "Coffee should be done. You want some breakfast now?"

Zane looked around at the gleaming kitchen and opened the refrigerator. There was nothing inside. It gleamed with cleanliness but there was absolutely nothing in it! Zane looked at Beth and shrugged. It looked, the chance of having breakfast, from what was in the refrigerator were slim to none.

"What do you want?" She smiled.

"Whatever you are having which appears to be nothing."

Beth picked up the phone and called for some breakfast. Zane looked at her and wondered where the breakfast was to come from and how long it would be before it showed up?

Beth poured the Coffee into a carafe and headed back to the living room. Zane followed her. He couldn't believe the view out of the windows. Beth was enjoying the view of Zane without his shirt as he looked out over the city from the high building.

In about fifteen minutes Beth answered the door and they had their breakfast delivered on a cart. Zane rolled his eyes as Beth gave the man in uniform some money.

"Do I want to know where this came from and what it cost?" He asked.

"No, and it doesn't matter either!" She laughed. They ate breakfast and Beth headed for the bath to get dressed. After a few minutes' Zane followed her and found her in a tub the size of a swimming pool. "Good!" He grinned, "You have plenty of room for me!" He shed his pants and climbed in the tub with her. They splashed and made love and had a grand time. Zane thought maybe this trip was not going to be unbearable after all.

After Beth emerged from another room dressed in a soft brown colored suit with her long hair tied into a knot on the back of her head. She was wearing heels and Zane whistled with appreciation. She smiled and she grabbed the phone. She poked a button without dialing. "This is Bethany, please inform John I am at the Penthouse. Thank you!"

"Who is John? Is that someone I need to be jealous of?" Zane asked.

"Not unless a fat middle-aged attorney is going to push your buttons? Now Zane, you cannot be knocking anyone through windows at this height!" She teased him.

"I promise to contain myself." He grinned. The phone rang. Beth answered.

Her conversation was brief. Zane could not make out what she was even talking about. He knew it was John and he knew the call had come promptly back from Beth's call. She said 2.00 p.m. and the conversation ended.

"Are you going to abandon me?" Zane asked

"Just for a couple of hours, unless you want to come with me?" Beth said.

"I don't think so. Attorneys make me nervous. I'll entertain myself with this spectacular view and all this electronic shit I see around here!" Zane grinned.

Beth opened a drawer in the table and handed him a couple of remote. "The one in the master bedroom where we slept is in the drawer beside the end table. I promise I won't be gone long. When I get back, maybe we can go do some site seeing or whatever you want." Beth kissed him and left the apartment.

After Beth left Zane looked out over the city and contemplated that it's size was small compared to the expanse of the mountains where he was so at home and never lost. He wondered how quickly he would be lost if he went out into the city even though it was smaller than his own stomping grounds. He marveled that the two very different places were even in the same world. He had never mentioned it to Beth but he now began to wonder if Bethany Robin's had also been overseas and out of the United States. Once she returned, he would ask?

Zane went in and noticed the big bed was not made. He made it and then sprawled on top of it and turned on the large screen television that hung on the wall.

The huge apartment had been very quiet after Beth left. Thinking about that Zane realized he had been in only a small portion of the apartment so he got up and went exploring.

He found a frilly looking girl bedroom; he surmised must have been Beth's room when her father lived. He didn't spend any time in the room as it was full of Beth's things and he didn't want to snoop. He also found an exercise room full of weights and treadmills and various exercise equipment. He noticed the exercise room had a sauna.

Zane found another large bedroom. There were in all three bedrooms all with their own bath.

The huge living room, a formal looking dining room and of coarse the gleaming kitchen they had made the coffee in.

Zane went back to the bedroom he and Beth had slept in. He watched the Television and fell asleep. He woke up when Beth came in. "Well, Bethany Robins Corporate Mogul, how were your meetings?" He smiled sleepily.

"Boring!" She smiled and shed her clothes and climbed onto the big bed with Zane while he drank in her naked loveliness with his eyes. They got into the big bed and made love hungrily.

"We going out and eat or you want me to order in?"

"We can go out if you want to? I guess you would know where to go?" Zane said. He was admittedly curious to see more of the city than he had seen from the penthouse and the taxi ride

"What are we to wear, for dinner?" Zane asked.

"There are several fine restaurants us hillbillies can go to without formal wear." Beth laughed.

"I'm the only one here that is a hillbilly." Zane reminded her.

"Not anymore!" Beth said softly wrapping her arms about Zane's neck and kissing him. She pulled away and on the phone without dialing she pushed a button and told someone, somewhere she wanted a car.

Zane and Beth went downstairs and the doorman named Fred opened the door on a black limousine.

After they got in Beth pushed a button and gave the driver an address.

"What are we doing in a limo?" Zane asked. "Is this necessary?"

"It's a company limo and it doesn't cost me anything. It is at my disposal as long as we need it." She smiled.

"Will it take us back to Idaho?" Zane asked amused.

"If I told them to, yes certainly." Beth said. The limo took them to a restaurant and Zane and Beth went in. It was a nice restaurant and Zane saw there were regular people in normal clothing mixed in with people in suits and dresses.

They were shown to a table and Zane and Beth both had steaks. When they were, finished Zane went to pick up the check left in a black folder but Beth put her hand on his and said "All her expenses on this trip were on an expense account and paid by the Corporation. She laid a card on the restaurant tab and she signed a slip when the waiter returned.

When they left the restaurant, the limo was still waiting.

Zane was startled. "We should have taken that poor driver in and fed him." He said.

Beth laughed and said she didn't see Zane at the dining room table when she and George ate at the Lodge. "Yeah, I guess that's true!" He agreed.

The limo, on Beth's instructions took them around town to see some of the sights. They went to the factory owned by Beth and Marion. It was huge. They went through a security gate but didn't go inside. Zane didn't want to, he could see the factory was a big place. When they returned through the security gate, they then drove downtown to a huge office building. A large sign read Belmont& Robins. Beth told Zane it was the corporate headquarters.

They went to the Dome where the Detroit Lions played and drove around and looked at other sights. Finally the limo took them back to the penthouse.

"I had no idea, this business of yours is so big!" Zane said.

Beth smiled and said, "Now you see why I can't sell my part and put it in the bank. There are thousands of people who have jobs with this Corporation. I could sell my share but my father would be turning over in his grave and besides what would I do with that chunk of money. Nobody would be happy but the Internal Revenue."

Zane could see very well what she was talking about. "I love you Beth and I want to marry you and I want us to have some kids but how are we to fit all this into our simple lives?"

"We have been living and loving each other in spite of all this. Why can't we go home and continue the way we have been? My attorney's can handle all this. They need me once a year and aside from that, can't we live as we have been? I love you and I also want to have some kids with you. So some day our children may discover they have rich parents, does that need to affect us? We are happy with our lives and I can't wait to go home." Beth said.

They were back at the Penthouse and the attendant; Fred opened the limo door and greeted Miss Robins. Zane and Beth went in and went up to the penthouse.

Zane gave a lot of thought the next few days to what Beth had said. He loved Beth and wanted her. He wanted to have kids with her and spend his life with her. Was it really possible they could go home and forget about this other world that Zane was getting a glimpse of? He did not forget she had also used the word 'Home' that night in the limo.

Zane wondered if his view of his home would be altered when they returned. Beth had one more meeting before they were scheduled to fly back to Spokane.

Beth attended her final meeting. The limo picked them up the day they left and they went to the airport. Zane had about all of Detroit he could stand, he was becoming bored at the Penthouse.

Beth and he were happy to be headed for home. Zane had spoken to Rachel and there were no looming problems at the ranch but Zane and Beth were both happy to be done in Detroit.

This time on the return trip they flew from Detroit to Salt Lake City and then into Spokane. Zane found the airport at Salt Lake was not nearly as big as the one in Chicago. The airport at Spokane even looked better. They claimed their baggage and got into Beth's Toyota and headed down the road to the Ranch.

"Thank you Zane! I am so glad you came with me. I was dreading this trip until you agreed to go with me. I hope it wasn't too unbearable for you."

"Enlightening, to say the least Beth! But one thing is not different, I still love you, but I love you more here than back in that strange world of yours. The only thing that bothers me is if you can always be happy with our simple life after seeing where you came from?"

"I have been happier here with you than I have ever been in my life. What makes you think it might change?" She said softly. "Can we plan a spring wedding, Zane?"

Zane grinned, he had an urge to get his hands on her but she was driving. It would have to wait but he didn't see any reason why they could not plan a spring wedding. As soon as those damned cows were out on grass he intended to take care of that detail.

Rachel was glad when Beth and Zane returned. She wanted to hear about their trip? She was also glad that Zane and Beth seemed to be as much in love as before.

Zane noticed their small home seemed shabbier. He wondered if Beth also saw that? If she did, she did not mention it. That night they were back in Zane's bed and the following morning they went to feed the cows. It was no longer dark when they fed and Zane saw the grass had grown some in his absence. Maybe they were to get those cows out by the first of May. He and Beth planned to be married in May.

Jack Cutler had called and when Zane returned his call Jack said he had some Bear hunter's and wanted to know if Zane could take a couple of them out. The spring bear season was such that no sows could be killed, only the male bears. Zane knew they could use the money so he agreed to take them.

The days he took the bear hunter's Beth and Rachel managed to feed. Rachel and Beth doctored a new calf and Beth gave her first vaccines to the newborn calf. She hated to put the needle in but she managed with Rachel's help. Rachel offered to do it but Beth insisted. She was to be Zane's wife she might as well get used to it.

Rachel asked Beth what her trip with Zane to Detroit was like?

"Zane is a wonderful man. He enjoyed himself but I believe he is still worried about the difference between his way of life and the kind of life he saw I came from."

"Yes, and I doubt he is going to stop worrying about it any time soon either." Rachel told Beth.

"Could you stop and imagine how you would feel, if you were able to make life for Zane and Matt so very much easier? Can you imagine what it would feel like if they would not let you do that even though you could?" Beth asked.

Rachel stared at Beth, for the first time she began to imagine how Beth must feel to have so very much and not be able to share it with the man she loves!"

"Do you think he will ever come to accept the fact that my money could make our lives, not just his but also yours, so much easier," Beth said her eyes sparkled with tears of frustration?

"This is exactly what Zane feared, your unhappiness in not having what you have become accustomed to. It is a matter of pride. Men are often that way. I told Zane when he found out about your fortune he should view it as a blessing in that finances should not be something you would have to worry about. I still don't think he has come to accept that. The important thing you and Zane need to remember is that you still have your love between you. That is the most important thing. Maybe eventually he will become accustomed to letting you help with things on down the road."

After Beth put her problem in prospective for Rachel. She began to see what a problem it would be if she were the one that could help Zane. She understood the frustration Beth was feeling.

On Mother's day Matt and his family came and Zane and Matt worked the cattle and opened the gates to let them out on green grass. It was the first time Beth had been around working cows. She hated the smell of the burning hair as they put a brand on the right hip of the baby calves. They also castrated the bull calves. The cows all went through the squeeze chute and had their ear tags renewed. They also received ear tags that contained pesticides. All the animals received vaccines for a couple of different diseases.

Matt ran the head gate catching them by the head as they came through. Zane ran the squeeze that immobilized the critter and held them tight so they could not struggle. Rachel kept records in a notebook.

They were finished up by afternoon and the family had a big dinner. Zane told Matt and Susie that he and Beth planned to be married in a week or so. Now that the cows had been worked and were out on pasture and Zane and Beth could get away.

Rachel had begged to put on a wedding at the ranch but Beth and Zane both wanted to go somewhere and get it done. Since it seemed to be what they wanted Rachel didn't argue.

Zane had enough money for them to go away for a few days. Beth argued that she should be allowed to contribute. It was commonly known that the brides' family paid for the wedding so Zane relented and Beth contributed a thousand dollars to the fund.

Zane took the money out of his Bonus savings to buy Beth a set of rings.

Just before they were ready to go, Jack Cutler called the Ranch one day when Zane was out with a bear hunter. He told Rachel Zane had been shot and was taken into Lewiston to the hospital. Jack told Rachel it was serious but Zane was going to be all right. The bullet from a high-powered rifle had hit him on the left side and traveled through his chest above his heart. It had done some damage to his shoulder but he was very lucky. Nobody knew where the shot had come from?

Beth and Rachel went to the hospital. Beth was frightened out of her wits when she saw Zane lying in the hospital bed looking pale. He grinned at her and said he was going to be fine not to worry. Zane had just come out of surgery and the surgeon explained to Rachel that Zane would recover and outside of a scar in his chest where the bullet had entered and the scar on his back shoulder where they had put a pin he would have no permanent injury.

Rachel and Beth talked with Jack Cutler and asked him how this had happened. Jack said he didn't know. And the sheriff's office also didn't know. There should not have been many hunters in the woods on the early bear hunt but the sheriff did not even have a clue where the shot came from.

Jack was surprised to see the blonde girl that had come with George Belmont still at the Adam farm. Rachel had forgotten that Jack Cutler had met Beth and she introduced Beth as Zane's Fiancé.

Zane was released three days later and went home with a sling on his left arm so the weight was off his shoulder to let it heal. Zane was anxious to return to where he was shot. They figured he was hit by a 7mm Magnum and Zane had not forgotten that George Belmont was also hit by a gun they figured to be that size.

Zane thought back to that day George was killed and how close it had been himself if not for him stepping off the log.

The sheriff also suspected Zane getting shot was an act of deliberation. They began to snoop around about who could have a reason to kill Zane Adams.

They came to the ranch after Zane was released from the hospital and talked with him about his fight with Punk Daniels. Zane said he didn't for one minute, believed Punk was capable or had any reason to shoot Zane.

It was near the end of May when Zane and Beth was able to get away and they were married at the hitching post in Coeur d'Alene. They went on North to Glacier Park. There they rented a cabin and spent a couple days alone. Bethany Robins was now Bethany Adams.

Beth quietly sent a copy of her marriage certificate to her Attorney in Detroit. She had made arrangement in April for Zane to have all she owned in case something should happen to her. She had never mentioned it to Zane.

Zane was still recovering when they returned. But upon their return he headed back out to where he was shot to look around for himself. Zane knew somebody was targeting him. He just didn't know who or why? There was no doubt in Zane's mind after he was shot that George Belmont had died because he, Zane had been missed as the likely target!

Why would someone want him dead? There was not any reason that Zane could think of but with two attempts he needed to figure it out. Since so much time had elapsed since George's death and the bullet in his chest, he had to consider whoever was after him, was deadly serious!

10

When Zane and Beth returned from their wedding trip Zane had begun to heal from the gunshot wound. Beth was fearful for Zane's safety. She begged him not to return to guiding.

"If someone is out to kill me, avoiding the woods won't save me! They will just find another way to do it. Why in the hell anyone would want to harm me doesn't make any sense. Usually People only kill, for a reason. Greed or hate, are the main motivators, and who would gain by my death? Who would hate me enough to want me dead?"

A few mornings later Zane awakened early. Beth slept contentedly beside him. Zane watched her. She looked so young and vulnerable but she slept with a slight smile on her on sensuous lips. Zane heart ached with his love for her. How in the hell, was he lucky enough to have her come into his life? He thanked George Belmont wherever George may now be?

Beth stirred and with eyes heavy from sleep she saw Zane watching her. She smiled slowly, "Why are you looking at me?"

"I was just thinking how you look so beautiful and happy while you were sleeping. Where you dreaming of something?" He asked softly.

"I'm always happy when I awaken or sleeping beside you." She smiled. "How long have you been awake?"

"I don't know, I lost track of time while I watched your lovely face Beth, but it must have only been a few minutes." With no cattle to feed they did not have to jump up and head down the stairs.

Zane kissed his beautiful wife and she wrapped her arms about him and responded with passion. She found she always felt passion when she was in Zane's arms. Beth was a very happy woman with Zane. He knew how to make her feel, that special way every time he took her in his arms. Seemed Zane was always thinking of her pleasure before his own and the result of that was most satisfying, for them. He now knew all those little, things that drove her wild.

Rachel heard Zane and Beth up stairs. She smiled, she had liked the girl the first time she saw her and Rachel was happy that she was now her daughter-in-law. But Rachel felt closer than that to Beth, she felt more like a daughter she never had.

Rachel had been busy trying to get the family vegetable garden planted. Beth was very interested and enthused about helping her. Beth was wide eyed at the prospect of them being able to grow food for their own use. Being raised in the city, she had never been around any gardening or anything like it. She admired and knew a few things about growing flowers.

Beth told Rachel before her mother died they had a home in the Hampton outside of New York and they went there in the summer to escape the heat of the city. Beth remembered her mother had flowers and Rose bushes. After her mothers death her father had sold the house in the Hampton and they had lived in the penthouse in Detroit continuously from then. Beth had gone to William and Mary College and lived on campus in the dormitories.

Beth told Rachel she had never known her father to be associated with a woman after her mothers' death. There were no other members in the Robins family. Beth had good memories of George Belmont, he was like an uncle to her growing up but after he married Marion he had stayed away because Marion had a jealousy of Beth.

Rachel began breakfast as she heard Beth and Zane awake upstairs. They finally appeared down the stairs and Rachel found herself wishing she had waited to start breakfast, as she had to keep it warm before they finally appeared. With all of them in the house Rachel tried not to interfere in the young peoples personal life as possible. She wished they could work on the old farmhouse and make it more accommodating for the newlyweds and her. Beth had brought the idea up one day and told Rachel she was trying to get Zane to agree to let her spend some money and do some remodeling. The old house was sorely in the need of updating.

Zane agreed it would be nice if they made some updates to the old house, especially if it gave them more privacy.

"As long as it's not something grand like I saw in Detroit" He grumbled. Something that fit in with the life style they had in rural America. Excited with the prospect, Rachel and Beth began to plan what could be done. Beth hired an Architect from Spokane. They decided to make the changes while Zane was at the Lodge. The Bow hunter's would be coming in the later part of August and Rachel and Beth would not have him underfoot when they tore into the old house.

Beth also wanted Zane to think about another truck. She told him they could then use his older Chevy to feed. "I like my truck, it's a perfectly good serviceable truck. Dependable also!" He added. Beth decided she would shut up about the truck.

The remodeling, planned on the house was something she assumed he would never consent to. She was happy that he had allowed her and Rachel to plan that much.

Matt and Susie were amazed that the Ranch house was going to undergo a renovation. They were aware Beth had some inheritance from her father but they had no idea, the extent of Beth's wealth.

There was still the constant worry about Zane's safety. Beth and Rachel worried incessantly. Zane refused to worry about it. He was more accepting of fateful events but he was more watchful after he was wounded in the spring bear season. The Sheriff's office had spoken to Punk Daniels and he had been logging at his job the day Zane was wounded. They had gotten rumor of Zane's altercation with Punk. Gina Daniels had been in Pete's bar that day and there were no other clues to who may want Zane Adam's dead.

After the authorities spoke to Gina, she wondered to Pete at the bar if it had something to do with the rich girl.

Gina couldn't believe it when she heard Zane and Beth had married. She saw them one evening in Pete's bar. They came with Zane driving his Chevy truck. Gina checked out the set of rings on Beth's hand and they were nothing spectacular. They were nice but nothing extravagant.

Pete began to wonder if Gina had been seeing things when she claimed to see a picture of Bethany Robin's in a magazine. It must have been someone who looked like Beth, who now was Zane's wife Beth Adam's.

The flowers and garden on the Adams ranch were beautiful as the early days of summer began. Beth took to mowing the lawn for Rachel because she enjoyed the smell of the fresh mown grass. And also it looked so neat when freshly mowed.

One day in early June Zane saddled Sonny and Dolly, the two Bays, and he and Beth rode into the Canyon to check on the cattle. Beth had never been on a horse. Zane helped her get on Dolly and he laughed as she tried to get her long legs over the saddle and seated without falling over the other side. Zane rode Sonny. He also had his side arm on his hip. Zane hardly went anywhere since he was wounded without the 357-magnum pistol with him. He didn't wear it into town but he always carried it in the holster in the truck and even in Beth's car.

The day they went to the canyon he also put the rifle scabbard on his saddle and took the 30–06 carbine. Beth who was afraid of guns did not object. Her fear for Zane's safety overrode any fear she had of guns.

Beth was so stiff and sore from the horse back ride she could barely get out of bed. Zane laughed at her. He said she needed to go again that day to cure the stiffness. She groaned in agony and came crippling down the stairs as if she was eighty years old.

"Don't you ever mention riding to me again?" She grumbled.

"You can't get used to it if you don't ride." Zane laughed. They were forced to postpone their love life while Beth recovered. Considering that disastrous consequence Zane decided he would also wait before insisting on Beth's next horseback ride!

Rachel still worked at Chuck Danner's store. She worked more as time went on because Mabel's health continued to decline. Rachel felt sorry for Mabel and Chuck. She was also aware Chuck had a crush on her but she figured it was because he was lonely with Mabel's declining health problems.

During June Zane worked on the Adams haying equipment. It was common practice to start cutting hay over the fourth of July. All of the haying equipment was old and worn but stump Ranchers like Adams were used to wiring things together and making them work once again another year. Sometimes a piece of equipment became so worn it was beyond repair. Then the small Ranchers would look around for a piece of used equipment that would not cost so much. That was the way it was with the New Holland hay baler. It was almost worn past repair. Zane done some emergency work on it and got it running. Beth thought with exasperation, she could easily buy him a new one and not even miss the money. The interest accruing on her money was enough to allow all Adams to live in luxury. Beth held her piece and let Zane do it his way. She was thankful he had consented to her working over the house. Beth had her attorney set up college trust funds for Jason and Levi. It would be available to them if they decided to go to college. She told Rachel so someone in the family would know but she did not tell Zane and neither did Matt and Susie know about it.

The weather cooperated and Zane began to mow hay first day of July. Matt and Susie came over the fourth. The weather stayed hot and they were able to begin to put it in the bale by the fourth. Matt, Susie, Beth and the two boys helped haul the bales in with the Chevy and a trailer they stacked the hay on. They had trouble with the bale elevator that put the hay up through the loft door in the old barn but Matt and Zane worked on it and also got it running.

It was terribly hot in the top of the barn. Only Matt and Zane could stand the heat to stack the hay in the top. Susie and Beth with the help of the two boys sent the bales off the trailer up to the men in the loft. Zane and Matt stacked; Rachel cooked if she had time off from the store. If Rachel had to work at the store, then Beth and Susie cooked. Beth had learned a great deal from Rachel over the past year.

It had been ten months since Bethany had flown out with George Belmont to get out of Detroit for a hunting trip George had planned. Beth had no idea how much that trip was to change her life. She was still sad that George had been killed but she thanked God every day she had become a member of, the Adams' family. She particularly thanked God for the man she loved, Zane Adams. She could not imagine going back to her lonely privileged life. At times she became aggravated that Zane would not let her use her money to ease their day to day burdens but if she had to make a choice she would give up all the money to be a part of the Adam's family.

Once the hay was in the barn it was time to celebrate. Zane, Beth, Matt and Susie all went to Pete's bar. It was late afternoon and all the local loggers and people returning from the Fourth of July holiday were in the Bar.

Adams family could not find a table so they sat on the pool table. Also, in the bar were Gina and Punk Daniels. Punk had avoided Zane since Zane knocked him through Pete's window. He also avoided him after being questioned by the authorities over Zane's shooting.

Punk and Gina were fighting as usual. Most people being aware of Gina's and Punks tumultuous relationship didn't pay any attention to their feuding. On this particular occasion Punk hauled off and hit Gina in the face. Gina's was bleeding profusely from her nose and her mouth was swollen.

When Zane saw Punk hit Gina in the face, he hopped off the pool table and headed for Punk and Gina. Beth knew very well what was about to happen. She had seen the look on Zane's face when Punk hit Gina in the face.

Zane pulled out his handkerchief and handed it to Gina. "Get to hell out of here Gina!" He said.

"What the hell you doing thumping on a woman?" Zane asked Punk.

"It's not any of your business Adams! It's my damn woman! Mind your own business." Punk growled at Zane.

"I'm making it my business Punk." Zane said. "Get out of here while you can!" Zane said to Gina who had stopped when Zane called Punk for hitting her.

The bar that had been noisy became quiet as the two men confronted each other. Punk came off his barstool and rushed Zane trying to get his arms around him.

Zane taller and with more reach hit Punk hard, with his right fist knocking him back but Punk scrambled and got Zane by the legs and brought him down to the floor. Zane had hoped to avoid getting in Punks grasps, as the barrel chest Punk was stout.

Zane was able to break Punks hold on him and he was able to drag Punk with him as he got to his feet. Zane was able to punch Punk a couple good punches and Zane knocked the wind out off him. He hit Punk hard in the Jaw with a right and that put Punk down and out.

Gina was still standing wide-eyed with Zane's handkerchief to her mouth. Beth had run over when Punk dragged Zane to the floor. Beth was worried about Zane left shoulder and if it was healed. It was over by then and Matt and Zane hauled the disoriented Punk out the door and threw him in the parking lot.

Gina was still standing in the bar. "Why don't you get to hell away from him, Gina?" Zane asked her with exasperation.

"Thank You Zane." Gina said. She still had feelings for Zane Adams and knew she would never forget the night she was with him. She wondered if that blonde knew what a special man Zane was.

"Get out of here, before Punk, comes, around!" Zane told Gina. She went out and got in the vehicle and left.

Beth was still worried about Zane. When she found he was all right, she became aggravated that he had stuck up for Gina.

"You know she probably won't get away from him, Zane. Gina likes that scrapping all the time and most of the time she starts it." Beth said with exasperation.

"Yeah, I know Beth! But I'm not going to sit on my ass and let any man hit any woman in the face. I don't care who she is." Zane said.

"Well at least this time you didn't break any windows!" Pete said as he brought Zane, Beth, Matt and Susie fresh, round of drinks. Zane went to pay but Pete said "On the house for throwing the bum out."

Pete didn't like Punk hitting Gina in the face but he had seen him do it before and there was little doubt Gina would have sense enough to get away from Punk and Pete doubted it would most likely happen again.

"What's this about the window?" Matt asked.

"Punk went to grab me one night and Zane knocked him through the plate glass window." Beth explained.

"Did they talk with Punk when you were shot?" Matt asked.

"Yeah," Zane said. "He didn't have anything to do with it. He is just a damned woman beater!"

"I doubt Gina will stay away from him though." Beth said. "If anything it might make it worse for her when you aren't around." Beth said.

Punk had gotten up from the parking lot and had tried to get back in the bar but Pete wouldn't let him. "Let me talk with him?" Zane said. Zane went out in the parking lot and without further altercation the people inside watched Zane talking to Punk. Punk did not look happy as Zane and he talked but he turned and walked up the street. Zane came back inside.

"What did you say to him?" Matt asked.

Zane shook his head like he wasn't going to say and they went back to celebrating the hay getting done.

Later in the evening Beth noticed Gina came back inside and made herself inconspicuous as she sat in a dark corner and watched Zane and Beth. Gina had cleaned herself up but she had a blackening eye and a swollen lip where Punk had hit her. Punk never returned that evening. When Adams, headed for home. Gina was still in the bar when they left.

When Rachel went to work the next day, Chuck was telling her about Zane and Punk fighting again. Chuck had finally found out who the unsavory character in Zane's bed that morning was when Zane put Punk, through the plate glass window.

"I know Zane thinks he is trying to help Gina," Rachel said. "But that won't do any good unless she decides to get away from her abuser."

Chuck listened and remembered the years he had seen Rachel with black eyes and swollen lips when Walt still lived. Rachel had never tried to get away from her abuser either. Apparently Rachel's sons took a dim view of that behavior. Chuck wondered if they remembered their father had abused their mother?

Rachel had never gone into the bars as Gina did but it was well known that Walt Adam's abused her. Chuck wondered if that was why Rachel had never seemed to be interested in another relationship after Walt died. Chuck and Rachel had never discussed their relationship but each knew nearly everything there was to know about each other as they had grown up together and went to school together.

Mabel Danner never came to the store again. Chuck told Rachel her weight had become so cumbersome she could barely get out of bed. Chuck didn't know what to do. He became more depressed. Mabel seemed to have given up on life and there seemed to be nothing Chuck could do to help her.

Chuck became more despondent over his wife and. he became more dependant on his daily association with Rachel. Rachel Adams was the only reason Chuck found to drag himself to the store. Rachel in turn felt very sad for Chuck and Mabel also. Many times Rachel stopped by the Danner home before going to work to visit Mabel and find out if there was anything she could do. One such occasion Mabel told Rachel straight out, she wanted her to look after Chuck once she; Mabel was gone.

"Oh Mabel, you are going to be fine!" Rachel told her. Mabel knew that was not going to be the case. But through the summer she lingered on.

The School board had offered Beth a permanent teaching position but she declined, as she wanted to help Zane with the cattle. She did however consent to be on the substitute callboard.

The unbearable heat of July beat down upon the countryside. Beth and Rachel canned green beans from the garden. Beth loved helping Rachel with anything to do with the garden and flowers. Beth tended to the watering during the heat. One day she happened onto a rattlesnake in the bean row. Beth didn't know what it was but by its actions she perceived it could be dangerous. Especially when Maggie began to bark furiously at it. Zane came out of the house to see what Maggie was carrying on about and he heard the rattler buzzing. Zane hollered at Beth to stay away from it and he got the garden shovel and killed it. Beth from Detroit had never seen a rattlesnake in her life.

"We, don't find, a lot of them but you need to be watchful, especially during dry spells and we are watering around the house." Zane told her. Beth carried a long stick and was more careful to poke the bean plants and squash when she picked from that time on.

In August the sweet corn matured and Beth about foundered on the fresh sweet corn. Zane laughed at her that she would be fat as a hog if she kept eating so much sweet corn. But he was just teasing her, as the tall lean Beth never seemed to gain weight whatever she ate. Although tall and lean Beth was very well endowed for breast size. She wore clothes like a model and looked good in whatever she wore. Often when on the ranch she wore shorts and had an enviable tan on her shapely long legs. She was a very beautiful woman and Zane and she made for a very attractive couple. Beth warned Zane they would more than likely have some very tall children. That had not happened yet but Beth had quit her birth control pills during the summer in hopes that she would become pregnant. Zane and Beth very much wanted to have a child.

The weather continued, hot and dry into August and the fire danger in the Forest became extreme. There were no campers allowed into the Forrest without ax, bucket, and shovels. As the dryness continued several fires got started. Smoke hung heavy in the air all over the northern part of Idaho. It never cleared out and the sun beat down day after day with no relief in sight. The sun-shined through the smoke and it were a strange looking shade of blood red as the smoke obscured the normal color of yellow. It was an eerie sight especially to Beth who had never seen a smoke laden sky before.

Jack Cutler stopped by The Adam's ranch one day and he and Zane talked about the dry conditions and the possibility they may restrict access to the bow hunters if there was no moisture to relieve the fire danger. The wolves working the Elk herds were still driving the elk deep into the brushy basins. The Elk could be called out during the rut but it was important to get some rain to quiet the Forest noise down. Jack congratulated Zane on his marriage. He wondered if Zane being married would interfere with Zane being the dedicated and experienced guide he had proven to be in the past. Jack hoped not, as he and Annie, still had plans to retire and turn it all over to Zane Adams.

Jack also told Zane he was worried about the cow and calf ratio on the Elk herds. Jack said he was seeing many cows that did not have calves. Jack didn't know if it was because it was a bad rut that the cows did not get pregnant or the increasing wolf population may have killed the calves. Jack said as a rule only the alpha male and the alpha female in the pack would have pups but several people reported seeing, several females in the pack either pregnant or with pups.

Also the packs with females and pups were splitting off from the main packs and the numbers of packs were rapidly increasing. Also the big breed brought in on the reintroduction program was breeding into the smaller species and the overall size of the average wolf being seen was increasing.

Between the drought conditions and the wolves Jack Cutler was worried they would be in for a dismal hunting season if conditions did not improve.

Zane told Jack about his loss of the spotted ass cow and her calf. He had turned it into the authorities and he received a visit from a federal man but when Zane showed him the photos the man told Zane they could not prove it a wolf kill and there would not be any compensation and it would not go on the record as an official kill.

Zane was frustrated it taken them so long to respond. If they had come when Zane first discovered the kill site it would have been easy to prove it was a recorded kill by the wolves!

Zane also mentioned a bear hunter in the spring had his entire bunch of bear hunting dogs wiped out and killed by a pack of wolves. The tracking collars on the dogs led the hunter to his hounds but there were very little left of the dogs by the time they were found. Men who run Bear hounds become very attached to their dogs and this man that had lost his entire pack of hunting dogs was done even trying to have dogs. He was too hurt to think about having dogs just to have them killed by wolves.

Zane Adam's was not old enough to remember but Jack Cutler remembered and talked of the loss of the Elk range along the North Fork of the Clearwater

River when they flooded thousands of acres of winter feeding grounds that supported a large and healthy Elk population. The winter feeding grounds were flooded from the filling of Dworshak Dam, which backed water forty miles upriver flooding the winter grounds of thousands of Elk. Not only were the feeding, grounds, flooded but also the slack water behind the dam caused ice to form on the huge lake. The Elk were used to swimming the river before the filling, ventured out onto the ice and plummeted through into the reservoir. Hundreds if not thousands of Elk perished unable to get back onto the shore because of the ice.

These perilous conditions persisted until a new generation of Elk began to realize they could not cross the expanse of water behind the large dam. The Elk had finally begun to flourish when the Wolf program was started to make life once more perilous for the wintering elk herds.

Some of the worst conditions for the Elk were when the snow became deep and it got cold where the wolves could run on top of the frozen snow and the heavier Elk were sinking in. A lot of observers reported Elk being killed and not even eaten by the wolves. The wolves were killing to be killing because in the deep snow it was easy for them.

The deer populations were not being impacted as much as the Elk herds. Deer are more solitary animals that live and die sometimes within a hundred acres. They don't herd up in such large numbers as Elk and therefore don't draw the attention from the marauding wolves as the Elk herds. The wintering herds on The Lochsa River were also being targeted by overabundance of wolves. The idea of wolves howling over Idaho might have seemed a romantic notion to some environmentalist but it was a nightmare for the people and animals that had to actually tolerate them!

There were plenty of concerns for Zane Adams hunting guide and rancher and Jack Cutler hunting and Guiding Contractor to be concerned about during their August visit.

Annie and Jack had already cleaned and moved into the Lodge for the coming season. Zane asked Jack about Jody Miller and Jack said he had talked with him and Jody would also be again joining Zane as one of the Guides.

"Well if we get rain, I imagine we will see you about the 29th of August?" Jack said, as he made ready to leave.

He had a good visit with Zane and Jack was gratified to see Zane so happy with his marriage. Jack still felt intrepid over the unsolved problem of Zane being wounded. Jack Cutler also realized George Belmont's death was a botched attempt by somebody most likely after Zane Adams.

"I'll be there if they don't shut down the forest." Zane said as Jack left.

A week before the bow season a strong front blew in off the Pacific and gave the countryside a long overdue soaking. It rained for two solid days but even at that the moisture only penetrated the earth about two inches. It would take a lot of moisture to soak things well.

However since the wind currents had changed, it did not turn off as hot. The Jet stream off the pacific had dropped below Oregon, Utah borders and cooler air from the north blew in across the parched forestlands of Idaho lowering the fire danger from extreme to moderate. With the Jet stream below there began to be some rain showers occasionally out of the Bering Straight dropping down and across keeping the air cool and sometimes damp. The big rainmakers over Idaho usually came in off the Pacific and were called Hawaiian express. These warmer rains were usually tropical and put down large amounts of moisture while the ones from the north were cooler but with less moisture.

In the area off India these fall rains from off a summer warmed, ocean, are known as monsoons. At any rate there was enough moisture came to drop the fire danger so the hunters would not be banned from the Forest. Extreme care and diligence were still required with campfires.

11

Zane packed his stuff to stay at the lodge. He was going to miss having Beth with him. He intended to find out if Jack and Annie could fix something different for accommodations so he could occasionally have Beth come out to the lodge with him. The way it was now he and Jody bunked in the same room and that certainly wouldn't work. Zane liked Jody but he didn't want him in the same room with him and his wife!

Rachel and Beth were poised to tear into the old house when Zane went to the lodge. The contractors had been hired and Zane had seen on paper the plans they intended to make. He teased Rachel and Beth about not being able to wait to get rid of him.

Although they were anxious to start, Beth and Rachel were both fearful for Zane's safety. Zane promised he would be extra watchful. He reminded her there had been plenty of opportunities for someone to pick him off through the summer. Although the case had not been solved, Zane had a feeling whoever it might be they weren't in desperate hurry as there had been no attempts made during the summer.

Zane had tended his business as usual and had not made any attempt to hide or protect himself other than packing his sidearm with him most of the time.

Beth made love to Zane the last night before he intended to leave as if she might never see him again. He teased her about that and said he would try to come home and leave more often if she was going to be that loving and intense. This was going to be a different hunting season with Beth now in his life, he hoped he could concentrate on the job he had to do and not his lovely wife waiting at home. It would be a nearly three-month season and the better job he did the bigger bonuses he earned and that is where most of the money the guides made came from. Jack paid a good monthly fee but three months of employment was not enough to average a decent income. The bonuses were usually twice as much as their monthly paychecks from Jack. More if the hunters were extra satisfied. Zane usually averaged a lot more in bonuses than Jody. Jody didn't develop a friendly relationship with the Dudes and Jody was also bashful and quiet. On top of that he wasn't the woodsman when it came to tracking and calling elk that Zane was.

Zane also had the extra income from the cattle. Zane didn't know what Jody worked at during the off-season. Jody had never told him. Jody didn't talk with Zane a lot either. He was just a very quiet man.

Zane arrived at the Lodge that evening. They had three bow hunters' for the week. Bow hunting was Zane's favorite season. He was very good with the Bull bugles and the cow calls. He could tease nearly any Bull in the rut into coming in. Most bow hunters were sitting in tree stands. The guide was usually upwind from the hunter and about twenty yards away. Depending on the calls used Zane had seen some big bulls so mad from the Bull bugle they were literally blind to a hunter when they saw them. The object was to make a bull Elk think another Bull was moving into his territory to take his cows.

When that happened for real under natural circumstances there would be some horrendous fights between the Bulls. They sometimes would get their horns locked and could not get loose. Usually it was a pushing match and the bigger Bull would run the smaller bull away.

Zane had an assortment of calls and hardly ever used a big Bull call as it would make the Bull who perhaps was not so big with the cows run away if he thought a much bigger Bull was moving in.

The first morning Zane called a big six point, in for his hunter from Texas. The hunter got Bull fever and fouled the shot and missed it. Zane was used to this from the Dudes. Many of them had never been close to a huge mad Bull Elk. Zane would laugh, and make a remark they can be scary when they are close enough to hear air blowing out both ends of their bodies. Jody and Charlie did not get a shot for their hunters but the Elk were answering the bugles well and it appeared it was going to be a very good bow season.

With Zane gone to the Lodge, Beth and Rachel had the contractors tear into the old house. Rachel escaped to the store to help Chuck but Beth hung around to supervise with the Architect they had chosen.

Beth drove in town in the afternoon to visit with Rachel. On her way back to the Adams farm she noticed Gina Daniels going into Pete's Bar. There were no cars at the bar so Beth decided to stop and have a word with Gina.

Beth found Gina sitting at the bar. She climbed up on a stool beside Gina and told Pete to bring her a beer. She also told Pete to bring Gina whatever she was drinking.

Gina rolled her eyes as Beth sat down beside her. She wondered what the Blonde would want to talk with her about. "What do you want, Beth?" She asked bluntly.

"Just wondering how you were doing? Have you been able to get away from your abusive husband?" Beth asked companionably.

"I don't see how that is any of your business!" Gina sniffed.

"It is my business when my husband feels he has to intervene on your behalf." Beth said.

Gina smiled smugly. "You're jealous! You should be. I know what a special guy your husband is. Believe me I would leave Punk in a minute for Zane Adams!"

"Well, that isn't going to happen! Zane and I are very happy with each other. I'm worried about you Gina, you are going to keep feuding with Punk until you get yourself really hurt or even killed. Why do you want to stay with somebody who treats you like that?"

"What else I am to do! I'm not some rich girl like you that can do anything I want. I have to live you know. I have no education and no family or anyplace to go."

"What if you did? Beth said. "What if someone would be willing to help you leave and get some education? Would you take it if you had the chance?"

Gina looked at Beth and smiled coyly. "I knew I was right. That was your picture I saw in, a magazine when they issued the one with some of the richest people in America, Bethany Robins!"

"You haven't answered me. Would you go if you had a chance?" Beth persisted.

"Sure." Gina said. "How much you willing to pay me to be gone."

"Not a dime!" Beth said. "But if you give me a plan of what you want to do and a school you want to go to, maybe I can help you do that. You are very attractive Gina and you could build a decent life for yourself but you have to get away from Punk before something bad happens!"

"Oh go play with yourself, rich, girl!" Gina said with ill humor.

Beth shook her head in dismay. "Let me know if you change your mind." Beth got off the stool and left.

"The nerve of that Bitch!" Gina grouched.

Pete had moved away from the two women after bringing their drinks but he had overheard every word that was said. He said to Gina "You might give it some thought, your going nowhere here fighting with Punk! Might be the break, your looking for?"

"Yeah, what I really want is that Bitches husband!" Gina said. "I told you she was rich!" She told Pete in triumph.

Beth got in her car and drove back to the ranch. She had found out from Susie that Rachel had lived a life of beatings and abuse when Zane and Matt's father Walt was alive. Beth had not mentioned she knew about it to Rachel but in her heart she hoped she could help Gina escape that kind of life. Beth could not imagine the gentle and caring nature of Zane and Matt being raised in a violent and abusive atmosphere. She would never have known about it if Susie had not told her. It explained why Zane was willing to defend Gina when he saw Punk abusing her.

When Beth returned to the house it looked as if it was a demolition site. She hoped they would have that part cleaned up by the time Zane came to spend the night. They had started upstairs. The three rooms upstairs were to become a suite of room that would give Beth and Zane more privacy. The small bath was to be over hauled. Once that phase was finished, they would start downstairs and redo that entire floor with a new modern kitchen, Bath and new windows for the whole house. There were also new energy efficient doors. The new floors downstairs would be the plastic laminate that looked like hardwood. It was tough and easy to clean with the same look as hardwood.

Beth thought about her conversation with Gina Daniels. She decided she would keep it to herself and not, mention it to Zane unless Gina decided to take her up on the offer. Then of coarse she would need to tell Zane.

Beth hoped the school would call and give her a chance to get out of the renovation zone. Perhaps she would go in and help Rachel in the store. If nothing else she was sure the store could use some cleaning. Beth had never met Mabel Danner but she knew Chuck well from her trips into the store. Beth also knew Chuck Danner was in love with Rachel. She was certain nothing unseemly had ever happened between them because both Rachel and Chuck were old-fashioned straight-laced people. Beth also knew how much Rachel liked Mabel. Rachel often talked about her friend's illness and her inability to get around.

Beth went into the store and found Rachel working alone.

"It's a mess at home!" She said. "Can I hide out here and help you?" Beth smiled. All of this looking forward, to the remodel, and on the first day Beth was looking for a place to hide. It was going to be a period of chaos.

Rachel laughed. "I'm sure Chuck would appreciate some help with the cleaning. He is at home now seeing to Mabel." At the mention of her friends name Rachel began to look sad.

Beth put on an apron and got some cleaning and dusting supplies from the back room. Rachel had earlier noticed Beth's car at Pete's Bar but she didn't mention it.

"Wonder how Zane's first day is going?" She said idly.

"I don't know, but I expect him to call this evening." Beth said. "He loves that job but I worry about him being out there after being wounded last spring."

"I know. I worry also but there is not much we can do about it. Zane is not going to hide from living his life. Zane has loved the outdoors since a little boy. He no doubt would have been a mountain man had he lived a hundred years ago."

"He is a mountain man!" Beth giggled.

"I guess he is!" Rachel agreed. A lot of people called Zane the mountain man.

"You want me to clean the produce cooler?" Beth asked.

"Yes, it needs it and I'm sure Chuck and the customers will appreciate it. You're a great gal Beth. It is so nice of you to help out. Our family is lucky to have you."

"Not nearly as lucky as I am to be a part of this family." Beth said. Rachel knew she meant it with all her heart.

When Chuck returned, he found both the Adams women busy cleaning the store. He appreciated their help and wondered what he would do if not for Rachel.

Chuck was having a hard time concealing his feelings for Rachel. He loved Mabel but he had romantic feelings for Rachel. Those feelings had died between him and Mabel a long time ago. Chuck still had needs but he was much to straight-laced to make a move on his old friend while Mabel was still his wife.

Beth stayed and helped until closing time and her and Rachel both drove home in their own cars. They were going home to the demolition. Sometimes things have to be torn apart to build them back again. They would just have to endure it! When they arrived there was a big pile of rubbish and sheet rock pieces in the front yard. The front yard that Beth had worked so hard on to keep lovely. Both women ignored it and went in the house. Beth was to sleep in her old room downstairs. She had moved all of their things out before the demolition began.

The second day Zane again called a big Bull in for his Texas hunter. This time the Dude made a good hit. Zane felt sure the Bull was mortally wounded but he had trouble convincing his hunter to give the Bull time to go down. Often when Elk are hit with arrows they don't know they have been hit until the blood loss forces them to lie down. When a high-powered rifle they are frightened first by the noise that puts the adrenalin to pumping hits an Elk and secondly they have the concussion or foot-pounds of energy behind the lead.

With an arrow it is a cutting wound like a razor blade and the animal needs time to lie down from blood loss. If pursued immediately, they may go a long distance. If left alone for about twenty minutes they have time to lie down and they often don't get back up on their feet.

Zane was having a hard time convincing his Texan that he had a good hit and needed to give it time. The hunter wanted to pursue the Bull.

Zane convinced him to wait and they found the Bull lying within 400 yards of where he was hit. A good blood trail led them to it. The Texas hunter was ecstatic with his trophy. Zane was as always sad until he had methodically reduced the animal to quarters and he could view it as another carcass.

Zane called the Lodge for the packhorses. He would not need to pack this one out of some deep hole on his back. By evening the carcass was hanging in the cooler and the Texas man gave Zane a $500.00 dollar bonus. Zane called that evening after dark and spoke to Beth. He missed her already.

"What is the situation with the Wolves?" Beth asked.

"There are tracks everywhere. Jody called a couple of wolves in when he was using the Elk Bugle. I guess they believed there was going to be an Elk battle and they could take down the weakened looser! I don't think it will affect our harvest during bow seasons but it will again rifle season, when the rut is over!

How is the remodeling going?"

"Oh Zane, I am glad you aren't here for that! The house is in total shambles! Be glad you are missing it!"

"What I'm missing is you!" Zane said softly. "I love you."

"I love you too. Good night Zane!"

Zane hung up and went to his room. Jody seemed to be already asleep. It seemed to Zane; Jody was even more moody and withdrawn this year. Zane wondered if Jody had a bad summer.

Zane got his second Elk for a hunter from Mississippi a few days later. Jody seemed to be in an even grouchier mood. Zane split the bonus with him for bringing the packhorses and helping pack it out. Not even half the bonus seemed to make the sullen Jody any happier.

Jody was just not as good at calling in the Elk as Zane was. And it was obvious even to Jack and Annie that Jody was envious of Zane's ability.

Since Jody had been a long and faithful employee Jack decided to give Jody a raise in his wages. He did not give Zane a raise because Zane had not worked for Jack as long as Jody and Zane was more capable of raking in the bonuses from the clients. That seemed to appease the sullen Jody to a certain extent.

Then the second week Jody called in a trophy Bull and tensioned eased at the lodge between the guides. Not that there was ever any tension on Zane's part. He was never envious of Jody and was happy when Jody called in the royal Trophy Bull for a guy from New York.

Shortly after Jody got the Royal the situation at the Lodge changed as a forest fire started below the lodge and the Lodge became the cookhouse and bunkhouse for a crew of fire fighters. That fire put the hold on the hunting for about five days before the fire crews got it under control.

It took a few days after that before the smoke began to clear out and the Clients came back to the Cutler Lodge.

A few days after that Zane had a hunter from Arkansas in a stand when he called in a pack of wolves. After that it was another week before any Elk could be called into that stand as apparently the wolves scent hung in the area and the Elk stayed away.

Zane had to move into another tree stand with the Arkansas hunter and was able to get him a rag horn Bull. The forlorn sound of the Wolves hunting and calling could be heard nearly any night at the Lodge. The sign from the wolves had also increased in the area from the year before.

As the rut began to decline, it became harder to call the Elk without dropping into the basins and brushy holes where the Elk were moving into for protection from the marauding wolf packs.

A government man showed up at the Lodge one day and wanted to fill out a questionnaire from the Guides. Needless to say he got an ear full from Jack Cutler and Zane both. Not Jody though, Jody never had much to say at any time. Even though he also hated to see the impact the wolves were having on the elk herds.

The local people were aware of the vigilante wolf hunters. These were hunters whose sole mission was to eliminate the wolves. If any of the locals knew who the vigilante wolf hunters were they weren't talking. They were not about to turn in guys that had guts enough to get out there and start thinning the wolves down to save the future of Elk hunting in Idaho.

Sometimes the vigilante wolf hunter was a single hunter with a 243 or a similar varmint rifle that was fast and had long range. All of the vigilantes' hunters were breaking the law under the federal endangered species act so therefore in addition to their gun they also packed shovels to bury the evidence so the feds couldn't find the wolf kills.

Many of the locals knew who the wolf killers were and that knowledge also made them guilty of a crime. But it is awfully hard to prosecute a man with a bad memory and most locals who knew who the wolf killers were had really bad memories. Sometimes a regular hunter would see a wolf and kill it and dispose of it. If this happened, the hunter never breathed a word about it. It is well known that if two people know a secret, it is no longer a secret.

One stupid wolf killer took the tail from his wolf home for a trophy and it was leaked and he was caught. He lost his hunting privileges and was rewarded with a huge fine and probation.

Another time a logger ran over a wolf with his truck. Everybody laughed, at that one! What a stupid wolf!

One cattleman running on the open range lost several cows and untold number of calves. The feds agreed to remove six wolves from the pack responsible for those killings but with a dozen wolves in that pack everyone wondered what good would that do? The remaining wolves in that pack had already feasted off beef; they weren't about to stop because six out of their pack were removed!

The Idaho archery season usually ran from August 30th until September 30th. The Cutler guide service did well on the bow season as they had the year before. The rifle season was to open October 10th and Zane headed for the Ranch to spend a few days with his wife before the rifle season.

The upstairs remodeling was finished. Beth and Zane were delighted with the improvements. The downstairs remodeling was in full swing and the kitchen was in shambles as was, the other rooms. Rachel was surviving. After looking at how great the upstairs looked she resolved the mess was going to be worth it.

It was difficult to get a meal. They were using the microwave and eating lots of sandwiches and snacks. They also trailed into town and about once a week ate in the café. The weather was still decent and they spent lots of time outdoors.

The suites upstairs were finished and Rachel joined Beth and Zane to watch Television. The contractors had put plastic across the upstairs openings to keep the construction dust out of the finished part.

Rachel got to use the new bath and shower upstairs to bathe but she used her toilet and slept downstairs among the mess. Zane could see the results were going to be well worth the mess but he was glad they chose to do it while he was at the lodge.

The ten days between the seasons gave Beth and Zane a chance to be together before the month long rifle season. One evening they got in the truck and went to Pete's Bar. Punk and Gina were also there but no fighting broke out between them. Beth was certain it was because Punk had learned his lesson about beating on Gina when Zane was around.

Beth told Zane, Susie had mentioned to her that his father was abusive toward his mother. Zane was very quiet about that and did not say much about it but

Beth could tell it bothered him a great deal. Beth asked Zane if he knew why Rachel had never become interested in someone else.

"I think she is interested in someone else." Zane said. "But the guy has a wife and my mother isn't the sort to interfere in a marriage."

Beth knew Zane also knew of the feelings between Chuck and Rachel. Beth did not mention her conversation with Gina Daniels. Beth had been serious when she spoke to Gina and still if Gina decided to leave, Beth intended to help her. Gina had not given Beth any indication she intended to do that. Beth wondered what made women like Rachel and Gina stay with men who abused them. Since it seemed to be a subject Zane didn't care to discuss, Beth was left to wonder

Beth did bring up Zane being vigilant concerning his own safety. Zane said he had no indication of anyone after him but he promised Beth he wouldn't let his guard down.

After a few beers Beth and Zane left and went home to their newly remodeled rooms and the mess the downstairs remained.

The next day Zane saddled Sonny and Dolly and he talked Beth into going with him and they rode the horses into the canyon to check on the cows. Maggie happily trotted along.

They rode across the canyon and into the old homestead where the wolves had killed the cow and her calf. Zane found most of their cows in that area. The old homestead was full of apple trees. Beth got off and gathered as many as she could. One apple tree had large striped apples on it and Zane said it was a breed known as Wolf River and it was a very good cooking apple.

Beth didn't know what that meant and Zane laughed and told her, it meant the apple had good flavor for pies and applesauce. Beth said she thought all apples were good for cooking.

"No, No." Zane said. "A Delicious apple is for eating not cooking. Sweet apples are to eat and cooking apples need to have a bit of tart to be good to cook."

"How do you know so much about things?" Beth asked.

Zane grinned and said he didn't know how Beth had learned anything in the penthouse in Detroit. "I'm a country boy, that knows about apples and horses and cows and trees and you're a city girl that knows about stocks and corporations and colleges and thing I don't know anything about." About that time Beth had both hands full of apples and the horses began to snort and Maggie began to bark.

"I also know Bears love apples!" Zane laughed.

A black bear had ambled out looking for his apple snacks. Beth dropped the apples and began to scream as she tried to get back on the horse.

Zane laughed until he cried. "Now look, what you've done! You scared the Bear away!"

The poor Black Bear became frightened of the screeching Beth and quickly ran away.

"That poor Bear may never come back to get him some apples here!" Zane laughed.

Beth this time managed to get herself up on Dolly without Zane's help. The woman from Detroit did not see one thing funny about Bears.

Zane was never going to let her forget how she scared the poor Bear away. They rode back across the creek and to the Ranch. Zane showed Beth how to rub the horses down after using them.

He had a great time telling Rachel about Beth scaring the poor Bear that only came to get himself an apple!

Rachel wanted to know if they brought any of the Wolf River apples with them.

Beth confessed to dropping them when the bear came but she blamed Zane for not gathering enough for a pie.

Rachel agreed Zane well knew those were exceptional pie apples. He should have brought some home.

Beth also discovered the Stanley prune tree on the Adams ranch. Zane warned her not to eat too many but they were so good she ate so many of them she couldn't walk without letting gas and she also had diarrhea

Zane also thought that funny. Try as she might Beth could not keep from farting nearly every step she took after eating so many of the prunes. Zane laughed and shook his head, "City girls'!"

The ninth of October Zane headed back to the Lodge for the rifle season. Rachel and Beth hunkered down to withstand the final part of the renovations on the main floor of the house.

Zane's first rifle hunter was a man from Michigan that reminded Zane very much of George Belmont. It had been a year since George's death. Zane decided not to take the Michigan hunter whose name was Sam Blake into the fern glades where George got shot. He instead took him into the basin and Sam Blake got himself a nice Bull the first day. They got into a herd and Zane used the reed in his mouth to cow call and settle the elk down until they spotted the five point, Bull, with a very good rack. Once again Zane had to backpack a Bull out of the basin.

The man from Michigan gave Zane a $1000.00. Zane thought George Belmont would have given a good bonus also had he lived. The way it turned out Zane got something more precious than money, his wife!

Jody's hunter also had luck and got a bull. The two guides skinned the bulls together at the meat house. Jody was still quiet.

"What kind of summer did you have Jody?" Zane asked as they worked.

"What makes you ask?" Jody wanted to know?

"Just wondering. You've really been quiet this year."

"I'm always quiet." Jody grunted.

Zane had to admit that was true. Jody didn't talk much. "Did I tell you I got married? "Zane asked.

"No, who did you marry?" Jody wanted to know.

"Remember the blonde I took home last fall?"

"You married her?" Jody's dark eyes sparkled with amusement. "If I remember right she was pretty good looking?"

"Yeah, good looking and good personality. I lucked out with her!" Zane said.

Jody thought everything Zane did he lucked out. They finished skinning the meat and washed up their tools and hands. Both guides went in the Lodge kitchen to get their supper. Annie Cutler was a very good cook and nobody at the lodge ever griped about the food.

As Annie brought their dinner, she wrinkled her nose. Both the Cutler guides smelled of elk.

"Sorry Annie, we'll find the shower after we eat." Zane said. After dinner Zane hit the shower but Jody just took off his clothes and crawled into bed. Zane didn't know how Jody could stand the smell. Zane knew it would transfer to his bed!

The remodeling was finished by the time the season ended at the Lodge. It had been a tense season between Zane and Jody for reasons Zane didn't understand. It seemed that Jody harbored feelings of jealousy for Zane. Zane chose to ignore him.

12

Zane was home for the winter. Nearly all of the cattle had come in from the open range. A couple cows and their calves were still missing. Zane hoped it was not going to be another loss to the wolves. He planned to go as soon as he had a chance and see if he could locate them.

With Thanksgiving a few days away he planned to wait until after the family dinner.

The truck Beth had bought to feed with was a couple years newer than Zane's truck but it had more mileage on it than his. It would require some work to get it into shape to be dependable. Zane had time during the winter months to do the work. He was grateful that Beth had not gone overboard and purchased a new truck as she had once mentioned. It would have been awful to throw hay out of the barn onto a new truck. He was grateful Beth, understood his reluctance to accept her money. He did not want his wife flaunting her wealth. He didn't want anybody to think he married her just to get her money. He didn't know how anyone could think that as beautiful as Beth was but never the less he didn't want Beth's fortune to be a factor in their simple lives.

The remodeling on the old farmhouse was nice but it was not outrageous for their life style and Zane thanked Beth for using restraint in not planning something extravagant.

Beth smiled and secretly wished he would allow her to do more. For instance that bunch of broken down hay equipment they owned. And the old Ford tractor that Rachel could hardly get to start. Oh well, Beth told herself Rome wasn't built in a day. She wasn't going to build Rome but she intended to use her money to make the life of her Adams' family better whenever she could.

Beth had also begun to make contributions to the area school district. She had her attorney set up charitable foundation so she could make contributions where they were needed without it being traced to her. Beth also continued to substitute as a teacher when she was asked. She also was able to contribute some of her money to people in the area that had unexpected disasters and health problems. The best part about the Foundation was that it helped Beth on her taxes. The amount of money she was showing as profits, from Detroit was causing her to pay a huge amount for taxes.

Beth also suggested to Zane the cost of the truck she bought would also help on his farm taxes.

The year before when they filed taxes Beth's personal income had to be filed jointly with Zane. He tried to not make too much of the outrageous amount that ended up on the bottom line of their taxes. Of coarse there were the Corporate taxes which Zane had nothing to do with but the earnings Beth got from the Corporate earnings was what she had to report on their joint form. Beth had made sure the Foundation tax breaks were reflected on her personal income.

Thanksgiving was a beautiful sunny day. The good dishes were once again set on the dining room. This year it was the remodeled house. Matt and Susie loved the changes that had been made to the ranch house.

Matt and Susie had been saving for several years to make a down payment on buying a house. Beth decided she would see if she could help without offending anyone. There was absolutely no sense to be made that she could not use her wealth to help if she could. And she easily could!

The men piled into the living room in front of the Television to again watch football. Rachel, Susie and Beth worked in the new kitchen to put the dinner on. Rachel put together a meal to run over to Chuck and Mabel after they were done with their own dinner.

After dinner and the dishes were done, Rachel took her meal for the Danner's to Chuck and Mabel.

Beth and Susie piled into the living room with the men and boys to watch the television. Matt and Zane had discussed Zane going and looking for the cows. Zane could not resist telling about Beth running the poor Bear out of the apple orchard.

Beth took it in good humor. She learned the Adams liked having something or someone to poke fun about. Beth remembered last year after dinner when Susie and Matt left and the kiss between her and Zane that had started their romance. She smiled remembering and was thrilled that she loved her gentle caring man so very much!

That evening as they made ready for bed Beth asked Zane if he wanted her to go with him to look for the cows?

"Sure Beth. I would love it if you would go but make sure you have warm clothes because sitting on the back of a horse can be a cold ride." Zane gathered Beth in his arms the idea of being cold quickly vanished from their minds. Beth and Zane had a very good marriage and they enjoyed their life together and had not yet grown tired of loving each other. Beth hoped they never would.

After feeding the cows, the next morning Zane and Beth left on the horses to look for the missing cattle. Beth did not remember which ones were missing. She recognized many of the cattle from when she helped the winter before but she was not yet familiar enough with them to know which one was missing as Rachel and Zane did. She recognized the calves that were born during the winter and some of their mothers. She knew, that in time she would also recognize all of them as Zane did. Once you had worked on a cow or a calf, they became familiar, to you and therefore you knew them.

There was about six inches of snow on the ground. Maggie trotted along. She almost had a smile on her face every time they took the horses. That was what she was born to do, work cows and go with the horses and her masters.

They rode down into the creek bottom and back over into the old homestead where Beth had scared the Bear. Outside of Elk and Deer tracks they didn't find any fresh tracks. Going up the other side of the canyon, they found fresh wolf tracks. Zane told Beth it looked to be two adults and three smaller tracks most likely pups half grown.

As they rode into the old homestead where the orchard was they found fresh cow tracks. Zane said there were two cows and two calves. Most likely the ones they were missing. He had no idea why they had remained behind and not come home with the rest of the herd.

"There won't be any Bears around here this time, will there?" Beth asked.

Zane smiled, "They should be finding a place to hibernate by now but I've seen them out once in a while in the winter during a warm spell. I'm sure if we see a bear he will be for getting away. Bears don't really eat Goldilocks!"

The cow tracks they had seen under the fruit trees were fresh so Beth and Zane began to look for the cows. Zane watched Maggie and Maggie went right to the cows and calves bedded down under some fir trees. Once Maggie spotted the cows, she looked to Zane to see what he wanted, her to do. He whistled her back and she fell in behind his horse as he expected her to. She would stay there until he wanted her to do otherwise.

They circled around behind the cows and began to herd them the way they had come from the ranch. The cows were stubborn about leaving the old homestead so Zane called on Maggie and she bit at their heels until she got them going. Then she followed along behind the cows to make sure they did not try to turn back.

It took them several hours to get the cows and their calves back, across the canyon. Once on the other side the cows lined out toward the ranch as if they knew where they were to go. Beth mentioned to Zane the cows seemed to know they were going home once they crossed the creek.

Zane looked at Beth with surprise. "They do know where they are going." He had not realized that Beth still did not know much about cows. He must remember he had known about cows his entire life and Beth had only helped the one winter. He should have known she could not yet think like a cow. He remembered a saying his Dad used to say, "There is nothing dumber than a damned cow other than the man that owns them!" It had been a long time since Zane had remembered his father saying that. Although Zane learned many things from his father, he had never forgiven him for mistreating his mother. He knew Matt felt the same way. It was for this reason Matt and Zane did not speak of their father very often. Zane was surprised that he had thought of him saying that about cows when Beth mentioned what the cows may or may not know.

Even Beth could plainly see that Maggie knew exactly how cows thought. Either that or she knew exactly what her master wanted! That black and white Border collie was an important member of the Adams farm. She kept the cattle in line and watch dogged the property. When she was bored and nobody was around to deter her, she also liked to chase Thumper, the tom car up the locust tree, but this was just for fun and was not normally part of her job description.

It was nearing dusk when Beth and Zane got back to the ranch. Beth was glad that Zane had warned her about the warm clothing. Even so, she was chilled by the time they finally got to the ranch and dismounted. Zane told her to go to the house; he would rub the horses down and care for them.

Beth declined and stayed to help him finish the job. He showed his appreciation with a kiss. Lifting her off her feet to his height. She laughed with happiness; they had a very good day and had brought the missing cattle home. There were no ear tags without the cows like there had been last year when Zane found the cow and calf, wolves killed.

When Beth and Zane went into the house, they found Rachel, her eyes swollen from crying. Her friend Mabel had passed away the day after Rachel had taken them Thanksgiving dinner.

The Danner store was closed for three days until after the funeral of Mabel. Chuck had been expecting her to pass on for some time but now that it had actually occurred he was not taking it well. He remembered the many good years he and Mabel had together. Chuck had become so used to going home and taking care of Mabel he now found the house where they had lived their entire married life silent and empty. He also felt empty. After the funeral and Chuck opened the store he found he did not even want to go home to the now empty house. He began to stay at the store. He had a camp cot he opened at night and slept in a sleeping bag. He only went home to shower and change clothes.

Chuck was spending the entire day and night at the store. His car was being used so Rachel did not catch onto what he was doing until she came early one morning and found the cot Chuck had not put away.

"Why aren't you going home, Chuck?" She asked.

"The house seems so empty with Mabel gone, I can't stand to be there for long."

"What are you eating?" Rachel asked.

"This is a grocery store, Rachel." Chuck pointed out.

"Well tonight you are going home and have a hot meal, because I am going with you."

Rachel called the ranch and told Beth she would be late. She was going to Chucks.

When Chuck and Rachel entered the house, it was musty smelling because there had been no one in it for about two weeks. Rachel opened the refrigerator and found the left over she had brought Chuck and Mabel for Thanksgiving. She began by cleaning out the refrigerator.

Chuck went in and took a shower. He had not even made the bed since they had taken Mabel away. Chuck found clean linens and made the bed. He went in the kitchen and found Rachel had cleaned the fridge. "Now there is nothing in it. Why don't you go to the store and get something I can cook?" She asked Chuck.

"I believe the store is closed." Chuck said and laughed for the first time in months. He went out and got in his car and went back to the store. He picked up some pork chops, some instant potatoes and some salad fixings and returned to his house.

He found Rachel in his bedroom folding Mabel's clothing and putting her things in some trash bags she had found in the kitchen.

"I could have done that!" Chuck said.

"When, next year some time, you have to get on with it Chuck." Rachel said firmly.

Chuck took over bagging Mabel's things and Rachel went to the kitchen to fix the pork chops. When Chuck finished the clothing he took the bags to the garage. He would donate the stuff to the church rummage sales. When he returned to the kitchen, Rachel had the food cooking and had turned on the Television in the family room and was watching the news as she cooked. Chuck thought the house was already beginning to feel different. He hoped it would be the same once Rachel left to go to her own home.

After they ate Rachel and Chuck did the dishes. Rachel got her coat.

"Are you going to stay in your own home tonight?" She asked as she put her coat on.

"Yes, I'll stay. I changed the bed and thanks to you Rachel, I have my belly full. How can I thank you?"

"You don't need to, that is what friends are for. Good night Chuck, see you tomorrow." Rachel pecked Chuck on the cheek. Chuck resisted the urge to put his arms around her and beg her to stay. He knew it was much too soon.

After Rachel left Chuck sat down in his recliner and watched the television. The house did not feel quit so empty. The smell of the cooked food lingered. He got up and went to his bedroom and went to bed. For the first time since Mabel died Chuck slept soundly.

When Rachel got home Zane and Beth had already retired upstairs. She went in and took a long hot bath in her newly remodeled bathroom. She hoped her old friend Chuck would get a decent night sleep. After her bath she got in bed and read for a while. She heard Zane and Beth laughing upstairs. She smiled, they seemed to be so happy with each other, and she hoped her friend Chuck would also find some peace and happiness. She briefly thought about Chucks long-standing crush on her and what that might mean for her and Chuck. She quickly put the thought out of her mind, the man's wife and her good friend were barely gone and she should not be having such thoughts, it was too soon!

The next morning Beth and Zane headed for the barn. Zane put the coffee on as usual. Beth climbed the loft and Zane warmed up the truck Beth had bought. Zane had been working on the truck and it was beginning to sound better. Beth turned on the barn lights and when Zane pulled under the loft door she began to push the bales out. Beth had a much better appreciation on how the bales got into the loft after being part of the hay crew the summer past.

When the truck was loaded, Beth climbed down and got in with Zane. They had moved the cattle off the field and into the feedlot right after Zane came from the Lodge. They filled the feeders and pulled out of the feedlot with Maggie helping keep the cattle out of the trucks way.

The Bays were fed and the barn lights turned out but not before Beth and Zane had their morning kiss before they left the barn. It had become a ritual after feeding since the year before when Beth waited for him that morning with a tear on her cheek.

Together they went to the house. Rachel was up and putting Breakfast on the stove. They had coffee while Rachel cooked Breakfast.

"How is Chuck doing?" Zane asked.

"Not good. He has been staying at the store and only going home to change or shower." Rachel said sadly.

"You mean he is sleeping at the store?" Zane asked.

"Yes, I made him go home last night and fixed him a hot meal. We also packed some of Mabel's things. He is going to have to get on with it." Rachel said firmly.

Zane looked at Beth and smiled. They had talked before, about Chuck's interest in Rachel. The secret smile between them, they both knew Chuck would get on with it, most likely with Rachel!

Rachel, went to the store, about ten and Chuck was looking much more rested and relaxed. He started to thank Rachel again but she cut him off. She did not want any thanks; she put on her apron and went to work as usual.

Beth and Zane went in the afternoon to Pete's bar to have a beer. There were several people in the bar and as usual Punk Daniels and Gina was there. Punk was on his best behavior when they came in, after two fights with Zane Adam's Punk didn't want any more.

Gina however was in the mood for a fracas. She deliberately tried to piss Punk off but with Zane sitting in the bar but Punk wouldn't fight with her. Punk finally got up and left to avoid trouble. With Punk gone Gina decided to see what she could stir up with Zane and his rich wife Beth.

Zane and Beth were sitting at a table. Gina sauntered over and sat down between them without being invited.

"What are you up to, Gina?" Zane asked. He knew she was trying to start something with Punk before he left. He also knew she was now up to something at him and Beth's table.

"Did your wife tell you she tried to pay me to leave town?"

"Why would she do that?" Zane asked smiling at Gina with tolerance.

"Because she is jealous! Ask her?" Gina asked of Zane.

Zane looked at Beth with a question in his eyes and then told Gina, "I don't own my wife and I have no intentions of asking her anything about you. Do you mind sitting someplace else? You are interfering, in us having, a peaceful drink." Gina was taken aback by the cold look in Zane's eyes. This was not going as she planned so she got up and took her ass away from Beth and Zane's table.

Beth looked at Zane with amusement. She was surprised that Zane had not bit on Gina's attempt to start something. "I'll explain that to you later." Beth said softly.

"You don't have to unless you want to." Zane said smiling at his wife. He knew that Beth wasn't jealous of Gina and whatever Beth had said or offered

Gina was Beth's business. He knew she would tell him if she wanted but he wasn't going to insist.

After Beth and Zane had a couple of beers they left and Gina glowered as they went out the door. Pete stood behind the bar and smiled. He knew what Beth had offered Gina and he admired Zane Adam's for the way he handled it. Hell, Zane could have known all about Beth's offer to help Gina but if he did not then Zane Adams was even cooler than Pete had thought him to be.

Beth did tell Zane that she had offered to help Gina, get away from Punk, and help her go to school.

Zane didn't say much. He just told Beth what she was already beginning to suspect. "Gina doesn't want to get away from Punk, hell she likes the turmoil of fighting with him. Some women are like that. I would not be surprised if one of them ends up dead by the time it is all said and done!"

Beth just shook her head in dismay. "Wouldn't that be awful?"

They pulled into the Ranch. Thumper was waiting on the porch to get his dose of daily attention from Beth. Zane pet Maggie to keep her from getting jealous over Beth giving attention to the cat. They went on in the house. Zane pulled Beth to him. "How about a nap?" He said nibbling on her neck.

"A nap?" Beth smiled knowing a nap was not what he had in mind.

"Well, maybe eventually." He said softly and they headed up the stairs.

Rachel stayed at the store until time to close.

"Since you cooked for me last night Rachel, will you let me buy you dinner at the café?" Chuck asked, as he was reluctant for Rachel to leave.

"Yes, that would be nice. At least I will then know you have had something to eat." She said laughing.

When Chuck and Rachel walked across the street to the café nobody inside was the least bit surprised to see Chuck Danner and his long time friend Rachel Adams dining together.

Beth and Zane were not surprised to find Rachel was again not home at closing time. Zane grinned and told Beth, "You may have to learn how to cook better."

"I have learned how to cook better." She retorted, frowning at him.

"I mean you may well be the next chief cook around here! Our present cook may decide to find employment elsewhere! Oh I guess if worse comes to worse we can go to Chuck Danner's and eat!" He grinned as Beth made a face at him.

"Do you really believe Rachel has feelings for Chuck?" Beth asked Zane.

"Oh Yeah, they both had feelings for a long time. I think Chuck is why Mother never encouraged her other would be suitors."

"Really, there were others interested in her?" Beth was surprised.

"Yeah, there were several guys came around here after Dad died. Mom was indifferent toward them and they eventually gave up and went away. We always knew she was partial to Chuck but she also was a good friend of Mabel's. Now that has all changed, it won't happen overnight because Chuck and Mom are both conservative people but mark my words there is a future for Mom and Chuck Danner." Zane was certain.

Beth had also noticed Chuck was taken with Rachel but Rachel had not acted that way with Chuck. It was as Zane said because she was a very close friend of Mabel's.

The Christmas season was a festive year for the Adams. There had been no attempts through the summer and hunting season on Zane's life. He and Beth were ecstatically happy and Rachel was spending more time with her friend Chuck. Susie and Matt had found a house and their loan had been approved even though they did not think they had enough for the down payment. Beth's attorney in Detroit on her instructions had assured the bank doing the mortgage that the money was there. Matt and Susie were not to be told or were, any of the other Adams to know that Beth was behind it.

Christmas Day the entire Adam's family as well as Chuck Danner was at the Ranch for Christmas dinner. At least the family had their good cook for the time being. Zane was right Rachel and Chuck had not become involved. Chuck was not a man that would invite people to gossip about Rachel Adams and he had not declared his feeling for her or done anything that might be construed to be unseemly. Never the less it was obvious the way Chuck felt about Rachel when he looked at her. The Adams brother's looked at each other and smiled. Both had known about Chuck and Rachel's feelings for years.

Through the winter Rachel fixed dinner for Chuck at his home once a week. The grip of winter loosened and signs of spring were in the air. The robins had returned and Zane and Beth noticed a few flocks of geese heading north as they tended the cows. They had a good calving season. This year they had only lost one calf. They had a bit of a hay shortage and Zane had to buy some hay in March to get them through.

Beth told Zane she would transfer some money into his account if he needed it. Zane told her it wasn't necessary. Beth had bought Zane a tractor for Christmas. She had paid for it and it was to be delivered in the spring. Beth cut out the picture of the tractor she bought and that is what was in his package under the tree. With Rachel's help Beth picked a modest tractor that would do for the kind of work that needed to be done on the Adams farm. Zane didn't gripe about it.

Just kissed his wife thanks and was glad she had not spent a fortune on some big thing that was over the top. The tractor was delivered in April when the load limit was off the roads so it could be hauled into the ranch.

The middle of April Rachel cooked her weekly dinner at Chucks. It was a lovely evening for April. The golden daffodils were in bloom. After Rachel finished cleaning up after their meal, she got her coat and prepared to leave.

For the first time Chuck put his arms around her and softly asked if she would stay? “I don’t want you to go, Rachel.”

“I don’t want to go, either Chuck.” She said. It had been years since Rachel had a man’s arms around her and as Chuck drew her to him she began to tremble.

“Is it too much, too soon?” Chuck asked as he held her.

“No I want you Chuck, but it has been years, I’m afraid and I’m not sure I even know what to do.”

Chuck went to take her into his bedroom but Rachel refused. There were tears in her eyes as she told him, “Mabel died in this room and you and she was man and wife here many years, I can’t be with you in Mabel’s bed.”

Chuck took her in the guest room. They undressed and got into bed. Rachel still trembled and Chuck took her in his arms. All the years he had dreamed of being with Rachel and now that he held her in his arms and in his bed, he found to his horror he could not get an erection.

Realizing Chuck was having difficulty Rachel assured him, “I want your hands on my body, I want to feel your arms around me. I want to know you want me and care about me in your heart. Don’t worry about performing, just love me.”

Chuck did. He found Rachel still had a lovely body. Her breast still firm and filled his hand without being overly large like some older women. He also found he loved stroking her body and he felt the swell of her hips. Her buttocks were still firm and as he caressed her he found he began to get an erection. All of the time he had dreamed of being with her, he guessed he had stage fright because as he began to explore her body his began to react and he felt aroused. He was able to make love to her.

It had been many years since Rachel had felt any kind of sexual feeling and she thought those feelings were long gone but she was wrong. Her years of loneliness and the warm and caring hands on her body awakened feelings of passion she had thought were no longer possible for her to feel.

She spent the night with Chuck. They made love and talked. Chuck asked her why she had put up with Walt’s abuse all those years.

"I had Matt and Zane to think of. They needed their father in many ways and I never had anywhere to go. The farm was the place to raise my boys. It was not that way when Walt and I were first married. He never hurt me until several years of excessive drinking changed him. I probably would have left once the boys were raised if he had not died. People get into a rut and years go by before you realize it."

Chuck knew what Rachel said was true. He and Mabel had many good years before the bad. He neither could call it quits with her when he looked back over the good times. He felt compelled to see it to the end. His time was gone with Mabel and Rachel's time was gone with Walt. Chuck just hoped that he could continue to find the happiness and satisfaction with Rachel that they had just shared in the future. But as one grows older, he had learned to take one day at a time. His years, of wanting and dreaming, of being with Rachel Adams, were everything he had dreamt.

Rachel spent the night with Chuck and neither of them regretted it.

Zane and Beth were neither one surprised when that first night Rachel did not come home. Neither of them said anything to her and life went on at the Adam farm as if everything was the same. But everyone knew things were about to change.

The customers to the store found Rachel Adams and Chuck Danner were both beaming with happiness. Nobody resented or begrudged them a little happiness.

13

The beautiful month of May brought the flowers Rachel had planted around the Adams house in full bloom. Rachel and Beth had planted many spring flowering bulbs in the fall after the remodeling mess was cleaned up.

Thumper did his job and kept the gophers from eating the bulbs. Maggie had also done her job and kept the deer from eating the emerging tulip foliage. Beth who had kept the yard mowed the summer before was delighted with the spring bulbs blooming in all their glory. Being raised in the city she found it fascinating that she and Rachel had planted all of those bulbs and they had slept under the winter snow to come up in the spring and turn the Adams yard into a riot of color.

Beth resisted the urge to pick the flowers and bring them into the house. She knew they would last much longer in their outdoor location and could therefore be enjoyed by all who saw them longer.

On Mother's day Adam's family again worked the cattle and opened the gates to let them out on the summer range. This year Chuck Danner had come and joined them in the evening after he closed the store. Rachel was spending several nights a month at Chuck's house but Chuck had never spent the night at the Adams farm. However, the morning after Mothers day Beth and Zane came downstairs to find Chuck and Rachel at the kitchen table sharing morning coffee.

Zane looked at Beth with a knowing smile. He greeted his mother and Chuck with a good morning and he and Beth went out to do morning chores. By the time they returned Chuck had left for the store. Neither Beth not Zane said anything to Rachel about Chuck's apparent sojourn the night on the Adams farm. It had been expected eventually.

Zane had taken a couple of Bear Hunter's out for Jack Cutler. Beth worried about it, not forgetting it had been during the spring season someone had put a bullet in Zane's shoulder.

The Sheriffs' office still had the investigation open into Zane's shooting but the trail had grown cold and they were no closer to figuring out who would want Zane Adams dead than they were when it happened. Zane at times would forget it had even occurred. Beth never forgot. She wondered if she could use her money to secretly hire some expert investigators to find out who was involved? She decided to look into it and she didn't mention it to Zane.

The middle of May the ongoing tumultuous marriage of Gina and Punk Daniels came to a sudden end. Gina staggered, into Pete's bar about six p.m. covered in blood. She was hysterical and screaming. Nobody could find out what was going on, as she was incoherent. As they examined Gina and called for the Sheriff it was determined that Gina was not the source of all of the blood. She was apparently other than bruised and abrasions unwounded. When the Sheriffs' office went to Daniel's home, they found Punk Daniels dead of multiple stab wounds. There was blood all over the house. They transported the incoherent Gina to the mental ward at the nearest hospital where she was sedated and put under guard until further investigation.

After they investigated, Gina was booked and held in the county jail on suspicion of murder in the death of her husband. The obituary in the county newspaper reminded folk's that Punk's real name was, Dale Daniels.

After arraigning her they released Gina on her own recognizance pending future charges. She had nowhere to go. Daniel's house was a grizzly crime scene.

Beth again intervened on Gina's behalf and sent an attendant to take Gina to an apartment that had been rented in the town at the county seat. Gina would have an Attorney appointed for her by the State but the attendant that Beth hired anonymously was a psychiatric nurse. She was to see that Gina did not harm herself and was not alone. The attendant told Gina she was sent to care for her by the State. Beth felt better knowing poor Gina was not alone. She remembered that Zane had said this might be what happened to end the fighting between Punk and Gina. Nobody figured Gina would be the one to survive. The odds had been that Gina would die because Punk broke her neck or injured her internally beating on her. Nobody ever dreamed Gina would be the survivor in that relationship. It became unclear given the tumultuous relationship between Punk and Gina what the prosecutors was going to be able to prove. There could be plenty of possible evidence Gina had merely been defending herself.

One thing Beth thought of and she brought it up to Zane was how Gina was going to be able to reconcile herself with what happened and build a life for herself.

"I don't know Beth, that kind of woman may very well find another man to abuse her. It is sometimes an unconscious need for that type of relationship." He added, "Or so I've read and seen on Doctor Phil."

Beth laughed, "Since when have you been watching Doctor Phil?"

Zane just grinned and shook his head. Beth wondered how much of what Zane knew about abusive relationships he had garnered from his own parents. She realized it had more than likely been a subject that weighed on his mind even after all the years his father had been gone.

Beth decided to make sure Gina got all the professional help she needed!

The relationship between Rachel and Chuck seemed to be satisfying for both of them. Zane knew the type of man Chuck was and knew he and Matt would never have to fear Chuck would abuse his mother in any way! Rachel appeared to be a woman fulfilled and happy these days and they could all thank Chuck Danner for that.

In June Zane and Beth rode the Bays into the canyon several times to check on the cows. Beth was getting used to riding and found she was beginning to enjoy her trips with Zane and Maggie.

Beth had begged off her April trip to Detroit this year but she had promised her advisors and Attorney she would make the trip in July. Beth began to pester Zane to come with her. Zane did not want to go. He asked Beth why they needed her back there at all, why couldn't they fax or mail whatever documents they needed to? Zane reminded Beth they would have to be cutting hay over the fourth or as soon as the weather allowed. He had the new tractor but was trying to get the old worn hay Baler to work!

"Why don't we just buy another one?" Beth asked.

"I guess we could look for a used one?" Zane conceded.

"If you can't find a used one, we can easily buy a new one. Don't be so stubborn about this Zane; we are now family and my money is also yours. If you don't believe me ask the Internal Revenue service." She said with exasperation. It seemed everyone in the family knew Beth had money; they just had no idea how much?

They mowed hay the second of July. This time it took a week to get it in. There was a thunderstorm that blew through and Zane had to turn the hay to get it to dry for the new used baler. He and Matt were happy with the new tractor and the new used baler was also working well. The storm was the only delay they had. Matt took a couple days of his paid vacation from the mill to help get the hay in the barn. Once finished Zane figured he would again have to buy hay in March. The cattle herd was increasing. They had not sold, the amount of calves they had before Beth came to the ranch. With the extra household money she provided they had held some extra heifers. Those heifers would next spring begin to have calves.

With the hay in the barn Zane ran out of excuses to get out of the trip to Detroit. He agreed to go. Beth Was ecstatic she would not have to go alone.

They flew out of Spokane and as before went through Chicago and onto Detroit. Fred, the doorman greeted Beth as he had before.

"Nice to see you Miss Robins."

"Mrs. Adams! Fred, this is my husband, Mr. Adams."

"Mr. Adams." Fred acknowledged and observed the tall young man that was with Beth the year before was once again getting the baggage from the Taxi driver without waiting for Fred to get it.

Beth smiled sweetly as she waited for Zane to get their baggage. Zane packed it and Fred opened the door and trailed behind them to the elevator. Fred tipped his hat and returned to the door as Mr. And Mrs. Adams rode the elevator up to the penthouse.

This trip Beth had promised they would finish up her business in three days. Zane thought it was a good thing because it was oppressively hot in Detroit. Not hot like in Idaho on the temperature gauge but hot with humidity, which made the heat unbearable. The penthouse was as cool and elegant as Zane remembered. This time he wasn't sure he was even interested in leaving the penthouse until they were ready to return home. The dreaded trip was over and Beth and Zane flew back to Spokane via Chicago and were relieved when they got in the Toyota they had left at the Spokane airport and headed for the Adams ranch.

A few days later as things begin to return to normal Beth received a fax from her Attorney in Detroit. On the society page was a picture of Beth and Zane as they left the Penthouse. The caption read, "Heiress marries Idaho Mountain Man"

Beth was horrified. She had not even known that some Paparazzi had snapped the picture. She dreaded having to tell Zane about it. She also knew it may not be on the front page across the country, but could be picked up and printed somewhere in papers across the country. She wondered how they had found out about Zane and what he did? The caption would not have been nearly as salacious if it read she had married a rancher!

The headlines, was the worst. The picture of her and Zane was actually very good. Zane looked tall and handsome. His longer than normal curly hair showed plainly and the picture depicted the handsome couple Beth and Zane were! How had they tracked down what Zane did as a guide? Beth was afraid that everyone would now be privy to the fact she was a very rich woman. She knew Zane was not going to like it but the proverbial cat was out of the bag and there was nothing she could do! Too late, she wished she had made the trip alone.

Since Zane had accompanied Beth the year before, Beth knew her mistake was informing Fred that Zane was her husband. She was angry that Fred had probably sold the story. She could have him fired but it would not undo the damage that had been done. Fred had worked at the building for many years but Beth intended he was going to get a piece of her mind if she ever saw him again. One thing she was certain of, that Zane would never go with her again.

Beth knew she needed to tell him before someone else did. Zane came down the stairs about that time and Beth handed him the fax. "I'm afraid we have bad news Zane!" She said miserably.

Zane's color blanched as he read the caption under their picture." Oh Jesus Christ! How in the hell did that happen?"

"Probably when I told Fred, you were my husband." Beth said tears in her eyes.

"Where was this printed?" Zane asked.

"In the Detroit society news. But the associated press probably will pick it up. It may even get on one of the celebrity gossip Television programs." Beth was miserable having to tell Zane their business could be plastered across the country.

"Well I guess it was bound to happen sooner or later. We have had nearly two years of privacy." Zane gathered Beth in his arms. "I guess we can just hide out on the farm and wait for it to blow over." He said softly." Maybe it won't penetrate in this backwoods area?"

Beth was afraid that was wishful thinking on his part. "I hate the headlines." But she said, "The picture shows how handsome you are, they can't blame me, for falling for a guy that looks like you!"

"Right and especially since you are such an ugly rich girl!" Zane laughed.

Beth and Zane kept quiet and waited to see what the headline in Detroit would do to their quiet happy lives. It took a while but eventually everyone had either seen the picture and caption or had heard about it. Most people didn't have the bad manners to mention it but they began to look at Zane Adams, pretty blonde wife differently. Beth even began to get calls from strangers with sad stories wanting money. The first thing they had to do was get an unlisted private number. They found satellite news feed truck in front of the ranch house and Zane ran them off and started building a gate that blocked the driveway up to the house.

Beth suggested they get a fencing company and put a gate that could only be opened by remote in their vehicles or from the house. Zane agreed they needed to do something. It was not the local people that were giving them trouble, as it was outsiders, trying to gain access to the wealthy heiress.

Matt and Susie were astonished, they had known that Beth had some money but like Zane they did not have any idea it was so much money that would cause headlines and Paparazzi interest across the country.

Rachel and Zane had known and had hoped it would not affect their lives but it was obvious now that it was going to. Especially since Zane and Beth were now married. Chuck asked Rachel if she had known about Beth being an heiress and Rachel admitted she had. Beth had told her shortly after she came to the ranch.

"Did Zane know?" Chuck asked.

"Not until they had fallen in love." Rachel told him. "He knew Beth had some money from her father but he had no idea it was millions or hundreds of millions. He wanted Beth to sell her share of the company she owned and put it in the bank when they planned to marry but when he found out the size of the company he realized she would be unable to do that. Zane had hoped they could be a normal family and this wealth would not affect them but now that everyone knows?" Rachel shook her head." It is going to be something they will have to deal with. Maybe the thing will blow over somewhat!"

Chuck looked doubtful and Rachel felt doubtful. There was not much chance the locals were going to forget how rich Zane's wife is! Rachel knew they had gotten the information locally to dub Zane a mountain man. That could only have come from a local, but who! It would be a witch-hunt to find out and there was nothing to be gained.

Zane called Jack Cutler and gave him the new unlisted phone number. The first thing Jack wanted to know was if Zane would be coming back to the lodge. Zane was speechless.

"Of coarse, nothing has changed except what people know about Beth. That hasn't affected what I do, I still get up and take care of the cows and I still intend to Guide for you unless you don't want me?"

"Of coarse I want you! You're the best Guide I've ever had and this notoriety can only help our business. I'm sorry about that but you know it will help?" Jack laughed.

Zane said he supposed that was true. He promised to be at the Lodge for the Bow season which was only a little over a month away.

With the unlisted number and the locked gate it was beginning to quiet down at the ranch. The gate was something the family would all have to get used to. Beth hung onto her husband, she was sad that things had changed because she was foolish enough to be proud Zane was her husband. Thank God they still loved each other passionately and some how they would learn to live with it, even if it was behind a locked gate.

Beth and Rachel canned the green beans from the garden. Beth mowed the grass and her and Zane had time to be together before Zane was to go to the Lodge. Beth packed sticks when in the garden ever mindful of rattlesnakes. Maggie also scouted for tress passers, snakes in the grass or two legged snakes that crawled over the gate and walked up the driveway. Beth and Zane rode often. They still went when they felt like it to Pete's Bar and had a beer. Nobody bothered them and everyone locally knew Zane was a force to be reckoned with when riled so nobody bothered Zane or Beth.

The locals didn't know why Beth and Zane still drove Zane's old Chevy truck when they came to the Bar as everyone knew Beth had money enough to buy a fleet of new trucks but nobody had nerve enough to ask.

Zane was asked by different ones if he was going to the Lodge for the hunting season and he replied he was, they looked at him oddly. Beth and Zane smiled at each other and said nothing more about it.

One night in each other's arm Beth was complaining about how their situation had changed because of her and her wealth.

"Beth, just forget about it." Zane said. "I knew you were wealthy when I married you. You're still the woman I want to spend my life with. Nothing has changed, we still love each other and so people know you have some money. Let us just go about our business and not forget how we feel about each other. It isn't anybody's fault! It is what is!" He pulled her to him and they made love as they always did and made each other happy.

Beth resolved to quit beating herself up over it. One thing, she was certain, that she was never going back to Detroit again. Her damned Attorney would need to find another way if he had to bring a boardroom to Idaho. She was going to sell the Penthouse.

The next day she fired a fax off to her power of Attorney and instructed him, to sell the Penthouse.

Zane made ready to go back up to the Lodge for bow season. Rachel was often gone to Chucks and Zane began to worry about Beth being alone at the Ranch. Since so many people knew about her wealth, he began to fear she could become a target for someone to extort money from her. He even began to worry she might be kidnapped or harmed. He decided they needed to spend the money for more security and perhaps even some guard dogs.

Another possibility was she could go with him to the Lodge. When she was there the year before she had been helpful to Annie. Zane wondered if he could talk it over with Jack and Annie. He knew he would feel she was safer with him.

Beth on the other hand was still worried about Zane's safety. The investigators she had hired had come up with nothing more than the local sheriffs office.

Zane and Beth drove to Lewiston and talked with Annie and Jack. Zane explained he was reluctant to leave Beth alone with all the commotion over her being an heiress.

"Are you suggesting we hire Beth to help Annie?" Jack said looking at Zane in amazement?.

"I wouldn't need to be paid," Beth said. I could work for my board and room?"

Jack began to laugh. He thought it was insanity that a rich heiress was going to be willing to help Annie for her board and room.

"Of coarse you would be paid." Annie said, throwing a look of disapproval at Jack. Annie could see Beth and Zane were both aggravated by Jacks humor over the situation. "You might as well know Zane, Jack and I for some time have planned to offer you to take over the Lodge when we retire."

"Well, what about Jody? He has been with you guys longer than I have?" Zane was surprised as he had not known Jack had intended something like that?

"Jody is just not the kind of fellow that could run a business and although he is a good guide he doesn't get along well with the clients. Jody is too bashful and shy."

"Does he know you have planned for me to take over?" Zane asked. He knew that Jody was jealous of him as it was. Jack had often made it clear he was partial to Zane.

"I don't know. Unless he overheard us discussing it, we haven't told him." Jack said.

"If Beth would come and learn the business and you would consider taking it over, it would please us very much. We are getting too old and would like to think about getting out the next couple of years. We would not expect Beth to work for her board and room, we would welcome her as your future partner and she would be paid a wage same as anybody else who works at the lodge. However since we know that you and Beth don't have to worry about money, it probably doesn't sound like all that attractive of a deal?"

"Oh Yes, It does sound good. I have been teaching school off and on and I want to be involved with Zane. We work the cattle together and my money is something that seems to hang around our necks like an albatross. I would get rid of it but the company continues to grow. Zane and I have tried to live a normal life but now that everyone knows I have money it has become tiresome, especially for Zane."

"Yeah," Zane grinned, "I would hate to think people believe I married this ugly woman for her money!"

Jack and Annie laughed. Anyone could see Beth was far from ugly.

On the way back to the ranch Beth was ecstatic she was to go with Zane to the Lodge. Last year she had missed him terribly and had enjoyed the night she spent there with him. Jack had ribbed Zane about keeping his mind on his hunting with his beautiful wife at the lodge but Jack knew Zane loved the guide business and he knew he could always count on Zane.

Zane was thoughtful and quiet on the way home. He had a sneaking suspicion his old partner Jody might have figured Jack had chosen Zane to take over the business. He remembered Jody was quiet and sullen last year and Zane had wondered what was bothering him. He wondered if somehow Jody had found out about Jacks plans for Zane.

Zane also wondered how long Jack and Annie had these plans in their mind. It was an opportunity Zane had never even thought about. It was something he was very much interested in. There was a great deal to learn about the business end of the Guide business but Zane knew Beth had the education and experience to be partners with him.

He was looking forward to having her with him at the Lodge this year. Rachel and Chuck would have to hold down things at the Ranch. It seemed to Zane with Chuck's business and the Ranch and Beth's Corporation and now the possibility of him and Beth taking on the Guide business; Adams family had far too many irons in the fire!

The only good part was the Guiding Lodge was only open for about three months but Zane had a feeling the business end was more complicated than that. There was the ongoing job of recruiting hunters across the country. Jack may be right, Zane's, wives' fame may be an unexpected bonus since the headlines had announced Zane was a mountain guide!

Rachel and Chuck prepared to hold down the Adams farm as Beth and Zane made ready to move to the Lodge for a three-month stay. Zane and Beth went several days before the first hunters came in so Annie could begin to show Beth what needed to be done. They also made some adjustments to the private quarters and Beth and Zane was to have accommodations in the area that Annie and Jack had their rooms. This meant Jody was going to be alone in the Guides quarters.

Jody came the day before the season began. He was surprised to see Zane was already there.

"I wondered if you would even be here this year?" He told Zane.

"Why is that?" Zane asked.

"Well with your wife having all that money, what are you doing up here?" Jody wanted to know. He did not act as if he was happy that Zane had returned for the season.

"My wife has money, I don't, and I'm just the mountain man that married her!" Zane said. "Did you expect I would sit around and spend my wife's money?"

Jody was even more surprised to see Beth with Zane at the Lodge. He watched with amazement as the heiress, his guide partner had married brought his dinner to him. It all seemed rather confusing to Jody who never being around anybody that had money and he was under the assumption that kind of person did nothing but sit around and spend their money!

Beth found most people who had not been around the rich had no idea what rich people do with their time. Beth told Zane one time that when one is rich, money becomes, without value. Money, after all is only worth what you can buy with it. If one has everything or wants nothing, money in itself, lose its value.

It is nice to think the money is there if one needs it, but it is easier to use it to help people who really have a need for it. That becomes another problem, many people think they would have a need of money and it would cure all their problems. Beth said her Dad used to say if you have a problem that can be cured by money, you truly have no problem at all!

Beth mentioned the fact that all the money in the world will not help if you are terminally ill or suffering the loss of a loved one and a myriad of problems that no amount of money could cure. Being lonely for instance, which Bethany Robins had been all too aware of even with the money?

Beth was grateful for her love with her husband and she knew the money was one of the least important things about her life. She found her life with Zane to be fulfilling and she was looking forward to sharing this new adventure at the Lodge by his side.

The first day of the Bow season Zane called a six point into a client from Wisconsin. The man made a clean kill and they were able to get the packhorses into the carcass. Jody was grouchy that Zane had bagged the first bull of the season. He was also jealous that Zane had his rich wife with him. Jody's animosity toward Zane was boiling just below the surface. Zane knew Jody was unhappy with him but he had no idea of the hatred Jody Miller felt for Zane. Jody felt Zane had everything handed to him and him, Jody was given little, he figured mostly because he was Indian.

After the first week Beth got up feeling ill one morning. Annie had enjoyed having the help Beth gave her but when she noticed the girl felt ill she sent her back to her and Zane's room.

Beth protested she was fine but Annie reminded her it could be cold or flue, which might get transferred to the clients. Beth felt better in the afternoon and Annie let her help with the evening meal.

The next morning Beth was again ill and Annie put her on housecleaning and told her to stay away from the kitchen. Zane was worried. He suggested that Beth should go into town and see a doctor.

Beth felt better in the afternoon. Annie asked Beth if it were possible she could be pregnant when Beth once again got out of bed feeling ill?

Beth looked at Annie in astonishment. She had not been on the pill since Zane and she had been married. In fact she and Zane had not even given it any thought. They had planned on having children, someday? But Beth realized when Annie mentioned it that she did not remember when she had last had her menstrual cycle. She told Annie it could be, and decided she would not mention it to Zane until she was sure.

She wondered what how Zane would feel if they were to be expecting a baby?

Zane came back with his client around noon and went to check on Beth. She had not felt good that morning and he worried.

Beth told him she thought she would drive into town and get some medicine. Beth had brought her car to the Lodge. She drove into town and got a pregnancy test kit at the Danner store. Chuck happened to be working and Rachel was no place in sight. Beth assumed she might be at the Ranch.

Beth drove back to the Lodge and took the test. Zane was still out with a client. The test was positive! Beth was pregnant. Her mind reeled as she tried to imagine how Zane would take the news. Beth was overjoyed. She wanted to have a baby with Zane the man she loved more than anything in the world. The idea they could have a family made Beth so happy she was not sure she could contain herself she felt like going to the woods and finding Zane to tell him. Of coarse she could not, she would have to wait?

Beth felt such overwhelming joy to think this man she loved so much and loved her back, that now within her that love had created another person growing within her was such an intense feeling of joy and gratitude she began to cry.

She was crying when Zane returned. He had been worried about her and when he found her crying he became alarmed.

Zane gathered her in her arms. "What wrong Beth?"

"Nothing is wrong, I'm so happy I can't help but cry!" She blubbered aware she looked terrible. This is not the way in her mind she had intended to tell him.

"We are going to have a baby, Zane," She cried.

"Are you sure, Beth?" He said softly. He was afraid she was mistaken; he knew Beth had wanted to get pregnant for several months. He had hoped it would happen also."

"I'm sure," She said choking back tears, "I went in town and got a test kit. We are going to have a baby!" She threw her self back in his arms and Beth cried and Zane laughed.

With tears running down her face, she began to kiss him. Her kisses became passionate. Beth wanted him to make love to her. She had this overwhelming need to be joined with him. She wanted to share the joy inside of her with him. Zane began to also want her. They made love and it was more intense between them than it had ever been. Beth wanted him as close to her and what grew within her as he could get.

Annie came down the hall to check on Beth. With Zane and Beth's door shut she went back to the kitchen. Jack was having a cup of tea. "I believe the Adams, family is about to grow," She smiled.

14

Jody and Jack were the only ones at the table for the evening meal. Beth and Zane didn't appear.

"What's up with those two?" Jody asked his dark eyes looking around wondering why neither Zane nor his rich blonde wife was about the kitchen.

Annie laughed and said she thought, the Adams family was having a reunion. Jody looked at her strangely; he had noticed Zane's truck and Beth's car both out behind when he came in.

"What did you find out there this afternoon?" Jack asked.

"Not much of anything." Jody said.

"What do you have planned for tomorrow?"

"I don't know," Jody said. "I planned to talk it over with Zane, see where he is going in the morning."

"I have an idea that might have to wait until morning." Jack grinned. Something was going on around there. Jody could feel it and the way Jack and Annie was acting, he was sure it had to do with Zane.

Zane was at the breakfast table the next morning. He looked rested and happy. Beth finally appeared and she looked like hell warmed over.

"Where you going today?" Jody asked.

"Taking the guy from Missouri over into the Armstrong tree stand. The bulls are still squealing well and I had one over there the other day that nearly come in. I figure I can get him if the Bowmen from Missouri can put him down. What about you? That guy you have from California is one of those heavy weights; you need to get him where he doesn't have to expend too much effort. I always worry about those type having a heart attack."

"Yeah, I hate to even put them in a tree stand." Jody agreed. "I think I'll take him up on the high road and put him in a blind. Maybe I can call something in." It seemed to Jody Zane always got the best clients. He hated taking the fat guy. Jody was also not as good as Zane with the calls and he wished he could get the fat guy in a tree stand as Jody was better at running game to a tree stand.

Jody had really grown resentful that Zane was at the Lodge when he found out Zane's wife was wealthy. Why didn't Zane just stay home and leave the job to people who needed one, also Zane's skill made Jody look bad? He had looked forward after finding out about Zane's wife to working with a novice where he would be the more skilled guide.

Jody noticed Beth and Annie had their heads together in the kitchen. Beth didn't look well but her and Annie were smiling and laughing. Jack had already eaten. Jody met him on his way out when he came to the table. There were only the two clients at the lodge. Since Jack was leaving so early Jody surmised, he must have some clients coming in he had to meet at the airport.

After breakfast Jody went out to put his gear together. Zane stayed behind to say goodbye to Beth. With just Annie and Beth in the kitchen, Annie smiled and said to Zane, "Going to be a papa, I'm so happy for you and Beth."

Zane said, "Thank you Annie, we are ecstatic." Zane kissed Beth and went out to get his gear gathered.

Zane was back before noon with the guy from Missouri to get the packhorses. He had called the Bull in on the Armstrong tree stand and the hunter from Missouri got his Elk. Zane took the horses and the trailer. The Hunter from Missouri went with him. He was not, one of those hunters that were done with his hunting experience when he made the kill. The Missouri hunter, helped get the Bull packed.

Jody didn't get back until afternoon with his portly hunter from California. Jody was disgusted he had gotten a Bull into the blind but the California hunter had missed. That miss caused Jody aggravation but he was even more aggravated that Zane had gotten a nice Bull for his client and the client had also helped get it out.

Zane and the Missouri man had already skinned the bull and were finished up by the time Jody showed up. Jody tried to act pleased but he was thinking that without help from him, Zane would not share the bonus on that Elk. Jody needed the money and he knew full well Zane did not!

Seems that those who have get more and those who have not get less, Jody thought as he watched the happy Missouri hunter talking with Zane. One of the reasons, Zane got on well with the clients was that when Zane talked with anybody he looked at them directly and everyone knew he was interested in what you were saying. It was a trait that attracted Beth to Zane from the first time she met him.

Zane also had a smile that was engaging. He had perfect teeth, which Beth once asked him if he had to wear braces when a child. Zane just smiled and shook his head no. Beth remembered she had worn those damned braces on her teeth for months. Beth hoped their child would inherit Zane's teeth. Matt also had nice teeth so it must be a family trait.

Beth made an appointment with a Doctor that specialized in babies' and went to Lewiston. Zane was busy with the hunters but Rachel went with her. Rachel was also ecstatic for Beth and Zane.

Chuck and Rachel were spending more time at the Ranch with Beth and Zane both gone to the Lodge. When the bow season came to an end Zane and Beth came home until the rifle season was to begin on October 10th.

Since there, seemed to be more Wolf signs than even the year before, Zane was expecting to have to hunt the deep holes and brushy basins to get any success for the rifle hunters. The rifle hunters had been declining the last few years because the Elk were holed in rough country where they could best protect themselves from the wolves and hunters alike.

When rifle hunters paid big bucks for an Elk hunt in Idaho and when they went home without success they were less likely to return the following year. They were also less likely to recommend a hunt to their friends.

The vigilante Wolf hunters were making a dent in the numbers in some of the packs but the Feds had also caught a few and levied some hefty fines and those hunters were unable to procure a hunting license for some time, often several years. No hunting license in Idaho meant you could not even pack a gun. The need for secrecy among the dedicated vigilantes was becoming more important. Zane had never shot a Wolf. His livelihood depended on his guide license but he admired and hoped the vigilantes could make a dent in the Wolf population. There was talk of taking the wolves off the endangered species list. If they lost protection from the Feds Zane knew lots of guys would be on a mission to eliminate as many as they could. The idea they had been introduced to the Idaho Forest did not set well with the folks that had to coexist with them. The fact that the residents of Idaho had not even been asked was also a sore spot with many. All Idaho residents who had livestock were adamant about getting rid of the Wolves.

The ten days, before the rifle season, when Beth and Zane were home was a time they could get lined out on Beth's doctor and prenatal care. Their love for each other took on even deeper meaning now that they were sharing the fact that their baby was growing within Beth. That seemed to be a sexual stimulant for Beth. She was insatiable and Zane wondered if that was healthy for her pregnancy. Beth asked the Doctor and he said it would have no adverse effect.

Beth had always enjoyed making love with Zane but now that she was pregnant, he teased her she was about to wear him completely out. Of coarse he was teasing her. Zane first consideration had always been to satisfy her first and it seemed to work the best for him also. A warm and receptive woman was an ego boost for any passionate man and especially a man as much in love with his wife as Zane was.

October 9 Beth and Zane packed up and returned to the Lodge for the rifle season. The first week they had four hunters and Jack, Jody and Zane were very busy trying to handle them. Having more hunters than guides meant that they would need to be sure one hunter was on a stand or safe place where he would not apt to get off alone. A lost hunter did not bode well for a Guide, reputation.

The Elk as expected were hard to find. Zane took a man from California into a brushy basin and they got a nice bull for him but Zane had to back pack it as it wasn't a place to get the horses.

Since Jack and Jody were busy with their own hunters Zane had to pack the bull out on his own but he earned a nice bonus and a hunter from California left happy. The second hunter was a man named Clyde Baker from Texas and Zane decided to take him into the glades where George Belmont had been killed. Zane knew there were some elk in that area. It had been two years since George's death and over a year and several months since Zane had been wounded in the shoulder.

Although those incidents had not been resolved, Zane had relaxed and hoped whoever was behind it had now given up or moved or abandoned the idea of wanting him dead. With this much time gone by it was plausible that whoever was behind it had abandoned the idea

That morning Zane took Clyde Baker up on the high ridge and they went down through the glades seemed like a different time and place. The brush had grown some during the two years. They began to hit fresh Elk signs, as soon as they started working down through the glades. It had rained well that fall and it was quiet hunting. Clyde Baker was a man in his early forties and seemed to have some idea of what he was doing. Zane could tell he had hunted quit a bit before.

As they worked their way into the glade where George was shot Zane was concentrating on playing with some cows below with the cow elk reed in his mouth. He chirped the cow call and got an answer. Zane made a calf call and a cow answered.

Clyde Baker was watching carefully down below trying to spot a Bull.

When the rifle shot rang out it caught Zane totally by surprise. The bullet tore into Zane's abdomen and he hit the dirt in the Bracken ferns. Clyde Baker stood with his mouth agape as he saw Zane go down. "Get down!" Zane told him and Clyde Baker dropped down on one knee along side Zane.

"What the hell is going on?" Clyde Baker asked. His face turned white as he saw the blood stain spread across Zane's abdomen. "Your hit!" Clyde said.

"Yeah," Zane gritted his teeth with pain. He knew the wound was on the left side and he hoped it had not hit his spleen. "Stay down!" He told Baker.

"Give me your damned gun!" Zane told Clyde.

"Maybe I should keep it. They may hit me next!"

"No," Zane grunted. "They are after me and I know where the shooter is!" Zane struggled the pack off his back. And rolled onto his belly. The moldy smell of the moss and ferns was strong in his nose. "Give me the gun and stay down" Zane told Baker.

Zane remembered where he had seen the tracks on the ridge two years before. He also knew he needed the shooter to believe he was down permanently. Baker handed his gun over to Zane. Zane knew Baker was packing a 300 Weatherby magnum and he also knew the gunman was 430 yards away. He had checked the distance two years ago when he saw the trampled spot that day. The problem was that a certain amount of time needed to pass to make the gunmen believe he had a killing shot before Zane dare make a move. He would need a clear shot himself if he were to reach the position he believed he knew the gunmen in.

Zane checked the wound in his side. He was losing too much blood. He wadded his handkerchief up and put pressure on the wound. He slid his belt up and tightened it to put pressure on and cover the makeshift bandage.

Zane waited. Clyde Baker lay still beside him and watched as Zane made ready to move. Zane Belly crawled up through the ferns to get away from the area where he had went down when he was hit. He was now almost to the log where George Belmont had been killed.

Clyde Baker stayed where Zane had told him. Zane dove over the log and brought the scope of the 300 into the place he had seen the tracks two years before. Through the scope, which was a top of the line Leopold, Zane could see someone wearing camouflage clothing. They were standing and looking over toward the area where Zane and Clyde Baker had hit the dirt.

Zane whispered a prayer that Clyde Bakers gun was accurately sighted in. He squeezed the trigger as he sighted on the man on the ridge 430 yards away. As the rifle roared, the man went down.

"Get me my pack." Zane said to Clyde Baker who still was on his belly below. The recoil of the 300 was all the strength Zane had, to keep from falling over.

"Do I dare move?" Clyde asked.

"Yeah," Zane said. "The shooter is on the ground."

Clyde Baker wasn't sure so he threw Zane's pack up the hill toward him. Zane's wound felt like it was on fire. The man on the ridge was still down as Zane looked through the scope. Painfully Zane dragged himself back over the log and dug in his pack for the radio.

Zane got Jack on the radio. "I've been shot Jack. I need help the same place George Belmont was killed."

"Repeat that Zane!" Jack Cutler thought he was hearing things.

"I've been shot and we need medical help." Zane said. "The guy who shot me is also down and maybe dead."

"I'll get a chopper right in there!" Jack said. "How bad are you hit Zane?"

"My left abdomen but I've got a pressure bandage on it. I'm going to see about the guy who shot me."

"Who in the hell would do something like that? Do you know who it was?" Jack asked.

"I think so," Zane said. "Just get someone in as quick as you can. I might make it but I don't know about the other guy." Zane put the phone down and looked at Clyde Baker. "How you holding up Clyde?" He asked.

Clyde Bakers face was ashen but he wasn't wounded, just half scared to death.

"I'm heading over there to see what I can do for the other guy." Zane struggled to his feet. With pain etched on his face he told Clyde Baker, "If you don't mind I'll keep your gun just a little longer. Stay here and make yourself visible, there will be a helicopter here soon."

Zane headed over toward the ridge where the downed shooter lay. Clyde Baker could see a large blood stain across Zane Adam's back. He wondered how the guide was still even on his feet.

Zane painfully made his way down the first draw and dropped off the ridge and climbed up the ridge from the second draw. He knew exactly where the man he shot had gone down. It was the same place he had noticed the grass trampled down two years ago. As he climbed up the last ridge he felt as if his side was afire. It burned where the bullet had passed through. He found the man he had cut down with the 300 magnum laying on his side right where Zane knew he would be. It was his long time partner and hunting guide buddy Jody Miller and he was still alive.

Jody's eyes fluttered open when he heard Zane walk up to him

"How bad you hit Jody?" Zane asked. Zane could see a bloodstain on Jody's chest and blood trickled from the corner of his mouth.

Zane knew he had probably hit him in the lungs. It had missed his heart and hit him on the right side of his chest. Zane, bent over Jody and pulled his shirt back. Jody tried to speak.

Zane located Jody's handkerchief and put it on the wound and put pressure on it trying to stem the flow of blood.

"Why?" Zane asked.

"You were going to get everything." Jody gasped. Zane felt tears sting his face. His heart was heavy to think Jody had wanted him dead because Jody was jealous.

"Don't talk, help is coming." Zane said gently and cradled Jody head in his lap as he held pressure on Jody's chest wound.

Zane didn't know how long he sat there and held his friends head in his lap. Zane finally heard the chopper overhead and it landed in the glade by Clyde Baker. Clyde pointed toward Zane and the chopper lifted off and set down in a clearing a short distance where Zane sat with Jody's head in his lap.

A medic and an Emergency doctor made their way toward Zane and Jody. "Take care of him first. He's hit the worst!" Zane said. Jody's eyes fluttered as they lifted his head and Zane crawled out away from him so they could work on him

"Sorry," Jody said and he looked right at Zane but his voice was barely audible. Zane turned away sickened. His side burned but his heart, hurt worse to think his old friend and partner had tried to kill him. Possibly three different times; Zane choked back a sob thinking about it.

They worked on Jody but Zane was afraid there was not much they could do. They loaded Jody onto one of the cages that they could fasten on the chopper. Then they came back to see how Zane was doing. The Doctor was alarmed when he saw how much blood was across Zane's back but Zane still had the entrance hole plugged with his handkerchief and his belt tied over it.

"Can you walk?" The Doctor asked Zane.

"Yes," Zane struggled to his feet. His knees felt rubbery but he managed with help to walk to the chopper and climb inside. He sat in a seat and with Jody in the basket stretcher below they lifted off. Zane was barely conscious when they set down on the heliport at the hospital.

Zane tried to ask about Jody but he was lapsing in and out of consciousness. He remembered thinking about Beth and then it was the last thing he remembered.

Zane opened his eyes and saw Beth sitting beside him in a chair. He thought he must have been dreaming. He didn't say anything, just looked at his beautiful wife.

Rachel came through the door and saw Zane's eyes were open. "You're awake!" She said.

Startled Beth turned her head and saw Zane was looking at her. "Oh Zane, you are a wake!"

Zane closed his eyes and tried to concentrate. Where was he? What was he doing? Had he just been asleep, he didn't recognize the room he was in?

He opened his eyes again and both Beth and Rachel were standing over him.

"What the hell is going on?" He didn't know if he said it or if he imagined he said it. He struggled to sit up. He had a terrible pain in his side.

Another person appeared with Beth and Rachel. He could see their mouths moving but he wasn't hearing what they said. There was a roaring sound in his ears. The man with Beth and Rachel pushed him back down on the bed and the roaring sound in his ears stopped.

"You're all right, just take it easy." Zane could hear the man's voice as the roaring in his ears stopped. Zane had shut his eyes but he opened them again and he could see Rachel and Beth were still there. They had stepped back and the man whose voice he could hear was listening to his chest with a stethoscope. Zane knew he must be a doctor but he still didn't remember how he got there. Was he sick?

"Sounds good." The doctor said. Zane looked at Beth. Her eyes were wide and she looked at him as if she were frightened.

"Why am I here?" Zane struggled to speak. He still looked at Beth.

"You don't remember?" Beth said. She carefully put her hand on his face. The man with the stethoscope had disappeared. Zane struggled to clear the fuzzy images in his head. He saw Beth and he knew Rachel was there but he no longer saw her. Where was the man? He felt Beth's cool hand on his face. He was so tired, he tried to open his eyes but he felt Beth's hand on his face, it felt reassuring and Zane slept.

The next time he awakened Zane remembered. He remembered sitting on the ridge with Jody's head in his lap. He remembered everything that happened that day in the glade. The tears slipped down his face. Beth was beside him; she was trying to comfort him. The pain in his side no longer hurt. The pain in his heart was unbearable.

"Jody?" Zane asked looking at Beth.

Beth shook her head, "He didn't make it Zane."

"I killed him." The tears still slid down Zane's face.

"No, you didn't. Jody killed himself." Beth said gently and bent over and laid her head on Zane's chest. Zane lifted his hand and felt her soft silky hair.

"Do you remember everything?" Beth asked softly.

"Yes." Zane said and held her head on his chest.

"How is the baby?" He asked.

"We are fine, and you will be also." She said softly.

Zane was a week in the hospital. The Sheriff came and talked with him. They had gotten the story from Clyde Baker and the Sheriff told Zane he just needed his version to collaborate what Baker had told them.

"I don't suppose, there is some way this could go down in the record as a hunting accident?

Zane asked.

"No," Sheriff Anderson said.

"I was just thinking of Jody's family." Zane said.

"Jody's brother told us Jody had been saying he hated you for about three years. He told them you were going to get the Lodge handed to you when he was the one that deserved it. Apparently he knew a long time ago Jack planned on you taking over the lodge. Jody's brother didn't know Jody was trying to kill you though."

"He intended to kill me the day George Belmont died. I should have known sooner it was Jody. I knew it was when that bullet hit me in the side that last day. I knew it when I went over to him." Zane told the sheriff.

"Clyde Baker told us about you making your way over there to the gunmen. Don't know how you were able to do that as badly as you were wounded."

"I had hoped I could do something to help him. I knew, when I shot him, with Bakers Rifle, it was bad. I also knew it was Jody. I should have figured it out when George Belmont got killed but I didn't know Jack and Annie planned for me to take over the lodge until a couple weeks ago."

"You didn't have that much of a target, at that range. You couldn't have just wounded him, you're lucky you got him."

"I don't feel lucky. I wish I could have helped him when I got over to him." Zane said sadly.

"Well Adams, I guess you can quit looking over your shoulder now, we know now who was gunning for you."

"Yeah, I said at the time it had to be hatred or greed. I didn't know anyone felt that about me. Now I know poor Jody was feeling both."

"Yeah, that brother of his, said he was livid when he found out about your wife being rich."

"Yeah, but I didn't have any rich wife when George Belmont died. The strange part is that if not for George Belmont, I would never have even met my wife. It seems that Jody must have been mentally ill. I worked with him for years and at one time we were very close. I will never think of him badly, something went wrong in his head and that wouldn't have been the Jody I intend to remember."

Sheriff Anderson looked at Zane Adam's with admiration. He was a tough bastard, but the Sheriff couldn't believe he had compassion for the man that tried to kill him.

Zane went home after ten days in the hospital. Jack Cutler had closed the Lodge for the remainder of the season. He was out of Guides with Jody dead and Zane in the hospital. Jack intended to come back next year with Zane and Beth as proprietors and help them through their first season. Next year Beth would need help, as there would be a new Adams in the family.

Once home Zane was strangely quiet. He was still trying to reconcile what had happened. Zane didn't say it to Beth but he kept thinking if Jody, his friend was capable of killing him over his greed for the lodge, what was some stranger capable of over Beth's wealth. For the first time Zane began to seriously wonder how much danger his family and his coming child could be in from the greed of strangers out in the world?

How could he hope to protect them? Zane knew he was being paranoid but he didn't know what to do about it. For the first time Zane mentioned to Beth they should get a guard at the gate.

Zane no longer thought the remote controls and the access, code on the gate was sufficient to protect them. As much as Zane hated it they were going to have to spend Beth's money for more security. Beth agreed and they began to build a guard's house down at the gate.

Beth contacted her security people back east and told them to find men who would qualify to man the small house being constructed to guard the gate at the Adams farm.

One thing Zane and Beth were both happy about was Beth's morning sickness had subsided and the pregnancy was going well. When Zane came home from the hospital he was still sore from his wound. He was able to get up and down the stairs but the cattle were coming in and Zane didn't want Beth out helping Rachel feed. He bitched about it and asked Rachel to find someone to hire to help until Zane could get around enough to handle the bales and climb the loft.

Nobody could be found so Chuck came and stayed and he and Rachel took care of the cattle before going to open the store. Zane grinned and said, "I guess we are a couple of invalids and are going to have to depend on the old folks to take care of things."

"There is nothing wrong with me except I'm pregnant! I could help feed."

"You shouldn't be climbing the loft. What if you fell?" Zane said.

"I won't climb the loft but I can take care of the Bay's and the henhouse. I can help Chuck and Rachel and they can get done sooner." Beth felt Zane was looking for trouble where there was none. She had noticed when he came home from the hospital he seemed to be more paranoid about things. She had gone along with him on the guards at the gate but she had long thought they needed more security.

Lying around the house was also not helping Zane get over what had happened. He had too much time to think about it.

The first snow fell at the ranch by Halloween. It was early this year. It melted in a few days but about the tenth on November it began to snow and didn't stop for a week. It finally stopped shortly before Thanksgiving and there were also about four heads of cows and calves that had never come in. Zane knew nobody but him would be able to ride the Bays across the canyon and look for them. He was out in the barn one morning saddling Sonny to go look for the cows when Chuck and Rachel were getting ready to feed.

"You are not going by yourself Zane." Rachel said with exasperation.

"Why in the hell not. It isn't going to hurt anything. It's been over a month and I'm able to do anything except heavy lifting. I don't need to lift to get on this damned horse." Zane had already heard all this from Beth when he got up early and told her, he was going.

Rachel gave up as Zane led the horse out. She noticed he had his side arm on. He got up in the saddle and rode down around the field and through the canyon gate and out of sight. Rachel looked at Chuck and shook her head.

Sonny, slipped a bit in the snow as his shoes got packed with snow but other than that it was not bothering Zane to ride. At least Zane knew he had done the right thing when he shoed the horses after the bow season when he and Beth had come home for the ten days.

Zane noticed some wolf tracks not far below the Ranch. He felt alarmed they were that close. He had known there was a pack working the canyon since he had found the remains of the spotted ass cow and her calf. He and Beth had also seen tracks when they brought the four head, from across the year before. This was the first time Zane had seen tracks right below the Ranch.

Rachel had seen the three in the hay field the summer before the wolves got the spotted cow.

Zane didn't run onto any cow tracks on this side of the canyon. He rode down and across the creek. The action of riding was beginning to make his wounded side hurt some by the time he crossed the creek. Maggie was beginning to fall back behind the horse so she could travel in the horse tracks and she would not have to break trail, in the snow, which was up to her belly. Zane finally found cow tracks in the old homestead. But it was only one cow and her calf. He had a feeling it was bad news that the other cow and calf weren't together. He and Maggie took the cow and calf and headed them down to the creek and home.

As the pain Zane's side worsened he began to wonder if Rachel had been right. He could have waited for Matt to go with him over the Thanksgiving holiday. Zane and Maggie got the cow and calf back to the ranch but Zane wasn't certain the way his side hurt if he could dismount. Beth put on her coat and came out when she heard him out by the barn. Zane had not yet gotten off the horse. Beth could see he looked as if he was in pain.

"What's going on Zane?" She asked anxiously

"Just a stitch in my side." He said and started to dismount. He damned near fell to the ground but held onto the saddle and kept his feet under him. He was walking gingerly as he led Sonny into the barn and began to unsaddle him.

Beth could tell Zane was in pain and she helped him rub the horse down after the saddle was put up. Beth got Sonny his grain. She didn't say anything to Zane but she could see he was hurting. She knew him well enough that he would not let on if something was wrong. She took his hand and they went to the house. Zane was walking gingerly.

Beth asked if she could do anything to help. He grimaced and went into the house and sprawled on the sofa with a groan.

"Should I call the Doctor?" She asked feeling his forehead to see if he had a fever.

"No, just some hot tea. Thank you Beth?

"For what?"

"For not saying I told you so!" Zane grinned weakly.

Beth smiled and went to get his tea and a couple of the pain pills he had from the doctor when he came home from the Hospital. She brought the tea and handed him the pain pills without comment. He took them gratefully. In about twenty minutes he was asleep on the sofa. He still had the pistol strapped on his side. Beth couldn't get the holster off him so she took the gun out and laid it on the coffee table.

Zane slept peacefully for about two hours and then he began to awaken, the pain pills were wearing off. He got up and went in the downstairs bath and Beth heard the bathtub running. She went up and got him some clean underwear and a pair of sweat pants.

When Zane took his clothes off to get in the tub Beth could see the wound on his side looked red and irritated. It also was swollen a bit. She helped him without saying anything and he got into the tub. He groaned as he settled down and let the jets on the tub work. Beth heart ached as she looked at the ugly scar on his left side and the one on his chest and shoulder.

Jody Miller's attempts to kill her beloved husband had left some nasty reminders behind on his body.

15

After the Thanksgiving holiday Zane began to take over the feeding. He was a bit laid up a few days after the ride but when the soreness went out he began to get his strength back.

Neither Beth nor Rachel said anything to Zane about his ill-advised trip across the canyon. They knew Zane well enough it would be of no value to say anything to him. Zane's frame of mind improved after that ordeal. He knew he had pushed himself too soon but he also felt he could once again take care of things if he needed to. He would go back after Christmas and look for the remains of the missing cow and calf. Zane feared the Wolves had got them more than likely.

By Christmas the guards were at the gate. Once the guards were on duty, the gate was left open. That became a relief to Rachel who went almost daily to the store with Chuck. It had been over a year since Mabel passed away. Rachel and Chuck talked about marriage. Rachel was dragging her feet. She had been Rachel Adams for many years and she was reluctant to change that. It wasn't that she didn't love Chuck it was she was happy as things were.

Beth was beginning to look very pregnant. She was nearly five months and the baby was moving inside of her. She still had not lost her sexual appetite for Zane. She seemed to feel their making love joined the three of them together. Zane had finally recovered enough but the wound on his left side remained tender to touch. He had not been back to his doctor since before the horseback ride into the canyon and Beth thought he should go back and find out why the wound was still tender to touch. Zane didn't think it was important. It would go away in time.

Zane began to keep busy with the cows. Beth still went to help him feed. He just wouldn't let her climb the loft up in the big barn. Beth had the best boots she could buy for traction on the snow and ice. She was bound and determined to be with Zane when he fed the cows. Maggie also was always there to help.

Zane went with Beth to her Doctors' appointments but he still refused to go back to his Doctor to see about the soreness that persisted around the wound.

Zane and Beth stopped one day at Pete's Bar. When Pete saw Zane's wife was pregnant, he realized why he had seen little of Zane since the shooting. Zane had a beer and Beth had a soda.

They still drove the Chevy truck Zane had always had. Zane was thinner and looked as if he were tired. From what Pete had been told it was a miracle that Zane still was alive. Everyone had heard how Zane crossed the two ravines to get to Jody Miller and try to help save him. It was a feat no body could believe. To Zane it was no big deal but a hurtful aching memory of what happened that day.

Pete had heard about the guardhouse at the Adams gate but he didn't mention it to Zane. Pete did ask when they expected the baby and Beth told him about the first of May. Beth was beaming. She was a beautiful woman anyhow but she definitely shined when pregnant. With Beth's height she did not look as pregnant as some women that were smaller that may have when that far along. Pete reflected to himself that Adams was going to have some tall children. Pete also reflected back to the day Zane had knocked Punk out through the window. He had never seen anybody pack a punch like Zane Adams. It didn't surprise Pete when he heard about Zane's attempt to save his intended killer. Pete had never known a man with Zane Adams strength.

The Prosecutors' office had dropped charges against Gina Daniels and Pete had heard that Gina was over at Moscow taking classes at the university. He wondered, remembering Beth and Gina's conversation that day, if Beth Adam's had anything to do with helping Gina. He had heard Gina was getting help from somebody. Pete had a feeling that somebody was Zane's wife.

Zane told Pete he was missing a couple heads of livestock and was afraid the Wolves got them.

Pete said he didn't know there were any in the canyon behind the Adams farm.

"Yeah, I found a cow and calf, wolf killed two years ago. Mom saw three in the field behind the house the summer before that"

"Jesus, I thought they were to get it on the Idaho election ballot. What happened to that?" Pete wondered. He had not seen anything on the ballot even though Pete had expected it after the petitions were circulated.

"Guess half the signatures on the petition weren't registered voters." Zane said.

"Yeah, well nobody a resident of Idaho wanted the wolves brought back, we should have been asked before they did it!" Pete voiced his opinion with disgust. Zane had heard a lot of people say the same thing.

Zane drank two beers and him and Beth left. When they went out the door, Pete felt something about Zane Adam's had changed. He still had that engaging smile, but there was something sad and different about him. The Jody Miller incident had taken the boyishness out of Zane Adams.

January was a snowy gray dismal month. Beth still went out with Zane to do the chores. They were now beginning to get calves. Zane had to fight to save a little one as he did the first one Beth, helped him work on the first winter she was there. Beth now knew how to help him

February the icy grip on winter let up some and there were days of some sunshine and the snow banks and ice began to give way to mud.

It was shortly before Valentines Day, Zane and Beth were startled awake by the blood-curdling howl of a wolf right at the area of the Barn.

Zane scrambled into his pants and grabbed his pistol and raced down the stairs. He grabbed a powerful beam flashlight and slipped into his boots and ran out into the night, bare chested.

Beth got her boots on and in her robe she also went out to see. Beth could hear Zane calling for Maggie. She could also hear the cattle bawling. By the time Beth came out Zane had turned on the barn lights. She went into the barn and Zane had Maggie lying on the barn floor in the hay. She whimpered and looked at Zane with sad eyes and hope that her master could help her.

Zane had blood all over his chest where he had cradled her in his arms to pack her in. Zane had tears in his eyes. He knew there was nothing could be done for Maggie, her artery had been torn in her throat. She died as Beth came into the barn.

"Oh no, Zane" Beth cried.

"Stay here", Zane said and with the flashlight and his pistol he went back out into the night. Beth knelt down and stroked Maggie's wet fur. Beth wondered how they would do without her.

Zane came back and said. "They got one of the calves also, dragged it through the fence away from the cattle.

Zane picked Maggie up and laid her in the calf pen stall. "I'll bury her in the morning. Come Beth you will get chilled out here."

Beth thought it was an odd thing to say as Zane was without a shirt and had nothing on his chest but Maggie's blood where he had hugged her to him to carry her to the barn.

Sadly Zane and Beth went back to the house. Zane washed Maggie's blood off and then he put on his shirt and coat.

"Where are you going?" Beth asked.

"I need to get the calf carcass in before the wolves come back for it. It is proof of what happened. After that I'm getting the rifle and wait for the son of Bitches to come back."

Zane went back out into the night. In a short time he came to the house and took a rifle with a telescope, out of the gun case.

He hunted up another high beam flashlight.

"How do you know if they will return?" Beth asked.

"They will come back for their kill and the cattle will let me know when they are here" Zane said his lips thin and his jaw set hard with anger. He went back out in the darkness to wait.

Beth made some coffee and sat down at the table. In about forty-five minutes she heard the rifle crack, not once but three times in rapid succession. Then she heard the cattle bawling again.

In about ten minutes Zane came in and put the rifle back in the case.

"Did you get any of them?" Beth asked.

"Two, both adults." Zane said but there was no satisfaction in his voice. "Two for Maggie."

"What are you going to do with them?" Beth asked. She had heard how the wolf vigilantes had buried them to conceal them.

"I'm going to leave the son of a bitch, lay so no more wolves will come in around that fence." Zane took off his coat, poured himself a cup of coffee and sat down with Beth. Beth had never seen him with such a hard look in his eyes.

The next morning Zane had to feed without his faithful helper. The cows crowded the feedlot gate and Zane had to get out and hurry to get the truck through after he ran the cattle back. The Cattle also crowded the truck loaded with feed. Beth offered to shoo them away but Zane told her to stay in the truck. He thought he could not stand another tragedy.

After they had done the feeding, Zane dug a grave for Maggie in the orchard where her grave would not be disturbed. He asked Beth to find something to wrap her in. Beth took a soft polar fleece blanker from the bedroom.

"You couldn't find anything older?" Zane asked.

"It's of no consequences, I can always buy another, but we can't ever have another, Maggie." Beth said tearfully.

Zane wrapped Maggie tenderly in the soft blanket and laid her in the hole he had dug and covered her up. Zane's lips shook at his pain of losing his faithful helper and Beth wept openly.

Beth and Zane went to the house.

Thumper was sitting on the porch and Beth stopped to pet him. He looked around as if he expected Maggie to be there to chase him any moment.

Zane went on into the kitchen. He was sipping coffee when Beth comes in from petting Thumper. He was in a morose mood. Beth put her arms around his neck and Zane pulled her onto his lap and buried his face in the fragrance of her hair. At six and a half month Beth's baby stomach was beginning to be sizable and the Baby could be felt moving within her. The baby kicked Zane as he held her on his lap. He smiled and Beth kissed him softly and got up to go take a shower.

When Rachel and Chuck came to check on Beth and Zane, she was saddened to hear they had lost Maggie. Outside of the joy of Beth's pregnancy it had been a tough year for Zane. He still had tenderness in the wound on his side and still refused to see his doctor about it. Rachel tried to get him to go see about it, as did Beth, but Zane just said it would go away.

Shortly after the Wolves killed Maggie Zane began to wake during the night drenched in sweat. The first time it happened Beth thought he had dreamed about the wolves. His curly hair was soaked as was the bedding. Beth changed the bedding and Zane took a shower and went back to bed. A week later it occurred again. Beth had noticed Zane was groaning in his sleep before the sweats occurred.

By the first of March the signs of spring began to appear. Zane was still having the sweats and Beth was still trying to get him to see a doctor. In desperation Beth spoke to her Doctor about Zane's symptoms. He asked Beth if Zane was having a fever?

Beth didn't know but the next time she heard Zane groaning in his sleep she awakened him and took his temperature. It was 102 degrees. Shortly after he began to sweat, and this time he wasn't asleep but awake. Once the sweat stopped and he showered Beth checked his fever and it was back down to 100. Obviously something was going on and it was more than a dream about the wolves and Maggie.

Beth made an appointment for Zane to see his doctor the middle of March. "You are going!"

Beth made it clear she would not let him delay it.

Zane's trip to his Doctor revealed he had an infection on the inside, of his wound. When his whites count, come back on his blood test the doctor growled at him he was lucky it had not become gangrene. It explained why he had not gained back his weight. It also explained the night sweats and fever. The doctor put him on some strong antibiotics and said if that treatment didn't work he would need to get a drain tube in the wound area to drain the infection.

The antibiotics worked, and Zane began to feel better. Beth was getting close to her delivery date. By the first of April she was a month away and she began to go weekly to her doctor.

Zane had made up his mind; he was going to eliminate the wolves from the canyon behind the Adams ranch. With Beth's due date closing he had to wait but he intended after they had the baby to hunt Maggie's killers to extinction within the canyon.

April 25 Beth and Zane had their baby boy. He weighed in a hefty eight and a half pound. They named him Tyler Douglas Adams after Beth's father. Her fathers name was Douglas and Beth and Zane both liked Tyler or Ty as he would be nick named.

Needless to say Ty Adams had everything a baby could need. Zane and Beth were thrilled. Rachel took time off from the store to help Beth. Beth had mentioned hiring someone but Rachel wouldn't hear of it. She would take time to spoil her new grandson herself.

Chuck didn't mind. He put in some extra hours but he followed the proud Grandma to the Ranch to spend the night. He didn't mind that he and Rachel were often the ones up with Ty for the night feedings.

Rachel and Beth got the family vegetable garden in during the month of May. With Zane home and Rachel spending as much time as she could help, things were getting done even with the new baby.

After Ty was born Zane began to spend a lot of time on Sonny riding the canyon. He left early and came home late. Beth noticed he was taking his rifle and wearing his pistol. When she asked what, he was looking for, he said, "The remains of the missing cow and calf."

He wasn't lying to Beth because he was looking for the bones and ear tags of the missing cows. He did not tell Beth he was after Maggie's killers but she guessed and knew Zane did not want to discuss with her or even mention it. Like a man on a mission Zane hunted down and eliminated four adult wolves, and three fall pups. One of the adult females was suckling some pups and even Zane in his anger could not leave the pups to starve. He hunted the den and killed the pups.

He did not quit until he was certain there were no wolves left in the canyon. He also found the bones and ear tags of the missing cattle.

Done by June with his quest to eliminate the wolves and having turned the cattle out on pasture, Zane settled down at peace to enjoy his son and wife. Beth and Zane were as much in love as ever and they had resumed their sex life interrupted occasionally by the demands of baby Ty.

Zane began to work on the haying equipment. Beth had found and purchased a young Australian Shepard dog that was started on cattle. She got him from a breeder at Kendrick that had a reputation for good cattle dogs. They called him Bowser, and Zane, looked him in the eyes and decided Bowser was intelligent and would be satisfactory.

Beth also bought a black and white six week old, a ball of fur they called Missy. She was a purebred border collie. It was hoped since she came from working parents she would have natural instincts for cattle. Whatever Missy was to be, it was already apparent she was adorable.

Bowser seemed to like her also. But they would need to get her spaded before she was six months or so or the Adams ranch would have a litter of Missy Bowser pups!

Matt, Susie and the boys came over the fourth of July and with Rachel and Chuck at the ranch they again put the hay in. This year, Matt's two boys were also getting big enough to help. When finished Rachel babysat and Matt, Beth, Susie, and Zane went to Pete's Bar to celebrate. Hopefully the past year of disasters had come to an end.

Things were as they had always been on the Adams Ranch except for the guards and the little house they manned at the gate. Nobody got through the gate without approval from the house or was recognized as safe by the guards.

Jack and Annie found this out when they tried to visit Beth and Zane after their baby was born. Zane straightened out the guys at the gate about Annie and Jack Cutler when Jack called on the phone a few days after they had been turned away at the gate. It seemed everyone was gone that day at the Adams Ranch. Jack and Annie made a return visit. They got to see Tyler Adams and Beth and Zane. Zane had returned to his former health after they healed up the infection in his wound. He had also found some peace of mind when he avenged Maggie's killers and he was as much in love with his wife and son as a man could be. Jack and Annie were glad to see Zane seemed to be his old self.

Annie had put together a book of recipes for the lodge and she brought it for Beth to look over.

Jack and Annie both intended to be at the Lodge to help Zane and Beth their first year. During their visit Jack and Zane discussed the wolf problem. Beth told them they had a bunch of wolves in the canyon and they had killed their dog and a calf.

"Had" Zane said, and looked at Jack and smiled. He said nothing further and he didn't need to. Jack knew exactly what Zane meant when he said, "Had!"

Jack knew Zane had superior tracking and hunting skills. If Zane had been on a quest to eliminate the Wolves from the canyon behind his house, Jack would bet money they were gone!

The Cutler's stayed and had dinner with Beth and Zane. Jack mentioned to Zane they would have to begin to look for another guide. Jack thought they should run an ad now to see if they could line someone out for a bow season. It was only about six weeks away.

Zane talked with Beth and Rachel that he wanted to talk with Matt. Matt already would one day have an interest in the Adams Ranch. Zane wondered if Matt would consider a partnership in the Ranch herd and also the Guide business?

Rachel was thrilled that her two sons would be working together. They would need an additional living place on the ranch. Zane pointed out Jason and Levi was getting to be teenagers and would be a great deal of help. Beth would have to put up the money to put another home at the Adams ranch but there were three hundred acres and room for Matt and Susie to build wherever they wanted.

Zane and Beth drove to Matt and Susie's home one weekend and Zane asked Matt if he was interested.

Matt was not only interested but also thrilled. He told Zane he did not relish the idea of working in the sawmill the rest of his life. When Zane suggested Beth would front the money for them to build, Matt said they could repay her for some when they sold their house.

Matt and Susie by then both knew Beth had set up trust college funds for Levi and Jason. They were thankful for that gesture on her part. They also had a sneaking suspicion Beth had a hand in their getting financing on their house. Matt, had no idea, the extent of Beth's fortune but when the story broke after Zane and Beth's marriage they knew her wealth was sizable. The guardhouses, on the gate were also an indication she was more than merely rich.

Matt was not as good as Zane with the game calls but he was an accomplished hunter and with help from Zane he could also learn the calls. Zane wasn't offering Matt a job but he was offering a partnership. Matt could not afford to work three months as a guide and support his family.

A partnership in the cattle would help but Zane and Matt also talked of increasing the herd. Zane didn't yet have the books on the Guide business but he knew it was lucrative business and he was certain there would be money enough for both families especially since they would not have payroll expenses with a partnership. Zane had discussed it with Jack Cutler and Jack told Zane it was however Zane wished to do it. They would pay a rent to Jack for the lodge and that was all he and Annie expected.

With that plan they did not advertise for an additional guide. Zane reflected he would not have to watch his back with his brother as partner.

Susie Adam's had never held a job but she was a good housekeeper and cook. She had experience as a housewife and she would be valuable at the lodge to help Beth who didn't have so much experience cooking but brought knowledge of business management to the team.

Both families would have to rely on Rachel to hold down the farm during the hunting season. Zane figured to expand the spring bear hunt and that could be done behind the Adams ranch and they would not need to open the Lodge for that.

The first thing to be done was for Matt and Susie to pick a place to build. They moved quickly, on that decision, and picked a spot up the road from the ranch gate. Neither Matt nor Susie felt the need to live behind the guard gate.

They chose a manufactured, home and the foundation, septic, and well were being done in August. The house it's self would be installed within days after the site was prepared. Beth told them they could custom builds, but both Matt and Susie were happy with the manufactured home they chose.

Matt went to the Lodge the last of August with Beth and Zane. Ty also went but Levi and Jason stayed at the ranch with Rachel to start school and Susie was at their old house packing up for their move to the Adams Ranch once their home was ready to be occupied.

It was middle September before the home was placed and Susie and the boys began to move furniture. Matt was at the Lodge with Zane.

Beth was learning a great deal from Annie. The Lodge had a relaxed feeling this year. Zane was no longer fearful of who could be gunning for him and he was comfortable with Matt and him guiding. Matt was picking up fast on what he needed to learn. Matt was also good with the Hunter's coming in. Matt was perhaps more social able and comfortable with strangers than Zane.

Jack, had opened up his books, and Zane and Matt, were both surprised at the money to be made. The Guide business was a most lucrative business and barring the extinction of the elk herds had a promising future.

Zane had become a secret vigilante and he knew his future hinged on no one knowing. Not even his wife. Zane would take no chance he would be caught. He kept a close eye on the canyon behind the ranch in case a pair of wolves came into the area. He would best be able to patrol the canyon ground when the snow came and they were done at the Lodge.

The Bow seasons in the past two years went well and Matt was doing a much better job than Jody. He had to learn the area but his ability to get along and work well with Zane made it easy for him to quickly pick up the business. He also was better at the call; he also had to listen to Zane blowing on the damned things since Zane was just a child. Although Zane had driven his mother to the brink of insanity, Matt had picked up the way they were supposed to sound. And it did not take him long to get onto it and the way they were to sound. Something he had more trouble with was the reed that imitated the cow call and the calf chirps.

Matt practiced with the things in his mouth until he about gagged. Zane laughed and told him, more practice. While the Bull calls were effective during the rut, once they moved into rifle seasons past the rut the cow calls would be needed.

Under Annie's capable hands Beth was learning how to cook for the Lodge. Beth was grateful that Annie and Jack had come to help, Adam's family through their first season. Jack also liked Matt and found he was as easy to get along with as his brother. Matt was also energetic and quick to see things that needed to be done.

Matt was particularly good at any maintenance needed at the lodge. Matt was definitely a better handyman than Zane. Zane excelled in the Forest with the hunters, tracking and locating and calling the Elk!

All and all the Adams brothers were a good combination that Jack was well pleased with.

At the ranch Susie was getting things in order. Rachel helped as much as she could. The Adams boys, Levi and Jason were settled in their new school. Beth had withdrawn the winter before as a substitute when she was pregnant with Ty.

Ty was happily in the mountains at the Lodge with his parents. He was beginning to sit and play in his playpen. He put up a howl every time he saw his Daddy and Zane always picked him up and spoiled him. Zane was crazy about his baby boy. Beth smiled with indulgence but she suffered the consequences of Zane spoiling him rotten. Ty soon caught on to the fact his howling didn't work as well on his mother as it did on his Daddy.

Beth's business advisors in Detroit were having a fit that she refused to make her annual trip to the city to sign and tend to the part of her business only she could handle. Beth was adamant if they needed her signature they send a notary and any legal advisors needed. She was not going to Detroit! She sold the Penthouse and the sales from that were immediately transferred into the charitable Foundation she had set up in Idaho. With the help of some savvy tax attorneys she also established other trust and foundations getting much of her fortune off the internal revenue grab.

It became obvious to Beth that the Lodge was going to be a profitable enterprise. She knew the deficit on the ranching operation and the split in the income with Matt would take care of the Profits to be gained at the Lodge. Still it was important to keep track of each, expenditure and they hired an accountant to handle both the Ranch and Lodge and set up an incorporation between Matt and Zane. Beth and Susie were also members of that enterprise and all four were the board of directors.

Zane chuckled when they did it, because he knew by his trips to Detroit what a real business was. Beth told him not to laugh it was important to be savvy about taxes and investments and expenditures no matter what the size of a business. And of coarse she was correct, her years of college had stood her in good stead for business acumen

The rifle season at the lodge was better than expected. The ratio of Bulls taken was higher not because the Bulls were increasing and the wolves were less but because neither Matt nor Zane was afraid to go into the brushy holes and basins after them.

They closed up the Lodge the 20th of November and headed down to the Adams ranch to feed cows. They had a big party the last day and celebrated the successful season and the last year they would have Annie and Jack Cutler to guide them.

"You know where to find us when you need to." Jack laughed." Unless Annie and I are on a trip or fishing!"

16

Rachel Adams planned a special Thanksgiving this year. Her son's were both living on the ranch. She had a new grandson and her other two were just next-door. The mystery of who was after Zane was behind them. Beth seemed to have handled the notoriety about her wealth. Things could not have been going better than they were.

Rachel and Chuck were settled into a satisfying relationship. She had love in her personal life and a kind, gentle handsome man in her bed. Life was great. There was plenty of reason for a special Thanksgiving in the Adams house.

Winter had also held off and the cattle that had come home grazed in the hay field. Rachel and Chuck had not yet needed to feed much when Matt, Zane, Beth and Ty came moving down from the Lodge.

Zane and Matt had both come home from the Lodge with a sizable sum of money saved from the hunting season. Jack had refused to take any more than Rent for the Lodge. Even though he and Annie had worked the entire season with the brothers.

Matt knew him and Susie didn't have the romance in their marriage they had once had. He did not give it much thought. He was too busy trying to make a living and although he and Susie never fought it seemed they never made love much anymore.

Once in a while Matt would coax Susie into it but it didn't seem she enjoyed it and it became a occasional desperate release for Matt only. Matt didn't know but he wondered if that was the way all marriages became after time. He knew there was little use in speaking to Zane about it because Zane and Beth could hardly keep their hands off each other. They had only been together for three years and obviously the relationship was nowhere near stale.

Matt never dreamed that Susie could be having an affair. After they moved to the Ranch, it seemed Susie was finding reasons to be gone. Matt knew she had friends in the town they had lived but she was gone all the time, or so it seemed.

They all gathered for Thanksgiving dinner at the Ranch house. Rachel had the girls set the good dishes at the dining room table. She and Beth had baked the day before. Beth noticed that Susie was unusually quiet. Beth and Rachel had planned on their early morning shopping trip the day after Thanksgiving. Zane was going to watch Ty and Beth urged Susie to join them. Rachel also thought it would be great fun, but Susie declined. She made some excuse that she had already made plans with another friend.

Zane and Matt had planned to sell calves around the first of December. They had agreed to split the calf crop this year because of all the years Matt had helped Zane brand and put up hay he had never taken anything for his help except for some beef when they occasionally butchered one.

Beth worried that maybe Susie felt she didn't have enough money to be able to go with them. She mentioned it to Zane and he assured her they had more money than they had ever had when Matt worked at the mill. His share from the lodge equaled about ten months of wages Matt had earned at the mill. Zane was certain it wasn't a money problem. Zane had for some time felt Matt wasn't happy with the way he and Susie's relationship was going. Zane didn't know what the problem was. Only that he felt there was one.

Zane thought about bringing it up but he was afraid Matt would think he was sticking his nose in his business. Since Matt was now his business partner, Zane was reluctant to get into his personal business.

Zane had brought it up to Rachel. She was thoughtful when he mentioned it and she said she thought what was wrong had to do somehow with Susie. Rachel said she didn't know what was the matter? She said she hoped it would work out when they moved but Susie was spending a lot of time away from home. With Levi and Jason old enough to be left alone it was easy for Susie to come and go as she wanted.

Rachel and Beth went to Lewiston and spent the day shopping, dining out and enjoying themselves. When they arrived home late, Beth found Zane had fed Ty and he was down for the night. Beth went in and took a shower, when she came out Zane was lying on the bed waiting. He had that hungry look in his eyes as he looked at her. Beth had not yet put on her nightgown. She went to Zane and he pulled her naked body to him. He had been thinking of her all day.

Zane could always make Beth's blood boil. After they made love Beth lay in his arms.

"Is it this way for everyone?" She asked suddenly.

"What do you mean, is it this way for everyone?" Zane grinned, not sure what Beth wanted to know.

"You've been with other woman, was it this way? I mean, was it satisfying. Zane, you make me feel like the most loved woman in the world. I was wondering if it was that way with other people."

"I've never been with anyone that makes me feel the way you do Beth. Sex is sex and although it can be satisfying, I think we have something special between us. I think that something special is love and I've never felt that with anyone else."

"I was wondering as I had a brief experience with a boy who took me to the prom and I drank too much alcohol but I don't remember that. I had never wanted to be with anyone until you. Do you think Matt and Susie feel about each other the way we do?"

"I don't know Beth. I just know how we feel together. I hope other people feel as we do but I don't have any way of knowing."

"What about Chuck and your mother. Do you think when we get older we will still feel this way?"

"Oh God," Zane laughed. "Please don't ask me about my mother's sex life. I don't have a clue and I really don't want to think about it."

"Well, as happy as Rachel, is there must be something between her and Chuck that makes her happy?" Beth pointed out.

"Yeah, well I don't want to discuss it or even think about it!" Zane shook his head and Beth could see her conversation about his mother's possible sex life was making Zane very uncomfortable. She decided to drop it. One thing she knew is that she never grew tired of being with Zane. He always made sure she was feeling satisfied first. If she was tired, he seemed to sense it and very rarely, she was not in the mood and he always seemed to sense that also. Beth thought her husband was the most capable lover in the world and she never thought of being with anyone else. She never had any reason to, she was a very satisfied, woman, with the man she was married to and deeply in love with.

The next morning Zane went down the stairs fixed coffee and went out to feed. He warmed the truck and waited for Matt to show up.

Beth cuddled in their warm bed and waited to see if Ty was going to want a bottle. She missed feeding this year with Zane but he seemed happy to have Matt helping him. Rachel was not yet up, their shopping had tired her yesterday and Beth thought it would do her good to sleep in a bit. Chuck had not been at the house when they got back but Beth had heard Rachel on the phone with him. She heard Rachel tell him Goodnight and she would see him tomorrow.

Zane waited, the truck was warmed and he was just getting ready to start loading without him when Matt showed up.

"Sleep late this morning?" Zane asked, as he was about to go in and climb the loft.

"No, didn't get any sleep at all. It seems my wife wants to leave me."

Zane froze, as he was about to open the barn door. "You want to come in a minute and talk?"

Matt walked over and they both went in the barn. The Bays came tromping in for their grain.

Zane gives them their grain. "What seems to be the problem? Did she say?"

"Not exactly, it all seems like a bunch of googol gunk. It is this excuse and that excuse. I don't think she is giving me the real reason she wants to leave. She just say's she's unhappy! Hell I've known that for some time. I think there is more to it."

"Yeah, I've felt for some time you and Susie weren't on the same track. Is there someone else?"

Matt looked startled as if it had not occurred to him. "I don't know. Let's get these cows fed."

Matt went back out and got on the truck. Zane climbed the loft and began pushing the hay out through the loft door."

Once they fed, Zane suggested they have some breakfast. He also suggested they saddle the Bays and go for a ride in the canyon. He had been anxious to see if he could find any wolf tracks. All of the cattle had come in this year but Zane wanted to keep an eye on it and he also wanted to spend time with Matt. It was obvious Matt wanted to talk.

After they fed, the two brothers went to the house. Rachel was up as well as Beth. Rachel was cooking breakfast. As she saw Matt come in, she asked him if she should fix an extra egg?

"Sure, Zane and I are going in the canyon." He said taking off his coat and going down the hall to wash. Zane washed at the kitchen sink.

Beth was feeding Ty some baby cereal. He grinned at his Daddy and cereal came squishing back out of his mouth. He banged his hands on the high chair to get Zane's attention.

Zane washed his hands, kissed Beth and poked his finger at Ty and sat down at the table. Rachel gave him a cup of coffee. "Why you guys' going in the canyon?" Rachel asked. "All the cows are here?"

"Checking for Wolf tracks." Zane said. "Also it is a good day to go."

Matt came back and sat down with them to eat. Rachel thought he looked tired. "Susie gets her shopping done yesterday?" She asked.

"I suppose she did. I didn't ask." Matt replied, and since he didn't say anything else the conversation drifted to Rachel and Beth's trip to the city. As usual they had a great time. The car was still full of stuff.

"By the way," Beth said to Zane. "Let's go see about trading the car for one of those SUV's one of these first days. It would be easier to haul things to the Lodge and also we could get a four-wheel drive."

"Good idea, "Zane said.

When they finished breakfast Zane and Matt saddled the Bays and headed into the canyon. Zane had his side arm and rifle both. Matt didn't take a firearm. He had been thinking back on Zane's question about if there was someone else in his marriage problems.

After they rode down around the field and headed into the canyon Zane asked Matt, "What did Susie say exactly."

"That she was leaving. She needs time to be alone."

"What about the Boys?

"She talked like I could take care of them. She was very vague about what she felt our problems were."

"Well, Susie has never worked outside the home, I wonder how she intends to support herself if she leaves the boys with you? Zane said. It was apparent to Zane there could be someone else in the picture she was going to depend on to stay with and support her.

"Yeah, I think you may have hit the nail on the head! There must be someone else, she just hasn't admitted it and I think she hopes to hide the fact." Matt was beginning to get a clearer picture of his problems since Zane had pointed out a few things he had not thought of.

"You have been married since you got out of high school. I doubt, if you or Susie had any experience other than being married and with each other. It must be hard to spend fifteen years together and not pay much attention other than trying to raise the boys and make a living."

"Yeah, we've kind of been in a rut all right." Matt agreed. "Don't know what I can do about it now, though."

"I'm no expert on marriage either," Zane grinned. "But I do have a little more experience than you, my big brother, when it comes to different women. I spent a little more time out here playing the field before I met Beth so I might be inclined to give you some brotherly advice on chasing after women if it comes to that."

"Thanks," Matt said gloomily. "I think I will try to get Susie to delay making a move until after the holidays. It will ruin the holiday for the boys. I am going to try to keep it civil if at all possible."

"Yeah, I can't imagine anger would help the situation and it will only make it worse for Jason and Levi to live in a war zone." Zane said. They had ridden a couple hours and Zane had seen nothing but coyote and game tracks. He decided to turn back. He was certain he had eliminated the wolves but he would need to keep vigilant as the game moved down into the lower country for the winter. Often wolves followed the migrating game.

When Matt and Zane returned they rubbed the horses down and Matt left for his house. Zane did not say anything to Rachel or Beth about his conversation with Matt. It was after all Matt's decision to tell his mother when he decided to.

The Family gathered again at the Ranch for Christmas day. Matt's boys seemed happy and content. Susie and Matt had not let on there was trouble brewing in the marriage.

Matt had made an extra effort to make the time between Thanksgiving and Christmas a peaceful and non-combative atmosphere in their household. Susie agreed to stay until after the New year on the condition she and Matt would not discuss their problems.

Although Matt and Susie were still sharing the bed, Matt didn't make any demands on her and they coexisted until after the holidays. At Christmas Zane noticed Susie was more relaxed and friendly than she had been at Thanksgiving. He and Matt had not discussed the situation after the day they rode in the canyon.

After the first of the year, Susie packed and moved out. Matt tried to accept her decision and he tried to explain to the boy's what was going on. He told them him and Susie decided they needed some time apart.

Since Matt was at home and no longer working at the mill, he had plenty of time to spend with the boys. Rachel went to help him with his housework and cooking but Matt turned her down and said he could handle it himself.

After Susie had been gone a couple months, Matt asked Zane about those pointers for dating.

"Getting lonely, or just horny?" Zane laughed.

"Some of both." Matt growled.

"Not much choice around, very rarely does anything available shows up at Pete's." Zane told him. "You might have to look out of town."

"Well there is always some other poor sucker's wife, isn't that kind of what happened between you and Gina Daniels?" Matt grinned. He remembered helping pack Punk out after haying when he and Zane got into it.

"Hey, Pete tells me that Gina is over at Moscow going to college." Zane said. "You might go look her up, she's hot though, I'm not sure an old guy like you could handle something like her!"

Matt threw the bundle of hay strings he was tying at Zane.

As spring began to break, Susie was spending more time visiting with her boys. Matt wondered if the romance Susie had with whoever was cooling off. Zane had once mentioned she might get it out of her system and come back?

Matt had never fought with Susie and had treated her with respect when she came to see the boys. He had not pried into whom she was with and he had never mentioned getting a divorce.

He had managed to keep things civil and friendly. His own pain he dealt with and never let it show to Susie and the boy's. He did make sure the boys knew he was going over to Moscow some on weekends and in turn, they told Susie about his absence.

Susie began to worry about Matt was going to move on and since her affair was wearing itself out she began to spend more time with her sons, and of coarse Matt.

Zane and Matt had some personal conversations while feeding the cattle. Matt was surprised when Zane offered advice on sex. Zane mentioned he had found out if he worried more about the person he was with and less about his own gratification it worked out better in the long run. Matt thought about that and since he had not had the experience Zane had he began to remember he had always been after his own gratification and had given his partner little thought.

Matt had been just out of high school when he and Susie got married and naturally had been ruled by his hormones. He had never given much thought to sex and realized he may have been pretty self-centered about it. He wondered if that was one reason his wife had began to search elsewhere.

Matt knew Zane had never had a serious relationship before Beth but he did recall that Zane always seemed to be trying to outrun someone he had been with. Maybe his little big brother did know something about women after all. Beth certainly seemed to be very well satisfied with his brother. Matt was going to try being more thoughtful, that is if he ever again found someone to have sex with!

As the spring flowers began to bloom Matt and Susie seemed to find each other again. This time Matt was paying more attention to the needs of his wife. Susie had begun to worry about Matt moving on and as she spent more time at the house she eventually spent the night. She found herself with a different and thoughtful Matt.

By the first of May Susie had come back. Matt vowed to pay more attention to his marriage. Levi and Jason were thrilled to have their parents back. Rachel, Beth and Zane were also glad that Matt and Susie worked it out. The fact that nobody had interfered and there had been no animosity in the family made it easier for Susie to return without any I told you so!

Matt and Zane worked the cows and turned them into the canyon. Zane had also booked a few Bear hunters and they perhaps bagged the poor bear that Beth had frightened away from the apple trees.

Between their savings from the fall hunt and the cattle sales and the spring bear hunters, Adams Brothers, had done very well.

Matt was much more content in his job and also since he had his family back together. It was looking to be a very good year. Matt and Zane occasionally took their wives down to Pete's to have a few beers and dance whenever Pete booked some music.

Matt also took Susie and they went for a trip to the coast, the two of them and left Rachel to oversee the boys. They no longer needed a babysitter, just a little supervision.

Ty had his first birthday in April and by May was walking and getting into everything. Knickknacks, that Grandma Rachel had been sitting around for years were now put up on shelves out of reach.

Beth was having trouble with her business advisors in Detroit. They were pushing for her to make a trip east to Detroit. She had not been east since the picture of her and Zane had been published.

Beth had expanded her Foundation she set up in Idaho and she was pouring more of her profits from the business into the Foundation. Beth hoped to help many more people in the area. She had the Foundation offices in Moscow.

Beth had discussed the Foundation with Zane. He knew what she was doing and he told her.

"It is you're business, do as you wish."

"Yes, but in the event something should happen to me, you need to have some idea of my holdings for Ty's sake."

"I don't want to hear you even talk about something happening to you!" Zane said, clearly frightened about the prospect.

Beth could see that Zane didn't want to discuss her mortality but she nevertheless kept him up to date on what she was doing. Especially with the Foundation because she was very proud of the work they were doing. Also the existence of the Foundation was providing huge tax breaks on the earnings from her Detroit business. There was also other, various trust.

Beth made the Detroit advisors and Attorney's make a trek to Idaho. She had decided she would never return to Detroit. When the entourage showed up at the Spokane airport, Beth scheduled meetings in Couer d'Alene, in early June and made sure that Zane accompanied her.

Zane wasn't happy about it but when Beth insisted he went with her. Beth they would need to deal with Zane and her son as the heirs in the event something was to happen advised her attorneys.

Zane wasn't bored during the meetings in fact he understood a lot more of what was going on than Beth's sophisticated group of attorneys and advisors from Detroit thought he did. He smiled to himself as he realized they had taken the caption in the press about him being a mountain man to be interpreted as someone simple minded.

Beth had also hired a couple of Idaho attorneys, one an expert in taxes and another knowledgeable in the fact that Idaho is a community property state, which put Zane right in the middle of Beth's business.

Beth and Zane had two days of meetings. Zane was quiet and had little to say. Beth noticed he didn't like the discussions that were held about the possibility of something happening to her. But she noted he didn't say anything but listened attentively as the required points were discussed. Beth signed the required proxy's and Zane also found he was required to sign also as his wife's business under Idaho law was also partly his business. The Proxy's give Beth's advisors and Attorney's the right to conduct business, in Detroit in her name and make the necessary decisions.

The crew from Detroit returned east with a newfound respect for Bethany Adams Husband

Beth and Zane and the Advisors and Attorney's they had hired were controlling the disposition of the income pouring into Idaho from the Detroit business. That was beyond the scope of the Detroit crews business.

Zane noted that the advisors and Attorneys were all making salaries higher that he and Matt made in their business. But if Beth's fortune was to be managed he knew the hiring of those professionals was necessary. He also knew Beth was correct; he needed to know what was going on! Zane was thoughtful for a couple days after they concluded the meetings. Beth knew he was mulling something over in his mind. She found out what it was one day when he asked her, "I wonder if we shouldn't draw some papers up to turn the guide business over to Matt and list me as an employee. Seems to me the profits I'm making are ending up being paid out as taxes. That mean, I'm working for nothing but the Internal Revenue Service when I contribute to the bottom line?"

Beth smiled. Seemed her husband was beginning to understand what big business meant and to think of ways to preserve what he had worked hard to gain. "Yes, it might be worthwhile for you to do that and then you could carry the farm on your side and list what Matt does as wages. The farm is a bigger tax break for us and the guide Business would not be taxed so heavily if Matt was the owner. Those profits are being consumed in our bottom line."

Zane discussed it with Matt and they agreed to confer with the tax attorney Beth had retained for her business and the Foundation.

Beth found out her husband and a quick and intuitive grasp, of the business world his association with his wife and her entourage of business advisors had dragged him into.

When Matt and Zane met with the tax attorney they did divide their partnership into two divisions, Zane with the farm and Matt with the Guide business. They still split the profits, fifty, fifty but on the books it became separate.

With Beth's business meetings behind them, Beth and Zane began to concentrate on their life on the farm; Such as getting in the Garden and the upcoming task of putting up hay.

That year on the fourth the entire Adams' family worked at putting in the hay. They bought a new baler. Zane grinned at Beth and said he was, "beginning to understand how one spends money to save money." The new baler would be more depreciation for the farm.

Zane rode often through the summer into the canyon to check the cows and he kept a watchful eye for signs of wolves. None had followed the wintering game herds down the winter before. At least he didn't believe they had and he had gone often when the snow was on the ground.

After the hay was in the barn, they began to ready the Lodge for the fall Bow season to open the 30th of August.

Zane and Matt were out checking the tree stands located on main game trails and blinds where game came to feed. There were plenty of Wolf signs in the mountains.

The vigilante's hunters had not been able to slow down the proliferation of the packs in the high country. Zane felt certain he could control the canyon ground behind the ranch but he dare not attempt to thin the wolf population in the mountains. There was too much chance of being caught as the game wardens kept close watch on the activities of the Packers and Guides.

He and Matt's livelihoods were too precious to take a chance. Although Matt was technically the Guide owner, Zane could still lose his license to operate. Since Zane and his years of knowledge was essential to their business he knew they would be in for another season of having to hunt the Elk in brushy inaccessible holes and basins.

Beth and Susie pitched in to do some painting. Susie would have to be at the Lodge this year there would be no help from Annie Cutler. Annie and Jack had retired and they had indicated they were going to visit but they were permanently out of the Guide business and enjoying their retirement. Beth had the benefit of Annie guidance the pervious year but now she would need Susie's help.

17

The third week of August Zane drove up on the high ridge road where he had parked that day when George Belmont had been killed. It would only be a few days until the Dudes would be at the Lodge and the season would begin.

He got out of the suburban that now had 'Adams Guide Service' written on the side. He was looking over from that viewpoint a large portion of the mountain area they were allotted and licensed to Guide upon.

The peaks and ridges that Zane could see in the distance from the high road were all very familiar to Zane. He had hunted and been all over the areas he could see. He knew where all the big meadows were; he also knew where the fern glades the Elk liked to inhabit were.

Zane ruminated about that day he had brought George Belmont up on the high road and how his death had ended up changing Zane's entire future. He sadly remembered the last day him and Jody had ended things in the same fern glade.

He also pondered the end of Georges life had been the beginning of his life with Beth. Without George's death she would have without a doubt returned to Detroit. Zane would never have gotten to know and love her. He wouldn't have his precious child. The actions of Jody Miller had changed everything for Zane in a way that Jody had not planned. Also in a way that Zane could never have imagined.

When Zane remembered Jody, he felt sad that it must have been a mental illness that caused his old friend and guiding partner to have wanted to kill him. Jody's thinking that Zane was going to get what he thought he deserved was not rational. In all likelihood Zane and Jody would have been partners in the business instead of his brother Matt.

That afternoon alone on the high road Zane gave thanks for his wife and son and the fact that he was still a part of this beautiful country he loved. He knew he would never forget the part Jody and George's deaths had played in his good fortune. He had met Beth, the woman who was the center of his life. He never dreamed he would love someone as much as he did her. It had been a bit of an inconvenience in dealing with her wealth but for one second Zane had never regretted meeting and loving her. He could not imagine his life without her. It had been nearly four years since it all began. Zane hoped the next four years would not be so dramatic but he hoped his happiness with his life continued.

Zane heard a couple of Bulls squealing far down in the glades below him. As he listened, he knew one was larger than the other. Zane got his bugle out of the Suburban and joined in with the Bulls. They immediately answered. As Zane played with the Bulls, the larger sounding Bull began to move up the glade toward Zane. Apparently he was not worried about the smaller Bull squealing but when Zane bugled the larger Bull perceived him to be a potential threat.

Zane played with the Bull with his bugle for about twenty minutes. Zane knew he had the Bull riled enough to call him in so he quit and left him be. He would return another day with a hunter and have another go at him.

Zane drove back to the Lodge. Beth and Susie had finished painting and cleaning. The large propane tanks and the generator that provided power were ready to go. They had filled the fuel Barrel and hauled the pack stock in.

Zane had been wintering the packhorses and mules on the Adams farm the last two seasons.

They were scheduled to pick two bow hunters up at the Lewiston airport.

Matt had volunteered to pick them up. Beth and Susie had gone on this day to stock the groceries and lodge supplies.

Things had straightened out for Matt and Susie and Zane was glad to see that Beth and Susie were also beginning to establish a close relationship. They worked well together. Zane was looking forward to a pleasant season or so he hoped.

Zane had read in the newspaper recently that the Feds were considering taking the wolves off the endangered species list and turning their management over to the Idaho Fish and Game. They had reported in the article they figured there were 500 wolves in the Idaho Forest. Zane laughed. He knew there were in excess of 300 in the North Fork drainage alone.

He had eliminated six adults, three adolescent and three pups from the small canyon behind his house. And that was down in the lower country close to town.

Zane knew if the wolves had proliferated in the South Fork, The Lochsa, The Selway and the area south around McCall there could be at least 1500 if not more. He knew there had been livestock and hunting dogs attacked in the Elk City, Red River area. Also there had been attacks on hunting dogs and on livestock in the Elk River and Dent Bridge area.

Last year some muzzle loader hunters which hunt from November 21st to December 9th had road tripped from outside of Pierce over French mountain and came back through Sheep mountain and Eagle Point into Headquarters and had seen nothing in the snow but a few Elk tracks and Wolf tracks everywhere they went.

The idea, that there were only 500 Wolves in Idaho Zane knew was ludicrous. There was probably that many in the Idaho Forest through natural migration before the introduction program began! The wolves they reintroduced weren't conforming to wolf behavior patterns. Zane had read that Alpha Male and one Alpha female were the only ones that bred and had pups. This wasn't the case. Many of the packs were breeding like dogs and several Bitches were having pups in the same pack. They were seen and one could count the tracks. Often the pregnant females would split off from the original pack and start a pack of their own.

Also the Lobo males were stealing mates from the main pack and starting their own packs. The vigilante Wolf hunters seemed to know more about the behavior and numbers of the Wolves than the Federal Conservationist did!

There was hardly a single local hunter that wasn't bitching about the situation. The entire thing was grossly out of hand and there were many hunters that intended to kill wolves if they saw them and never say one word for fear of getting caught!

Beth and Susie came driving in and jolted Zane out of his morose mood thinking about the Wolf populations. "Caught you napping, didn't we?" Beth teased as Zane helped them unload the supplies.

"Not exactly, more like Day dreaming or having a wide-awake night mare."

"What's wrong?" She asked, concern for him on her face.

"Just thinking about the Wolf problem!"

"Well you know that won't do you any good." Beth said. She knew Zane had been nearly obsessed since the Wolves had killed Maggie and the stock. She also knew he had hunted them in the Canyon even though he had never told her one word about it.

Zane and Beth had bought a Toyota four runner and traded Beth's Car. The seats folded down in the four runners to make room for plenty of supplies. Beth and Susie had it packed with foodstuff for the lodge. Zane lugged it into the kitchen as Beth and Susie put it away.

Zane checked his watch. "Matt should be coming soon with those bow hunters he went to pick up?"

"He will be here." Beth smiled. They had two days to feed them before they could even hunt.

"Both of these guys are from California." Zane told Beth and Susie.

He hated to see the Californians come. They often came back to retire and live once they saw the beautiful country. Being from California was almost as bad to the locals as an illegal alien from Mexico. Especially since they always had solutions to problems there were no tax dollars to fix. All of the California transplants thought they had the solution for bad roads, under funded schools and any myriad of problems that Idaho seemed to have because of lack of tax dollars.

Zane heard a vehicle come and he saw Matt had driven in with two passengers. The season had begun!

Two mornings later Zane took one California hunter and Matt took another. The Elk were bugling well and Zane had no trouble, bugling a Bull in for his hunter. The Hunter underestimated the yardage and didn't allow the Elk to come into the tree stand before he tried a shot. He missed.

Zane grinned to himself and thought it typical for a Dude; it was the first bow hunt for this California hunter. Zane let him use the range finder and the Dude was surprised that he had no clue to the actual yardage the Bull had been when he unsuccessfully tried the shot.

The next morning the same scenario except this time the Californian made a hit. Zane was disgusted that it was not a killing shot and had wounded the Bull. They sent several hours trying to track the wounded animal but the blood trail quit and Zane was sure, the Bulls wound had sealed. The California hunter was objecting, to having to spend hours tracking the Bull and they had to cover some rugged country. Zane told the hunter that it was necessary for him to try and retrieve his wounded animal and Zane could not be the one to track down and kill that wounded animal.

It was required by law to be the hunter that had the tag and had made the shot.

Zane thought with satisfaction that long and arduous trek after the wounded animal may teach the Bow hunter to have more patience before making a bad shot!

They did retrieve the arrow and by the location of the blood trail and the fact the blood was low on the brush Zane figured it to be a cut from the arrowhead on the lower front leg.

Zane knew this particular hunter was not going to bag an Elk unless he got the yardage problem figured out. He did not have to worry about that as that hunter left the next morning disgruntled.

Meanwhile Matt's hunter had bagged an Elk the second day. It was a small rag horn that came right into the tree stand as Matt called him. Matt's California, hunter was happy, as it was also his first Bow hunt.

The first week they had one happy hunter and one disgruntled hunter. Zane knew that was the way the Guide business was!

The second week Susie made a run into Lewiston and met the next two hunters. One came in from Texas and the other came from Florida.

Beth was doing the cooking. Ty was a year and a half old and Beth was on the run trying to keep up with him. He was especially difficult to watch at the Lodge because Beth and Susie were busy with the cooking and cleaning. After trying the first week, Zane begged Grandma Rachel into watching him. She agreed.

Zane was glad his mother had Chuck Danner in her life. Chuck had decided to sell the store. After nearly forty years he had a couple from Washington that had taken over the store. When Zane asked Rachel to watch Ty he knew Chuck and Rachel now had the time. Chuck had kept his home and him and Rachel was often there but that was mostly when Beth and Zane were at the Ranch.

Beth and Zane had kept the small guardhouse manned at the gate to the Adams ranch. It provided peace of mind for them. They hoped Ty would be able to attend public schools as his cousins did but he would most likely need to be taken to and from school. There would be no school bus for Tyler Adams! He would be too vulnerable to persons interested in Beth's wealth!

Matt and Zane did better this year for the bow season. They were now preparing for the rifle hunters. They had three hunters that needed to be met and picked up at the Spokane Airport.

Since Beth had business she needed to take care of at the Foundation in Moscow, she volunteered to go on to Spokane and meet the hunters.

When Beth stopped in Moscow, that day she met with one of the heads of her family distress units, which was one division the Foundation funded heavily.

The head of that division, were the rehabilitated, Gina Daniels. Beth had funded her education and extensive counseling. It had been a hard struggle for Gina to come to gripes with what she had done. Beth Adams had been her major supporter. Beth and Gina had become friends and Gina was now one of Beth's most trusted advisors in the Foundation.

Beth got into Moscow at noon and went to the Foundation. Gina was waiting in her office. Beth had called her that morning and told her she was coming.

"Hi, Gina." Beth said as she went into the office that Gina now had in the Foundation.

"Hi Beth, glad to see you. We have a couple of family situations I need to discuss with you?

How is your family?" Gina always asked but she never mentioned Zane specifically.

"Great" Beth said digging a recent picture of Ty out of her wallet. The photo of Ty showed he had a head full of curls like Zane.

Gina smiled when she saw the picture. "He is adorable."

"You want to discuss these cases over lunch? I'm afraid I have been in such a rush I haven't eaten since breakfast?" Beth asked.

Gina grabbed the files she was working on and she and Beth went to a nearby restaurant.

As they sat down at the restaurant Beth noted that no one who knew Gina from when she was with Punk Daniels would now recognize the capable composed young woman that she had become. Gina was one of Beth's most trusted advisors and Beth was extremely proud of how far Gina had come. Beth knew that Gina had her life together but she was bothered that Gina had resisted dating anybody. She didn't seem to be interested in moving on with that part of her life.

Gina had plenty of men interested in her but she had not come to place where she was interested in forming another relationship. Gina had told Beth her counselors had said she was ready but Gina herself wasn't ready. She was being fulfilled in the kind of work she was doing and that seemed to be all she was interested in.

Beth would not have been surprised to know Gina still thought about Zane Adams. She had come to care for Beth but Gina had never forgotten being with Zane that one night. She knew Beth was a very lucky woman, and it was obvious. Gina didn't feel resentment about Beth and Zane but she hoped sometime she would meet someone like Zane Adams that was gentle and caring. That had not happened.

Beth and Gina went over the files during their lunch. Beth told Gina to use her own judgment, She had come to trust and rely on Gina. After their lunch Beth said she had to run to Spokane and meet some hunters coming in. Gina never saw Bethany Adams again!

Zane, Matt and Susie were making the Lodge ready for the rifle hunters. Rachel Adams came driving in with Sheriff Anderson.

When Zane saw his mother with the sheriff his heart jumped in his throat and he felt a cold chill. When he saw, the look on Rachel's face Zane knew it was Beth.

"There's been a car accident!" Rachel said, tears, running down her face.

"Beth!" Zane said. He felt sick. "How bad?" He felt he was choking as fear clawed at his throat.

"Bad, Zane, they have taken her to Spokane, they need you as soon as possible."

"Take our car." Matt said. He had been standing with Zane when they noticed the Sheriffs' vehicle drive in.

"I'll drive." Rachel said as she could see Zane was in no condition. He already was moving like a man in shock.

Sheriff Anderson could not believe he had seen Zane Adams with his side blown out and with a dead hunter but he had never seen him crumble as he did when he found out his wife was in a wreck and had been taken to the hospital.

The trip to Spokane was a daze for Zane. He remembered very little except his urgency to get to Beth!

Once they arrived at the hospital, they went directly to the ICU department. They were met by a neurologist as soon as the receptionist found out whom they were.

He introduced himself as Doctor Hill and he was the Doctor in Charge of Bethany Adams. He began to try and fill them in on Beth's condition but Zane wanted immediately to see her!

"Of coarse." The Doctor said and showed Zane and Rachel to a room. There were many machines in the room. Beth's head was bandaged and her face was pale. The heart monitor was steady and Zane was encouraged although he could see that Beth was unresponsive and unconscious "When will she awakens?" Zane asked.

Doctor Hill shook his head and said, "She won't! That is what I was trying to explain to you. Your wife is what we call brain dead. She won't wake!"

Zane stared at the Doctor with horror. "Could this be a mistake?" He asked?

"I'm sorry, Mr. Adams, it is no mistake. We are keeping your wife's body alive on the respirator but she is technically gone. Mrs. Adams had on her drivers license she would be an organ donor. We need your consent and then we will take her off life support."

Zane looked at his beloved Beth in disbelief. She was just lying there! It was impossible that she could be gone. He could not grasp the thought that the stupid doctor wanted him to give permission for them to cut her up. To take her body parts. He had not had her long enough! He and Ty needed her! This had to be a bad dream.

Rachel wrapped her arms around Zane and began to cry. "It would be what Beth would want."

"Get out!" Zane glared at the Doctor.

Doctor Hill left the room. He had seen many other survivors react the same way. Denial was the first reaction. He knew he needed to give Mr. Adams time to realize what he had told him.

Zane pushed Rachel away and went to Beth. Her skin, felt warm to his touch as he took her hand. "Oh God, this can't be happening, Beth. We need you!"

Beth lay still and unresponsive, as the machines were the only sound except for Rachel's soft crying. Zane pulled up a chair and sat holding his wife's hand. Rachel put her hand on Zane's shoulder. He pushed her hand away as if her presence was the cause of the nightmare.

Rachel went out of the room. Clearly Zane needed to be alone with Beth. Rachel hoped he could come to realize it was a hopeless situation but as usual Rachel knew Zane would need to wrestle with it himself. He had always been that way. All she could do is a wait and see if he needed her.

In about an hour Rachel went back and Zane was now leaning his head against Beth and crying. Rachel knew he was beginning to realize.

Another hour Zane came looking for Rachel. He was now dry eyed and his jaw was set and his face was like stone.

"You want to go find that Doctor, Mom?" He said and went back to Beth's room.

Rachel went and asked at the nurse's station for the Doctor. In about twenty minutes Doctor Hill came in. "He wants to see you." Rachel told him.

Doctor Hill and Rachel went into Beth's room. Zane had been sitting in the chair, when he saw the Doctor come in he stood up.

"What do I sign?" He said.

Doctor Hill explained to Zane they would not remove life support until Zane was ready. He explained they needed to get the transplant teams in place.

Zane knew he had to let her go! He signed the papers. He and Rachel were in the room when they unplugged the machines. It was moments and her heart stopped and then they took her away. Zane refused to leave the hospital until they told him the harvest had been complete. He signed the papers to have her remains cremated and Rachel and Zane finally left the hospital. It had only been ten hours for Zane's life to fall apart!

Rachel drove home with a stone faced and silent Zane. She could almost feel the pain he was in. Maybe when they got home where Chuck was watching Ty, would Zane realize Beth was not completely gone, she had left him her precious son, a part of her.

When Rachel and Zane reached the Ranch Chuck came out with Ty in his arms. He looked at Zane and Rachel with a question in his eyes. Zane brushed by Chuck holding Ty and went into the house and up the stairs.

Rachel began to cry again, "She's gone! Oh God what can I to do to help him?"

Chuck also felt his tears well up as he seen, the terrible pain Rachel was in. "Nothing Rachel, he will have to deal with it alone. Death is so final nobody can help!"

Rachel and Chuck went in the house. That evening Rachel fixed Zane a tray and took it upstairs and knocked on the door. Zane opened the door and he was dry eyed but his face was without expression.

"You need to eat, Zane, keep your strength up."

"Thanks Mom." Zane took the tray and shut the door.

Rachel went down the stairs and called the Lodge to tell Matt and Susie what was going on.

"How is he taking it?" Matt asked.

"You know Zane. It is hard to tell." Rachel told Matt what had happened at the hospital.

"I'll try to keep things going here but I will need to refund and pay for the hunters Beth was to pick up in Spokane. I'll call the airport and see if they left messages when nobody met them. Call me if there is anything I can do. Sometimes Zane will talk with me, when he won't anybody else. Call me and I'll be there. What has been done for arrangements?"

"Zane signed to have Beth cremated. Apparently they had talked about it at some point, although I'm sure he never dreamed it would need to be done. With that there will be no rush to make arrangements. It is all in Zane's hands and I don't know if he can handle it?" Rachel said. She was uncertain, what to do next?

Rachel heard Zane moving around upstairs during the night. She knew he wasn't getting any sleep. The next morning she heard him come down the stairs. When she put on her robe and went to the kitchen Zane was making coffee. He had laid a folder on the table.

He looked at his mother and didn't say anything.

"What is this?" Rachel asked about the file lying on the table.

"You know how to run that damned, fax machine?" Zane asked tersely.

"Yes, what do you want to fax?"

Zane looked at his watch. "It's nine a.m. in Detroit. I want you to fax that advisor of Beth's a copy of that death certificate. The Fax number is on one of those letters. I can't call them and I don't wish to speak to them. This fax will set the ball rolling with that bunch! It has to be done!"

Zane said tiredly sitting down at the table to wait for the coffee.

"I suppose it does." Rachel picked up the file and opened it. The first letter was Beth's advisor, the one that had her proxy and power of attorney. The second document was the death certificate they had been given at the hospital. Rachel went to fax the death certificate to the advisor.

Zane was drinking coffee when she returned. "Matt is trying to locate the hunters that came into the airport yesterday. He said he would handle that." Rachel told him.

Zane looked at Rachel as if he thought it was ludicrous to be concerned about hunters at a time like this.

The phone began to ring. Rachel got up to answer it but Zane stopped her. "Let the machine get it." It was already the advisor in Detroit.

The phone continued to ring throughout the morning. Some calls, Rachel took, others she didn't. Zane had enough of it and at noon he told his mother he was going to the Lodge.

He got in Matt's, car they had taken to Spokane and left for the Lodge. Rachel called Matt to expect him.

When Zane got to the Lodge, Matt was waiting. He hugged his brother. Zane was still stone faced but Matt could feel the pain in him as he hugged him.

"Why aren't you out with a hunter?" Zane asked.

"I was trying to locate the ones in Spokane. We will need to pay their airfare back and reimburse them their fee." Matt told him.

"Why is that? Get someone up there to get them." Zane asked?

Matt looked at him in astonishment. "Aren't we going to need to handle Beth's death? You aren't going to take anybody hunting are you?"

"There is nothing to handle. She's gone! Beth wouldn't want me sitting around wringing my hands. It won't bring her back! I need to do something to stay busy. You know there is going to be a storm with those ass holes in Detroit.! The busier I am the better." Zane said grimly.

Matt looked at Zane and wondered to himself if Zane was in control or was in shock! "What do you want me to do?" He asked?

"Find those hunters! Apologize and get them in here."

Matt went into the Lodge to get on the phone. He had located two of the three hunters in hotels in Spokane. One of them had called the Lodge and Matt had already sent him back. Matt got the other two in the hotels and assured them someone would pick them up today. When he finished, he found Zane talking in the great room to the only hunter they had at the lodge. Zane was planning a hunt for the afternoon.

Matt called Rachel and told her what Zane wanted him to do?

"Go to Spokane and get them, if that's what he wants. I will try to handle the storm here since Beth's death came out in the newspapers this morning."

Matt took off for Spokane and returned well after dark with the remaining two hunters.

The next morning Zane was up well before daylight. He was in the kitchen talking with Susie. He wanted to know if they should try to get someone in to help her. Susie assured him she could handle it a few days but in the long run she would need to have some help. Zane told her to call the unemployment office in Moscow or Lewiston or both.

Zane took the hunter out that day. He felt himself beginning to rejuvenate in the forest. It took his mind away from what he had refused to think about. That he would never see his beloved Beth again! On a conscious level he knew she was gone but in his heart he had not yet accepted it!

That evening Rachel called and wanted to know what she was to do about a memorial service.

"Schedule it for two weeks, at Moscow." Zane said. "That should give those Detroit people time to get here."

"Beth's Foundation Attorney called and wanted you to attend a meeting of the board of Directors, what should I tell them." Rachel asked. "You know the Foundation was very near and dear to Beth's heart, she would not want you to neglect it."

"Schedule a meeting the day after Beth's Memorial. I can have someone else take over on recommendation from that board. I don't know anything about running the Foundation but Beth had people she very much trusted. I'm sure they can handle things. Is that all?" Zane sounded to Rachel as if he was operating on autopilot. He was abrupt and unemotional. She was very worried.

The twenty eighth of October Beth's memorial was held in Moscow. The whole affair was a fog for Zane. He held Ty on his lap and there were literally hundreds of people there. The Foundation had picked the location and it was the biggest Church in town but it still did not hold the people that came. There were many local people attended that Beth had helped.

There was also the troop from Detroit. Zane recognized the same ones that had been at the board meeting Beth had set up in Idaho. They were giving their condolence to Zane in one breath and clamoring for a meeting in the next.

After the memorial Beth's Detroit Attorney came to the Ranch and told Zane, he had Beth's will. He wanted a reading and needed to meet with her Idaho Attorney to begin the probate.

Zane told them all to be at the Foundation the following day at 1.00p.m.

The next day Zane went to the Foundation. The receptionist told him that a meeting had been arranged in the conference room. Rachel had offered to go with Zane but he said he could handle it. When Zane entered the conference room, he found it packed with Attorneys and Advisors.

Zane spoke to Beth's Idaho Attorney and suggested they split the meeting in half. He and the Attorney would first, meet, with the Detroit bunch and after that he would meet with the Foundation advisors and board of directors.

The Detroit men were all men Zane had met. He listened as Beth's attorney read Beth's will. She had left everything to Zane. Beth had drawn the will before Tyler's birth but Zane knew that she had set up a trust fund for Tyler.

Zane signed the papers to allow the Attorney that Beth had chosen to continue to represent the estate and vote Beth's proxy. Things would continue in Detroit as they had been. Nothing was changed except they now needed to deal with Zane.

After the Detroit troop filed out the Foundation crew came into the conference room. That included two Attorney's and two board members that Zane had never met.

The Attorney that represented the estate told Zane they needed to appoint a third member to the board of directors to replace Beth, unless he was willing to do it himself?

Zane said he didn't know anything about running the Foundation and he was certain Beth had people more qualified than him.

The other two board members suggested the head of Family Services Gina Daniels be appointed to take Beth's place on the board.

Zane was surprised that Gina was employed by the Foundation. He was assured that Gina was one of Beth's most trusted and capable advisors and was the one most qualified to sit on the Board. Surprised but certain that it was most likely something Beth would have done, Zane signed the papers appointing Gina Daniels as the third Board member. He also found that Gina had Beth's power of attorney but that would need to be changed to Zane. Zane agreed to sign it once the attorney drew it up. At last done with the meeting Zane made a hasty retreat back to the safety and sanity of the Ranch.

When he drove up and got out of the car he looked weary and depressed. All this Beth business had taken a toll on him. He wanted to escape back to the Lodge. He played with Tyler and told Rachel he was going in the evening back to the lodge.

Zane went upstairs and lay down on him and Beth's bed. He thought back to the night she had come in his room and stripped her nightgown off. That memory caused tears to flow down Zane's cheeks and he felt the pain in his heart was unbearable. For the first time since the day in the hospital room Zane was overcome with his grief.

18

Zane returned to the Lodge that evening. Rachel had tried to get him to eat before he left the Ranch but he did not. When he drove by Pete's Bar, he remembered he had seen Pete at Beth's memorial. That day was a haze in his memory but he remembered bits and pieces of people whom he had seen there. There had been so many. He knew Beth had helped many people in the Foundation but he had no idea there would be so many come to pay their respects.

He remembered the next day much better. He remembered everything that happened when he met with the crew from Detroit. He remembered what happened at the Foundation. He was not surprised that Beth had helped Gina Daniels but he had no idea that she had become such an important worker for the foundation. It was hard for Zane to equate the Gina Daniels he remembered, to the Gina Daniels that they recommended to take Beth's place on the Board of Directors. If Beth had chosen Gina to head up a division, Zane was not going to second-guess, her decision.

He pulled into the Lodge. They only had one hunter left. Matt had covered the days after the memorial. Zane wondered if Susie had found someone to help out in the kitchen.

Zane was pleasantly surprised when he saw that Jack and Annie Cutler were at the Lodge. Annie hugged Zane as he came in the kitchen and Jack got up and soberly offered his hand.

"Figured you could use some help Zane? We are so sorry!" Jack said.

"Thank you," Zane felt he was about to choke up. He got control of himself and smiled. There was nobody in the world he would be happier to see right now as much as Jack and Annie.

Zane noticed Jack and Annie were looking rested and happy with their retirement.

"Matt tells me you intend to handle the hunters you have scheduled. We are here to help." Annie said.

"I appreciate it. Susie has been overwhelmed trying to do things alone. Matt also has been spread thin but I'm here now and I hope we can get things back on track!" Zane said.

"We'll hang around a couple of days and help." Jack said, worried about the dejected look in Zane's eyes. Matt had told him Zane wasn't doing well. Jack and Annie had been at Beth's memorial service but they had not tried to speak to Zane as mostly people who looked to be business people surrounded him. Zane looked a bit better than he had that day but he was a long way from being himself and Jack, bet it was going to take him a while.

Matt came driving in about then with two hunters he had run to Lewiston to pick up. Annie was already helping Susie in the kitchen.

Jack and Annie stayed and helped Matt and Zane finish out the season. Zane had become used to Beth not being at the Lodge but he knew he was going to have to face going home to the Ranch and her not being there, would be like he losing her all over again!

There was already a foot of snow at the Lodge as they closed up for the winter. The season had turned out to be not too bad considering the time they had to take off for Beth's death. Matt had held things together very well and Zane was grateful. He was also grateful, for his friends, Jack and Annie.

"You need help next year, let us know." Jack said, as they got ready to head down the mountain.

"Thanks again!" Zane said as he loaded up to leave. Matt and Susie had already left.

As Zane drove up to the Ranch house he saw that Chucks car was there and he was glad Rachel had help with the chores since she was taking care of Ty. Zane had missed Ty and was anxious to see him. Rachel and Chuck had brought him to the Lodge one Sunday but it had been a couple weeks since Zane had seen him.

As he entered the house Ty came running to him. Zane picked him up and hugged him. Zane searched his sons' face for resemblance of his beloved Beth. He did not see it yet, as Ty looked so much like Zane with his towheaded curly hair and blue eyes. Maybe in his smile and his nose Zane saw resemblance to Beth. Ty was so young it was hard to tell but Zane felt Beth's spirit watching as Ty put his little arms around his Daddy's neck and hugged him.

"How is it going, Mom?"

"Glad you are home. We missed you, especially Ty. Ever since we went to the Lodge he has been wanting his Daddy to come home?" Rachel had also heard Ty ask for his mother but she had told Ty his mother had to go away and since Ty's attention span did not last long at his age he didn't ask again.

"Have you been able to handle the blizzard of problems with Beth's business?" Zane asked.

"They have been pretty quiet. Apparently you handled things the day you spent at the Foundation. The cows have come in and you will be glad to hear they are all here."

"You and Chuck having to feed much?" Zane asked. There were a couple inches of snow at the Ranch already.

"We moved them into the feed lot. I have been putting Ty in the car seat in the truck but now you are home, you and Matt can take things over."

"You have the spare room made up? I think I will sleep downstairs with Ty and you this winter."

"Of coarse Zane, Chuck will help you unload your things. Do you want me to move some of your clothes down here?"

"Yes, Thanks Mom! Thank you also Chuck. Don't know what we Adams would do without you. I know my mother doesn't want to try!" Zane grinned at Chuck who had been standing there with Rachel to greet Zane.

"I'll help you with your things." Chuck said and he followed Zane back out to get the stuff out of Zane's truck. Zane was still driving the Chevy Truck he always had. Chuck and Rachel had been using the one Beth bought to feed with.

The Toyota four runners had been totaled in the wreck that took Beth's life. The other driver had been in Beth's lane, passing when he hit her head on. Beth's attorney had suggested to Zane they sue the driver that survived but Zane refused. There would be little sense in suing for more money when there was already more money than could be spent.

By the time the truck was unloaded Rachel had moved part of Zane's clothes into the spare room. It was only a few days until Thanksgiving and Rachel just planned on Matt and Susie and their boy's as well as Chuck. It would not be a very festive Thanksgiving this year.

The next morning Zane got up made coffee and went out and started the feed truck. Matt soon came and they fed the cows. Zane had tied the Bays in their stall when he grained them.

"You going for a ride?" Matt asked when he saw Sonny and Dolly with their halters on.

"Yeah, I'm going in the canyon." Zane said and since he did not ask Matt to go with him Matt returned home after they finished feeding.

Zane went to the house. He got his pistol and told Rachel he was going in the canyon. He tied Bowser, the Australian shepherd, but he let Missy go with him. She was reminding Zane more all the time of Maggie. She seemed to have a natural ability to work the cattle and she had been spaded to insure there were no puppies. She pulled her lips back and smiled when she was happy. On this morning she was happy that she was going to get to go with the Zane and the horse.

With the skiff of snow on the ground Zane was wanted to check the canyon for wolf tracks. For that reason he did not want Matt to go with him. If any Wolves had come into the canyon, Zane did not want Matt involved.

Zane and Missy made a long ride and there did not seem to be any sign of wolves but Zane would be vigilant and make sure they did not get in and pose a threat to their cattle and dogs.

When he returned, he rubbed Sonny down and turned both of the Bays out. When he walked up on the porch Thumper was sitting there and Zane remembered Beth had always pet the cat when they finished the chores. He bent down and petted him. "Yeah, you miss her too!" He said and then he went into the house.

Ty came running when he heard Zane come in. Zane picked his son up in his arms and hugged him. Rachel smiled at Zane's affection for his son.

Thanksgiving was a low-key dinner that year. Matt, Susie, Chuck, Levi and Jason sat in the dining room and the family ate off the good dishes.

Rachel had made arrangements for Susie to go with her the next day to shop. Zane was going to watch Ty.

Winter set in at the Ranch in December and the snow got too deep to go into the canyon looking for a Christmas tree. They had to buy one.

Ty was beginning to be of an age that he was wide eyed at the Christmas season. The whole family enjoyed watching the child as he opened his gifts and played with his new toys. Susie and Matt's boys were getting to be teenagers and they were no longer much fun to watch at the holidays.

Matt began to bring the boys to help with the feeding on those days there was no school. Levi had been taking drivers training and soon he would have his license

On New Years Eve, Matt, Susie, and Zane went to Pete's Bar and had a few drinks. Zane did not stay long. He was bored and there was music and he left early. Matt and Susie stayed and saw the New Year in.

Three days later after their morning chores Zane was working on his truck when Rachel came out.

"Gina Daniel's is on the phone and wants to talk with you." Rachel's mouth was drawn in a thin line of disapproval.

"I'll be right there." Zane said. He wiped his hands off and followed Rachel into the house.

"Yeah, Gina, What do you need?" Zane asked as Rachel glared with disapproval.

"I'm sorry to bother you Zane, but we need you to sign off on the expenditures for November and December. Do you want me to bring them or how do you want to handle it?"

"I'll take care of it there. Will tomorrow afternoon is all right?" Zane told her.

"Yes, of coarse whenever it is convenient for you. We will be expecting you. Goodbye Zane."

"See you tomorrow. Goodbye Gina." Zane hung up the phone.

"Why on earth would you be meeting that woman?" Rachel said with disgust.

Zane smiled with amusement. "That woman is one of the directors on the board at the Foundation. Gina was one of Beth's most trusted employees and she heads up one of the departments. Beth poured a lot of money into Gina's education and she always believed in her."

"Unbelievable!" Rachel said. "Have you seen her?"

"No, I haven't seen her. Not since she left town when Punk died."

"You mean when she killed Punk!" Rachel reminded Zane.

"Things change Mom. People change." Zane went back out to work on his truck.

The next day Zane drove over to Moscow and met with Gina at the Foundation. He had not seen her for several years. When he entered, he noticed Gina's name on the office door.

Gina got up from her desk when he came in. "I'm so sorry about Beth. We had lunch, on that day she went to Spokane. I miss her very much." Gina blinked back tears. "I owe Beth my life, I don't know what would have happened to me without Beth's support."

Zane could see that Gina was sincere. He also noticed she was still a very good-looking woman and now had an air of confidence about her.

"I'm glad for you that things have worked out. I'm also glad to see Beth's confidence in you has been rewarded with your being a valued person here at the Foundation. Beth felt this Foundation was the most important thing she had ever done. Thanks for helping keep things going in her memory. What do you need me for?" He smiled with amusement. Zane had no idea they would need him for anything.

"These monthly expenditures have to be signed off by the owner of the Foundation. That is now you." Gina said handing, him a sheaf of papers. "Please sit down."

Zane sat down and asked. "Am I supposed to know what these mean? Don't we have an accountant that handles the Foundation?"

"Yes, of coarse we do, these are the reports from the accountant. We just need you to sign off on them. You should probably read them before you sign or if you don't want to?" Gina looked at Zane expectantly.

Zane scanned through the papers. "Where do I sign? And will you give me a copy of them?" He asked.

"Yes! You sign here," Gina got up and leaned across the desk and showed him. "I'll make copies. Would you like coffee or something? This will only take a moment."

"No thanks. Just get me the copies and I'll be out of your hair."

Gina took the papers and after a couple minutes she returned and handed the copies to Zane.

"If it would be easier next time I can run them out to you?" She asked.

"We'll see. You might not get through the gate, call and then we will decide. Goodbye Gina. Nice to see you doing so well."

"Goodbye Zane." Gina watched him get up and walk out the door. She had noticed an air of sadness about Zane and Gina knew it was going to be some time before Zane got over the loss of his wife if ever. After he left, Gina knew she had never gotten over being with Zane Adams. She hoped in time he would be ready to look at a woman again and she knew however long that took she would wait, and hope he would look at her. Somehow she had a feeling Bethany Adam's would approve!

On the way back to the Ranch Zane gave some thought to the remarkable transformation of Gina Daniels. Beth had never mentioned she had invested in helping Gina but Zane had known Beth felt empathy for Gina. He should have known she would get behind her. Somewhere in that Foundation was a file on Gina Daniels. Zane decided he would take a look at it one day when he had time. He felt Beth had no doubt paid for Gina's counseling on top of her education. He had noticed on the expenditure list there were a lot of fee being paid for counselors and psychiatrist.

Zane was glad he had Gina copy the expenditures. He was very much interested in finding out more about Beth's Foundation and all the good work she had done that promoted the good will so many people had told him about.

Zane had once heard Beth say she felt the Foundation was the most rewarding accomplishment she had achieved. He knew he wanted her legacy to continue. If Beth was proud of it, so would Zane be and someday Ty also!

When he got back to the Ranch, Rachel nagged him about his meeting with Gina Daniels. She wanted to know in detail what Gina did at the Foundation and what she had said to Zane.

Zane didn't tell Rachel much because he really didn't know that much about what Gina's department in the Foundation did but he was going to look into it. He trusted Beth's decisions though and he was certain Gina was qualified or Beth would not have put her in a position of trust and for the other board members to recommend Gina, replace Beth on the Board meant they, also had great faith in her abilities to do her job.

Zane settled down to the job of feeding the cows. They had increased the herd size since Matt had become a partner. They no longer had the capacity to put up enough hay to get through the winter. By mid January they bought a semi load and Zane and Matt with the boy's help put it up in the barn loft. The physical labor felt good to Zane. He was having a rough time through the winter. Zane felt a part of him was missing without Beth at his side. He began to wonder if that feeling would ever go away.

Zane began to spend more time down at Pete's Bar. There wasn't much else to do. Zane began to also spend more time looking into the Foundation.

In February when he went to sign off on expenditures, he asked the receptionist to give him the file on Gina Daniels. Zane was aware she would tell Gina he had asked for it. Because he didn't want to take the file from the Foundation Zane had the receptionist copy the file. He also told her to inform him of the next board meeting. Zane intended to be present and take in what the board meeting was all about.

The Attorney that handled the Foundation Business informed Zane that he had not received the quarterly deposit from Detroit and Zane told him to get after them about it. In a few days the Attorney called Zane again and told Zane, he was not getting any response from Detroit.

Zane called the Attorney in Detroit that had his proxy and power of Attorney. "What the hell is going on?" Zane wanted to know?

"We are waiting for the probate to be completed." The Attorney told him.

"You get the payments into the Foundation or I will find someone else to handle things back there, do we understand each other?" Zane said.

"Yes Mr. Adams, I will make the transfers to the account within a couple days. Anything else I can do, Mr. Adams?"

Zane hung up and smiled with amusement. Who in the hell did they think they were dealing with, the mountain man? He called the Foundation Attorney and told him to contact him if the money wasn't received within a couple days.

Zane didn't hear any more from the Foundation Attorney. He was notified in February and went into the Foundation and sat in on the Board of Directors meeting. He was there as an observer and the other two members seemed to be nervous that Zane was attending. Only Gina was unruffled and composed. It was obvious to Zane that Gina was the leader of the Board members.

While Zane listened in they discussed a family in Kendrick that had their home destroyed by fire and what the foundation could do to help. They also discussed a woman and her children that were living in an abusive household. The woman had access to a safe home but she could only stay a certain period of time.

She would need help with reeducating herself to support her children. Also, Gina pointed out it was uncertain that she would not return to the husband. Gina suggested they offer counseling to the entire family in that event and if the woman intended to get out on her own she would still need counseling as well as help funding for her education.

After the meeting Zane asked Gina if he could speak with her?

"What can I help you with Zane?" Gina said after the other two members of the board had left.

"Aren't there federal programs that can help this abused wife?" Zane asked.

"Yes of coarse, but they don't usually, provide funding for counseling. They also will provide support if there are children but their education is mostly Grants and student loans. The loans put the student under a financial burden when they try to get going on their own.

It is a complicated scenario to deal with the bureaucrats and we try to take up the slack between approval on the federal and state programs.

As you know from my file, that counseling is extremely important in changing the mind set of the abused victim." Gina smiled. She had been told Zane had her file!

"Anything else I can help you with? I'm glad to see you are taking an interest in the Foundation, Beth would have been pleased." Gina saw the pain in Zane's eyes when she mentioned Beth.

"I know Beth felt this Foundation was her most important legacy. I hope someday Ty feels the same way. In the meantime it would behoove me to learn more about it. The Attorney for the Foundation called me that funds had not been transferred from Detroit. I imagine that has been taken care of?"

"Yes, the funds are in the account. You might some time want to think about sitting down with the accountant and going over the accounts. I try to keep an eye on things, but we are talking a great deal of money and the chance for abuse is always tempting without some ones watchful eye. I know it may seem tedious but just thought I would mention it." Gina was afraid someone would think Zane wasn't watching and she had been!

Zane smiled with amusement, "I'm sure you would be able to spot any irregularity before I could. Thanks Gina, I appreciate your dedication. Call when you need something otherwise I'll see you when I need to sign the expenditures."

"Yes, I'll see you then Zane. Thank you for your trust."

"It's not my trust, its Beth. I trust her judgment and don't worry anybody else will have access to your file. I have destroyed the copy I had." Zane left the boardroom.

Gina gathered up the files that had been discussed and returned them to her office. She could still see Zane was grieving for his wife. Gina herself missed Beth very much!

Zane was driving Rachel's car when he went into Moscow for the foundation meetings. He began to wonder if he should not replace the four runners, that Beth had been killed in. The insurance company had paid for the vehicle and Zane decided he should get something to drive so he would not have to use Rachel's car. After the meeting at the Foundation he stopped at a few dealers and looked at different vehicles. Zane had always hated making decisions about vehicles; he missed Beth making the decision. He left without deciding and took some brochures home for Rachel to look at.

When Zane got back to the ranch he played with Ty for a while and then asked Rachel if she had some boxes.

"What do you want with boxes?" She asked.

"I need to box some things for you to give the good will or somebody."

Rachel realized he was ready to box Beth's things up and she went out on the porch and got him two boxes. "You need help?"

"No, thanks!" Zane took the boxes and went upstairs. The rooms had been shut up nearly all winter. Zane began by emptying the drawers. On top of the dresser Zane noticed Beth's laptop.

Zane did not even know how to turn it on. Wondering what could be on it that was important, he decided the next time he went to the Foundation he would take it with him.

Zane soon realized he was going to need more than two boxes. He hollered down to have Rachel bring more boxes. The clothing he packed smelled like Beth. Zane found handling the cloths was extremely painful for him but he continued.

Once the clothing was all packed in boxes, Zane grabbed the laptop computer and went to his bedroom downstairs.

The next time Zane went to the Foundation he took the laptop. When he entered Gina's office she grinned.

"You are serous about being involved in the Foundation. You turning into a computer geek?"

"It's not mine." Zane said grimly. "Its Beth!"

Gina got a serous look on her face. "Do you know what is on it?"

"I don't even know how to turn it on. I thought maybe you could help?"

"I don't know! Are you sure you want to know what is on it?" Gina looked at the computer with concern. She was surprised it had not been in the vehicle with Beth.

"I need to know! There may be instructions I don't know about?" Zane said. His eyes grave and his jaw fixed like stone.

Gina plugged the laptop in and immediately the screen was asking for a password. Gina tried Zane, Tyler and Robins. "Can you think of a word she would pick for a password that not everybody would know?"

"Try Douglas, it was her father's name." Zane was standing behind Gina as she tried to access the computer.

Gina typed in Douglas and the computer allowed her to enter. She went directly to Beth's documents. There were many listing about the Foundation. There were also many documents marked as Detroit. One file was marked Zane and when Gina opened it she saw immediately it was a letter to Zane from Beth.

"This is personal for you Zane and only you should read it." Gina got up from the desk and let Zane sit down. Gina showed Zane how to scroll down to read the letter and then Gina hastily left the room. She had seen the first line where Beth had written if Zane was reading it, no doubt it was because something had happened to her!

Gina waited outside in the waiting room with the receptionist. It was nearly an hour before he came out. Gina had taken her calls at the reception desk so Zane would not be disturbed.

When Zane emerged from her office, he was packing the laptop. Gina could not tell what he was thinking as his face was without emotion.

"Anything else I can do, Zane?"

"No thank you, Gina. I appreciate your help." Zane went out the Foundation door with the laptop and Gina went back to her office. Gina hoped the letter from Beth would give Zane some closure but it was hard to tell by his expression what effect the letter had on him.

The next morning after chores Zane saddled Sonny for a ride in the canyon. He went in the house and come downstairs with the urn that had Beth's ashes in it. Upon her death Zane had purchased a plot at the cemetery outside of town and had a stone put on it with her birth date and death but her ashes had sat in the urn, as Zane was undecided, as to what to do with them. Rachel had tried to get him to bury them where the stone was but Zane had resisted.

Rachel, seen Zane with the ashes but she said nothing as he went out and got on Sonny and rode away into the canyon.

Nearly three hours later he returned with the urn. He took it back upstairs and when he came back down Rachel asked him what he was doing with the urn?

"Putting her ashes where she wanted." Zane replied tersely.

"How do you know where she wanted them?" Rachel asked.

"She told me on her computer." Zane said. "There was a letter on her laptop on what she wanted if something happened to her. It was addressed to me. I did what she wanted."

"How did you find it?" Rachel asked?

"Gina and I opened the computer yesterday at the Foundation. Beth wanted her ashes spread under the Wolf River apple tree where the bear was that day. That's what I did." Zane took a can of beer out of the refrigerator and sat down at the table." I should have known Beth would leave something for me, she was no stranger to losing people close to her and she thought of everything. I knew she wanted to be cremated. I just didn't know what she wanted done with her ashes. There are also some messages for Ty when he gets old enough."

"Why did you take it to Gina Daniels?" Rachel still was dismayed at Zane's connection to that woman.

"She is the only one that Beth would have trusted to help me open the computer. She would have been correct. Gina has been, a God, send for me in trying to gain some knowledge of the Foundation and what Beth's vision was to be concerning it. Zane smiled with amusement. "I know you don't like Gina but Beth did and believe me she knew what she was doing when she hired her for the Foundation."

There was nothing about Gina Daniels that evoked fond memories of her in Rachel Adams mind.

Zane thought there was little about Gina other than her looks that resembled the Gina that he had brought home that night but unlike Rachel there were a couple things that Zane remembered about Gina Daniels that were not bad memories. He smiled when he thought of that and wondered wryly if everything about Gina Daniels had changed. There were a couple of things he hoped had not changed.

The letter on the laptop was a turning point in Zane's attitude. Whatever Beth had said in the letter seemed to give him closure of sorts. Matt and Rachel noticed he was more his old self and he began to talk about the future and the Lodge and his plans for Ty.

The next time he went to the Foundation Zane asked Gina to have lunch with him. While they ate at a restaurant Zane asked Gina if she had moved on in her personal life.

"There won't be some big burly guy come in here and knock me out through a window?" He asked with a grin that reminded Gina of the old Zane.

"No, there won't be anybody. Actually I haven't had time to build a personal life. Beth used to encourage me with that but it has been difficult for me to let go of everything. I fear my choices might get me involved with another guy like Punk and so I've not been interested in dating. Besides the work I'm doing is very rewarding and keeps me busy."

"Yeah, staying busy helps." Zane said. "But it doesn't help when you wake in the middle of the night and you're alone."

Gina smiled, "I don't wake in the middle of the night. I drag myself home too tired."

"Aw come on Gina, all that counseling could have not stifled your natural inclinations. If I remember right that would take more than counseling?" Zane smiled with amusement.

Gina's face was red with embarrassment. She jumped to her feet and excused herself to the restroom. She splashed cold water on her wrist and tried to compose herself. She was shocked that Zane had said anything about her and him being together.

While she was gone Zane, decided he should let poor Gina off the hook and quit bringing up things she was obviously embarrassed about.

When Gina returned to the table, Zane didn't say anything else of a personal nature. He asked her if she wanted a desert and she said she did not.

"We, ready to go back to the Foundation?" He asked as he left money to pay the check.

Zane helped Gina into her coat and they went back to the Foundation. Zane signed off on the expenditures and asked Gina to call him for the next board meeting.

Gina told him she would and she was surprised he was coming again to a meeting. "Thank you for lunch." She said.

"You're welcome. Maybe next time we can make it Dinner?" He grinned at her and left.

Gina reflected she had begun to see the old Zane Adams since the day they had opened the computer. She didn't know what was in the letter Beth left for Zane but whatever had been in it had seemed to give Zane a sense of peace. Gina knew Beth would have done something to help him and by the first line of the letter she had written in it with the expectations she would be gone from his life.

Spring came in the Northwest. The spring bulbs, planted by Rachel and Beth burst forth in March. It had been a cold and snowy winter. The snowdrops and crocus had multiplied and bloomed profusely along the edge of the lawn. The years, Beth had been at the Ranch she had taken over the lawn care and had also done the gardening. She had managed all of this in spite of her busy schedule with Ty and the Foundation.

Zane began to wonder if they were going to have to hire help for Rachel. He decided to speak with Matt about Levi and Jason being paid to care for the Ranch lawn. He was certain the boys would appreciate the extra money. Levi and Jason had been helping through the winter with the cattle. Zane figured Matt had given them some incentive for their help but the care of the lawn would need to be paid by their Uncle Zane. Both of the Adams boys knew they had the funds to go on to college set up that first year in trust funds by Beth. It was uncertain what their plans was to be but they knew the money was there when they decided.

Zane continued to take an interest in the Foundation. In April when the grass had turned green and the spring daffodils were in bloom Zane had Gina Daniels drive to the Ranch for him to sign off on the March expenditures. He instructed the guards at the gate to allow her in when she arrived.

Gina showed up that day wearing a beige suit and her dark hair pulled back away from her face. Gina was still a very beautiful woman. However, Rachel answered the door with her lips in that fine line of disapproval.

"Hello Mrs. Adams," Gina smiled. "I have some papers for Zane to sign."

"Yes, of coarse." Rachel reluctantly let Gina into the house. Zane was sitting at the kitchen table waiting for her. He grinned with amusement when Rachel showed Gina into the kitchen to the very table Gina and Zane had drunk coffee at that morning Rachel found Gina in Zane's bed.

Rachel never bothered to excuse herself; she just disappeared down the hall to her room. Ty had climbed into his Daddy's lamp and looked at the stranger with curiosity.

"Hi, Gina, come in and sit down. You want some coffee?" To Ty, Zane said, "Can you say hello to Gina?" Ty hid his face against Zane. He was not used to strange people at the ranch.

"Yes, thank you, I would like some coffee." Gina was remembering the morning she had coffee at the table with Zane and Rachel also. "He is so cute, Zane." She said as Ty peeked at her.

Zane got up still holding Ty and got a cup for Gina. She jumped up to help him as he had Ty in his arms.

"Seems strange to drive through town. I've not been back since I left." Gina told Zane.

"Yeah, I bet it is strange, I hope it wasn't too much of an inconvenience, it could have waited until next week when I come for the board meeting?" Zane told her.

"It's fine. You are coming for the meeting?"

"Yes, schedule, it in the afternoon. I planned to take you to that dinner I promised." Zane smiled at Gina's surprised look.

"I will look forward to it. Here are the monthly reports." Gina dug them out of her brief case as she sat down with her coffee. Ty wriggled out of Zane's arms and ran off to find his grandmother.

Zane ignored the papers and sat visiting with Gina. He was in no hurry to sign them and have her leave. Zane had come to be better acquainted with Gina and found he liked her company. She was intelligent and he enjoyed visiting with her. It would have surprised him a few years ago when she and he had their brief encounter.

Matt came through the door and stopped short when he saw that Gina Daniel, was sitting at the table with Zane.

"You remember Gina, don't you?" Zane asked Matt. Zane could see Matt was taken aback at Gina sitting at the table with Zane. Apparently Rachel had not said anything to Matt about Zane working with Gina Daniels at the Foundations.

"Yes of coarse, how are you?" Matt said and looked at Zane with a question clearly in his eyes.

Gina also noticed. "I must be going. You sign those papers, and I'll see you next week. I'll call you about the time of the meeting."

Zane signed the papers and escorted Gina out to her car. When he came back in the house, Matt was sitting in the chair that Gina had occupied. "Gina Daniels?" Matt asked.

"Yeah, she works at the Foundation. Beth has had her working there since she finished her schooling." Zane looked at Matt with amusement

"Whew, her looks haven't diminished one bit!" Matt said.

Rachel had come back into the kitchen when she heard Gina leave and heard what Matt's, remark, had been. She grunted with disgust.

"I think Zane should fire that woman." Rachel growled.

"Why would I do that? I've depended on Gina to keep the Foundation going! You know how important it was to Beth?" Zane said.

"Oh I wouldn't fire her!" Matt said, "Not the way she looks!"

Zane grinned at Matt and Matt grinned back as Rachel slammed the cupboard doors as she started dinner.

Zane headed for Moscow the next week and told Rachel when he left he could be late. Rachel watched him go worriedly.

Zane sat in on the Board meeting, which Gina had scheduled for four in the afternoon. They had finished their business by five. "You didn't forget we were having dinner?" Zane asked.

"No, I didn't Zane. But I need to go home and change. Do you want to meet up later or would you rather go with me?"

"I'll go with you and then I'll know where you live. Why don't I follow you and then we can take one car.?" Zane said. "If you don't mind?"

Zane followed Gina to the outskirts of town toward the highway from Lewiston. She pulled into a small white house with a neat, well kept, yard. Gina got out of her car and waited.

Zane pulled in and noticed a horse from a lot next to the house came and stuck his head over the fence. Gina patted the horse as she waited for Zane to park.

"Your horse," Zane asked as he got out.

"No, my neighbors horse. The horse is my friend." She laughed. "Come in Zane, while I change." It was the first time Gina had ever had a man in her house since she moved after Punks death.

Gina's house was neat and clean. Zane noticed a bookcase well filled with books. He would never have guessed Gina to be a reader.

"I won't be long. You want something to drink?" She said.

"Do you have a Beer?" Zane asked.

"Yes I do, but I can't tell you how fresh it is, you still want to try it?" Gina smiled.

"Sure! It won't be the first stale beer I've drank." He grinned.

Gina brought the beer and disappeared into the back of the house. In about fifteen minutes she appeared ready to go.

Zane helped her into the car him and Rachel had picked out. They went down town to a better restaurant that Gina said was good. Zane didn't know as he had not spent much time around Moscow and he had asked Gina to recommend a place.

As they were seated Gina asked him how the beer was.

"I drank it. It was all right. You don't drink any more?" He asked.

"I can, for a long time I was on antidepressants but now I'm not and I can drink but I don't.

I would need to drink alone and there is not much sense in that."

"What do you do for recreation?" Zane asked.

"I go to a gym, the university library and sometime my neighbor lets me ride her horse that was begging for attention over the fence. Other than that I work on the Foundation. I'm afraid I'm a very dull person these days." Gina smiled. "What about you, what exciting things do you do?"

"Yeah, you got me there." Zane admitted. "I feed the cows, go for an occasional horseback ride and play with Ty. I still go to Pete's Bar and play a little pool and of coarse come over here on Foundation business. Nothing, really exciting."

Gina smiled. Seemed Zane was also whiling away his time. But he had Ty! She wished she had a child. She wondered if her biological clock was ticking, Gina was just thirty years old.

"What are you planning for the future of the Foundation?" She asked.

"The Foundation was Beth's other baby. It started as a tax hedge but seemed to grow into something she believed in very much and I intend to continue that, with your help of coarse. You have proved to be invaluable, to me Gina."

"I'm glad you feel that way. It is gratifying to see all the good that has been done."

"I also need the Foundation, even with the big tax break the Foundation provided the Attorney that handles our taxes tells me I'll still pay in excess of a million in taxes for last year. Beth set up trust and other things to handle the huge amount of income from the factory in Detroit but still it is mind-boggling. I sometimes wish I could give it all away but of coarse I can't, it is Tyler's legacy someday."

After Zane and Gina ate Zane asked her if she wanted to go to a club or movie. She said she didn't so they returned to Gina's. Zane followed Gina to the door but he said he wouldn't come in. "I know where you live though." He grinned.

"Good night Zane, Thanks for dinner." Gina said.

"Not yet!" Zane said and pulled Gina into his arms and kissed her gently. "Good night Gina."

He let her go and got in his car and left.

Gina went in the house. Her legs were trembling, she remembered what it was like to be in Zane Adams arms and she knew she wanted more. She had hated to let him go but she felt he would be back. He needed more time and like he had told her the first time she was with him, what the hell was her big rush? Better to take time, slow down and enjoy it!

This time she would make sure she did.

978-0-595-43456-5
0-595-43456-8